THE EXODUS GAMBIT

THE EXODUS GAMBIT

HOUSE ADAMANT
BOOK 1

GLYNN STEWART

FAOLAN'S PEN
PUBLISHING

This edition published in 2024 by:

Faolan's Pen Publishing Inc.

22 King St. S, Suite 300

Waterloo, Ontario

N2J 1N8 Canada

ISBN-13: 978-1-989674-47-5 (print)

A record of this book is available from Library and Archives Canada.

Printed in the United States of America

1 2 3 4 5 6 7 8 9 10

First edition

First printing: March 2024

Illustration by Elias Stern

Faolan's Pen Publishing logo is a registered trademark of Faolan's Pen Publishing Inc.

Read more books from Glynn Stewart at faolanspen.com

VISIT ME ONLINE

For Glynn Stewart news, announcements, and more, visit
GlynnStewart.com

ONE

"You know, I'm pretty sure being a bodyguard is easier when the principal *doesn't* strap herself to half a megaton of nukes."

Major Vigo Jarret swallowed a chuckle at his subordinate's comment. He didn't entirely *disagree* with Lieutenant Jelica Laurenz, but he couldn't let his people *see* that. His detachment of the Adamant Guard was aboard a Royal Kingdom of Adamant Navy frigate on sufferance at best.

"Archangel has a job to do," he murmured into the encrypted network his people shared, even aboard the frigate *Goldenrod*. "We are here to protect *her* while she does it. If she can't do her job, we are failing at our duty."

The Major eyed the shuttle in front of him with scant favor. *Goldenrod* normally carried twelve modular combat shuttles, but the Guard had crammed four more in. Sadly, he *knew* that the RKAN— pronounced "Ar-Can"—crew had left them the worst corner.

Vigo was a big enough man that just cramming himself into an MCS's pilot seat was a struggle. A *familiar* one, as the gold ace wings on his dark gray uniform declared, but a struggle nonetheless—and the cramped space was going to hurt.

"Bravo Flight! On me!" his principal's voice barked through the shuttle bay. *Archangel* was the Guard's code name for *Goldenrod*'s Bravo Flight commander, Lieutenant Commander Lorraine Adamant.

Aboard *Goldenrod*, Lorraine Adamant would only go by rank and her base names. It created an illusion of separation between Lieutenant Commander Adamant and Her Royal Highness, Lorraine Alexis Elouise Nala Adamant, Fourth Pentarch of the Kingdom of Adamant.

It was only an illusion, one made harder by Vigo's own presence —with sixty-one *other* Adamant Guards—aboard the frigate.

Watching the pilots and copilots of Bravo Flight gather around the elegant young woman he was sworn to protect reminded Vigo of the task at hand and he gave his shuttle another grim look. Getting into the small craft was going to be a pain, so he turned back to *his* pilots.

The biggest visible difference between the eight Adamant Guards assigned to Charlie Flight and the twelve RKAN officers of the Pentarch's Bravo Flight was age. Only veterans who'd served a ten-year service term—requiring a reenlistment after five years—were considered for the Guard.

"Guards," Vigo addressed his people. "Let's keep the snarking about the job under control, please. The Pentarch is a Navy officer, and we do *not* get in the way of her job. Understood?"

His people were too experienced to snap to attention at being gently rebuked, but he could see the urge in the stiffening shoulders. They *knew* better—but they were also, to a one, older than their principal.

As he surveyed his people to be sure the message had landed, he heard Lorraine start briefing *her* shuttle crews. They weren't actually close enough for her speech to be clearly audible, with half a dozen shuttles and most of the workbay between her and her bodyguards' flight squadron, but Vigo's neural link was synchronized with hers.

Everything she heard, he heard. Balancing the inputs wasn't easy, but he'd learned it.

"Briefing time," he told his people after he was sure he had their attention. "You know most of the drill. Alpha and Bravo flights are rigged up in bomber mode. This is an *endurance* maneuver, not just a live-fire exercise, so the plan is to be out in space for six hours.

"First five hours will be practice shots with training warheads. Eight of the bombs on each shuttle are training rounds." He smiled with wry humor. "So, for those worrying about Archangel strapping herself to half a megaton of nuclear weapons, I can reassure you that she is *only* strapping herself to a hundred kilotons!"

Given that a bomb was a ballistic weapon until its last twenty seconds of life, the training weapons gave up the warheads and even that twenty-second terminal drive for a bunch of electronics that allowed them to mimic an entire ten-shot salvo.

Bombers generally dropped their entire load at an appropriate distance and velocity, then ran for home. But for a *training* exercise, they wanted to repeat that process multiple times.

"The last hour of the exercise *is* a live-fire maneuver, of course," he continued. "Captain Stephson has designated an ice asteroid that she doesn't like. The bomber strike is going to make it go away."

Lieutenant Colonel Sigrid Stephson was *Goldenrod*'s Captain, a broad-shouldered blonde Valkyrie of a woman as tall and large as Vigo himself. He figured she had an ancestral hatred of ice, hence the selection of target.

The irony was that if *Goldenrod*'s shuttles hit the asteroid with *every* bomb, they were doing it wrong. An asteroid wasn't evading—an actual target would be.

And while most of the shuttle crews were inevitably green, the COSH—Commanding Officer, Shuttles—was Commander Olavi Chevrolet. Chevrolet was a solid officer, one Vigo had served along-side before he'd joined the Guard.

"Our job is the usual," Vigo reminded his people. "Charlie Flight has been rigged as interceptors. We aren't carrying nukes," he told them. A rueful chuckle told him he could stop belaboring the point.

"We will hang back from the main exercise zone with our sensors peeled, with a tightbeam link to *Goldenrod* herself," he continued. "We are in position for search and rescue if there's an accident—and my Charlie One and Archie's Charlie Three will carry S and R modules."

They gave up a measurable amount of maneuverability to do that, but Vigo agreed with Chevrolet and Stephson. It was more likely they'd have to clean up after an accident than shoot down assassins—and the loss of maneuverability wasn't *that* much.

There was a reason Vigo had put the modules on the shuttles assigned to himself and his best pilot. He was confident that he could outfly the handicap.

"Any questions, people?" he asked them.

"Any intel suggesting an unusual threat level?" Lieutenant Major Archie Patriksson asked. The slim redheaded officer was one of Vigo's three "section leaders" and was nominally in charge of the shuttle section.

Unfortunately for his independent authority, the principal was a shuttle pilot, and that meant that Patriksson's boss went out with him as often as not.

"All threat environments are currently quiet," Vigo told them. "Both military and civil intelligence are sounding warning notes about the Richelieu Directorate again, but that's at least partially *habit* and the fact that they've finally rebuilt the ships they lost the *last* time they went around with us.

"But we do not accompany the Pentarchs to protect them from the threats we can foresee, people," he reminded them. "The Guard exists for the threats that cannot be foreseen.

"So, if *I* see any one of you slacking off out there today, there will be hell to pay. Slack enough, and I'll send you to Brave's detail!"

That got him the laughs—and the understanding—he was after.

Brave was the Guard code name for Admiral His Highness

Benjamin Adamant, the Fifth Pentarch. The oldest of the Pentarchs —the current King's older brother, in fact—he was also the commander of the Adamantine Home Fleet and notorious for running his Guard as hard as he ran his crews.

When fate or exhaustion took King Valeriya Adamant from her throne, the Pentarchs would stand as candidates to replace her. If Benjamin Adamant had the poor luck to outlive his sister, he would have the rare distinction of standing for royal election *twice*.

Vigo had met the old prince—he'd met *all* of the current Pentarchs as part of his job—but he'd been Lorraine Adamant's shadow for twenty-two standard years. He had fewer illusions than most and had his own opinions as to which of the five Pentarchs should be the next King.

He figured Lorraine needed another decade to be *ready*—and he knew she didn't *want* the job—but the determination to learn and do her best that he could hear in the briefing she was finishing up would make for a brilliant King.

Vigo Jarret's job was to make sure she got that decade of seasoning.

Despite strapping herself to nukes on a regular basis.

TWO

The Midas-type modular combat shuttle was the backbone of the Kingdom of Adamant's military shuttle fleet. Depending on the modules hooked up to "the Cube" containing the engines and pilot compartment, it could do everything from hauling a thousand tons of cargo out of a gravity well to delivering a thirty-man platoon into the same gravity well and providing air support.

Vigo had flown it in every configuration that officially existed and at least three that *didn't* officially exist. Interceptor mode, designed to protect the mothership from missiles, shuttles, shuttle bombs, or any *other* projectile someone threw at the ship that held your bunk, was his favorite.

His neural link hooked up to the Midas's systems and augmented the direct physical controls. At his hands, the parasite craft could dance in space with a vectored thrust capability no larger ship could match.

Goldenrod was one of the few ships he knew of that could come close. A ten-year-old design now, the *Perennial*-class frigates had incorporated all of the lessons of the last war into a design that he thought was possibly the most gorgeous ship the RKAN had ever built.

She was two hundred meters from bow to stern, with rakish lines that drew the eye away from the box launchers, active heat-radiation vanes, and heavy laser emplacements. Dorsal and ventral sensor and communications towers gave her an almost sword-like appearance normally.

She was a fine-looking ship, though he knew his opinion was biased. The RKAN's frigates were built to be pretty—they were the most visible arm of the Kingdom of Adamant, the ships doing trade security and port visits throughout the Bright Dream Cluster.

And since there was no one *else* there to appreciate the view, Vigo gave the frigate an admiring portion of his attention for a few seconds before turning back to the situation around him.

They were a good three light-hours from home, well away from prying eyes in a zone of the Adamantine System's outer ice belt only the RKAN ever came to. The inner belt was far more interesting to miners, and the gas giant Orichalcum served as the main focus for gas refining.

Their exercise location was randomly selected—Vigo had triple-checked that himself, trying to calculate a guess of where they would be based on both Home Fleet's exercise schedule and *Goldenrod*'s own prior training runs—which meant they *should* be secure.

Should wasn't a word professional bodyguards hung the safety of their principals on, and he kept his sensors focused on Lorraine Adamant's Bravo Lead shuttle.

"Guard Actual, do you need our course?" Commander Chevrolet asked over a private channel. "Or do you want to work it out on your own for training?"

"We're not training today, COSH," Vigo pointed out. "Send it over and we'll shadow you out. We're rigged for S and R, if the Deck Chief didn't tell you that."

The Deck Chief had almost certainly told him that. But just as

Vigo was taking a shuttle flight out to play bodyguard around an exercise with no sign of danger, he was also going to confirm that all of the information was in everybody's hands.

"She did," Chevrolet confirmed. "I will admit, in private, that having an extra set of birds to fly overwatch does relax some of my hackles. But I will *never* say that where your people or mine can hear it!"

"We try to be *useful* as well as intimidating," Vigo told the other pilot. The course flickered up on his shuttle's displays. Forty minutes at four gravities to open distance from the frigate. Not a *pleasant* jaunt by any stretch of the imagination, but the pilots would be able to handle it easily. The angle, though...

"Got the course. We'll fall into your trails and keep our eyes peeled," he continued. "Any changes to the intended exercise area? I want to get some drones up to play backstop."

Redundant, probably. But Vigo's entire job was to *be* redundant. If he was actually needed, especially out there, things were already going very wrong.

"I'm sending you an update," Chevrolet confirmed. "You're getting it first. I'm relocating the entire maneuver zone and got the Captain to pick us a different asteroid to nuke."

Vigo took a moment to process that—and to take a second look at the course. That explained the angle being off. They weren't quite going in the opposite direction from *Goldenrod* than planned, but they were a good sixty degrees off from the original plan.

That *could* be a problem.

"Any particular reason, Olavi?" he asked softly, leaning on their old-comrade status and using the other man's first name. The reality of their ranks was more complicated than it sounded, since an Adamant Guard officer was generally considered to rank three levels up from the equivalent title in the rest of the military.

That meant that Vigo was regarded as Lieutenant Colonel Stephson's peer, *not* Commander Chevrolet's.

"Officially, to test my people's ability to adapt on the fly," Chevrolet told him.

"And unofficially?" Vigo prodded. Sudden changes that weren't cleared with the bodyguards were a problem.

"I can't put my finger on anything," the COSH told him. "Or I'd have talked to you about it. But my skin is *crawling* and the hairs on the back of my neck are standing up. Something isn't right, Vigo. So, I'm relocating the exercise and watching for Richards."

"You think the Directorate is going to try a sneak attack?" *Richard* was the radio code for Richelieu Directorate combatants: warships or shuttles.

"I don't think anything," Chevrolet admitted. "I'm just being twitchy, and shifting it up is good practice for my people. And I know *you're* paranoid enough to appreciate that the only person who knew where our final zone was until ten seconds ago was *me*."

He wasn't wrong there. If Vigo had trusted the COSH a bit less, it might have been a problem. As it was, though... Well, he'd flown a bomber with Olavi Chevrolet as interceptor escort.

There were few higher levels of trust.

THE NEXT TWO hours passed quietly. Well, quietly for the Guard shuttle flight—Lorraine and Chevrolet put their people through their paces, all the way up to the twelve-gee maximum thrust of a bomber-mode Midas.

Four training shots had been fired from each shuttle, each mimicking a full flight of bombs and allowing the two flight commanders to assess their people's performance in coordinating the drops.

Officially, Vigo Jarret had zero role in that assessment. Unofficially, he'd flown alongside Olavi Chevrolet when they'd both been wet-behind-the-ears rookie Lieutenants thirty years earlier, and he'd lived in Lorraine Adamant's back pocket for the last twenty-two years.

Both of them would both listen to and *solicit* his opinion, so he kept a good chunk of his attention on the exercises and kept a running tally. So far, *this time*, he wasn't seeing anything worth passing on to the flight commanders.

The bomber crews could be *better*, but that was always true. They *were* good, rising above base competence into a solid level of coordination that would leave any pirate or criminal needing new shorts.

Against an actual warship, they'd have more difficulty, but that, too, was always true. *Goldenrod* had a lovely array of beam weapons that no pirate would manage to keep operational for long, even if they managed to get them in the first place.

Those beams were intended to take down missiles and other warships, though not all could do both. Shuttles would often find themselves in the worst of all possible worlds if a warship dialed them in.

"Permission to take a nap?" Patriksson asked—and even with his senior pilot, Vigo had to check to be sure that was on a private channel.

There were jokes the Lieutenant Major could make to *him* that no one else could be allowed to hear. The Adamant Guard were *extremely* professional in how they presented to the outside world, but that came along with a certain degree of looseness behind the scenes.

There were limits, though. Patriksson hadn't broken them this time, though he was still pushing them.

"Archie, do I *need* to tell you to keep your eyes open?" he asked. "It might look like there's nothing out here, but we're not close enough to a gravity well to stop someone coming in translight."

It would take an incredible navigator and an incredible amount of chutzpah to do it, but it *was* theoretically possible to navigate into the ice belt under translight drive. And the kind of people who'd decide to pick off a Pentarch before she could ever stand for election could probably come up with both the navigator and the chutzpah.

"Fair, fair," Patriksson allowed. "Any idea when *Goldenrod* ships out next? Sitting around in Home Fleet is boring for everyone."

"You've served too long and done too much to want a *non*-boring life, haven't you?" Vigo asked. "Right now, she's part of the Escort Wing."

"Yeah, but the Escort Wing doesn't do solo exercises," his subordinate pushed.

Vigo knew perfectly well that *Goldenrod* would have been doing solo exercises *anyway*—so long as the frigate was carrying a Pentarch, she would train harder and more independently than any other ship, regardless of her official role—but he *also* knew that *Goldenrod* was slated for tour duty near the Sol-ward wormhole shortly.

That wormhole, in the Bright Dream System some thirty-five light-years away, was the only thing keeping a journey back to the old United Worlds and Earth from taking *years* at their best translight speed.

Even Bright Dream was over five months away. But the wormhole there would deliver them to a border system of the United Worlds, where another wormhole only a week or so's flight away would deliver them to Sol.

"So, we *are* getting deployed?" Patriksson asked.

"*We* don't get deployed," Vigo reminded his subordinate. "*We* go where the Fourth Pentarch goes. We effectively *are* deployed. If the ship Archangel is on gets a new mission, then we go wi—"

The great irony of the neural link had been the discovery that putting new *inputs* into the brain was far more dangerous than picking up commands *from* the brain. So, even though the sound that broke Vigo's train of thought arrived via his implant, it hit his auditory nerve and he *heard* it as a sharp siren wail.

One he'd been trained to recognize without hesitation. An emergency alert on the GuardNet—but he was *three light-hours* from the capital world of Bastion, where the rest of the Adamant Guard watched over the King and the other four Pentarchs.

"Critical alert," a neutral, computer-generated, voice said in his ear. "Critical alert. GuardNet compromised. Encrypted burst, incoming. Recipient, Major Vigo Jarret. Protocol, unknown. Breach, unknown. Source, unknown. GuardNet compromised. GuardNet compromised. Critical alert."

"Boss?"

Vigo had cut off in mid-word while talking to Patriksson.

"Give me a moment, Archie," he told the other man. The burst packet arrived as promised. It would have bounced through the GuardNet relay aboard *Goldenrod*, probably without anyone aboard knowing.

Well, officially. The ship's coms Chiefs knew perfectly well about the relay, and he wouldn't be surprised if they were watching to make sure the Captain knew if something *dangerous* went down.

The automated alert hadn't been kidding. *Nothing* on the packet was standard. The Adamant Guard had a *lot* of secrets, even from itself, and this didn't fit in the vast majority of anything he'd been briefed on.

An icon representing the compressed packet hung in his vision, rotating until it showed an icon that didn't belong *anywhere* on a Guard channel—it was the logo of a now-closed steakhouse in the capital city of Adamant.

Which was enough for the bits to click together—a quiet conversation with the then-head of King Valeriya's detail, one of the few times he'd eaten at the restaurant and the *only* possible work-relevant one.

They'd set up a private coms protocol, one just between them, in case even the Guard was compromised—a level of paranoia few professional bodyguards even would aspire to.

That woman was *now* Colonel Irina Roma, the commanding officer of the Adamant Guard and a woman who'd struggled *mightily* to avoid a desk job.

And that protocol was still tucked away in his neural link's storage. But what the *hell* was going on that they needed *that* level of secrecy?

Even as Vigo told his link to decrypt the message, contingency plans were already taking shape in his head.

Something had gone *very* wrong.

THREE

Unless Vigo missed his guess, Irina Roma had been shot. He couldn't *see* the wound, but there was a tension to her olive-skinned face and a grimness to her dark eyes he'd never seen on the older woman before.

He'd seen that tension a few times in others over the years. Somehow, being shot had an ever-so-slightly different edge to it than any other injury he'd seen.

Except there were very few, if any, scenarios he could think of that would result in the Colonel of the Adamant Guard, a mostly ceremonial position that was barely *administrative*, getting shot.

"Archangel-Lead, this is Central," she said. "If you are receiving this, you are still alive three hours after I sent it. Which is more than I can hope for, but it's all I've got left.

"We have been attacked. Guard Command is gone—a bomb. Adam and Armor are confirmed dead. Archer and Arrow are confirmed dead. Amber was separated from her husband, but both her and his aircraft were attacked and I have no confirmation of safe landing."

If Vigo hadn't been strapped into a pilot's seat, he might have fallen. That was the King and her husband—*Adam* and *Armor*, more properly King Valeriya Adamant and Prince Consort Frederick Adamant-Griffin—dead. That was the King's two eldest children —*Archer*, Prince Daniel, and *Amber*, Princess Taura—dead, with their spouses.

Vigo knew the risks of an aircraft under attack. If Central hadn't confirmed the survival of the Second Pentarch and her husband, they were dead.

"I have *zero* contact with Attila-Lead," Roma continued, her tone flat and level as she laid out the devastation of the entire royal family. "I have to assume that Attila is dead as well, but I have no information either way."

Attila was the second-youngest child of the King, Royal Kingdom of Adamant Army Colonel Nikola Adamant. He was surrounded by both Adamant Guard *and* loyal soldiers—which meant that Vigo had to agree. If Roma couldn't contact the head of Nikola's Guard Detail, Nikola was also likely dead.

"If you are receiving this message, I have to assume that Archangel is still alive and at large. I had to send this wide and broad, so everyone in the damn star system knows you got it, but if anyone knows where you are, they aren't telling me.

"And if you're alive, I'm guessing they *also* didn't tell Brave."

Vigo exhaled an explosive breath as *that* sank in. It couldn't be. But the only reason Roma would be worried about Admiral His Highness Benjamin Adamant knowing where Lorraine was...

"The bomb was infiltrated into Guard Command by a member of Brave Detail," Roma said flatly. "Security on Adam's transport was disabled by a member of her detail who *had been* part of Brave's, and I have suspicions about the source of the attack on Archer."

She snorted, and a terrifying bubble of red froth emerged from her nostril before she brushed it away angrily.

"Brave-Lead is dead," she told Vigo. "But he clipped me first. At this moment, Brave and Archangel appear to be the only surviving Pentarchs. Normally, the List would be rerun, but Brave wouldn't have done all of this to have an election.

"I am formally activating Exodus Protocols on Archangel," Roma finished. "You have full authorization to do *whatever* it takes, but get the Pentarch *out* of the Adamantine System."

She grimaced and wiped more red-tinged froth from her mouth.

"I have faith," she concluded. "Our will is adamant."

The message ended and Vigo forced his breathing and his heart rate under control.

Our Realm. Our House. Our Will. Adamant. The motto of the House he served—but if one of the Pentarchs had just turned on the rest, how "adamant" was any of that?

He had the grim suspicion that only the fact that he and Stephson had long insisted on truly random testing sites had kept them safe. Roma's message had been sent three hours earlier—which meant that similar wide-band omnidirectional messages would shortly be sent to *Goldenrod*, carrying the news of the King's death.

And, quite possibly, orders from Home Fleet Command to deliver Lorraine Adamant into a trap.

───────

TIME WAS THE PROBLEM. Three hours earlier, most of Lorraine's family had been dead. Depending on how many people Benjamin Adamant had looped into his coup, there could already be other frigates—maybe even cruisers or one of Home Fleet's battle-cruisers!—hunting the ice belt for them.

Given the clean sweep Roma had reported of Adamants on Bastion, the only reason Vigo could see for *not* hunting them was because there was already a plan in place to deal with Lorraine.

Either way, Vigo needed to keep her safe. Things had gone from very quiet to utter shitstorm very, *very* quickly—and he was half-consciously running a process to validate Roma's video was unedited as he assembled his plans.

His first step was to send a message to *Goldenrod*, to Lieutenant

Major Priskilla Blau. She was the senior of his three section leaders, responsible for Lorraine's close protection detail.

For all of the hours the shuttles had been in space, they were still close enough to *Goldenrod* for near-real-time communications. He considered that for half a moment but then realized they couldn't spare the time for argument.

Blau either trusted him or she didn't, and he had more steps to his plan.

He spared *one* moment for his copilot, looking over at Chief Iva Bevan with a grim expression.

"Shit is fucked, Chief," he told her. "I'm going to give some weird orders and you have to roll; I don't have time to explain."

Iva Bevan had been his copilot since Lorraine had first taken control of a spacecraft on her own. She simply nodded and wordlessly transferred control of the shuttle to her station as he turned to the coms and recorded a pulse message for Blau.

"Archangel-Alpha, this is Archangel-Lead. We have a Black Queen Scenario, I repeat, a *Black Queen Scenario*. Exodus and Praetorian Protocols are active. Implement Case Orange Glorious immediately.

"Priority is the semaphore. This is under the Praetorian Protocols, and these orders are nondiscretionary."

The mouthful of code phrases *hopefully* didn't mean much to anyone outside the Guard. Of course, *Black Queen Scenario* meant that the Guard was compromised and one of the Adamant family had turned on the rest, so even his code words and encryptions were useless against his real enemy.

The point was to avoid warning *Goldenrod*'s crew, because Case Orange Glorious—named, in a roundabout way, for the Glorious Revolution in Old Earth England—called for the Guard to *seize the ship*.

If Blau followed his orders, she'd shut down the frigate's communications and then move to seize Engineering, the bridge, and Main

Life Support in that order. It wasn't a plan they'd drilled outside of virtual reality, but it was one Vigo had made sure his people knew.

He didn't *like* it—he'd gone through the file of every crewmember aboard *Goldenrod* and had extensive interviews with the officers. He *believed* he could trust them.

But until ten minutes earlier, he'd considered Benjamin Adamant's role as Commanding Officer, Home Fleet, as the ultimate guarantor of the Kingdom's democratic monarchy, not the greatest *threat* to it.

So, he had to leave *Goldenrod* to Blau and trust his subordinate. There were more steps to his plan as it unfolded—and he grimaced in a strange relief as his analysis program came back.

It didn't detect any editing in Roma's video. It was a raw video feed, barely even compressed before it was encrypted and sent out to the entire star system to make sure he saw it.

He would have preferred her message to have been faked somehow, but he hadn't expected it to be. Even with the backing of the Praetorian Protocols, seizing an RKAN warship wasn't something he was going to come back from if he was *wrong*.

But his job was to keep Lorraine Adamant alive, no matter what it took.

The coms channel to Commander Chevrolet opened almost unconsciously as he moved through his steps.

"Jarret, we're about to start the last training run before the live fire," the RKAN officer told him. "What do you need?"

"We're aborting the exercise and falling back to *Goldenrod*," Vigo told him. "Praetorian Protocols are in effect; I can't say more."

There was a long silence.

"Vigo, I trust you, but that's a hell of a card to play," the Commander said slowly. "I need—"

"No, you don't," Vigo cut him off. "Praetorian Protocols give me full authority. The Pentarch is in immediate danger and the shuttle flights *must* return to the ship *now*."

"Okay." Chevrolet swallowed. "Assuming I don't want to just tell everyone that, I need a reason…"

"*Goldenrod* just lost long-range coms," Chief Bevan interrupted —and Vigo smothered a grim smile at realizing she'd made *sure* Chevrolet heard her, too.

"By the book, that means everyone falls back to the barn," Vigo said quietly.

"I'll push it to emergency accel, because you're calling it," Chevrolet replied. "But you owe me a beer and an explanation when this is over."

"Believe me, my old friend, I'm going to go through a *lot* of beer and explanations once I know we're clear," Vigo promised. "But we need to *move. Now.*"

Emergency acceleration for the shuttle flight was the full twelve gravities, which was *not* intended for long-range flight.

"At full thrust, we'll return to *Goldenrod* in twenty-six minutes," Chevrolet warned. "And I hope you have a good explanation for *her*, too. Because while *I* have to fall in line for Praetorian Protocols, my Bravo Flight Commander does *not*."

FOUR

Lorraine Adamant had done a lot of things in her now-decade-long career as a naval officer. She'd flown shuttles in every mode from heavy transport to assault. She'd handled the helm of a battleship—as a junior with her boss barely a shout away, but she'd still flown RKAN's ultimate leviathans of the void.

Despite what she suspected to be real effort by some of her superiors, she'd even been in combat twice—against pirates and similar low-threat-level hostiles, but that was all that RKAN had fought in the last decade.

She'd turned eighteen and entered the Adamantine Royal Naval Academy on Bastion five weeks after the Richelieu Directorate sued for peace. Family tradition said she had to make something of herself beyond being a Pentarch, and her time in the Navy had made her determined to do as well by her people as she could.

She was *good* at her job, though her discussions with the personnel office warned her that this was probably her last shuttle posting for a while. She had a year on *Goldenrod*, then she was moving to a tactical-officer slot—probably on a cruiser—as a prelude to a frigate executive-officer role.

In all of that, though, she'd never lived through emergency acceleration for almost half an hour. Twelve-gravity thrust was used for *emergencies*. Their mad dash back to the silent *Goldenrod* had probably cut six hours off the useful life of every shuttle's thruster nozzles.

And she had no idea what was going on. She didn't think anyone aboard the sixteen shuttles *did*. *Goldenrod* losing coms was a bad sign —but the sleek frigate had looked just fine when she'd come in, navigating by visual signal, as even short-range coms were being strangely finicky. *Goldenrod* was even sustaining standard one-gravity thrust to keep everything on her decks.

Her focus had to be Bravo Flight, her people. She'd be briefed on the issue with the frigate soon, but she also didn't expect to be needed to help fix it. First up on *her* list was making sure the Deck Chiefs knew her birds had come back in with nukes aboard—and that the thruster nozzles needed checking over.

All of *that* planning came to a crashing halt as she walked off the shuttle and six Adamant Guards in *fully powered battle armor* closed in around her.

"*Goldenrod* is under full security lockdown," someone declared over the shuttle bay announcement system. "All shuttle crew, please remain in the bay. *Goldenrod* is under full security lockdown."

Lorraine realized that her copilot had been intercepted by one of the Guards, an automatic boarding shotgun *barely* not pointing at the junior officer.

"What in blazes is going on?" she demanded.

"Your Highness," one of the armored Guards said crisply. "Security lockdown is in place for your safety. You will need to come with us."

"I have a job to do, Guard Sergeant Merle," Lorraine told the soldier. "I can't do that with you holding a gun on my copilot."

"*My* job is to protect you, Your Highness," Merle told her. "We have identified an immediate and active threat. Your protection is now the highest priority."

She glared at the Guard and then tried to stride past him,

heading for the main flight-control center. As she expected, the Guards moved with her, a hexagon of mobile statues armored in multiple centimeters of high-tech alloys making as much noise as a shuttle thruster on their own.

"Guard techs will see to your spacecraft, Your Highness," the Guard Sergeant told her. "Your munitions load is suspect. Your *shuttle* is suspect."

"What in *blazes* is going on?" Lorraine repeated, stopping and glaring at the Guard's faceless helm. "This is *our ship*."

"And we cannot trust it," Jarret's voice said in her ear.

Well, technically through her auditory nerve. Her keeper wasn't anywhere she could see, but he'd clearly synced with her neural link once she was in range. He was listening and watching as she spoke— and could insert his messages into both her optical and auditory nerves.

"These are *our people*," Lorraine protested weakly.

"I can't explain yet," Jarret told her. "The situation is fluid and critical. I need you to come with me to the bridge. Now."

He wasn't giving her orders. Jarret had *never* given her orders, even when she'd been very small and he probably should have. He'd been more patient with her than many of her other caretakers growing up, even when she hadn't deserved it.

Jarret had survived her being a teenager with hormones for brains. He had earned her faith.

"What about the lockdown?" she asked.

"That's *our* lockdown," Jarret admitted. "We need to get you out of the shuttle bay and away from the nukes. With everything going on, I have some *very* ugly suspicions about your test payload, Lorraine.

"And no matter what, we are running very low on time."

Guard Sergeant Merle, Lorraine realized, was surprisingly good at a part of his job the Princess had never recognized. Lorraine had started out heading for Flight Control, but with the distraction of Jarret's interruption, Merle had gently guided her to the nearest exit.

Four Guards in lighter gear—from the shuttle crews, she realized —were waiting with Jarret.

"Armor will slow us down," Jarret admitted. "I'm impressed Blau got any of you *into* it, but I need Archangel on the bridge ASAP."

"Understood, sir," Merle said calmly.

There was a momentary pause, then the Guard Major growled in the back of his throat.

"Leave two to watch this door, then back up the techs on Archangel's shuttle," he ordered. "I want every fucking nuke on those shuttles secured, and the armor should help with that."

"If nothing else, we can lift the whole assembly without extra gear," Merle agreed. "On it."

Jarret turned his attention back to Lorraine, who found herself swinging between wanting to trust him, being very confused, and being *utterly furious.*

"With me, Your Highness," he told her. "If you please?"

———

GOLDENROD'S INTERIOR was semi-contained chaos. Lockdown divided the ship into individual sections using bulkheads intended to contain damage or loss of atmosphere. Inside those sections, computerized warnings and flashing signs told people to return to whichever of their duty stations or quarters was closer.

The containment bulkheads slid open as they approached, and key passageways were barred by Adamant Guards in unpowered body armor. The crew was military, and clear voices with firm orders were buying time and order for now, but even in passing, Lorraine could tell that wasn't going to last long.

"You owe me one *hell* of an explanation, Vigo," she snapped at him as she watched a pair of Guards short-stop what looked like an emergency-repair team.

"I do, but we don't have time to stop," he agreed. "Bridge access is this way."

THE EXODUS GAMBIT 25

"No, it's *that* way," she argued, turning toward a different passage.

"That's the *elevator* that will take you to outside the bridge," her bodyguard reminded her. "*This* way is the ladder. I'm not putting you in an elevator until we've been through this ship with a fine-toothed comb."

"You think the bombs on my ship were rigged?" she demanded, thinking back to his orders in the shuttle bay. "And the elevators?"

"I don't know what to think," he admitted. "Beyond that, I need to be on the bridge and so do you."

Two of the Guard went up the steep stairs—not *quite* the ladder tradition labeled them—ahead of Lorraine, with Jarret and the rest following behind her. She was used to having the Guard *with* her wherever she went, but this level of being surrounded was far beyond that.

The ladderwell took them up the two decks they needed and let them out a single section away from the bridge. Here, there was no chaos. No flashing lights—even in the passage outside the bridge, a large portion of the alarms and alerts were muted to remove any impact on the command crew.

There were no *people*, either. They were halfway to the bridge security hatch before they saw *anyone*—and that was a power-armored Guard trooper.

"Bridge is secure, Major, Your Highness," the woman reported crisply. "Lieutenant Major Blau is on site. There are... problems."

"Then we will deal with them," Jarret replied.

The triple heavy-security doors to the bridge were open, Lorraine observed—but as she and Jarret stepped through, each of the doors slid heavily shut behind them like a tomb slamming closed.

That impression wasn't *eased* when she realized that there were already four Adamant Guards on the bridge and they had moved most of the bridge crew up against the wall, covered by their boarding shotguns.

They had *not* managed to get Sigrid Stephson to move. The Lieutenant Colonel stood at her console, her hand posed over the screens in a way that strongly suggested she was going to activate something drastic—and Lieutenant Major Blau stood facing her, her gun leveled at the Captain.

The word *mutiny* somehow hadn't landed in Lorraine's head yet, but at *that* moment, there was no doubt. Whatever his reasons, her bodyguard had just launched a mutiny against *her* commanding officer.

What the *fuck?*

FIVE

"Somehow, that was the problem I was expecting," Jarret said grimly. "Do I *want* to know what program you're trying to load, Sigrid?"

"Major, what in blazes do you think you're *doing*?" Stephson demanded. "Stand your dogs down."

"No," Jarret told her. He sighed, looking back at Lorraine.

For her part, she glared at him. She didn't know what was going on yet either, and the longer this went on, the more she was starting to think that *Stephson* had made the right call.

"And if *I* order you to stand down?" she snapped.

"Then I will ignore you, much as I did when you ordered me to ignore your bedtime when you were nine," he told her, his tone more exhausted than condescending. "Sigrid, it doesn't fucking matter what you think you're about to trigger. You're locked out."

"You... You can't *do* that," she snapped. But Lorraine saw the way her gaze sneaked back down to the console.

"I'm not *supposed* to do that, but I co-opted your Chief Engineer a long bloody time ago," Jarret confessed. "And I didn't have a choice. Please, step away from the console so that poor Major Blau can stop pointing a gun at you. It's making her want to cry."

Lorraine knew Priskilla Blau moderately well, and if the Guard wanted to cry, there was no sign of it on her near-black face. Her expression was flat, emotionless. Lorraine *knew* that mask on her personal Guard, and it scared her.

"I think you owe a lot of people explanations, Vigo," she told her keeper. "And I'll go this far and no farther without answers. Stephson is *my* Captain."

"I'm not sure how much I can do with that claim of loyalty," the blonde officer growled. "My link says I'm locked out. What the *fuck?*"

"Take the helm seat, Lorraine," Jarret told her.

She knew him well enough to pick up more than exhaustion in his voice now. Anger. Frustration. Grief?

Fear.

Vigo Jarret wasn't afraid of anything. The worst she'd ever seen him was the level of embarrassment he'd suffered when he'd had to explain to fourteen-year-old Lorraine that she hadn't *actually* disabled her link to him and that he had both heard and seen the entirety of her losing her virginity.

Because she'd *actually* disabled *his* ability to disconnect.

There was more fear in his voice now than there had been embarrassment and discomfort then, and *that* struck home.

"Please, Vigo, tell me what's going on," she begged.

"Sit down, Lorraine."

She didn't. He sighed.

"Your mother is dead," he said flatly. "Your father is dead. Daniel and Lavender are dead, I have to assume their daughters with them. Taura and Nelson are probably dead. Nikola is probably dead. Guard Central couldn't confirm Taura, Nelson, or Nikola were dead, but they had no confirmation they were *alive.*"

She sat down. The world swept out from under her feet, and even *Goldenrod*'s steady acceleration wasn't enough to keep her grounded. That was... That was *everyone.* Her siblings. Her parents. Her nieces. Taura had been *pregnant.*

"How... Why..."

"We were betrayed," Jarret told her, his tone flat. Not cruel. Not cold. He *knew* how much this hurt, but he'd clearly waited as long as he could to tell her. "Your uncle... *His* Guards turned on us. Undermined all of our security measures.

"Right now, I don't know the details of what happened to anybody, but the details I have, I trust. My orders are to get you out of Adamantine and reassess options once you're safe."

"Praetorian Protocols," Stephson said, her own voice suddenly as tired and grim as Jarret's. "Protect the Pentarch at any cost."

"I'm sorry, Sigrid, but yes," Jarret confirmed.

Lorraine couldn't find words. She couldn't even find tears. She just stared blankly ahead, trying to process the sudden seismic shift in her reality.

"You can't have me locked out, Major," Stephson said. Her voice was urgent, almost pleading. "If Admiral Adamant is behind this, we are in danger. I've served under his command; he will have a backup plan."

"More like three," Lorraine's bodyguard agreed. "But I don't know who I can trust on this ship. I'm sorry," he repeated.

"What *matters* is who *he* trusts in *Home fucking Fleet*," the Captain snapped. "Any intel you received is hours old. He almost certainly has Captains he can trust sweeping this belt, and while I played silly buggers getting us out here in translight, we *can* be followed."

Lorraine was reminded of where she was sitting. *Helm.* She hadn't navigated a frigate since training, but she knew *how*. A tap and a command from her link woke the console up, and she was surprised to realize *she* wasn't locked out.

"I can navigate us," she said, her voice hoarse with unshed tears even *she* hadn't expected.

"Fuck it. Pre-locked course Alpha Sierra Sierra Zero Uniform Tango," Stephson told her. "Plug it in and hit it; we can sort out the rest of the bullshit later."

Lorraine had the course up and loading before Jarret could say a word, then turned her gaze to her bodyguard.

"It's an emergency blast, straight ahead for twenty-four hours," she told him.

"We're out of *time*," Stephson growled. "Look at the plot!"

Lorraine looked and saw Jarret turning to do the same—relying, she presumed, on the other Guards in case it was a distraction.

It wasn't. Two brilliant green icons had just flashed up on the plot. Still distant, they were close enough for *Goldenrod*'s systems to automatically pick up their beacons.

Hermes and *Agamemnon*. Fast cruisers three times *Goldenrod*'s size and *far* more heavily armed. But *fast* was relative, and they were old. Their definition of *fast* was out of date—and fast for a cruiser wasn't fast for a frigate.

And *Goldenrod* was fast for a frigate.

Lorraine hit the command before Jarret or Stephson could say a word. A flare of light, its colors indescribable, washed over Lorraine's vision.

Then everything in the bridge started to shift away from the deck as the engines cut out. The translight drive was a miracle in many ways, but it didn't create thrust in the same way as a fusion engine did.

"Activating the zero-gravity alert," Lorraine said. "But... we're safe for a day. Wha..."

She couldn't even finish the question before grief punched her in the stomach.

SIX

"She's not going to be good for much of anything for a while," Stephson noted, her voice very gentle. "Why do I feel like I'm down my Bravo Flight commander?"

Vigo had expected his Guards to clear the bridge while he was situating Lorraine in the Executive Officer's office—the closest real quiet space for her to find some composure. Stephson speaking as he reentered was unexpected. The rest of the bridge crew had been escorted out, but the Captain was still there.

She was standing well away from all of the consoles, and Blau was right there watching her, but she was still on *Goldenrod*'s bridge.

He'd locked her out of her ship's systems, but he had no illusions about how long that would actually keep a starship's Captain out. One way or another, Stephson either needed to be contained... or trusted.

But she was a Home Fleet starship commander, under Benjamin Adamant's direct command.

"Right now, Lieutenant Colonel Stephson, I'm not sure *you* have anything left," he pointed out. "Priskilla?"

"She said she wanted to talk to you and has been behaving

herself," his second-in-command told him. "And we have to start *somewhere*."

"Start what?" Stephson demanded.

"Clearing the crew," Vigo said with a sigh. "Right now, my people will be sweeping sector by sector, chivvying people back to their quarters."

Zero gravity was going to make that *entertaining*. Uniforms included magnetic soles, but only a few paranoid souls would have had those online while the ship was under thrust. There was supposed to be a series of warnings before thrust went away, for just that reason.

"You need to trust me," Stephson told him. She held up a hand before he countered. "I use the word *need* very specifically, Major. If you don't trust me, we are fucked—but I recognize that right now, you feel you can't trust anyone."

She grimaced, an expression that turned her face into something out of a Viking's daydream or most people's nightmares.

"But you need to find a way that you can trust me," she clarified. "So, you need to do a clearing interview *right now*, with deep-synced links."

Vigo didn't necessarily disagree with her. It would make his life a *lot* easier if he could trust her, and he had implants most people didn't. A deep-link synchronization would allow him to not only tell if she was lying but even to pick up some of her surface thoughts.

It was also, even *without* the tech being installed in his head, extremely illegal under Adamantine law. A court could, in extreme circumstances, order a deep-synchronization interrogation. Even with consent, such an interview was supposed to take place with lawyers and doctors present.

"I cannot ask for or order that," he told her. "Even under Praetorian Protocols."

"You aren't asking. I am offering," Stephson told him, the tiniest of tremors in her voice telling Vigo she understood what she was saying. "If we are to save the Pentarch and survive what the *hell* is going on with our country, you need to trust me. I need you to trust me."

She'd done everything right so far, which meant Vigo was leaning that way *anyway*. But she was also *Goldenrod*'s Captain. At that moment, his people controlled the frigate and its key systems.

But if Vigo released the lock on Stephson's command codes, he was grimly certain she could take control of the ship away from his people. *Goldenrod*'s computers weren't sentient in any way—synthetic intelligences were citizens per the Asimov Convention and recruiting one to run a ship was difficult to impossible—but they were extremely capable and would do *whatever* the Captain told them.

"You understand that this cannot be a conventional interview and, by consenting to this, you are waiving rights even I'm not supposed to ignore?" he asked softly. "I have a full interrogator implant package. That's not even supposed to be turned *on* without three lawyers and a priest."

The joke was weak and her answering smile was no stronger. But it *was* there, and that was the best news he'd had since receiving Central's data burst.

"I understand."

"Take a seat, Sigrid," he told her.

He half-expected her to take the Captain's chair, but instead she crossed to an observer seat—one of the three that *normally* had view-only consoles. As he approached her, she carefully reached up and tapped what looked like an ordinary piece of her neck. A concealed panel slid open, and she tilted her neck to make his access easier.

The vulnerability she was offering *stunned* him, but he had a job to do. A similar panel on his left wrist disgorged a connector cable that he slowly and carefully seated in the port on Stephson's neck.

Data flickered across his vision as his interrogation software set to work on the connection between their neural links. It took a few seconds before he nodded down to her.

"Are you ready?"

"Ask what you must," she told him. "That feels... wrong."

"Function of the interrogator implant," he said. "I'm told it's intentional to avoid attempts at stealth usage."

Which meant there were almost certainly versions of it *without* that safeguard. The version provided to the Adamant Guard Detail commanders had it, though. Legally and officially, a Guard officer would *never* have a reason to use an interrogator implant.

In practice, well. The Adamant Guard's *job* was paranoia.

"Your name, please," he asked.

"Sigrid Jessica Stephson, Lieutenant Colonel, RKAN. Captain of *Goldenrod*. Ident key Papa Quebec Romeo Charlie Echo Foxtrot Seven One Nine Two."

Vigo didn't actually need a baseline, but the confirmation was useful and worked the way she was expecting. Stephson's entire file was stored in his link memory, too, which gave him a lot of questions he could ask if he needed more.

"What is your opinion of Lorraine Adamant?" he asked instead.

"The Lieutenant Commander is a competent officer, not spectacular but better than average at her job," Stephson said. "Honestly, my read of her record and her work here on *Goldenrod* is that I entirely agree with Personnel: she's not as well suited to the shuttle flight commander job as she thinks and is making up for it with base competence and a determination to do the job right.

"I *respect* that, but she's better suited as a tactical or helm officer. Personnel agrees with me. On the other hand, it's a pain that I've had to *have* more conversations with Personnel about LC Adamant than I have about any other O-Four on this ship.

"While I'm not aware of any occasion where she has actively leaned on her family name, it draws attention she either does not wish to avoid or hasn't learned to fully mute."

Through the link Vigo picked up a few pieces that Stephson wasn't saying out loud. She *liked* Lorraine, but had made an active effort to keep more distance from her than she did with the other Lieutenant Commanders on the ship.

At the end of the day, only Lorraine Adamant would have to stand for election as King, after all.

"Did you have any knowledge of a planned attack on House Adamant in general or on Pentarch Lorraine specifically?" Vigo asked.

"No."

The undertone to *that* was fascinating. It was a panicked guilt—a sense that Stephson, as even a junior-ish Captain in Home Fleet, *should* have known.

Even Vigo figured that was going too far.

"Was there any point where Benjamin Adamant attempted to sound out your loyalties to him versus the rest of House Adamant?" he asked.

"I..." Stephson paused. "I have met Admiral Pentarch Benjamin maybe twenty times in total, Major. Most were in larger groups, but Home Fleet has a total of forty-eight starships. Even a meeting of all of our Captains is larger than some might think.

"There were a handful of smaller meetings. Things were said that seemed innocent at the time but I question now." She cursed in a language Vigo didn't recognize—though the implant gave him a rough translation of the *painful* fate she was suggesting for Benjamin Adamant.

"At the time, I thought that if there was any kind of loyalty test being done, it was to see if I was reliable enough to be the captain of a Home Fleet frigate," she concluded.

Given that, between bomber munitions and *Goldenrod*'s own missiles, the frigate carried roughly a thousand nuclear weapons, that wasn't an unreasonable presumption. Vigo had a very good idea of just how many hoops *any* starship Captain jumped through, but trusting someone with a nuclear arsenal that was going to live near the capital definitely required something *more*.

"Where *do* your loyalties lie, Captain Stephson?" he continued gently.

"With the people, the laws, the government, and the monarchy of the Kingdom of Adamant," she told him. "In that order."

His implant danced along that sentence for a moment, slightly reordering it. Before today, he judged, the *true* order would have been *people, laws, monarchy, government.* Though she would have said the same thing.

Now, though, the monarchy and Pentarchy were in shambles. Whatever happened from there, Benjamin Adamant had cost his House a great deal of moral authority.

Vigo *guessed*, though his implant wasn't up to that level of analysis, that King Valeriya would have ranked higher—and also that Stephson didn't normally separate the government of the Kingdom from the monarchy.

Most people didn't, after all. The King was *part* of the government—and was elected like the rest of it, if for life instead of a fixed term.

"If Benjamin Adamant ascends the throne and orders the return of this ship and the surrender of Pentarch Lorraine, will you obey?"

"That has to depend on the information I see," she told him frankly. "Right now, you tell me he's behind a coup, so I cannot unquestioningly regard him as a legitimate authority... but I have seen little actual *evidence* either way.

"For now, I see my primary duty as protecting the Kingdom's succession—which means Pentarch Lorraine. Barring far greater clarity of what the *fuck* is going on, I cannot see any justification to surrendering her to anyone except under *her* orders."

Not necessarily the cleanest answer, but an honest one. Vigo wasn't sure he'd even needed his interrogator implant to know *that*. He disconnected the software with a thought-click and then carefully pulled the cable from Stephson's port.

"Thank you, Sigrid," he told her. "We're in a fine mess here, but I accept that you weren't involved."

"That's a start," she said, closing the port and smoothing her hair over it. "So, tell me, Major. I understand *why* you needed to fuck up my ship. How do we *unfuck* her so we can get to work?"

SEVEN

Before Vigo could answer Stephson's frankly reasonable question, a ping in his ear told him he had a call. He hadn't expected to hear from Archie Patriksson just yet, either, so that bumped his shuttle section leader to the top of the list.

"Archangel-Lead," he said aloud, gesturing for Stephson to wait. "I'm on the bridge; we've cleared the Captain, so that's a start."

"That's good news. *I* don't have good news," Patriksson said grimly. "There's a couple of Chiefs in the shuttle team that *my* Chiefs trust, so we had more hands on Archangel's shuttle than I expected."

"I'd like to say that *is* good news," Vigo replied, switching to subvocalizing now that Stephson knew what was going on. "Which tells me you found something."

"Two somethings, so far," the pilot confirmed. "First, the launch rig for her bombs was ever-so-carefully fucked. Those two nukes for the live fire would have failed to launch—and while we haven't finished breaking down the bombs themselves, I'm betting they were rigged to detonate 'accidentally' when the release failed."

"We checked that shuttle," Vigo pointed out.

"We did," his subordinate confirmed. "Four hours before launch, we ran the standard survey of the shuttle. *I* ran the survey, Major, and while it's *possible* I missed it, I think this was done afterward.

"Certainly, the fucking *bomb* wasn't there then."

Vigo exhaled sharply, feeling like he'd been punched in the gut.

"I'd really hoped that we'd be able to do a *relatively* light validation on the crew," he admitted. *Light* in these circumstances would still make them no friends, but *heavy* was going to take longer than he suspected they could afford.

"Someone installed a four-point-five-kilo charge of Composition D-X-Two-Fifty-Five along the air ducting under the cockpit," Patriksson said. "That was definitely *not* there for either our survey or the Deck Chief's survey, though it would have been invisible to cursory review.

"It's not a fifty-kiloton nuke, but it wouldn't have left much of the shuttle behind."

CDX-255 was approximately five thousand times as energy-dense as the TNT still used as a reference for explosives. Patriksson was right that it wasn't a nuke, but even *Goldenrod* didn't want that charge going off in her shuttle bay.

"I presumed all of that is disarmed?" Vigo asked drily.

"Yeah. Remote detonator via radio transmission," Patriksson noted. "There was a timer, but it hadn't ticked down yet. About an hour left still."

"So, the radio was the primary, and the bomb itself was a fallback anyway," Vigo concluded. "The plan A was for her nukes to fail and detonate in an ugly but not *completely* impossible accident. If that failed, someone on *Goldenrod* would have had to push the button, wouldn't they?"

"Receiver wasn't sensitive enough for anything farther away, according to the Chiefs. Someone on this ship, sir, was holding the button."

"Understood. Tear those bombs apart and confirm what we're looking at, then start validation procedures on the shuttle-bay crew,"

Vigo ordered. "I know you trust the Chiefs you pulled in, but check them, too. *Everyone.*"

"I warned 'em," Patriksson agreed. "I'll count this in their favor, but we have to interview everyone and see what falls out when we shake."

Vigo closed the channel with a thought-click and turned his attention back to Stephson.

"Lorraine's shuttle was rigged to explode two different ways," he told her. "One was by remote, but the command would have had to come from *Goldenrod.*"

Stephson had a *good* mask of command, one that had withstood most of what the day had inflicted. That was a step too far, and he watched the tremor of pure *rage* wash over her face for a moment.

"Someone on *my* ship," she ground out.

"At least one. Someone rigged the bomb, and someone—*not necessarily the same person*—was standing by to hit the button," he confirmed. "We need to interview and examine every member of the crew, Captain. Almost all of my people have the training to do that, but I'm going to need to keep most of them *watching* people."

"Clear Commander Cortez first," Stephson half-asked, half-instructed. "Rose can tear apart the engine room on her own if she has to—she came up the hard way, commissioned for being *spectacularly* good at her job.

"If she's our problem, we're fucked. If she isn't, she's the best chance we have to make sure our engines and reactors aren't going to kill us!"

"That's part of why my people are in control of the critical systems," he told her. Cortez *should* need less clearing than most—she was part of *how* his people had said control—but he truly couldn't trust *anyone* except his Guards. "I don't have a lot of people with the technical expertise to find traps in life support or power... but I *do* have them and they're in the right places."

"That helps," she allowed. "But you need a *real* engineering team to make sure we don't go *splat* when we leave translight."

That particular image sent a shiver down Vigo's spine. That wasn't, as she'd noted, something *he* could protect against.

"I'll let Lieutenant Major Klement know," he conceded, swiftly composing and sending a text message.

Avital Klement was his second section commander, the woman who usually ran backroom support for the other two sections. Her group handled tech, electronics, overwatch—everything from making sure nothing unacceptable ended up on the datanet to providing the snipers who watched Lorraine at events.

She could talk shop with Cortez long enough to get everything in order, he hoped.

"Not that we're safe even if we *do* land safely," he realized. "Those cruisers will be chasing us, won't they?"

"*Hermes* and *Agamemnon*? They can't chase us with anything but dreams," Stephson told him with a snort. "They know our exit vector but not how far we're going, and *we* make eighty cee. They max out at *seventy-two*."

She shook her head.

"*Fast cruiser* became a joke when we got enough seventy-two-cee translight drives to reequip the battleships. Home Fleet's frigates can chase us, but they need to get a ship they trust to our jump point within about two hours.

"And the frigates are only as fast as us. Only three things in the fleet faster than us, after all." She held up three fingers. "*One* frigate, *Estevez*. Courier ships—where we actually have a couple that can make *ninety-six* but the standard is eighty-eight—and, unfortunately, the battlecruisers."

"*Privateer* and *Buccaneer* can catch us?" Vigo said. "That doesn't make me feel better."

"Right now, I will bet you a large bottle of liquor that Benjamin Adamant is looking at the pair of absolute ironclad stick-up-their-ass orthodox Commodores commanding his battlecruisers and wishing he'd found an excuse to replace them years ago," Stephson told him. "Because neither Tatjana Nordberg nor Lance Kovachik are going to chase one of our own ships without orders in triplicate signed off by Central Command.

"How our stuffiest pair of capital-ship commanders got the Home Fleet battlecruisers, I do *not* know, but right now, that's our saving grace." She shook her head. "So long as we find whatever trap is in the translight drive—and I'm assuming there *is* one!—there are games I can play to keep dodging after that and get us somewhere safely."

"Wherever we *are* going."

"Okay," he allowed. "So, that's *one* fear reduced a bit and the other brought very much to the top of my mind."

"I am here to serve," Stephson said drily. "But I will do a *much* better job once I have my crew back and we know who the mole is."

"So... yeah. The sooner I have my XO, my Chief of the Boat, and my Chief Engineer clear, the faster we can plan for the future. My COSH and my Tactical Officer would be real handy too."

"Klement is already on Cortez," Vigo promised. "I'll pin down Commander Savege and Chief Roman myself, I promise."

He didn't offer to let Stephson sit in on the meetings and she didn't ask. The *last* few hours had been hell. The next few were going to suck in a very different way.

But he expected to have finished their current twenty-four-hour translight jump before he had a chance to sleep.

EIGHT

The universe felt gray. It probably didn't help that gray was the default color scheme of a warship office, given the preponderance of bare metal on all sides, and *Goldenrod*'s Executive Officer hadn't decorated her day office at all.

It still gave Lorraine somewhere to be that wasn't surrounded by people. She knew that Jarret would be watching their link carefully, just in case, but he would intrude as little as he could. She *trusted* that.

She trusted him.

But he was the only source of the worst news she'd received in her entire life, and part of her wanted to scream at him. It wouldn't *help*—but it also seemed to be the only thing she *felt* through a haze of disbelieving shock.

Sitting was pointless in zero gee, but she kept her magnetic soles turned on as she dared the bathroom. There were a lot more hoses involved in that process at that moment than she preferred, but she managed to get her face cleaned.

All she saw in the mirror, at that moment, was her mother. Everyone had always told her she looked like Valeriya—and Valeriya had been King by the time Lorraine remembered *anything*. Lorraine had never met her grandfather, who had died in the same car crash that had left Benjamin Adamant too injured to run a campaign for the Royal Election.

Never something Lorraine had thought much about, that memory made her wonder if that was *why*. It seemed so tiny a reason for *this* level of betrayal, though. Pentarch Benjamin was why Lorraine had joined the Navy, the glamor of his uniform and the responsible competence he projected a sharp influence on her younger self.

And so, Lorraine also saw *him* in the sharp-edged features looking back at her, a combination of angle and coloring rare outside House Adamant. From the permanently light-tan color of her skin and hair to her gold-centered blue eyes, she knew perfectly well that the *look* of a member of House Adamant was the result of expensive genetic engineering before the Kingdom had been founded.

Her trillionaire ancestor had done more than just fund three interstellar colonies to set his legacy in stone, after all.

What would His Majesty, Alexander Adamant, First of his Name and First of his House, say about this mess? He'd seen the end of the twenty-second century and the beginning of the twenty-third, and founded his Kingdom in the heady days of the second wormhole discoveries.

He'd founded it on the wrong *side* of the Bright Dream Cluster, as it turned out. When the long-sought wormhole farther out from Earth had been discovered, it was in the Kang Tao System. Almost directly opposite Adamantine across the wormhole back toward Earth.

Lorraine had to step away from the mirror. Looking at it reminded her of the family she'd lost and the family member who'd *caused* that loss. A spike of anger against her uncle made its way through the gray fog of her mind, but it was gone before she could even latch on to it as an anchor.

Only fog remained. Only gray. Bad enough, she realized, that her neural link had popped up a warning. The implants couldn't *do* anything about grief and depression, but they could recognize when her mental health was diving off a cliff.

But what could she do? Ask Jarret to prove his words? She doubted whatever transmission he'd received from Bastion was gentler than his explanation on the bridge had been. Probably *worse*, if that was even possible.

Tears had come for a few moments, but they were gone now. She couldn't even *sit*, not really. Translight left them in microgravity, which meant that sitting was effort, not relaxation.

She slumped against the empty air, letting her magnetic soles hold her in place as her thoughts whirled in circles.

They eventually landed in the only place they could: on *duty*.

Vigo Jarret had known she could only handle so much after being told. But the only person her bodyguard could be absolutely, without question, certain hadn't been involved in trying to kill Lorraine *was* Lorraine.

And while she knew it was no longer the most important thing in her life, she was a trained naval officer with almost a decade of experience.

The situation was a mess and she had skills that would help. She grasped that she needed to watch her own brain like a hawk—but right now, she *also* needed a distraction.

Work sounded about right.

WALKING BACK onto the bridge warned Lorraine that a great deal had changed in the—she checked—ninety minutes she'd been locked in the XO's office.

The bridge crew was gone. So were the Captain and Major Jarret, though the space was hardly *empty*.

Even under translight, a warship's bridge couldn't be empty. But where the Guard had detained a full crew of fourteen officers and specialists, only four people remained.

The bridge was designed to be as informative as possible while avoiding information overload. Lorraine wasn't sure how well the space walked that line, but she recognized that *her* ability to handle information was well above average.

Genetic engineering striking again, she presumed.

A large curved viewscreen, eight meters across and three high, dominated the front of the space. By default, it showed a tactical plot of the area around the frigate. In translight, it showed an astrographic chart with a calculation of their position.

After ninety minutes, that showed them to be roughly five light-days out from their previous location. The limited scan information they had showed that there was nothing near them, but about all they *could* pick up was a translight ship ahead of them.

Arrayed in front of the main viewscreen were three "team" positions—Helm, Tactical, Communications—whose officers on duty and specialists took up nine of the available seats. Each of them had a set of screens positioned to be out of the line of sight of the other two, though they *could* be read from the command position behind them.

Of course, the command position—a slightly elevated dais with the Captain's seat—had better data access via its own screens and a direct connection to the CO's neural link, but some wanted to watch over their people's shoulders.

To the port and starboard of the Captain's dais were the "solo" positions, usually occupied by the Bridge Intelligence and Engineering Officers. Both of those officers acted more as relays from other sections of the ship—the Combat Information Center and Primary Engineering, respectively—than as active command slots.

Behind the Captain's seat were what were called "hotel" stations, for reasons Lorraine wasn't entirely sure of. In her experience, those three seats were used by non-crew observers, but they *could* be rigged up to handle any bridge station except the Captain's.

There were fifteen seats including the "big chair," all set up with the straps and supports to be used under thrust or in zero gravity, but there were only four people in the room when she entered—and only one was sitting.

Two Adamant Guards in light full-body armor were standing outside the door to the XO's office, moving automatically to flank Lorraine as she stepped out of the room. Just from the way they *moved*, Lorraine knew they were Alvarez and Palmer, her usual close detail.

The pair of women made up what she referred to—inside her own head and occasionally to Jarret—as her *super* close detail. While her Guard Detail was sixty percent female, accompanying her into bathrooms and medical appointments was still limited to a very select few.

Usually, Guard Corporals Alvarez and Palmer.

A third Guard, Lieutenant Ulli Esparza, was at the Engineering Officer's station. Esparza was physically jacked into the console, but had enough situational awareness to give Lorraine a reassuring nod.

Esparza was the Guard Detail's ship's systems specialist. Lorraine knew she wasn't necessarily up to speed on the actual hardware of, say, fusion reactors or life support—but Esparza was probably more capable with the software and systems that *ran* those critical pieces than a lot of Navy officers.

And the bridge Engineering console was designed to allow the officer crewing it to coordinate damage control across a crippled starship while the Chief Engineer had their hands in the guts of the fusion plant.

Only *one* of the four people in the bridge was part of *Goldenrod*'s official crew, and Lorraine drew herself to a zero-gravity facsimile of attention and saluted the bald and visibly liver-spotted old man standing next to the Captain's chair.

Senior Chief Leonard Roman might "only" be a noncom, but he'd received the Adamantine Medal of Valor from Lorraine's *grandfather*. Well into his second century, *Goldenrod*'s Chief of the Boat was probably in the half-dozen most experienced individuals in

RKAN. He'd lived through all three decades of the twenty-sixth century and most of the twenty-fifth, and had spent somewhere around *seven* decades in the military service of Lorraine's family.

The wiry old man could have written his ticket to be *anywhere* but, for reasons Lorraine had never asked, had spent the last few years following Lieutenant Colonel Stephson from posting to posting as her senior NCO.

"Your Highness," Roman greeted her, bowing instead of returning her salute.

"It's *Lieutenant Commander*," she corrected him, the response automatic before she even paused to think. She hadn't had to make that correction aboard *Goldenrod* for months—and she'd *never* had to correct Roman.

"Not anymore, I'm afraid," the old man told her. He glanced at the consoles he was watching, then waved her over to him. "I'd say take a seat, but neither of us is going to take the Skipper's chair right now.

"So, just... float. And listen."

In theory, there was no universe or situation where Leonard Roman could give Lorraine Adamant orders. In reality, there were very few situations where even gentle suggestions from the ancient Chief would be ignored by *anyone*.

She took a spot next to Stephson's seat, surveying the bridge as she waited for Roman to speak.

"Right now, Pentarch Lorraine, you are wounded," he told her flatly. "As much, if not more so, than if you'd been shot. I want to be gentle, but I don't know how much *gentle* you can actually tolerate."

"Not much," she admitted. "I need to get to work."

"*Work* for you is going to look very different now," Roman warned her. "You..." He sighed, clearly considering his words for a few seconds. "You don't get to be Lieutenant Commander Adamant anymore," he finally said.

"Time to stop playing at being a naval officer, is it?" Lorraine asked. It came out more bitterly than she'd hoped.

"You were *never* playing, Your Highness," he said sharply. "House Adamant raises their kids well. I've never met a Pentarch who regarded their actual job as a game. I've *heard* of one or two, but they don't join the Navy."

He snorted.

"*They* go into politics, usually, and get a rude awakening about what the Kingdom's voters in general—and *Bastion's*, usually, in specific—will tolerate in both Pentarchs and regular politicians.

"But while you did a real job, a necessary job, and you did it decently, it can't be your job anymore," the Chief told her firmly. "Because we just bolted from Bastion to avoid two cruisers of our own Navy. Things have gone very wrong, which means your Pentarch status is no longer a *potential* but a *reality*.

"We *should* be taking you home to prepare an election campaign. Instead, we're running away. I've seen four Royal Elections in my life, Your Highness, and this..."

"Isn't going to be one," she finished for him. "I don't know enough to be certain of anything, Chief."

"I know this: your shuttle was rigged to blow," Roman told her. "Worse, Cheng Cortez is going through the translight drives and fusion reactors right now, and she's already found two worms in the engines. Something about *quanta destabilization on emergence*, which is a touch above my head."

Lorraine winced. She trusted the Cheng—the ship's Chief Engineer, Rose Cortez—to know her stuff. And, if nothing else, anyone aboard *Goldenrod* now would die if the traps weren't found.

"Do you *want* the explanation?" she asked. "Because my degrees are in higher-order physics, focusing on quantized tachyon phenomena."

"I know that we can only go translight in multiples of lightspeed, which is how we dodge the Einsteinian barrier," Roman said drily. "Given that I understand the tachyon quanta to be a pretty fundamental rule of the universe, I suspect falling off it is *bad*?"

"Two options," Lorraine said slowly, focusing on her memories of the complex nature of the translight drive. "Best option is the drive overloads and crashes us back into ordinary space in pieces that never knew what hit us. Because the *other* option is that destabilization *freezes* us—probably at one quanta, around eight times lightspeed—and we are stuck in translight forever."

Tachyonic speeds were quantized in a way that made relativistic calculations very, very, *very* strange once they got involved. Tachyons only moved in whole multiples of a specific velocity—the tachyonic quanta. With some *very* esoteric physics that Lorraine could only describe mathematically, a translight drive converted an entire ship into a faux-tachyonic state.

And because tachyons *only* moved at multiples of the quanta, that meant there was no real acceleration period and they never approached the lightspeed asymptote. Getting up to multiple quanta was almost as complicated as making the tachyon conversion in the first place, but tech was getting better.

"When instant death is the better option, you know you're having a bad fucking day," Roman muttered. "Cheng says she can't be sure everything is clear and she needs more hands."

"That's everyone's complaint right now," Esparza interrupted from the engineering station. "Klement is elbows-deep in life support and says *she's* found something suspicious, but Second Section doesn't have the hands to get the work done.

"First and Third Sections are working through interviews and clearing the crew as fast as we can, but..."

"But someone put a bunch of literal and electronic bombs on our ship," Roman finished. "So, much as I *hate* the mistrust and paranoia your bodyguards are bringing to this mess, I can't say they're wrong.

"All of this, Pentarch Lorraine, was aimed at *you*," he reminded her. "The *first* plan would *probably* have 'only' taken out one or two other shuttles in Bravo Flight, but once we hit the third or fourth layers of this attack, all three hundred and forty people on this ship were acceptable collateral damage."

"I know." Lorraine wasn't sure what else to say.

"And that's why you *can't* be Lieutenant Commander Adamant anymore," Roman told her, focusing on his original point. "Someone tried very hard to kill the Fourth Pentarch, which means that you need to *be* the Fourth Pentarch."

"First," Lorraine said very, very quietly. "If all of my sibs are dead, I think I'm *First* Pentarch."

"Yes." His tone told her he'd left that point out in an attempt at that gentleness he'd said they couldn't afford.

"In two hundred years, the Kingdom of Adamant has never *not* had a peaceful transfer of power via the Pentarchy," he continued. "But the choice wasn't yours. Our job is now to keep you alive to challenge whatever Pentarch Benjamin tries.

"But *your* job is to work out the best way to launch that challenge. The best way to save our Kingdom."

NINE

Habit and convenience took Lorraine to the Helm station, where her fingerprints and link code opened the consoles for her. A few more thought-commands to her link opened a status summary on the Adamant Guard.

She knew she wasn't as familiar with the tactical network for her Guard Detail as she should be, but she knew enough to read the icons and data updates streaming down the side of her vision.

Jarret had managed interviews for less than two dozen of the crew, focusing on Engineering so far. While Lorraine didn't fully understand the processes by which her Guards would be validating loyalty, she knew that Jarret trusted them.

Which had to be enough—not that the reality of the situation had wholly sunk in. It was easier, in some ways, to accept that assassins had murdered the rest of her family than that assassins had come for *her*.

Her acceptance of *any* of this was still intellectual at best—and she winced as she saw the data packet waiting for *her* on the network. Jarret hadn't sent it directly to her, where she'd have seen it, but he'd loaded it into the local GuardNet for her access only.

Lorraine didn't want to watch the video from Bastion. She wanted to find something useful to do, but her skills were... not critical at that moment. She could fly *Goldenrod*—but barring new information they couldn't *get* in translight, there was no reason to end their jump early. She could fly a shuttle—but even if she overrode every safety interlock created to *stop* that, a shuttle that left its mothership during translight travel would never be seen again.

She was qualified to handle *Goldenrod's* weapons—another useless skill—and could actually manage most officer positions on the bridge or in the Combat Information Center. The problem was that, right then, they needed engineering and software skills.

And Lorraine Adamant didn't have those. Not to the level needed to track down cyberworms meant to kill them all, anyway.

Poking at the console confirmed that Jarret had activated Praetorian Protocols, giving the Guard full control over the ship. Surprisingly, though reasonable once she thought about it, the same protocols appeared to have given *Lorraine* Captain-level access to everything.

That meant she could see that the lockdown was double-authorized now, with both Jarret's Praetorian authorizations *and* Captain Stephson's standard command codes. Looking at the time stamps, she concluded that Stephson must have been the first person the Guard cleared.

A smart decision, in her opinion.

Lorraine was familiar with the full suite of software and systems available aboard a starship, but she'd never had this level of access to a *live* system. The lockdown protocols gave her a *lot* more information than she would have expected on the positions and statuses of the crew.

They were... surprisingly quiet. She guessed that either an announcement or rumor—a communication method barely inconvenienced by sealed bulkheads—had managed to tell everyone what was going on, and the crew was working *with* the Guard to move toward feeling they were safe.

If nothing else, she suspected, telling everyone that Pentarch Benjamin's people had tried to sabotage the translight drive and kill *all of them* would buy them some patience.

The trick isn't to hide what you're doing, a familiar voice said inside her head, and she winced at the memory. *In chess, your every move is visible. Your opponent can see* everything. *In space, in politics —even in ground warfare most of the time!—it's the same. Perfect information.*

But perfect information isn't perfect intelligence. *You could see every move I made. But because I showed you the Alderaan Gambit, that was what you saw. And all along, I was setting up for the Gaspar Gambit. And, of course, if you'd seen the Gaspar Gambit and countered, I could have completed Alderaan. Let people see what they want to see—and always,* always, *have a fallback.*

And with that video note, her uncle had checkmated her in their play-by-mail game of chess. *Again.* That particular game had been... six months earlier? Maybe a bit more. They'd been playing chess against each other since she was fifteen, and only recently was she beginning to win or draw one game in five.

But she knew how Pentarch Benjamin thought. Someone else had been the hands, but the *mind* behind the scheme was his and she could *see* it. They'd found the traps on her shuttle. They'd found the traps on the translight drive. A status report said they'd found a series of worms and a physical *bomb* in the life support system—all being disarmed.

Those were the critical systems, where they'd focus first. But if she'd been setting up a layered trap, she'd have given them at least two possible lines to investigate. The critical systems were a clear one, where the ship's crew would automatically go.

What else? What could their supposed assassin already have access to that her people might miss?

Her eye fell on the *extremely* brief report Patriksson had written on the bombs she'd been carrying. While failures had been built into her shuttle, the *key* trap had been in the nuclear warheads themselves.

And *Goldenrod* carried almost a *thousand* nuclear warheads.

"Vigo, it's me," she said onto the GuardNet as a chill ran down her spine. "Patriksson still has those Chiefs who checked the bombs on my shuttle, right?"

"Yeah. They've got some bonus points, but we haven't got to fully clearing them yet," her bodyguard confirmed. He wasn't asking stupid questions. He *knew* she had a point.

"Get them and Patriksson to the magazines," she ordered him. "If someone rigged *my* warheads to explode, they had enough access to—"

"Do whatever they wanted to a whole lot of *other* nukes," he finished. "We're on it!"

LORRAINE COULDN'T GET a full link sync with Lieutenant Major Patriksson through the GuardNet. The 'Net could give her a helmet's-eye view, allowing her to listen and follow along, but it had less fidelity than a connection to his optic nerves would have.

But few datanets actually had the bandwidth for that. The only reason she and Vigo could share that synchronization without a physical connection was that both of them had upgraded implants to support both transmitting and receiving the hyper-encrypted datastream required.

Still, it was enough for her to watch as Patriksson and a team of experienced Guard and Navy specialists found the magazine doors sealed.

"That's not part of the lockdown," the Guard officer told his RKAN companions. "I already overrode all lockdown protocols for the magazines, plus the normal security systems."

Lorraine double-checked that on her other screen and saw that he'd set an extra layer of security bulkheads in place to close the area around the main magazine off once his party had passed through.

The compartmentalization might save the ship if, say, one warhead detonated. *Maybe*.

An RKAN Chief Petty Officer already had a hand-comp out and was linking it to the doors' systems.

"The lock is local," she reported. "In fact, the whole security system has been cut off from the rest of the ship."

"I'm not seeing that here on the bridge," Lorraine warned Patriksson. "I don't want to poke too hard at what's going wrong, in case I trigger another trap."

"Good call," he confirmed. "Chief, can you open it?"

"Whoever set this up thought they were real clever, covering up the local cutoff," the Chief replied. "But the local net they've created doesn't have the hardware for real security code and..."

The door slid open.

"And I am *good*," the Chief concluded in a satisfied voice.

Lorraine spent a moment looking up the Chief's name. Ubon Metharom was one of the senior shuttle techs—Lorraine had *definitely* worked with her, but the video feed made it hard to recognize people.

The sight beyond the door put her worries over not remembering names and faces into perspective. The personnel access for the magazine was a two-meter-long box—a gap in the similarly thick plating around the magazine—with a second door at the end, equally secured.

And only in the direst of emergencies would nuclear warheads be brought out this way rather than through automated systems. Yet three bombs, not even mounted in the chassis for their terminal attack mode, had been stacked into the access.

They half-filled the space, not even leaving enough room for someone to clamber over them. The radioactives were shielded enough that there wasn't *much* radiation coming off them—but it was enough to ping alerts on Patriksson's helmet.

"I... am going to guess that we don't want to move these without examination," the Guard officer said grimly. "Because, somehow, I doubt these are *only* here as a barricade."

Chief Metharom was already stepping forward, her hand-comp up as she reached for the top warhead. Lorraine suspected that she wasn't alone in holding her breath as the shuttle tech clicked the cables home with an experienced hand.

"Fuckers," she said calmly. "Anti-tamper code, set to trigger when someone accessed the bombs' controls."

"And do... what, exactly?" Patriksson asked, his voice more strained than Lorraine had ever heard before.

"Detonate the bombs," Metharom confirmed. "Except that I went in through the firmware instead of the standard controls." She sniffed. "I didn't see any *external* anti-tamper gear, so that was the logical threat."

"And if any of the rest of us had hooked up to those warheads?" the Guard officer asked.

"Oh, I'm certain any of the munitions techs would have done the same thing."

Lorraine, unlike Metharom, could see the expressions of the other four specialists with Patriksson and Metharom. The *Guard* tech had a thoughtful expression that suggested they *might* have.

The other three Navy shuttle techs—all of whom regularly handled nuclear weapons like this—looked different shades of sick.

"Can you disable it and disarm the bombs?" Patriksson finally asked.

"Yeees," Metharom said slowly. "Whoever did this was clever, but not *that* clever. I need to make *real* fucking sure there isn't something that I'm missing that will send an alert to another package in the main magazine.

"I'll need a few minutes."

"Can you tell when these were placed?"

"At least an hour after the shuttle flight went out, because that's when we finished the after-deployment magazine checks," one of the other techs answered Patriksson's question. "And *presumably* before the lockdown. I'd say the security systems would tell us, but we already established that those are *fucked.*"

"Wonderful," Lorraine muttered—and realized Patriksson had said the same thing in exactly the same tone.

"We'll get these clear and moved into the main magazine," the Lieutenant Major told her after a few moments' silence. "Good catch, ma'am. We've got it from here."

TEN

"If anyone managed to miss one along the way, there were two attacks built into Pentarch Lorraine's shuttle and *five* more hidden in various sections of *Goldenrod*," Stephson explained grimly, looking around the small group in her day office.

Vigo hadn't slept yet. Eighteen hours into their translight jump, he wasn't sure when he *would*. Of course, unlike the naval officers, *he* had toxin-scrubber implants set up to handle fatigue chemicals.

Those implants were about as restricted as something could be without being entirely illegal—because they were *phenomenally* dangerous. Without the chemical markers, it was theoretically possible to keep going until you just dropped dead. His system had a number of safeguards built into it to stop him before it got that far, but the dangers were such that Guard official policy on the use of the implant was *Do not use this*.

But section and detail leaders received them anyway—because while Guard *policy* was written for regular operations, the Guard *existed* for when everything collapsed.

So, Vigo remained fresh and awake even as the others in the room were starting to show the edge. They'd cleared the command crew at this point, which meant Stephson had left the bridge in the capable hands of her Tactical Officer and a full shift—more people, in fact, than would normally be on the bridge in translight.

Just in case.

That allowed her to drag her Cheng and XO into a meeting with Vigo, Blau, Klement and Pentarch Lorraine.

Three RKAN officers. Three Adamant Guard officers. And the Princess herself, who was *technically* an RKAN officer but now the core of everything.

"We can safely leave translight at this point," Cortez confirmed. "The fusion core, sublight engines, and life support also had... *fun* new additions. The nukes were not something I expected."

"Three munitions were armed and physically moved out of the armored magazine," Blau confirmed, Vigo's second-in-command looking grim. "They were on a timer that would have set them off before the next scheduled inspection—roughly ninety minutes after we found them."

"There is a team going through every other warhead in the magazine," Commander Savege noted.

The frigate's Executive Officer was a soft-edged dark-haired woman who normally wore a ready empathetic smile. That was missing today, replaced by a sharp, tired edge.

"So far, they have found *seven* munitions with arming triggers installed and code set to detonate them at further intervals," she continued. "Unfortunately, we haven't had time to inventory the arming triggers, and the system *says* we have all of them we expect to have.

"But since we've found ten armed warheads, either the system is wrong or someone managed to sneak their own arming triggers aboard."

"I'd guess the latter," Vigo admitted. "Though this whole process suggests a level of sophisticated intrusion into our systems that concerns me."

"It's no more sophisticated than your Praetorian Protocols,

Major," Cortez said grimly. "All of this has been achieved with override codes concealed in our software that we didn't know about."

Vigo grimaced.

"Some of it *with* the Praetorian Protocols?" he guessed.

"I... am not certain of that yet, but I have suspicions in that direction," the engineer told him.

"The warnings I received included the information that former members of Pentarch Benjamin's Guard Detail had betrayed us in multiple locations as part of the attack on the Royal Family," Vigo confessed. "Which means that it's possible that the Praetorian Protocols were used against us."

Which potentially explained the part that was concerning him. It made no sense for the warheads in the magazine to have been set up as visibly as they had been, not when the ship was still in theoretical regular operations. Yes, the timers had been set to go off before the *scheduled* inspection, but the nuclear magazines were supposed to get *unscheduled* inspections as often as possible.

No fewer than *nine* officers were expected to stick their heads into the control chamber and run self-test functions when they had time. His experience was that the average week would see at least a dozen random check-ins.

"Someone used our own protocols to move around the ship after we'd locked her down," he said grimly. "At *this* point, we've accounted for everyone and that shouldn't be an issue. But someone likely had the chance to rig up at least some of those problems *after* we moved."

"I would love to believe that no one on my ship was prepared to doom all of us and their shipmates," Stephson said. "The reality, however, is that most of these vectors of attack required physical access to either modify hardware or install software on fully isolated computers.

"We still have at least one mole on board. That, Major, is why I haven't objected to your continuing lockdowns and validations."

"Which so far have found nothing, but we've only cleared half of the crew," Vigo admitted. His math said there were probably at least *four* hostile assets aboard *Goldenrod* and he *should* have found at least one.

"Which is enough for us to do anything except fight a major battle," Stephson told him. "While we can't rule out being jumped by a battlecruiser, I *suspect* that anyone who tried to pursue us will expect us to go farther. That is part of the value of an emergency jump like this.

"We'll be seventy light-days from any sensors, and we're not on a course to anywhere specific. Cheng." She turned to Cortez. "How quickly after we drop out will we be good to go translight?"

"Basically immediately, if we have to," Cortez replied. "Standard cycle time and risk profile, but we're far enough from any gravity well that we can move within a few minutes.

"I'd *like* a couple of hours to go over everything externally, but an external survey shouldn't take more than... three hours, unless we find something."

"All right. Barring an active threat, we'll take six hours at our waypoint, and then I'm going to take us on a bit of a translight spaghetti knot," Stephson declared. "It won't help much if someone follows us right into translight, but if someone is following the trail from Bastion to our drop-out, I can make enough mess that they won't be able to trace us any farther."

"I'm not familiar with translight maneuvers and tactics," Vigo conceded. "I'll take your word for it."

"*Pursuit* is a lot easier than *tracking*, Major," she explained. "But it requires a ship that's enough faster to drop out every hour and re-fix our position. Most of the ships that are *faster* than us are *couriers*.

"There are only three *Martinez*-class ships—and the one here, *Estevez*, isn't worked up enough for pursuit. Other than those three frigates, the only eighty-eights in the entire fleet are the *Pirate* battle-cruisers."

"Because we *bought* their translight drives from Bright Dream,"

Cortez grumbled. "Same for the *Martinez* class, which is why we only have a class of six new frigates."

"And the reason three are late is because we played games with the deal and let Glorious Systems Technology have the three units for six months," Lorraine said, the first thing *she'd* said since everyone had sat down.

Everyone looked at her, and she smiled thinly.

"I don't *talk* about what my mother says, but I do *listen*," she pointed out. "The last half of the *Goldenrod* ships had homegrown eighties for drives, so we figure we can claim to have developed the eighty-eight on our own. But we let GST poke through the ones we bought to smooth the process."

Which, as Vigo's Princess carefully *didn't* say, was more than *playing games*. It was an outright violation of the deal with the Republic of Bright Dream, the star nation that held the wormhole back to the United Worlds.

While the United Worlds didn't sell *their* military tech to anyone, the systems at the heart of the first-order clusters had better access to the core worlds' general tech and research base. The Republic of Bright Dream Navy was built around the eighty-eight as their standard—which meant that, for example, their *battleships* were sixteen times lightspeed faster than RKAN's battle-line translight.

The reports Vigo had read suggested that the RBDN's *technological* advantage was eroded by weaknesses of both doctrine and ship design, but they were also a mostly friendly state over thirty light-years away.

Ton for ton, a Bright Dream ship outclassed an Adamantine one —but the Adamantine ship was slightly *bigger*, on average, and was commanded by officers who'd seen action against the Richelieu Directorate.

The Guard Officer didn't know how much weight to put on the Navy's insistence that it would balance out, because the star nations who were actual *problems* for the Kingdom were closer and more comparable to the Kingdom in tech.

"Bright Dream," Stephson echoed slowly. "I guess that brings me to my main question for this meeting: where do we go from here? We can't go *back* to Bastion—I am confident in my ability to lead this crew in support of Pentarch Lorraine, but asking them to go up against the rest of Home Fleet is too much."

Every eye in the room turned to Lorraine, even Vigo's—and he realized he should have talked this over with her in advance. He wasn't even sure *himself* what "Exodus Protocols" entailed beyond *get the Pentarch out of Bastion.*

He almost certainly had files in his link that had been unlocked by the activation of the Protocols, but he hadn't had time to review them. He'd needed to warn Lorraine that everyone was going to look to her.

To his surprise, however, she seemed to have been expecting the attention. She didn't look *comfortable* with it, but she wasn't surprised.

"Right now, we don't have enough information," his Pentarch admitted. "I have files from my mother and the Guard archives that I have barely begun to review, but the truth is that we need more confirmation of what has happened on Bastion."

She gestured to Vigo.

"I trust Major Jarret more than I trust *myself*," she told the others —which was a heartwarming, if terrifying, thing to hear from the woman you were charged to protect. "I've seen the message he received.

"I believe Colonel Roma told us everything she knew. But it's very little, in truth. I need to go over what is in place for this situation, but I think we will need to at least visit one of the other systems of our Kingdom."

Vigo nodded slowly.

"There may not be much to learn if we do," he warned. "Depending on what preparations Pentarch Benjamin had in place to cover his tracks, most of the Kingdom will *only* ever know his cover story."

"Our news media isn't *that* tame, Major," Stephson told him. "Much as the Navy and Government would *love* them to fall in line, they like to poke holes in the official story. If Admiral Adamant—Pentarch Benjamin—is expecting to keep his secrets forever, that's not likely to work out for him."

"It may work out long enough to get him into power, one way or another," Vigo said grimly. "And if the election crowns him, things get *much* more complicated."

"We won't know much for sure, no matter where we go," Savege reminded them all. "Yes, there are eighty-eight- and ninety-six-cee couriers both in civil service and the hands of the major newsies, so the news *should* be more up to date than we have, but the situation is likely going to remain confusing as all hell.

"And if the Pentarch is working a story and a line, that may add even *more* chaos."

"It will," Lorraine confirmed, the Princess's eyes flat. "I know my uncle. He will be pushing an official story—but he'll also have at least two sets of plausible false truths to conceal the reality."

"Like the layers of the attack on *Goldenrod*," Stephson agreed. "I've read war plans the Admiral has written. He often calls for layered approaches, keeping supporting forces far enough apart to confuse the enemy while close enough to support each other."

That was difficult, Vigo understood, given that travel times between even close stars were measured in weeks. To travel from Ominira—the system closest to Bright Dream—to Beulaiteuhom—the farthest from the center of the cluster—was fifteen light-years. Fifty-seven days for even a ninety-six-cee courier.

Both were eight light-years from Adamantine, though they were also the farthest away of the six stars of the Kingdom. Two systems, Tolkien and Maka'melemele, were less than two weeks' travel away.

But they were away from Bright Dream and the wormhole...

"We need to go to Ominira," he suggested. "Neither allies nor enemies of the Kingdom can truly be trusted right now. But the logistics base at Ominira should be enough for us to get any fuel or supplies we need for a longer journey."

"And one way or another, I think the wormholes are going to be top of mind," Lorraine agreed. "Is that enough for us to start with, Captain?"

"It is," Stephson agreed. "I will do my best to lose any pursuit, and then we will head for Ominira and the bases there."

"We can't trust *any* Navy personnel," Savege warned. "Pentarch Benjamin has been in the highest ranks of RKAN for my entire career. Most of our officers and specialists will follow legitimate orders, orders he can issue without question.

"More than that, though, I doubt he started this plan without making sure he had key station and capital-ship commanders whose loyalty he was certain of. I doubt he's brought many—if any at all!—of them fully into his plans, but he will have people he can send secret orders to.

"And those will have gone with whatever official update went out."

"I doubt he has gone so far as to proclaim that Lorraine was behind the attacks," Vigo said. From the way she winced at that, she hadn't thought of that possibility. "He will almost certainly *get there*, but I doubt he truly expected to lose a Pentarch in the mess."

"No. So, we will be very careful," Stephson agreed. "I'll cut our course for the fueling depot at the gas giant. Do you think your Praetorian Protocols can stretch far enough to fake formal orders for us?"

"I don't know," Vigo admitted, surprised. He hadn't thought of that—but given the level of access the Protocols gave him, they might. "We will have time to sort it out. Once we're finished the *spaghetti knot*, it'll be thirty-six days and some change to Ominira."

"We will." The Captain turned her attention back to Lorraine and sighed.

"We also need to decide just what we're going to do with you, Pentarch," she told her. "This entire mission just became about you.

Pentarch Lorraine Adamant cannot risk that someone will see Lieutenant Commander Lorraine Adamant and question her."

"I see no choice but to temporarily suspend my commission and act solely as civilian supercargo," Lorraine said, her voice level even though Vigo knew the words had to taste like broken glass.

She'd never told *him* she'd considered abdicating the Pentarchy to focus on her naval career.

She hadn't had to.

ELEVEN

Lorraine hadn't been able to stop herself from replaying Roma's message when she finally reached her quarters and collapsed. Zero gravity meant she didn't get to collapse *onto* anything. Even sleeping would require her to pull the hammock from its compartment.

But she could collapse in the air in private more than she could around her bodyguards. And she'd played the message that had destroyed her life again.

On the second viewing, she realized that the Colonel had been more severely wounded than her calm description implied. Had quite possibly been *dying*.

And Lorraine doubted that the Adamant Guard's commanding officer had been left to run free. One way or another, Irina Roma had not lived long after sending that message. Her last act had been to make certain that Lorraine's bodyguards knew about the attack in time to protect her.

Colonel Irina Roma's dying act had been to give Lorraine Adamant a chance at life.

"I won't forget that," she whispered to the empty air. "I promise you, Colonel. *I won't.*"

There was no one to hear her oath but the silence and the ghosts.

In that silence, she carefully crossed to her closet and opened a specific drawer. Money had never been a restraint on her life, so she had three different sets of her Lieutenant Commander's insignia.

The insignia was simple enough: three pips, two gold and one silver, worn on both sides of the collar. It was repeated in a badge above the row of markers for awards—a sparse collection on even her dress uniform, given her peacetime career—and again on the cuffs of her jacket.

Each set had all five trios of pips. Two were the standard gold- and silver-plated studs—one was issue, one was an optional purchase that almost every officer made.

The last set, reserved for the dress uniform of a Pentarch of the Kingdom of Adamant, was two solid gold pips and a *platinum* one. Because House Adamant understood that there were times to show off, even for the members of the House in one kind of service or another.

Slowly and carefully, Lorraine removed each trio of pips from her uniform and placed them in their case. The row of badges joined them in its own case, and she looked down at the nestled pieces of jewelry with sheer exhaustion.

She didn't even recall starting the video message. The most recent mail from her mother, it was flagged and easily accessible in her neural link, and while a thought-click required a conscious, active focus... Well, brains were brains, no matter how much molecular circuitry was listening to them.

A video screen filled about a quarter of her vision, expanding as she focused on it, with the form of her parents.

Lorraine and her mother, King Valeriya the First, shared features and a build. At sixty-three standard years old, Valeriya showed few signs of age. She was tall and slim, with the same light-tan skin, golden hair, and hazel eyes as Lorraine. There was an elegance and a confidence to her that never faded, even when she was recording a message to her daughter in sweatpants.

Her husband, Prince Consort Frederick Adamant-Griffin, had been a diplomat for the Concordat of Amal Jadid before falling for his Adamantine counterpart. Despite his very German-sounding name, he had the dark hair and skin of the Concordat's ethnically Arab majority.

From what Lorraine understood, he hadn't expected Valeriya to become King when he married her—but he had moved cultures and star systems and convinced his own family and government to let him go so he could marry her.

Many gave their marriage credit for turning the Concordat from a stiffly polite rival into a solid ally. Certainly, the difficulties the Griffins and other leading families of the Concordat had put in the way were near legend—and House Adamant had hardly encouraged Valeriya in the matter, either!

Theirs was a romance to sway the hearts of millions, a romance that had cut through national rivalries and eventually *ended* those rivalries. Concordat ships had fought alongside RKAN against the Directorate in the last two wars.

Mostly, Lorraine was just glad they'd made it work and were still so *disgustingly* happy with each other. Even recording this message, which she knew had been hard for her mother at least, they'd been sitting next to each other with Valeriya's sweatpant-clad leg draped over Frederick's still-formally dressed lap.

"We listened to your last message," Lorraine's mother started.

"And read the mail that came with it, I promise," her father continued with a chuckle, patting his wife's leg. "I think you made your point well enough in the video, but I will admit a fondness for well-organized position papers."

"Though you didn't need a sixteen-page position paper to ask anything of *us*," Valeria said quietly. "I understand, though. I also understand why you didn't want to have this conversation in person.

"I'd... rather we did, in some ways, but I know I wouldn't be able to resist trying to talk you out of it, and your mind is made up."

Lorraine watched the video as her parents shared a moment of silent communication that had nothing to do with their neural links.

"I think you would make a fine King, Lorraine," her mother finally said. "And the Kingdom will be worse off for you not standing for the crown. But all of your points about Lavender's twins and the value of House Adamant's service stand."

"And they don't really matter, either," Frederick added. "To either of us, Lorraine. All that matters, truly, is that this is what you want and you are certain."

He shrugged and gave his wife a one-armed hug.

"No one has actually abdicated the Pentarchy before," he continued. "But Adamant has a strong tradition of *Kings* abdicating, so while there is no *structure* for such an abdication, I don't see any real barrier to it."

"We've spoken to both House and Crown Counsel," Valeriya said. "No one sees an issue, though it will require a formal proclamation and some kind of ceremony before the House of the People at *least*—probably the House of the Realm, too, though we may be able to swing a joint session for you."

The House of the People was the primary legislature of the Kingdom, elected for three-year terms to a maximum of twelve years. The House of the *Realm* was the "chamber of sober second thought," elected for a single ten-year term and unable to initiate legislation of their own.

From a formal perspective, Lorraine knew that a "joint session" was inherently legally meaningless—the actions that required a vote in both Houses actually came with laws saying they *couldn't* communicate while parallel votes took place.

For an announcement that she was abdicating the Pentarchy to serve the Navy, it might have worked. That would have been a discussion with the lawyers.

"I presume you don't want to make special arrangements to leave your ship for this," her mother continued. "Let us know when you next have leave and we'll make sure we have the papers and lawyers lined up.

"We'll keep things quiet and under our hats until then, but I promise you, Lorraine, I will raise no barriers to this. If you feel you serve Our Realm better as an RKAN officer than as a potential candidate for King, that *is* your decision to make."

She hadn't even replied to the message yet. The rest of it was less important, but she let it run on anyway, the warm blather of family a soothing shield against the harsh reality she was facing.

Lavender's twins had been a year old. In seventeen years, they would have become part of the Pentarchy as the Fourth and Fifth Pentarchs, displacing both Lorraine and her uncle.

Now she could only hope they hadn't had enough time to be afraid.

She loved her mother, her brothers, her sister. She'd known their bodyguards, their drivers, the personal servants and advisors and staff who would have been there when the hammer fell.

For all of that, she hated what had happened. Hated her uncle for doing it, even if part of her wanted to cling to the frail hope that Roma hadn't *known* he was behind it.

But she couldn't believe that.

And for her nieces, she would never forgive him.

TWELVE

Knocking on Lorraine's door was redundant, Vigo knew. Part of the deal that Adamant Guard Detail commanders made with their charges was that the link sync went both ways. She could mute his visual and audio—did so *far* more often than he muted hers, in fact—but she would always know where he was.

Which meant that she knew he was outside her quarters—and *he* knew she was awake. The pair of Guards outside her door were watching him as he knocked, but there was no visible identification check.

His *link*, on the other hand, told him that both of the two women had independently demanded a digital call-and-response to confirm his identity. They were taking no chances with the Pentarch's safety now.

"Palmer has the door control locked to her link," Lorraine's voice said in his head. "I can override her, but *you* should play nice."

Vigo chuckled and gave the taller of the two bodyguards an arched eyebrow.

"I assume she told you to let me in?" he asked. "Since she says you have the lock control linked to your implants."

"I do and she did," Palmer confirmed. The door silently slid open. "Had to be sure she was ready for you."

"I don't think I'm going to be ready for much of *anything*," Lorraine told them as she walked to the door. "But what I have to do doesn't matter. What do you need, Jarret?"

"Your time, for now," he told her. "And privacy."

"Should I transfer lock control to you?" Palmer asked.

"No. Nobody comes in; handle all calls," Vigo ordered. "If Lorraine tells you I'm leaving, well, make sure I'm leaving."

That went more ways than one. He was *reasonably* sure his Pentarch wasn't going to have him thrown out... but he *was* confident that Guards Palmer and Alvarez *would* physically haul him out of there if Lorraine ordered it.

"Wilco."

Nodding to his two subordinates, Vigo entered his boss's quarters.

The room itself hadn't changed. A Lieutenant Commander aboard a frigate didn't rate one of the limited multi-room suites, but the single room they *did* rate was larger than the bedroom or office of the set a full Commander got. It had a separated sitting area, where Lorraine had replaced the furniture with that odd type of expensive that had endurance and comfort without screaming that it cost fifty thousand marks for a chair.

Delicate cloth privacy screens with a mural of the sprawling Adamantine Manse, House Adamant's main seat—as opposed to the *Kingdom's* state mansion or even the Crown Residence—separated the bedroom from the sitting area. All of the furniture was bolted to the floor, though they were back under thrust at last.

"We left translight, obviously," he told her. "It won't last, but it lets us sit down for a moment."

"My link says six minutes to translight," she replied. "I'm going to stand."

"Fair enough." *He* took a seat, relaxing into a chair that was comfortable enough that he had looked up what it cost.

The Adamant Guard was compensated *generously*, with all kinds of schemes to counteract attempts to bribe or blackmail them, but even so, he hadn't been able to justify the price of the chairs Lorraine had by default.

The only reason he had two of them at his apartment on Bastion was because *Lorraine* had bought them for him as a gift when one of his subordinates had sold him out on his whimsy.

"What do you know about the Exodus Protocols?" he finally asked her.

"That they involve getting a Pentarch out of the Adamantine System," Lorraine said instantly. "Which we have done. Once we're on our way to Ominira, that... about wraps up my knowledge of them. I'm assuming there's more."

"There is," he agreed. "I'd been briefed on some. Most of what *I* had been briefed on, of course, was about getting our hands on a ship to manage the evacuation. What I *hadn't* been briefed on was that Captain Stephson actually had sealed orders in her safe for this contingency."

As Lorraine nodded her understanding of that, he realized what he'd missed when he entered. She still wore an RKAN uniform—he had an inventory of what clothing she had aboard in his link, and she didn't have anything *else* practical to wear—but she'd removed all insignia. Rank, service branch, awards... Everything was gone.

Without that, it was a dark gray jacket over a lighter gray jump-suit with a high collar and thick gloves containing the systems to turn it into an emergency spacesuit. Even without the assorted insignia, it still looked like a uniform.

But it wasn't one. Not really.

"I don't suppose those orders give us a step-by-step plan to save the day?" Lorraine asked. "Because even when I'm not staring at a gray wall through gray vision, the task in front of me is overwhelming."

Vigo had lost his father a decade earlier to the normal ravages of time. His mother was still alive, though he knew he never saw her as much as he'd like. He didn't know what it was like to lose his entire family the way Lorraine had, but he knew enough to know *exactly* what she meant by *gray vision.*

"She'll present them to you when she gets a chance," he told her. "But the orders basically put her under *your* command as a special envoy of the Crown."

He watched her shiver and exhale, nodding as she tried to wrap her brain around that. He didn't *need* the link update on her biometrics to know she was stressed.

"I'm not processing ideas beyond *shove a bomb down my uncle's throat,*" she admitted. "I figured the Exodus Protocols might be, well, *more* than just *get out of Adamantine.*"

"They are," he confirmed. "But because they are the kind of thing that becomes less valuable the more is known about them, a lot of pieces of our various backup plans are buried and secured. There were embedded datacodes in Roma's message that unlocked files I didn't know were in my link.

"The main thing I got out of *those*, though, is that the main information on the plan and assets is stored in *your* link," he told her. "Roma included a code that should have unlocked some things for you, but I have the code for the rest."

She wasn't currently sharing her augmented vision—the one with all of her link software added to her sight—but he could tell that she was going through something on the implants.

"Send me the code," she ordered.

He did, and waited.

"That's a lot of data," Lorraine finally murmured. "I thought I *knew* how much storage this implant had, but if there's more than one of these hidden files..."

"I'm cleared for the full extent of your link architecture," Vigo said quietly. "There are at least two high-density data storage archives I don't believe you knew about."

Most of the neural-link hardware lived at the base of the skull, behind the left ear. There were pieces elsewhere—most people had an access-link cable in a self-sanitizing chamber in their dominant arm, for example—but that chunk anchored on the skull was not only the controller but almost *all* of the hardware for most.

Lorraine had a series of smaller modules positioned next to her spine, built to go unnoticed to all but the most discerning eye. Her normal uterine implants were used to conceal countertoxin hardware linked to her stomach. Where a neural link and link cable were default in the Kingdom of Adamant, she had somewhere in the region of twenty implants.

Most of them classified. Some of them secret from *her*.

"The fact that I have implants I don't know about is a touch concerning," she said drily.

"From what *I* have been told, you have been briefed on any and all *active* implants," he promised. "Covert-memory modules are the worst of it, I think. What have you found?"

"Most immediately important, I think, what appears to be a cover message," Lorraine told him. A window popped up in his sight as she shared the video.

Accepting it, Vigo took a moment to be sure they were synchronized for the playback, and then let it start.

THIRTEEN

Vigo was somehow unsurprised to see Irina Roma appear in his link, sitting behind her usual desk at Guard Central. She was visibly younger in the video, he realized, putting this around the time she'd taken command of the Adamant Guard.

"Lorraine, if you are watching this video, something has gone very fucking wrong," the Guard Commander said bluntly. "This is the emergency cover message for the data package for the Archangel Exodus Protocols, the ones specifically written and established to extract *you* and provide you with resources to handle whatever crisis has seen this code activated.

"There are very few scenarios I can anticipate that will see Exodus activated," Roma noted. "The most likely, frankly, is that we have gone to war with the Directorate again and lost. Badly.

"If you are heading out into exile with this as your sole guide, Bastion and the Adamantine System have presumably fallen to an enemy of some kind. The realities of the situation cannot be predicted from where I am sitting, at a comfortable desk in a time of peace—October twenty-five-twenty-nine standard dating, if you're wondering."

Almost four years earlier, Vigo realized. The message had been recorded within two months of Roma taking command of the Guard —which suggested that Roma had spent a lot of time in her first months in the top job reviewing the emergency plans and recording these messages.

"So." Roma cracked her knuckles and leaned closer to the camera. "You're supposed to be on one of our ships. The Captain will have sealed orders for this protocol, opened by a code that Major Jarret has encoded in his neural link.

"Assuming all protocols have been authorized properly, he gave you the codes to unlock the protocol archive in your link. There *are* other methods, but that's the most likely and it doesn't change much.

"Either way, this message is assuming the initial phases of the Protocol are complete and that Jarret has extracted you from Adamantine. From there, I see three main paths forward for you, all depending on what the situation is."

Roma's blithe statement that she assumed Vigo would be able to get the Pentarch out was heartwarming, if terrifying. He *had*, but he was all too aware of how close they'd come.

Pentarch Benjamin and his people had been ready for this. Vigo and his people really hadn't been. Fortunately, ready or not, they'd been paranoid *enough*.

"The first option is the Concordat of Amal Jadid," Roma said, holding up one finger. "Your blood ties to the Griffin Family will guarantee you at least a chance to speak to the Five Families of the Three Stars. And their Popular Assembly, of course."

There was no *official* special status for the Five Families of the Concordat of Amal Jadid, but they had both wealth and reputation enough to make certain that they and their proxies basically acted as the political parties in the Concordat's Popular Assembly.

And unlike the Kingdom, the Prime Minister wasn't required to give up their party to serve as head of state. Of course, the Concordat's First Minister had much less actual *power* than their Adamantine counterpart.

"Money will open more doors, of course, and you will find codes included for accounts in the Concordat of significant depth. There are also credit sequences drawn on multiple key banks that should be useful whatever your next steps are."

An alert rang in Vigo's link, and he made sure his feet were on the floor and his magnetic soles on before the engines cut out. He didn't lift out of the chair or anything as dramatic, but he was no longer being gently pressed into it, and it lost a lot of its comfort.

"Your father's family will keep you safe, but my honest assessment is that the Concordat is unlikely to be able to handle whatever threat has sent you into exile," Roman admitted. "They have three star systems and nine capital ships to the Kingdom's six and *sixteen*. Plus, thanks to your parents, they have become reliable allies.

"If Adamantine has fallen, I have to presume that either the Concordat has been badly battered in their own right or doesn't have the strength to stand up to whatever took us down."

"Or the strength to stand *against* our fleet in the wrong hands," Lorraine growled. "My father's people might fight for me, but they can't take Adamantine from RKAN."

"Unfortunately," Vigo agreed. Roma hadn't even *considered* the possibility of an internal coup, he suspected, though the plan was set up to handle that possibility.

"There are several more star nations in the Bright Dream Cluster that are friendly enough that you could approach them and ask for help, like the Republic of Bright Dream themselves," Roma continued, the recording unable to adapt to their conversation. "All of them suffer similar problems to the Concordat: the forces they could commit, even in the most generous scenario, fall short of what the RKAN already possesses.

"And there are enough *other* rivalries in play that you wouldn't be able to get them all on side." Roma shrugged. "Or you might. Your family has produced some silver-tongued diplomats over the years, and as I record this, I'm afraid you're too young for me to be certain where your skills will lie.

"I include any and all attempts to find allies in the Cluster as the same option as going to the Concordat. Your father's people should be your first stop if you take that route regardless, but I need to be clear about how unlikely it is to bear fruit."

The Guard Commander paused, settling her thoughts and taking a sip of water—this video was clearly too classified to have been edited after the fact.

"The second option is one I suspect will stick in the throat of any member of your family," Roma said wryly. "The accounts and secure credit sequences now available to you are more than enough to operate a starship for an extended period. Exile in the Concordat might be safest, but the Griffin Family would inevitably see you as an asset—to be protected, yes, but also used.

"With a ship and financial assets, you should be able to proceed to the United Worlds or to the Leonstar Wormhole in Kang Tao. In the Leonstar Cluster or the United Worlds, the funds set aside for you in this plan would allow you to live out your life as a wealthy, *safe* woman.

"If all is lost, which seems unfortunately likely, retreat and a quiet life may be the best choice."

"I'm surprised she even managed to suggest that with a straight face," Lorraine said. "Because she's right—she *does* know my family. And I doubt it's what *she'd* want me to do."

"You'd be surprised," Vigo told her. "The Guard's job is to *protect* you, Lorraine. Right now..." He trailed off and was surprised to realize Lorraine had paused Roma's video and was looking at him oddly.

"I don't see an answer to what has happened that doesn't involve a massive war," he confessed. "We *might* be able to convince a couple of the systems to defy Benjamin and join us, call on those friendships Roma mentioned, but a lot of people would die.

"And we might well see Richelieu move in while we're fighting ourselves. I don't want us to walk away"—he thought; he couldn't be certain—"but we need to face the costs of fighting back.

"We might take the crown from your uncle and *lose the Kingdom.*"

She grimaced, but she nodded her understanding.

"I don't think I have it in me to be a wealthy expatriate, even on *Earth,*" Lorraine told him. "But I see your point."

She resumed the video as Roma took another drink of water.

"The third option—and the one we've strangely put the most effort into in some ways—is a shot in the dark," the Guard Commander told her. "The Kingdom of Adamant, like most powers in the first-order clusters, is a signatory of and a contributor to the United Worlds Stability Convention Fund."

Vigo winced. *Shot in the dark* was probably a joke as well an overestimate there. There were several funds like the Stability Convention Fund that star nations on the other side of the wormholes from the United Worlds were *encouraged* to *voluntarily* donate to.

In theory, the Stability Convention was an agreement to respect the sovereignty of the borders of the star nations of the first-order clusters—the groups of stars one wormhole transit away from the stars around Sol itself. That agreement was supposedly backed by the power of the United Worlds Navy. The Fund was intended to underwrite the costs of demonstration deployments to tell would-be conquerors to go home.

Except that even in the case of open invasion, the Convention had *never* resulted in a United Worlds Navy deployment. On rare occasions, a United Worlds diplomat had shown up in a *courier*—though the proof that the Convention was being considered meant that said diplomats usually managed to resolve the issues with astonishing speed.

For an arguably internal dispute like this? It wasn't *impossible*, he supposed.

"Most of the secure credit sequences in your data files are drawn on United Worlds banks," Roma continued. "We have a significant and well-funded diplomatic and trade organization in the home stars as well that you will be able to draw on."

Maintaining that network of diplomats and trade officers was what required paying in to the assorted Funds, of course. No one was ever going to *say* that you wouldn't get the permits and licenses without doing so... but the evidence was quite clear.

"Your status as Pentarch, the resources this protocol makes available to you, and our diplomatic staff *should* make it possible for you to speak to the Grand Assembly," Roma concluded.

"We are not particularly relevant to them," she admitted. "But that also means that the resources necessary to save our Kingdom are minor to them. It is a shot in the dark, one where I can't really assess the likelihood of success.

"But if the UW agrees to provide support, *nothing* in the universe will stop them from restoring our Kingdom."

The Guard Commander looked down at her water, then back up at the camera.

"Lorraine, there are no good options in front of you if this protocol has been activated. I expect and hope that all of this contingency work, including this video, is wasted effort.

"But it is my job to prepare for all contingencies. Beyond the money we are putting at your disposal, your archives should have a relatively up-to-date listing of both overt and *covert* assets available in the Cluster and into the United Worlds.

"I can't know what scenario would possibly lead to the Exodus Protocol being activated. Go with God, Pentarch."

The recording ended and Vigo tried to collapse further into the chair. He failed, zero gravity meaning that the effort lifted him *out* of the seat, and he sighed as he turned his gaze on Lorraine.

"Well?" he asked.

"We don't have enough data," she told him. "It's possible the coup didn't close as tightly as we fear. That Benjamin isn't in control. Maybe... even if he *is* in control, there's still a chance he's planning on running the Royal Election and relying on the fact that the new Pentarchs haven't expected to be on the List!"

The List, Vigo reflected, did automatically update. *If* all four of

Valeriya's children were dead, then Benjamin was still merely First Pentarch. His son was Second Pentarch—though the three after that would be more distant cousins.

"House Adamant has ninety-five living members," he conceded. "If he runs the election, we can insert you quite publicly even from Ominira. That's part of why the election *has* to be as long as it does."

"Which gives us options," she said. "I don't want to be King, Vigo. I was about to give up the Pentarchy. I know you know, even if I hadn't told you.

"But with all of this?" She growled in the back of her throat, an angry and terrifying sound he'd never heard her make.

"I will fight a lousy election to keep my mother's crown out of his hands," she promised. "I... I am less sure if I will fight a war, but I'm not ruling it out. Ominira, Vigo.

"There, we will find more answers."

"And if the answers aren't what you want?" he asked.

"I don't even *know* what answers I want," Lorraine told him. "So, whatever they are, we will plan our next steps there."

FOURTEEN

Lorraine was far from an expert in interstellar finance—or finance in general, for that matter. She *had*, however, been raised knowing that she'd spend a good portion of her adult life as a Pentarch, with a nonzero chance of ending up as King of Adamant.

So, while her actual formal university education—first alongside her commission, then via correspondence because a master's degree looked good for promotion—was in tachyonic physics, she'd had the equivalent of a full minor program in... well, a *lot* of things, by the time she entered the Adamantine Royal Naval Academy.

She needed that background to understand the files hidden in the Exodus Protocols archive. The simplest piece was the secured credit sequences—encrypted one-time codes that told a bank in one star system that a bank in *another* system had a specific amount of funds set aside to honor that code.

Actual bank transfers were long, slow processes requiring back-and-forth validation via couriers and multi-week or more journeys. Money flowed at the speed of information and information only moved at the speed of the fastest ship.

But a secured credit sequence would allow the owner to access funds immediately, leaving the transfers for the banks to sort out in the background. Theoretically, they were unique and impossible to duplicate, though Lorraine knew that the reality was more complicated.

There were more complicated financial instruments tucked away in physical and digital archives that had been hidden in her Guard Detail's armory. Some of those chips had clearly been there for *years* —and some, like the data in the archive in her link, had been updated in the last few weeks.

Most of the resources and information, she presumed, were shared between multiple emergency protocols. She doubted, after all, that there was a hundred-million-United-Worlds-interstellar-credit fund set up for each emergency fund for each of the Pentarchs!

And that was just the amount she was *certain* of, which was mostly the credit sequences on UW banks—with about fifteen million credits in assorted "bearer bonds" and similar near-cash investment instruments.

The weight of United Worlds banks and United Worlds credits meant that the majority of the emergency assets were drawn on them. There were funds drawn on the Concordat and the Republic of Bright Dream, too, totaling about another twenty million credits' worth of taj and pounds.

The other, smaller banks made up about ten million between them.

It was notable, she knew, that there was *nothing* drawn on Adamantine banks. House Adamant had major ownership in several major banking entities, and the Kingdom's financial infrastructure *dominated* the chunk of the Bright Dream Cluster on the "wrong side" from the Kang-Tao–Leonstar Wormhole.

Money was only a tool, though, and it was her *people* who would be key to her next stages. And that thought carried her through *Goldenrod*'s corridors to her next meeting, four of her Guards in lockstep around her.

She doubted she was going to go anywhere on her own for a long, *long* time.

—————

"WE HAVE COMPLETED the interviews of the entire crew," Jarret told the gathered command staff.

There were a lot of theories available for the best way to "sit down" to a meeting in zero gravity, ranging from *just have it virtually* to *stand around via magnetic soles* to *strap people into chairs for tradition's sake.*

The meeting aboard *Goldenrod* was somewhere around the middle. The conference room was part of the so-called "presence section" of the frigate, which meant the ever-present gray metal had been floored in carpet, with wood trim and drywall covering the walls.

That created a very clear orientation to the room, and Stephson had mastered using the seats in zero gravity as she sat at the head of the table.

Lorraine, at the other end, lacked that skill and didn't even try. She had the magnetic soles of her uniform boots on and otherwise just hung in the air—and both Savege and Jarret were doing much the same.

The room was sized for up to twenty people, with one of the decorative bulkheads removable to merge it with the room next door to create a ballroom. Frigates were, after all, the most common RKAN warships seen outside the Kingdom, and they needed to show the flag and show it *well.*

Not least because with fourteen six-ship squadrons in service, they were simply the most common RKAN warship, period.

The tools built for that reality would serve Lorraine's new mission well.

"I haven't heard anything requiring Lieutenant Commander

Zdravkov's Marines," Stephson noted. "So, either you handled whoever you found with your Guards, or..."

"We found nothing," Jarret said grimly. "We've pushed the constitutional rights of our people and their dignity as far as I feel we *can*. Given the techniques and tools available to my people, we *should* have IDed our problem.

"But so far as we can tell, everyone aboard this ship is clean and loyal. I would *love* to believe that, but..."

"Someone rigged this ship to explode—or to kill us all in other ways," Savege finished for him, glancing at her boss. "So, you think someone got past your validation tests somehow? We still have a threat?"

"People did leave the ship the day of the attack," Lorraine pointed out, thinking back. *Goldenrod*'s shuttle wing handled a lot more personnel and cargo transport than they did strike ops, which meant she'd known about most personnel movements.

"We were prepping for a strike exercise, so I remember the hassle of arranging the transport," she continued. "A few back-and-forths. Mostly with *Sultan*, I think."

"Which seems stickier in hindsight than swapping bodies with the flagship would normally," Stephson said sadly. "I don't recall any permanent orders."

"No," Savege agreed, staring off into the distance as she consulted her neural link. "We sent some people over for a logistics planning session. Three of my admin staff were on *Sultan* when we fled the system. We didn't have any extra hands with us."

Lorraine shook her head, grimacing.

"There is no way everything was done by people who left before the exercise started," she told the others. "Some of the cyberworms, maybe, but too many pieces of the other problems required someone on hand."

"Exactly," Jarret agreed. "Just the bombs set up in the magazine alone required someone to move those weapons. We *should* have security footage, but..."

"*Goldenrod* is pissed about that," Stephson said. "A ship's computer net isn't a synthetic intelligence, but the human interaction protocols mean it has *some* personality."

About as much sense of self as the average dog, was how it had been described to Lorraine. There were hard limits set of what could be built to have a specific purpose—synthetic intelligences were people and citizens, and had to be recruited—but the level of capability and complexity necessary to run a starship inevitably resulted in some level of personality.

And while *Goldenrod* wasn't necessarily aware of *herself* in many ways, she could definitely be frustrated when she kept not being able to do things she *should* be able to do.

And the lace and spiderwebs that were all that remained of hours of security footage and trackers after the cyberworms had finished with them was useless. The ship's computer should have been able to answer a lot of questions about who had done what and when.

Instead, the security memory of the key twenty-four hours was a mosaic of copied data, with no clarity as to when the original seconds were from.

The live data at the time had appeared correct, so no one had realized that a virus was shredding it behind the scenes.

"The ship will get over it," Savege told her boss. "I'm not sure *I* will. We need to trust our crew, and you're telling me that everything we have done isn't enough for that?"

Jarret sighed, glancing at Lorraine for support.

She shrugged. This was his realm of expertise, not hers.

"We can assume that the vast majority of the crew are exactly what our efforts show them to be: loyal and dedicated, with a full understanding of what has gone down and a commitment to help finish the job," he told them all. "We have a few—twenty or so—who have asked to be left at the next place we stop. They don't want to go against the Pentarch, but a run to unknown destinations with questionable missions... It's a lot to ask.

"I'm surprised more haven't asked what the exit options are."

"Are you comfortable letting them go, Major?" Stephson asked. "I don't want to keep anyone who doesn't want to be here, but if they are a security threat..."

"They'd be more of a security threat if we forced them to stay, frankly," he admitted. "We're better off short a few crew than we are locking them in the brig—and they won't be able to tell Benjamin's people anything they don't already know, either.

"They can't betray our plans, because they don't know them."

"*We* don't even know them," Savege pointed out.

"I need to see the news updates from home," Lorraine reminded them. "The civil-service couriers should have updates from as much as a week after we left. Some of the news carriers might be a bit behind that, but this is going to be the breaking story of the decade.

"The news ships will be *desperate* to get the scoop to our systems and sell it."

The news carriers and mail carriers for most systems were the same companies—because they were the same *ships*. They'd started as mail ships but realized they were also the ones carrying the news updates.

There was a complex structure of interwoven licenses and corporations, but the most basic fact was that if you wanted interstellar news when it arrived, you paid the primary mail carriers. Otherwise, you waited to see other people's interpretations and analysis of what the news ships sold *them*.

The Kingdom's government and Navy both maintained fleets of ninety-six-cee couriers, but even they depended on civilian mail ships for a lot of day-to-day traffic.

"And then?" Stephson asked.

"I don't know," Lorraine told her. She had a *leaning* toward one of Roma's suggested plans, but none of the plans were *good* ideas. "We still know so very little about what happened," she reminded them. "All we really *know* is that my family is dead."

That silenced the room and she grimaced.

"So, in Ominira, we find some answers and updates. Then we

decide where to go from there. Hopefully without Lieutenant Admiral Tunison ever realizing we were there."

Because she'd checked. Lieutenant Admiral Are Tunison had been her uncle's Chief of Staff as a Commodore. Now he commanded the Ominira Fleet Station, the battle group watching the route toward the wormholes.

Lorraine saw absolutely *no* way that Tunison wasn't her uncle's man through and through.

FIFTEEN

Lorraine's sleeping habits were, normally, extremely fixed. The duties of a naval officer required fixed duty shifts and a vast amount of data-work, meaning that her day was scheduled tightly.

Like everything else, that had changed drastically since the assassination attempt and flight from Adamantine. Her entire universe had been turned upside down, and while the habits of her adult life weren't completely gone, she now lacked an external schedule.

Fourteen days into their thirty-six-day journey, that left her half-seated, half-hooked-on-the-chair at the desk in her office. She hadn't moved out of the Bravo Flight Commander quarters, though she knew there were a dozen arguments in favor of her transferring to the guest quarters reserved for civilian dignitaries.

The main one, though, was that the guest quarters were more easily secured—but her quarters had been upgraded and modified over the last eighteen months to be more secure than any other place on the ship.

It had separate life support, carefully managed wireless blocking only permeable via specific hardware points linked to specific link IDs, bug sweeping—the works. There was nowhere on the ship safer for her to sleep—and nowhere more secure for her to go through the highly classified documents that had been buried in the back of her brain.

The official trade organization of the Kingdom of Adamant was anchored on a line of star systems stretching from the Bright Dream Wormhole's inner end in the Tavastar System toward Sol itself.

That was an eighty-two-light-year journey, a full year at *Goldenrod*'s best speed. Plus the time to get to the wormhole itself, it would be almost three *years* for them to get to Sol and back.

A tickle in the back of her throat forced her to cough and take a sip of her lukewarm coffee bulb, reminding her that she was up late and she'd let the hot drink cool.

Part of the security for her quarters was that she had a wholly self-contained coffee unit that needed its water tank refilled rather than drawing from a water line like most aboard the ship. There was still enough for another pot of coffee, and she started it up as she tossed her existing drink.

The tickle remained and she opened a bulb of water as she considered the physical path for their craziest options. According to the notes she now had, there was a wormhole that would take them right to Sol roughly a week's flight from the Bright Dream Wormhole. That made... very little sense, honestly, though it looked to have filtered into broader awareness closer to Bright Dream over the last decade.

If there'd been a wormhole from Sol to near Tavastar, that would have been found before the Tau Ceti Wormhole. Any wormhole from *Sol* would have been a major historical note, not a small aside in her notes.

As the machine bubbled and her throat scratched at her, she dove into the information for the key, the piece blandly concealed in a pile of corporate speak and technical jargon—and almost forgot her coffee as she stared at what she'd found.

The Tavastar System didn't have a habitable world, rendering its only value the wormhole outward. While some people lived there, the nearest settled world was the Greenhall System, two light-years away.

Greenhall and Tavastar were both arguably secondary stars of the supergiant Calypso, not quite orbiting but forever caught in the trail of their immense neighbor. Tavastar anchored a gas giant, a few dusty balls of rock, and a wormhole that jumped about six hundred light-years.

Greenhall anchored asteroids, gas giants, and a terrestrial garden world that had proven habitable—everything for a major civilized star system. But at eighty-four light-years from Sol, it was pushing the limits of even the United Worlds' ability to maintain connection and authority.

And now it was home to one of three *artificial* wormholes linked to Sol that the United Worlds had built fifteen years earlier. The Charon Complex, the Sol ends of the three were called. *That* was a game changer, one that she was surprised hadn't come up before.

A bit more poking, interrupted by another bout of the annoying new cough, gave her the answer. *Officially*, the Sol-Greenhall Wormhole was a fluke, a newly developed natural wormhole. The United Worlds had not *admitted* that they were building wormholes, and the Kingdom's intelligence had only truly confirmed it in the last couple of years.

Universities and even junior-officer intelligence briefings couldn't challenge the official position of humanity's unquestioned first power. The more complete notes she now accessed said that the Charon Complex hadn't been repeated—something to do with questions around the stability of running three wormholes to one place.

The best guess was that the UW had built at least ten more point-to-point wormholes, at a pace of roughly one a year. If the Kingdom of Adamant had any information on *how* it was being done, Lorraine didn't have it. Some information on cost had been acquired, though, and *that* was sobering enough.

To build one wormhole required resources equivalent to the gross economic production of all six star systems of the Kingdom of Adamant. *For three years.*

No one except the United Worlds could do it—but it was the existence of the Sol-Greenhall Wormhole that turned Roma's third option from *impossible* to *improbable.* She *could* get to Sol in time to ask them for help that might matter.

They just might not *give* it—a thought that triggered another round of angry coughing before she could swallow her coffee.

She froze, staring down at the steam venting from the bulb. The coughing was... odd, but she spent enough time around people that colds were inevitable. Her healthcare implant could deal with it, but she'd still cough.

But despite her magnetic soles, she was still in zero gravity. The steam from her coffee bulb would go toward the cycling vent concealed near the top of the room.

Instead, it was forming an expanding cloud around her hand and the container. There was no airflow.

"Computer, air scan of the room," she ordered aloud.

"Scan reports N-two, seventy-seven percent. O-two, twenty-two percent. CO-two, one percent," a voice immediately replied.

That was normal. The standard mix on any spaceship, basically—slightly more oxygen-rich than Earth-normal, but comfortable and easily measured. It was actually slightly *less* oxygen-rich than, say, Bastion—but also lacked assorted other trace gasses.

That shouldn't have been making her cough. Or her mouth dry. Her breath was starting to come short, and the air *tasted* wrong.

A silent command to her implants brought back the same result. The *exact* same result, and she slapped in an override to confirm what she suspected: her link was checking the ship's systems for the air data.

That made sense, since any trusted environment would have better sensors than she did in her implants. Except at that moment, she didn't *trust* her environment, and she should have changed that toggle.

A new report appeared in her vision, drawing from a tiny—and hence unreliable!—sensor chip at the top of her left lung.

Oxygen was correct, which was what would have triggered an alert. Carbon dioxide was high... and nitrogen was low, replaced with CO_2 and other things her implanted scanner couldn't ID.

Her life support had been compromised.

———

LORRAINE'S first response to *any* danger had been drilled into her since she was old enough to have a neural link. Before that, even. From the moment she was able to understand the idea, she'd been taught to go to the Guard if she was worried.

That had morphed over the years into *call on your link* and specifically *call Jarret,* but the instinct had become so ingrained, she barely even *thought* before triggering the emergency connection on her link.

And the NO SIGNAL response tore the ground out from under her in a way even the lack of gravity couldn't.

Her room was secured against all connection. There were six— she thought—hard-wired connections through that security, linked to her implant codes on this side. No one could call *out* from her quarters without her authorization.

Except now her authorization apparently meant buzzer shit. And unlike buzzers, a strange insect-like bird native to Bastion, that absence *wasn't* harmless.

A thought-click ordered her room door to open as she crossed to it, but Lorraine wasn't surprised when that also failed. She'd been so lost in her research, she'd missed when she'd lost connection.

She might be able to find it later, but right now, the sharp dryness in her mouth told her she didn't have a lot of time.

What she *did* have, though, were ways to *buy* herself time. A specific sequence of three presses on her uniform collar resulted in a puff of air, a warning beep to remain still, and a hood-like clear plastic helmet emerging from the back of the collar and sweeping over her head.

Habit ran her through the full drill, locking seals against her boots and putting on the gloves, without even thinking. The helmet was what she needed right now, sealing her against whatever was going on in her room.

Her implant happily reported that the air from her emergency suit, at least, wasn't compromised. A few deep breaths cleared *some* of the dryness in her throat—and the spots in her vision she hadn't even noticed yet!

But the suit wasn't intended to be a long-term solution to anything on its own. The concealed microreservoirs throughout the fabric only contained a *ten-minute* air supply. In combat, she'd have been wearing a secondary oxygen bottle in her harness.

She could extend the air supply further if she could trust the outside air, but while it hadn't *looked* like there'd been any poison in the air, that might not *remain* that way.

Lorraine hammered sharply on the door, once, twice, three times. There wasn't so much as an answering knock, which left her worrying about Palmer and Alvarez.

She needed to look to her own safety first, though. Everything in her closet was designed for both thrust and zero gravity, which sometimes made it hard to sort through but also allowed her to throw the entire compartment wide open to check for her combat harness.

If she'd been going drawer by drawer, the explosive might have taken out her hand. It would *definitely* have breached her suit integrity—but most critically, at that moment, the tiny blast wrecked all three of the emergency oxygen tanks she'd stored away, cracking their shells, and sending all three bottles careening around the room as they lost the precious gas she needed to survive.

Who in all stars had managed to sneak even a tiny—almost prank-level, really—bomb into her quarters?

No one was supposed to have access to her quarters when she wasn't around. While she'd been senior enough to warrant sharing a steward, she'd declined for security reasons.

Lieutenant and full Commanders shared steward noncoms, except for ship commanders. Only Lieutenant Colonels and above would have a permanent assigned steward, and Lorraine had been a long way from there.

She'd refused to push that standard and so cleaned her own quarters and maintained her own uniform and such. That way, the Guard could simply not let anyone *into* her space when she wasn't there.

No one should have had access to her closet at all, let alone sufficient access to plant a bomb that had just taken her from three hours to solve the problem to nine minutes.

"Think," she ordered herself, stepping back from her smoking closet—and *that* should have been setting off sensors too, alarms that her implant could tell her weren't activating.

The room's sensors were compromised. The pass-through systems for her coms were either broken or had seen her access revoked.

"The sensors have their own connection," she said aloud, looking for the dome she knew had to be *somewhere*. She *knew* where at least two of the coms pass-throughs were, but they were behind plates she couldn't remove without tools.

There. There were likely other sensor clusters, but there was one in the corner by the entrance. It wouldn't have cameras—even her room wasn't wired for video, though everywhere aboard the ship *outside* of personal quarters was—but it did have a stack of *other* scanners and would need a wired connection to the rest of the ship.

The sensors in there would go to a closed console under Guard control, not the general ship network, but the link still had to *exist*.

And because they were in translight, it being on the ceiling and tucked into a corner wasn't the problem it could have been. A touch of half-remembered teenage acrobatics got her walking up the wall and into position to examine the dome.

It took more effort to remember how to interface her shipsuit with her link to give her an estimated countdown before the air in her suit would start to go foul. At that point, she'd have to risk any poisons in the room and see how long she could keep going.

Seven minutes.

The dome was a solid black thing, roughly half the size of her fist. Its cover would be transparent to thermal and motion sensors, and she could see the intake for the atmosphere scanners, but the opaque material reassured people on the *we're not filming in your quarters* promise.

The irony was that sufficient members of the crew *shared* quarters that Lorraine figured that the cameras *outside* the designated private zones picked up a lot of naked aerobics anyway.

For now, she was half-hoping the sensor cluster had a link connection for maintenance work. If there was, she couldn't find it and stared at the smooth plastic dome hopelessly for a second.

"New design instructions for all new sensors," she muttered to herself, then set about getting into a position where she had a grip and leverage—critical when relying on magnetic soles to keep from flying off!

Her first attempt to twist the dome off failed, her hands sliding clear of the smooth plastic and the contortion twinging a muscle in her back.

Six minutes left, and she glared at the device.

"You're *supposed* to be removable for maintenance," she accused it. "Which means..."

It took her a minute to track down the heavy gripped gloves she used when working on her shuttle with the tech crew. Sturdier and higher-friction than the shipsuit gloves, they *did* stick to the smooth dome.

The dome still resisted her for a few moments, but this time, it came off in her hands. Tossing it aside, she looked at the array of chips and probes that watched her quarters for problems.

Those sensors *should* have been sending an alert. Stars knew that *removing the dome* should have sent an alert—that was her first hope.

Her second was that she *had* spent a lot of time with Guard and Navy techs over the years, poking at shuttles and other gear. There were the *official* ways to link into hardware, and then there were *other* ways—one of which she'd kept stored with the gloves and thankfully hadn't been damaged by the bomb.

Three minutes left as she snapped clips onto cables that were intended to carry one type of data and one type of data only. She couldn't connect the interface box directly to her own link without opening the suit, but the very situation making all this *necessary* meant that she could risk opening her firewalls and creating a wireless link.

It just wasn't fast.

Two minutes. She had a connection, but her link wasn't configured to make sense of the data flowing along the cables. So, she overrode it all, killing the signal entirely and overwhelming it with a Guard emergency code.

Then another. And another. She *knew* she didn't have the tools or time to breach the door from the inside, whether directly or going after its controls. This was all she could manage, and she was left hoping that whoever was supposed to be watching the feeds would see the chaos she was creating.

And hoping that whatever had been done to mask the warnings from the sensors wasn't ready for her hammering the channel with every emergency code the Adamant Guard *had*.

The silence that continued told her part of the problem—hopefully, at least. If the room was so separated from the exterior that she couldn't hear anyone trying to break *in*, no wonder her Guards hadn't heard her hammering to get their attention.

Silence.

Thirty seconds. The air in the room *probably* wouldn't kill her on first breath. It wasn't safe, but someone had been aiming to make it look like an accident.

Twenty seconds—and then the cable she was hooked up to pulsed with a return message.

GET BACK.

Her sensor dome was next to the door.

Oh. Her sensor dome was *next to the door.*

Lorraine turned off her magnetic soles and kicked away from the wall in the same moment, sending herself hurtling toward the cushion of her bed on the other end of the room.

Sound and light alike broke the sanctuary of her quarters as bright-white fire highlighted the door. Even at the far end of the room, heat washed over her—but she'd moved far enough to be safe and to avoid the heavy chunk of metal as the hatch hurtled across the room.

And then Jarret was there, almost *riding* the still-glowing door as microjets hurled him across the room.

She barely had time to register Palmer and Alvarez entering the room before her head bodyguard had her by the waist and boosted back for the exit.

Zero gravity, she weakly supposed, had some *definite* advantages.

SIXTEEN

With the Pentarch ensconced in what Vigo figured to be the safest place on the ship at this point—*his* quarters, with her close detail *in the room*—he stood in the center of her quarters, surveying the space.

There were few signs of the nearly successful assassination attempt. The closet door was open, with a clear scorch mark where the explosive had cracked the tray of emergency oxygen tanks. The dome from the sensor cluster Lorraine had detached still hung in the air where she'd dropped it.

The most blatant sign was the armored door's presence on the wrong wall, where it had been flung by the force of the explosives they'd used to cut it free.

Priskilla Blau stood behind him at stiff attention. The only parts of the tall Black woman that were moving were her eyes as she studied the key points.

"I don't know what happened," she said grimly. "If the situation permitted, you'd have my resignation. This *should not* have happened."

"If the situation was different, this would call for *my* fucking resignation," Vigo told her. "At the *fucking* ease, Lieutenant Major. Tell me what you *do* know."

He could... *feel* the shape of the thing. The problem. The only possible problem, but Blau had been running the investigation while he'd moved the Pentarch.

"Everything in this room was controlled by a separate terminal," Blau reminded him. "That terminal was directly linked to this room's systems and fully airgapped from *Goldenrod*'s, with no wireless access at all.

"All of the equipment for Her Highness's quarters was in a utility closet that backed on to the room. We carved approximately seven percent of the volume of the original room away to install separate security and environmental systems, including soundproofing to prevent any form of eavesdropping."

"Which is why no one heard the Pentarch hammering on the door," he conceded. "I know all this, Major."

"Laying out the background," she said. "The utility closet isn't accessible from the same corridor as the Pentarch's quarters. Without a review of the schematics, it would be difficult to realize the two are connected.

"Access to that closet was fully controlled. Only the Guard should have been able to enter the space, and it was being checked a minimum of once every ten minutes except for the first forty-eight hours after the coup."

Which had been reasonable enough, but...

"I'm guessing something happened during that window?" he asked grimly.

"I can't be certain *when*, but that seems the most likely time period," Blau told him. "No less than *seven* encrypted wireless bridges were attached to the security and life-support controllers. All were receipt-to-activate, not transmitting until pinged, and passed our bugs and security scans."

"Even inactive, that shouldn't have been possible," Vigo observed. He wasn't arguing—the reality was obvious.

"In *theory,* there are particular triggers our security scans are looking for," she admitted. "I don't see any way someone could build a bug that missed them all."

"Unless they had the full documentation of our security scanners," he said quietly. "And probably access to test—but we *know* that Adamant Guards loyal to Pentarch Benjamin were involved in the coup.

"If anyone would be able to circumvent our scanners, it would be another Adamant Guard."

Which meant that somebody on *Goldenrod* wasn't who they said they were. He supposed someone who knew the full doctrine and tools of the Guard could fool their validation methods and loyalty checks.

Vigo couldn't see a Guard member turning assassin, but it would fit the evidence in front of him... except that Blau was shaking her head.

"Colonel Roma had a moment of paranoia about... six months ago? Do you remember? She instructed us to reconfigure all of our scanners to a unique scan metric. There's overlap with the other Guard Details, but even another Adamant Guard would have real difficulty building something to elude our scanners.

"Plus, I see nothing suggesting there was unauthorized access to the room."

The shape that Vigo had been prodding at in his mind came into stark clarity, the answer that explained how all of the odd side cases had occurred. The problem he hadn't foreseen, that felt *impossible.*

"One of ours," he said softly. "One of *our* fucking Guards."

"Nothing else makes sense," she admitted.

Vigo finally turned to look back at her, reminded that they were alone. A single Guard stood watch outside the hatch to Lorraine's quarters, and he had to decide in an instant how far he trusted Guard Sergeant Harold Merle.

Pretty far, he realized. Merle was the man he'd sent to pull Lorraine out of her shuttle and get her to the bridge, after all. The man had been in Lorraine's detail for the entirety of his Guard career —and he'd been Royal Adamant Marine Corps before that. The first few years of Merle's career in RAMC and the last few years of Vigo's career in the Navy had overlapped, with Merle serving two years as part of the security detail for Vigo's shuttle flight.

"I trust Merle," he murmured, nodding toward the man. "I'm assuming this room is secure *now*?"

"Even with the crap in the utilities, no one could ever have eavesdropped in here, sir," Blau promised. "Though I do have Esparza analyzing the bugs to see if she can rig up a means to trace anything built on the same principles.

"It's *possible* that similar tech is being used to listen in, but it's not actively transmitting and... we are in as much danger anywhere aboard the ship."

"Eighteen days left," Vigo noted. "Eighteen days until we reach Ominira and hopefully find more information. Assuming most of my *oddities* were the same person, our potential mole appears ready to die for this cause.

"Because if one of *ours* rigged the nukes, that answers a list of questions *there*."

"It does," she agreed. "I was assuming that Benjamin's people got Praetorian Protocol codes and some nasty viral attack code into an asset's hands, but if one of ours..."

"We didn't loyalty-validate our own people," Vigo realized aloud. "Hell, they're supposed to have gone through *deep-sync* interviews."

"They have. *Regularly*," Blau agreed. "My people, at least. I have no reason to assume Guard Central was any more lenient on Second or Third Section."

Vigo turned to study the scorch mark of the tiny explosive. Just enough to crack the oxygen bottles, not even enough to ignite the oxygen itself.

"A larger bomb would have triggered a question in *Goldenrod*'s security systems," he observed. "This is a *warship*; unexpected explosives get picked up and questioned."

"Whoever this is, they're operating inside the limits of the current high security level we're running," Blau agreed. "They have viral tools to help cover their asses, but they *know* that every time they use those, *Goldenrod* is going to get better at tracking them."

"We have our own watch set now," Vigo noted. "But that's parallel to the Navy's. Even if someone on Klement's team is screwing with it, I suspect Stephson's people will be watching their systems like hawks."

"So, what do we do?" his subordinate asked. "I... Hell, you can't even be sure you trust *me*."

It would be a spectacular degree of double bluff for her to tell him there was a mole in the Guard while *being* the mole... but he couldn't rule it out, no.

"You're right," he conceded. "Which means I have some work to do."

There was one advantage, he supposed, to knowing the *Guard* was compromised. Because he knew who was *least* likely to be compromised *other* than them, and if the main mole was in the Guard, well...

He needed to talk to the Marines.

SEVENTEEN

Marine Country on *Goldenrod* was both smaller and quieter than Vigo was used to. Normally, an RKAN frigate carried two platoons, totaling eighty Marines. With the Adamant Guard aboard his frigate, Lieutenant Commander Enitan Zdravkov only had one platoon under their command.

Tradition said that a frigate's senior RAMC officer had to be at least an O-4, though, so a Lieutenant Commander commanded a single platoon on an independent command that could probably have been handled by an experienced Lieutenant *Major*.

To make room for Vigo's Archangel Detail, the barracks and armory sections set aside for the Marines had been chopped in half. Adjustments had been made throughout the ship for the lack of the ground troopers, who usually filled other roles where they were needed.

Even considering all of that, Vigo would have expected the quarters of the forty Marines still aboard the ship to be loud. The Corps had a reputation to uphold, and he'd never known them to decline to live down to it.

With the Guard taking over shipboard security duties, the

Marines were present. That might be the problem, Vigo realized—not just that the Marines had been reduced to little more than virtual training, but that *he* had been the one to make that call.

He was regretting it now, though the dark looks that followed him as he approached Zdravkov's office weren't why.

The door slid open before he could even knock.

"Come in," Zdravkov ordered. They were a squat bull of a human, nearly as broad as Vigo himself but only a hundred and fifty-odd centimeters tall. A heavyset but unusually pale face regarded the Guard officer as Vigo stepped into the office, ice-blue eyes glaring.

The office, like everything else in the abbreviated Marine section, was smaller than it should have been, and Zdravkov had space for exactly two chairs in front of their desk. They didn't invite Vigo to sit, though zero gee made it pointless.

The Guard Major sat anyway, returning the Marine's level regard as he hooked a mag-booted foot around the chair to anchor himself.

"Well, Major?" Zdravkov finally asked. "Did one of my Marines step outside the door or something?"

"Your Marines aren't restricted to quarters, Lieutenant Major," Vigo told him. "You *do* have other jobs than the security role my people took over."

For that matter, RKAN military police normally handled at least half of the duties the Adamant Guard had taken over.

"We were the last to be cleared. The last to return to any semblance of duty. And still much of our *duty* has been taken over by the Guard." Zdravkov shrugged, still staring impassively at Vigo.

Unblinkingly. That was starting to get strange, though Vigo had been glared down by some of the best. Zdravkov was good... but they were also the same age as Pentarch Lorraine, which meant they needed a *lot* of seasoning before they'd be able to stare down Guard Detail commanders.

"I think you and your people have misinterpreted something,"

Vigo suggested gently. "Do you recognize *why* your Marines were the last people we interviewed and cleared?"

"Either because you thought someone in the platoon was the problem or because you thought we weren't a threat," Zdravkov growled.

"The latter is closer," Vigo replied. "I didn't *need* extra hands—the Guard was enough—and it was critical that I clear people to repair the ship's systems.

"We left the Marines for last, Major Zdravkov, because I *knew* that the Marines weren't going to be a problem. We needed to assess and clear everyone on this ship. Someone had to be last—and I *trusted* your people to not be a problem."

The officer behind the desk snorted, clearly not entirely believing him, and then spread their hands wide.

"I will pass that on to my people," they allowed. "It may help. Bored, angry Marines are the most dangerous kind, sir, and we are at risk of that.

"I have a handle on them, but if it is possible to restore some security duties to my people, that would be... helpful."

Vigo wondered how much the Marine disliked admitting that. It couldn't be *easy* to tell an officer who wasn't even technically in the chain of command that your people were going to snap if they stayed cooped up.

"That may help, actually," he murmured. "How secure is this room, Zdravkov?"

"As secure as anywhere on this ship," the Marine replied instantly. "Should be more so, but I heard some rumors about what happened in the Pentarch's rooms."

"Indeed." Vigo removed a tool from inside his uniform jacket and put it over the table. He fiddled with it for a moment until the tripod legs clicked open uselessly, then watched its lights turn on.

He saw Zdravkov wince and glare balefully at the device.

"Enhanced hearing, I take it?" he asked. "This is a portable security jammer. White noise, radio jamming, ultrasonic emitters—everything we can think of."

He chuckled.

"It gives *me* a migraine if I'm around one for more than twenty minutes," he conceded.

"My grandmother was a musician with a budget and a doctor who had clever ideas," Zdravkov replied. "I don't think she saw passing an expanded hearing range down to her kids as a problem. Hell, *I* don't usually."

They shook themselves like a wet dog, then gave Vigo a very flat look.

"You're the boss, Major. What's going on?"

"One of my Guards is a traitor," Vigo said flatly. "I have people I believe I can trust... but I thought my entire detail was absolutely beyond reproach.

"But too many incidents, from the nukes in the magazines to the incident last night, only make sense if one of my own was behind them. Someone who knew our protocols, our gear, our access codes..."

The office was very silent.

"So, you come to the Marines."

"So, I come to the Marines," Vigo confirmed. "Because despite how your people took it, you were left for last because I trusted you. And all of your people did pass my screenings."

Of course, so had everyone else on the ship, and he doubted his Guard mole had acted alone.

"What do you need from us?" Zdravkov asked crisply, their doubts still clear in their voice.

"We'll start with what you asked for," the Guard officer replied. "Returning your people to their security roles, freeing up more of my people for other duties. We're barely two weeks into this voyage. Sixteen days left until we reach Ominira. I have no idea what's waiting for us there... but I suspect that our mole will make a move before then.

"My job, above all else, is to make sure Pentarch Lorraine

survives," Vigo warned. "While I *care* if I devastate the carefully balanced structure of this ship's company, it won't *stop* me. I'm going to break the chain of command six ways from Sunday and rely on people I *personally* know in the ship's crew.

"But if I can't rely on my Guards, there is only one other source of armed force on this ship."

"Our oath is to the Kingdom, the Houses, and the King," Zdravkov pointed out. "*Pentarchs* aren't in there for a damn good reason."

"Your point?"

"This is a giant clusterfuck, mostly," the Marine replied. "And I have an allergy to people who try to blow up ships I'm standing on. Tell me what you need, Major, and we'll keep this ship safe.

"If that also involves protecting the Pentarch, well, *coups* are bad for the Kingdom, aren't they?"

EIGHTEEN

It stung, a little, that the first time Lorraine managed to get back to the shuttle bay to check in on her people was part of a scheme. A *necessary* scheme, but still. She should have checked in on her people directly before day *sixteen* of their journey to Ominira.

Day nineteen, give or take a few hours, since the assassination attempt.

Some of that was her inability to just casually *do* things now. Even aboard *Goldenrod*, they knew she was under threat. Palmer or Alvarez were with her everywhere—at least one of them, though the other members of her close detail rotated—but electronic eyes followed her as well.

The level of security should have felt ridiculous. The only time she'd ever seen this level of security before, she'd been sixteen and accompanying her father—*not* her mother, for security reasons—on a state visit to the Richelieu Directorate.

Given that they'd gone to war with the Directorate a few months later, it was a safe guess that the state visit hadn't worked out as anyone had planned. She'd spent her entire time on Richelieu, the capital planet of the Directorate, under a close watch by her security detail. And *almost* as close a watch by a Directorate Security Service team to make sure she wasn't trying to leave behind covert agents or something.

To have the same level of security on *Goldenrod* was uncomfortable, and she'd reacted by keeping to herself outside of meetings with what she couldn't *quite* call her command staff.

Now, though, she needed to be seen, and the first place she was going with that excuse was to check on her people.

"Your Highness!" Commander Olavi Chevrolet greeted her, his tone both enthusiastic and awkward. The frail-looking redheaded Ominiran native grinned up at her. "I'm not sure if I should salute, bow—or tell you that you still have to salute *me*!"

She offered her hand instead.

"Sadly, it's safe to say that I no longer have to salute you," she told him. "We're basically on election rules for my naval commission—which means it's suspended until there is a new King."

Rules Chevrolet *should* have been briefed on when a Pentarch was placed under his command. Effectively, from the moment of the King's death or abdication to the election and coronation of the new King, all five Pentarchs were legally obliged to step away from any existing civil or military role to run an election campaign.

That was part of why Lorraine had wanted to abdicate, so that nightmare wasn't hanging over her head. *She* had figured her mother, like most Kings before her, would abdicate at some point and then serve as the Crown Regent herself for the traditional six-month election period.

Without more information from home, she wasn't sure what Benjamin's tack was. While the other four official preexisting Pentarchs were "dead," there were still, legally, *always* five Pentarchs. The other four wouldn't be ready to run, which meant he could probably manage to get elected no matter what.

But she wondered if he would risk the election, after everything he'd done.

"Well, rank or no rank, you're still welcome in this shuttle bay," the COSH told her, gesturing around the cramped space with its too many spacecraft. "I presume you want to see your people?

"Major Watanabe has been handling things in your absence, though she hasn't let me officially put her in permanent command."

Isabella Watanabe had been the second-in-command of Bravo Flight, the most senior of Lorraine's pilots and one of only two Majors in the shuttle group. The small group on a frigate ended up with a surprisingly steep rank chart, since a full pilot was expected to be a Lieutenant Major with a Lieutenant as copilot.

"You'll need to," Lorraine told Chevrolet. "I... One way or another, Commander, I'm not coming back to Bravo Flight."

He glanced past her at the trio of Guards barely two steps back.

"I figured. But I think Isabella needs to hear that part from you," he said. "She told me she was just keeping the seat warm for you. Metaphorically, I suppose."

"Hard to sit down in translight, yeah," she agreed. "Shall we, Commander?"

"After you. You *do* still know how to get to the ready room, right?"

LORRAINE HAD ALWAYS THOUGHT the ready room set aside for a single shuttle flight was undersized. Part of that was that *she* would have preferred to pull the chiefs in—the flight had six Chief Petty Officers to go along with its six pilots and six copilots, though only three were actually rated to serve as Crew Chief on a shuttle—and the space was only sized for the twelve officers.

The rest was that it was a cramped fit even for that twelve. It had just enough space for seven seats facing the front and, *barely*, for one person to stand in front of them. Adding in the VR gear necessary for simulated training ops—because there was nowhere *else* to put it—made for a room that was politely described as claustrophobic.

In zero gravity, it was a *bit* better. The seats folded to the floor, and while the VR gear was cabled, the cables were long enough to allow the pilots to use it on any of the six surfaces.

That left the eleven men and women of Bravo Flight scattered all around the space, locked in to an exercise that was playing out in a virtual world shared between their neural links and the frigate's computers.

Chevrolet stepped up to the front of the room, leaving Lorraine standing at the door in easy sight of her bodyguards, and cleared his throat loudly.

She knew from personal experience that no one would *hear* that, but he would also accompany it with a ping into the simulation itself. It took a few seconds for everyone to disengage—but Watanabe was first.

The Major's dark hair could stretch all the way to her waist if she let it, but it was usually tied up in a twisted bun that fit surprisingly easily under a helmet. Lorraine wasn't sure *how* Watanabe managed that—even though the other woman had *shown* her.

"Isabella," she greeted the junior officer. "Apologies for interrupting, but I wanted to check in on everyone."

Several iterations on "Commander!" and "Your Highness!" followed as the other members of the Flight removed their VR helmets, but Lorraine kept her attention on Watanabe for a moment.

The gorgeous woman was lithe and graceful in a way that left even Lorraine, with her genetically enhanced reflexes, feeling gawky. She moved from "sitting" cross-legged on the normal ceiling of the ready room to standing in front of Lorraine in a perfect dismount and flip.

Lorraine was *quite* certain of her interests as far as sexual partners went, but in a different circumstance, she could have seen Watanabe challenging that certainty.

"Your Highness," Watanabe greeted her, putting her hands together and bowing over them. "I'm delighted to see you." She glanced over her shoulder at the other pilots. "The rest of you are too, right?"

"Glad we didn't get forgot!" someone said—Lorraine didn't even *try* to identify the voice, but she could guess. Every small team had its troublemaker, and Bravo Flight's was Lieutenant Major Hiro Baier, Bravo-Three.

"I'm sorry I didn't get to check in on you all sooner," she told them, moving over slightly to lean against a wall and ease the strain on her neck from looking at the pilots on the ceiling. "As you can imagine, the Guard is being paranoid of my person and my time!"

"Only one question." This time, it was *definitely* Baier, and she looked over to meet his gaze. "When do we vote for you?"

She chuckled.

"You know as much as I do," she admitted. "Things got very ugly before we fled Adamantine, people, and *voting* might not be enough to fix things. We're heading to Ominira, hoping to get more information without drawing attention.

"But you all knew that. And..." she shrugged. "If my uncle is playing the game we think he is, we may have some of our own people shooting at us before this is over."

"They'll regret that," Watanabe said firmly. "This Flight—this *ship*—isn't going to take what happened lying down, sir. If they come for you again—"

"They ain't gonna get a *chance* to miss," Baier interrupted fiercely.

Lorraine flushed with a warmth she didn't let reach her face. She'd believed, *hoped*, that her people would understand. That they'd take her stepping away to deal with the crisis and the attack on her family as the duty it was.

"Thank you," she told them quietly. "Now, I have one ask of you in turn," she continued, pointing to Watanabe. "Play nice with Isabella, okay? She's going to take over as Bravo Flight Commander— whether she likes it or not!"

Since every one of the officers in the room would know perfectly

well that Watanabe had been fighting against that permanent decla-
ration, she got the chuckles she'd hoped for.

"Now Major Watanabe and Commander Chevrolet and I need
to catch up," she said. "I needed to check in on you all, but the Guard
are twitchy about letting me stand in one place for too long.

"Magic space fairies might kidnap me!"

NINETEEN

"Things are still that uncertain?" Chevrolet asked as they crossed the shuttle bay to his office.

The shuttles couldn't be used in translight, but that didn't mean the bay didn't see activity. The Navy flight officers might be doing training, but several of the Guard Lieutenants were working on their shuttles with the Deck Chiefs.

Lorraine gave one of those Guards—Lieutenant Laurenz, the woman she could see most clearly—a small wave and got a grin back.

"The Guard aren't working on their shuttles because they *need* to," she murmured to the ship's COSH. "They're adding an extra layer of security, keeping an eye on me."

Everywhere she went, it seemed that there were already Adamant Guards waiting for her. That was just the more *visible* security, what with Section Two living inside *Goldenrod*'s computers and Lorraine's suspicions that Vigo had gone outside the Guard after the attack on her quarters.

He hadn't *said* so to her. But she could put together the pieces too. Someone *in* the Guard had been involved in the attack on her quarters.

"Your quarters are a wreck. They've put you somewhere safe now, right?" Watanabe asked as the door to Chevrolet's office slid closed.

None of the three bothered to sit as Chevrolet fiddled with a coffee machine to produce bulbs of hot caffeinated liquid. The same microgravity that made sitting useless made the coffee bulbs necessary.

"Civil-service wing," she told them. She didn't narrow it down from there—though the "wing" was a single corridor of rooms close to the shuttle bay. It defined one end of the presence section of the ship, which had more decorative flooring and walls.

It *also* had a bubble of seven centimeters of vacuum on all sides and limited access via two securable airlocks. It *should* be secure against any threats, but the people doing the securing were the Guards.

Lorraine did note that Watanabe hadn't actually *asked* where she was, either. The scheme Vigo was playing called for her to give various people different information, so she gave more information than she would otherwise.

And if Chevrolet or Watanabe noticed, well, she trusted them more than most.

"The Pentarch is on Election rules now," Chevrolet told Watanabe after a moment of thought. "She effectively doesn't *have* a commission until the election is complete. Whenever the hell that will be."

"In theory, six months from my mother's death," Lorraine said quietly. "So... end of September, standard dating. Enough time for each of the Pentarchs to set up a campaign in Adamantine, then make at least a passing visit to each of the other five systems before the votes are cast."

Getting to all six systems of the Kingdom took time, even with the fastest ships available to the nation. When Lorraine's mother and uncle had stood for election—alongside three of their cousins—it had taken thirty-five-plus days just to get the votes from Ominira and Beulaiteuhom to Adamantine.

That had been with eighty-cee couriers as fast as *Goldenrod* was now. With the ninety-six-cee couriers available to the Kingdom now, the votes could be held closer to the final date.

"Something tells me that the election isn't going to take place on schedule," she told the two pilots. "I don't know what plans my uncle has in place, but if he's done everything we're told he did in Bastion, he isn't going to calmly run an election campaign and risk losing.

"Not even to Oliver, most likely."

Oliver Adamant had been the Fifth Pentarch until Lorraine had turned eighteen—but given that her cousin, Pentarch Benjamin's only son, was only three years older than her, he'd known his turn in the Pentarchy would be short.

"Who else *would* be running?" Chevrolet asked. "I assume there's a list?"

"Every member of House Adamant is on the List," Lorraine told her ex-boss. "So, me, Benjamin, Oliver... Jessica and Hans."

Jessica and Hans were older than Lorraine or Oliver. The fraternal twin children of Valeriya's late cousin, Jessica Adamant was a diplomat and Hans Adamant was a serving member of the House of the Realm—AKA the Long House, whose Realm Representatives served a single ten-year term.

Neither had ever been a Pentarch. Their *mother* had been, before Oliver Adamant turned eighteen, but Irmentrud Adamant had passed away five years earlier.

"While I doubt Oliver ever expected to run in an Election, his father would have made sure he was ready in the three years he was a Pentarch," Lorraine said. "Benjamin, I have to assume, has as much ready to go as he could without it looking strange.

"If he's counting me as dead... I'd have to actually look at the family tree to sort out which cousin ends up as Fifth Pentarch, but I *think* it's Travis."

"I figure he is, so our first order of business might be to give him the headache of knowing you're alive," Chevrolet said with a chuckle. "Won't *that* muck up a lot of things?"

"Well..." She sighed. "Do you know Lieutenant Admiral Tunison?"

Lorraine felt the chill wash over the other two officers.

"I do," Watanabe said slowly. "I flew a shuttle off of *Il Duce* back when he was her Captain, before he made the bump from Commodore."

"I've never met him," Chevrolet said. "I've served on ships in the same *formation* as him—Third Fleet during the war, mostly—but never under his authority."

"Like most of the officers who were high in Third Fleet, he's Pentarch Benjamin's man through and through," Watanabe told the Commander. "He wasn't under the Prince's command when *I* served on *Il Duce*—we were on Greenrock Station, playing nice with the Concordat.

"Still, even then there was no question who *he* thought the best tactician and admiral in the fleet was. And, though he never said as much around a brand-new Lieutenant Major, who he figured was the best choice of the Pentarchs."

"If you'd asked me three weeks ago, *I* would have said it was a toss-up between him and Daniel," Lorraine said grimly. "With it only going to Daniel because a three-decade age difference means Daniel would provide stability to the kingdom for longer."

Her brother had been twelve years older than her, and she'd been at her uncle's seventieth birthday party that January. Modern medicine meant that her uncle had at least three decades more of healthy life in him—but the odds were that Valeriya had *four*, being ten years younger than *her* brother.

By the time Valeriya abdicated or passed on, Benjamin would have been too old for most people to elect him as King. And that, as Lorraine was grimly struggling with, was likely part of what had led to the attack on her family.

"I would never have seen this coming," Chevrolet agreed. "I

mean... he's always been the one to see the most pragmatic, even ruthless, solution. Not many would have pulled Third Fleet out of Tolkien and abandoned the system to the Directorate."

Third Fleet had been the main offensive and defensive arm of RKAN during the war with the Directorate, three battleships and a pair of battlecruisers operating out of the Tolkien System.

But when the Richards had arrived with *six* battleships, a full half of their fleet, Third Fleet had been outmatched. A fight in Tolkien would have cost the Kingdom a third of their fleet, making kicking the Directorate Navy out of Tolkien that much harder.

Lorraine wasn't sure she could have left a billion people behind like that, but hindsight made it clear it had been the correct call.

"The Army never forgave him for that," Watanabe murmured. "It was a whole *thing* when I was under Tunison. There were, what, four entire *corps* he left behind? Plus the civilians."

"Roughly," Lorraine agreed quietly. "My mother stripping Home Fleet to relieve Tolkien with *ten* battleships certainly left an impression on a lot of people, though."

"The Admiral is ruthless and pragmatic, yes, but this is treason," Chevrolet said. "Do you really think Tunison would back him so far as to move against *Goldenrod*?"

"I know my uncle," Lorraine told the COSH. "No plan of his lacks a backup. He wouldn't have *launched* this coup without being certain that he had officers in key positions to catch any of us who escaped.

"Tunison is his protégé. There is no way he hasn't made certain the commander of the Ominira Station isn't loyal. We have to step carefully in Ominira—but that's a conversation for me to have with the Captain and Major Jarret."

"Well, if you need a place to drink coffee and bitch about the universe, my door is always open to you," Chevrolet told her. "So long as you get *this* one to accept command of your shuttle flight!"

Watanabe chuckled as he indicated her with his coffee.

"I give up, I give up," she said. "We'll need to see if we can pull someone in to backstop pilot seats, though. Bump a Lieutenant?"

"Exactly. We can talk without the Pentarch," Chevrolet observed. "Unless you want to get drawn down into all of the data-work you have finally escaped?"

"Temporarily escaped, hopefully," Lorraine said. "When this is all over, I'd love to go back to the Navy."

She knew perfectly well she'd make a better naval officer than King. But she also didn't see many ways out of her uncle's scheme that *didn't* involve kicking his ass in an Election and taking the crown, either.

Getting to that point, though...

TWENTY

According to the tracker Lorraine was keeping, there were four versions of her schedule floating around the ship—and *six* different places where she was supposedly sleeping.

If she was being honest, she figured *she* was the most likely to slip up and say the wrong thing to the wrong people. So, her neural link was running a program that was tracking which story she gave to whom—and reminding her when she bounced off them.

"Where now, sir?" Palmer asked, the Guard's dark-eyed gaze flickering across the corridors as they moved away from the shuttle bay.

"Don't you have my agenda, such as it is?" Lorraine asked wryly. If there was anyone who *couldn't* have a false itinerary, it was the people who would be living in her immediate back pocket.

Plus, if the mole was in her close detail, she was already dead. She just didn't know it yet. She trusted those women with her life and her dignity. They were the ones who'd had to interrupt her in the middle of time with lovers for assorted reasons over the years, after all.

Not even her entire Guard Detail was really privy to the particulars of her love life, after all. Jarret was—he *pretended* not to, because they both found that awkward, but he was fully informed. Otherwise, not even Priskilla was fully in the loop.

That kind of intimacy was limited to the eight members of Alpha Section Squad Three, co-led by Corporals Palmer and Alvarez. The other fifty-odd members of her detail were supposed to be a few steps back, so to speak.

"Just because I know the schedule you gave me and I'm about ninety percent sure it's even the real schedule doesn't mean it didn't *change*," Palmer reminded her. "Plus, the next thing up is to check in on the bridge, which can be delayed, and random adjustments are a *good* thing."

Lorraine sighed.

"You're not wrong. I'm just not sure what else I'd do other than return to my quarters. Anything else feels like it's creating risk and work for you lot."

"We're here to protect you, including your sanity," Palmer reminded her. "Staying in those rooms... you will go nuts."

Rooms was a generous description of the Pentarch's current quarters. She would, eventually, move into the guest quarters. Right now, though, Bravo Section was reengineering the entire support system for that section of the ship, which meant that Lorraine was entering the main envoy's quarters and taking a brand-new temporary connection out into one of *Goldenrod*'s storage compartments.

Two cargo containers had been cut open and fitted with lights and other equipment by a trio of engineering techs Jarret trusted. They were perfectly functional, especially in microgravity, but they made her previous quarters look like a luxury penthouse in downtown Adamant City.

"Let's stick with the bridge plan for now," Lorraine decided. "Unless something new has come up with us in the middle of nowhere, utterly incommunicado?"

"Nothing good is going to come up, that's for sure," Palmer muttered. "Posey, move up. You've got the route loaded."

Lorraine made it about five steps toward the bridge before the local GuardNet catastrophically failed. A feedback pulse hammered into her neural link as a brilliant flash of light and crash of thunder, and she stumbled against a wall.

From the complete freeze on her bodyguards' part, they'd been hit even harder. For *her*, GuardNet was one of three networks she was linked in to, and she only really had one small window open in her vision linked to it.

For her Guard Detail, it would have been the primary interface they were using with the ship and with each other. Lorraine wasn't sure just how secure the GuardNet *was*, but she suspected a direct attack like that should have been *impossible*.

She went for the weapon holstered at the small of her back. A shockwhip was far from a *pleasant* weapon, even if it was theoretically guaranteed to be nonlethal due to a set of sophisticated sensors.

What it *was* was incapacitating. Lorraine was *qualified* with small arms—that had been expected of both a naval officer and a daughter of the King—but she was far more comfortable with the less-lethal weapon.

And something was very, *very* wrong.

"Link overload," Palmer finally gasped out. "I... can't actually *see* anything. We need a medic, Your Highness. Can you—"

"Thank *God* I found you!"

Lorraine turned to the speaker, checking to see if her link to *Goldenrod*'s network was intact enough for her to summon medical help. GuardNet going down was bad enough, but what appeared to be a broad-spectrum cyberattack on the network was at least not *jamming*.

What was blocking her from *Goldenrod*'s wireless *was* jamming. She didn't have the gear to locate the source, but the presence of the electronic static left her eyeing Archie Patriksson with scant favor.

"Lieutenant Major, what are you doing here?" she asked the Guard shuttle commander.

"I got a handwritten note left *on my shuttle* that GuardNet was about to be attacked, then all of my coms failed," Patriksson told her grimly. "I was trying to find someone—*anyone*—but I remembered Laurenz saying—"

For all of her training, Lorraine's actual combat experience had been behind the controls of a shuttle. She'd helped deal with a pirate attack once—but that had been a very sterile, almost surreal experience.

It took her a full half second to put Patriksson ceasing to talk and the sudden crimson flowers on his chest together and realize he'd been shot. At least three times, with fragments of the frangible rounds scattering down the hall.

Lorraine discharged her shockwhip without even thinking, the paired darts, linked to each other with a charged wire, flashing past where Patriksson's body hung in the microgravity.

"Watch it, watch it!" a more feminine voice snapped. "Patriksson was the traitor—he's *carrying* the damn jammer, Your Highness!"

Lieutenant Jelica Laurenz stepped around her boss's body, her pistol held loosely off to one side as she approached.

"I know how this looks," she said quickly. "Check his jacket. You can kill the jammer and call a medical detail for Palmer and the others."

"Palmer?" Lorraine asked.

"Still blind," her bodyguard ground out. Something in her tone and posture warned Lorraine that Palmer didn't trust the situation.

That was fair. Neither did Lorraine.

Holding the shockwhip in one hand, she pulled Patriksson's bloody jacket open. She had hardware in her implants few others shared, which guided her to the jammer in the inside pocket.

Just as Laurenz had said.

Patriksson betraying her didn't make *sense*. But *none* of the Guard betraying her made sense!

"Call for medical help for your detail, but then you need to keep moving," Laurenz told her. "We have to assume that Patriksson has co-opted others—among the crew if not the Guard. We need to keep you radio silent until we get to Major Jarret."

"As it happens, there's a medic with my squad here," another new voice interrupted, and Lorraine tried not to reel from the mental whiplash.

"We can take care of Corporal Palmer's detail and then reinforce your security, Lieutenant, Pentarch."

The sight of a full squad of ten Marines *shouldn't* have been a relief at that moment, Lorraine suspected. She did, however, recognize Lieutenant Commander Enitan Zdravkov. She and *Goldenrod*'s Marine CO had been the same rank, which always lent itself to a certain degree of solidarity among the handful of O-4s on the ship.

"I think you understand, Commander, that we can't allow that," Laurenz snapped. "We have no idea who is moving against the Pentarch. You or one of your people could be working with Patriksson."

"Except I'm operating under direct orders from the Captain and the Major," Zdravkov said calmly, their tone unflappable as they stepped forward.

Unlike Patriksson, Lorraine noted absently, the Marines were in armor. The ceramic breastplates and support plates weren't full body armor, let alone powered combat armor, but it was enough that Laurenz's sidearm *probably* couldn't hurt Zdravkov.

Without GuardNet, though, Lorraine couldn't confirm the Marine's statement—until she noticed a tiny icon pop into her vision. The floppy-eared long-haired dog wasn't even of a *breed* she was familiar with, but it suddenly rolled across the bottom of her link feed, presented its belly to her, then sprang up to pant at her.

She treated it like an icon, thought-clicking it—and was unsurprised when it triggered an automatic challenge-response sequence from her implants.

Whatever the *hell* was going on, Zdravkov had full authentication from Vigo Jarret. *Why*, exactly, those two had hidden said authentication in an animated icon of a dog, she wasn't entirely certain.

"Stand down, Lieutenant Laurenz," she told the Guard officer. "The Lieutenant Commander and I know each other—and he *is* operating on orders from the Major. LC, can you get your medic to check on Palme—"

Lorraine was suddenly painfully aware that she hadn't noticed Laurenz shuffling closer—and that while the *Marines* might be in body armor, *she* wasn't. The shockwhip went flying away and she found herself locked down by the Guard, her arm twisted behind her back and a pistol pressed to her temple.

"Get back," Laurenz snapped at the Marines. "Get back *now*."

"Lieutenant, please think through your situation," Zdravkov said, their tone and body language shifting into a form Lorraine recognized instantly.

It was drilled into every police constable and military police agent in the entire Kingdom before they were even allowed to pick up a gun. Adamantine constabulary prided themselves on de-escalation and getting the right resources in place to handle a situation once they'd de-escalated it.

She knew that Zdravkov had done time as an MP, but it was still quite a surprise to see them go into full police de-escalation mode.

It was less reassuring, of course, when *she* was the hostage.

"You can't get off this ship," Zdravkov told Laurenz gently. "I don't know what your plans or goals are, but I do think you want to live. Otherwise, you wouldn't be trying to take hostages.

"Right now, if you pull that trigger, you die. You're Adamant Guard. You *know* how good, how tough the people on this ship are. You might buy yourself a few minutes. Maybe even an hour or two.

"But you're going to have to hold a gun to the Pentarch's head forever, and the moment you blink, it's over."

Reassuring and gentle as the Marine Lieutenant Commander's voice was, their words only resulted in Laurenz jamming the gun into Lorraine's head harder.

"Don't push it, Marine," she growled. "I *will* shoot."

"That's not the course that gets you out of here alive, Lieutenant Laurenz," they told her. "There's only one option that does that, and that's you putting down the gun. You'll go to the brig, yeah, and it won't be fun for you... but you'll live.

"That's the only way you do. There are too many Marines and too many other Guards on this ship for anything else. Work with me here, Lieutenant. I don't want to lose the Pentarch; you're right. But holding her hostage isn't going to help you."

Lorraine could feel the barrel of the pistol *burning* into her temple, the cold steel an eerie foreboding of death. Laurenz's hold was *perfect*, using the lack of gravity against Lorraine to limit her movement and negate any leverage she tried to create.

"This is the mission," Laurenz growled. "I'm going to keep walking and you're going to let me go."

"I can't do that, Lieutenant. This doesn't need to get uglier. We've already lost a good man today. Put the gun down."

Lorraine could feel the moment of weakness. The gun didn't really *move* so much as just relax a touch. Not enough to even reduce the chill on her forehead. Not enough for her to think that Laurenz was buying what the Marine was selling.

Just enough for an armored hand to *bounce* off Lorraine's head and take the gun with it. The pistol discharged into the bulkhead, but Palmer was still moving as she peeled Laurenz off the Pentarch.

The pistol came around again, back toward Lorraine—and then kept going as a sickening *crack* announced that Palmer had broken the younger Guard's arm. A moment later, a second pair of uncomfortable noises announced the end of the fight.

"Blind," Palmer repeated in a cold growl at the woman whose arms and left leg she'd just broken. "*Not* useless."

TWENTY-ONE

There were no Adamant Guards in *Goldenrod*'s brig other than Vigo Jarret himself. And, he supposed, Jelica Laurenz.

Lieutenant Commander Zdravkov was waiting for him at the entrance to the cell block, the Marine clad in standard body armor that looked both too long and too narrow for their frame. They gave Vigo a crisp salute.

"Prisoner has been fed and allowed access to hygiene facilities," they told him. "She's been uncommunicative but cooperative. We're keeping an implant lock on her for her own safety. While I don't *believe* we have anyone on board who would trigger a suicide implant, we can't take chances."

"In theory, if she'd acquired an unauthorized suicide plant, that would have shown up on her regular checkups," Vigo said, but he shook his head as he looked down the utilitarian corridor of cells. He couldn't see his subordinate, but he knew she'd be in one of the two high-security cells at the end of the passage—past the secondary security post where two Marines stood a careful watch.

"But her being co-opted by a hostile actor should *also* have been picked up," he conceded. "There's a reason my people didn't get subjected to the same interview and validation process as everyone else."

"I presumed you went through something more intense on a regular basis," Zdravkov admitted. "Not everyone on the ship is quite so generous, though."

"And they shouldn't be," Vigo agreed. "I am surprisingly okay with the crew being grouchy at us, Lieutenant Commander. We did what was necessary for Her Highness's security, but it wasn't nice or fair.

"Worse, with Laurenz turning out to be the traitor, it now looks hypocritical."

"I'm no systems specialist," the Marine told him, gesturing for him to follow them, "but my impression is that Laurenz couldn't have done all of this on her own."

"No," Vigo conceded. "But being a shuttle pilot requires more system-specialist skills than you might think. It's the engineering work of the original traps that I'm less sure about."

"She had help," Zdravkov stated. "We both know it. The question, I suppose, is whether her help is still aboard the ship."

"I don't know," Vigo said. "And that, Commander, is what I am here to sort out."

───────

WITHOUT GRAVITY, securing a prisoner for interrogation became a messy process. Normally, Vigo would have expected to see Laurenz cuffed hand and ankle to a chair bolted to the floor. The interrogation room he entered even had a clear spot for both the chair and its stereotypical accompanying table.

Instead, Jelica Laurenz was suspended in the middle of the room. Each of her limbs was cuffed and hooked to a cable with enough slack to avoid *too* much discomfort, but she didn't have enough mobility to threaten anyone unless they did something *really* dumb.

"Lieutenant," he greeted her, stopping halfway between the door and the prisoner. The door closed behind him as he spoke, leaving them alone in the room.

Mostly. Vigo could tell that Lorraine was riding their implant link. He trusted her to stay silent and just listen, but he understood her need to know just what had happened... and *why*.

"Sir."

Well, that was a start. The single word sounded like it had been dragged out of her with pliers, but at least she was acknowledging his existence.

"I have a lot of questions," he admitted after a moment, studying her. Laurenz was typical for the natives of Tolkien. The Tolkienites were sufficiently pale and skinny as a group that Vigo personally suspected genetic engineering to make them look more like the twen- tieth-century author's elves.

In Jelica Laurenz's case, he knew the apparent wispiness of her build concealed wiry muscle and a mental toughness that had seen her into first RAMC and then the Adamant Guard. She had just turned thirty-eight and had served three years as a Guard officer after fifteen years as a Marine NCO and mustanged officer.

"Nothing in your file, your interviews, your assessments... *nothing* in any of the documents I have—even the ones I can only see now you're accused of treason!—lets me understand this any better," he told her. "Archie Patriksson is dead. We're back-tracing your movements against the problems we've had with *Goldenrod*'s cameras, and we have confirmed you were responsible for placing the wireless bridges used to launch the attack on the Pentarch's quarters.

"That's enough, really."

He let that hang. He didn't explain what it was *enough* for. She'd been an officer in the Adamant Guard. She knew at what point, espe- cially in an emergency situation like this, Vigo could shoot her out of hand.

Laurenz said nothing, just glaring at the wall away from him.

"I don't understand," he repeated. "You were loyal to the

Kingdom and the Pentarch. I *know* that—I conducted enough of your assessments myself to be certain of that!"

He hadn't conducted all of them, but that was because the Guard made sure no one person conducted all of someone's loyalty and health reviews. If the Guard leadership could *think* of the angle, they had tried to cover it.

Which was part of why Vigo needed to know what had happened. Mostly, though, it was very personal.

"You betrayed the Pentarch. You betrayed *me*, Lieutenant Laurenz. *Why?*"

Vigo began to walk in a slow circle around her, waiting for an answer. He completed a full rotation—a slow, far-from-silent process with the magnetic boots—and faced her again, his hands behind his back in near-parade rest.

"Well?" he asked. "What *happened*? Did the Pentarch accidentally insult your shoes or something?"

"Maybe she should look in a *mirror*," Laurenz growled, then snapped her jaw shut.

"A mirror?" Vigo asked. That didn't actually help, but it gave him a string to yank on. A thread to hopefully unravel Laurenz's defenses if not the deception that had carried her this far.

He waited, but Laurenz said nothing more.

"Most people say that the Pentarch looks like her mother," he finally said. "The resemblance is uncomfortable, even, to those who recognize it as the result of forced-dominance genetic engineering.

"So, she also looks like her *uncle*, who you know is behind this whole mess. Even if you didn't before, you have for a while. And yet you still tried to kill the Pentarch. So, *why?*"

It would have been *difficult* for Laurenz to get away with that. Even with GuardNet overloaded—and the only thing keeping Vigo from a skull-splitting migraine was medication and neurotransmitter management by his implants—and a dozen random jammers throughout the ship, if Laurenz had taken over Lorraine's security and Lorraine had died, everything would have been dissected to the nth degree.

But *difficult* wasn't *impossible*. He could think of a few ways, most of which would have left them thinking they still had a traitor on the loose—and several of which would have ended with Laurenz herself in sickbay.

"You're blind."

Even *that* was an improvement over what Vigo had been expecting, but he concealed his triumph as he carefully faced Laurenz and met her gaze.

"Then enlighten me," he murmured. "What do *you* see when you look at the Pentarch?"

"Her father. The Muslim bastard who wants to drag us all down to his level, put women in veils and make them *cattle* like the rest of his scum kind. He's all smiles and cheer to the cameras, but he's one of *them*, all right."

The sheer breadth of the phobia and blind... *bigotry*, for lack of a better word, stunned Vigo.

My father isn't even Muslim. He's Baha'i.

Not that Vigo needed the text from Lorraine to know that. Most of the Concordat of Amal Jadid *was* Muslim, yes. But even the majority of the Muslim population followed the Wahida Qadir version of the faith born in the twenty-second century, one of several major branches that rejected *any* mandated differences between genders.

And it took a very... *specific* perspective to consider the Concordat's Baha'i minority as Muslims in *any* sense whatsoever.

"You thought Prince Consort Frederick was trying to... impose some form of religious law on the Kingdom's women?" he asked, trying *not* to let his tone turn too dry. The problem wasn't even that he could say Laurenz was insane. That would be too easy an out—and likely detected by the screening systems.

Sadly, bigotry wasn't insanity. It was something they screened for, but it was harder to pick out than some others... and he wasn't sure they even *would* have screened for Islamophobia as part of the security tests for the Guard.

Why would they, since even Frederick Adamant-Griffin *hadn't been Muslim*. He had been ethnically Arabic, but it took a massive leap to get from that to a threat of some kind of misogynist movement.

Laurenz said nothing. He suspected he hadn't kept his tone as neutral as he'd hoped, but he waited anyway.

"Why, Lieutenant?" he finally asked, echoing his first question even as he tried to expand on this revelation. A check of her records told him she hadn't actually met the Prince Consort, so none of this would have come up.

"They're all that way," she insisted. "Like the bastard who killed my mother."

At least a few pieces clicked into place. Except one. Jelica Laurenz was *adopted*, and her birth parents weren't on her Guard record. The Guard wouldn't have left that blank unless they couldn't find any information on them at all.

What was a private matter for most people could be a security threat for a member of the Adamant Guard. They wouldn't necessarily give that information *to* the individual Guard unless asked, but Guard Central needed to know if there was a possible threat.

"Your adoptive mother was still alive when we left Adamantine," he said quietly. "What did you find out about your birth mother?"

"She was beaten and left for dead by a Concordat diplomat," Laurenz told him. "Not even... not even a targeted attack. Just in the wrong place at the wrong time, beaten because she, a *woman*, dared defy him.

"Hospital saved me but couldn't save her. My birth father couldn't handle things, put me up for adoption, and vanished. But it was a dark-eyed bastard like 'Adamant-Griffin' who killed her."

Vigo wasn't sure how to respond to that. *He'd* have needed a lot of proof to even *begin* to buy that story, himself—but he was guessing whoever had played Laurenz had possessed that proof. It might even have been real; he couldn't be sure.

Transforming *that* into a conspiracy theory to tar the Prince Consort and turn one of Pentarch Lorraine's Guards had to have been an impressive leap. He would love to meet the spy behind it—if only so he could punch the bastard before he made the universe a better place by removing them from it.

"Lieutenant..." He paused. There wasn't much point in coddling her, he supposed.

"You realize you fucked up, right?" he asked. "Even *if* your mother's death was what you're telling me, going from *that* to the Prince Consort being a threat is a hell of a leap. And even if I could concede *that*, going from that to murdering the Pentarch was worse.

"You got played. And because you couldn't see that, Archie Patriksson is dead and everyone on this ship very nearly died. If Zdravkov hadn't been there, you might have even managed to kill Pentarch Lorraine—a woman who never did anything to you and is our best chance of stopping a coup in our Kingdom.

"A coup you knowingly contributed to, didn't you?"

Laurenz said nothing, not even looking at him.

"I need info from you, Lieutenant," Vigo said with a sigh. "I need to know who recruited you, what you know about Pentarch Benjamin's plans—and who on this ship *you* recruited. I know you don't have the skills to set up the traps in Life Support or the power core.

"I'm guessing the nuke magazine was you? Though I almost figure you *wanted* us to find that one," he admitted. "Once you were back on the ship with the rest of us, you didn't have the option to bolt and wait for the cruisers to come pick you up."

She was still staring blankly at the wall.

"There are two choices here, Lieutenant," he said gently. "The first is that you tell me what I want to know. Preferably with voluntary deep-link sync. We make sure this ship is safe and no one else dies by your actions.

"Help me with that, and we'll fudge some datawork and clean

things up. We'll drop you off somewhere along the way and we forget you were ever an Adamant Guard."

Probably *not* in Ominira—he was thinking somewhere along the way to the Republic, possibly even in Bright Dream itself. But he'd spare her life and let her go, in exchange for enough information to make sure his people and the Pentarch were safe.

"Like you've a choice," she said, her voice low and scratchy. "Only way you're getting that data from me."

"That... is not as true as you think," Vigo warned her. "There are ways around your anti-interrogation implants, Lieutenant Laurenz. We gave them to you, after all."

The ways weren't *easy*, but on the other hand, it wasn't like the Guard issued lethal anti-interrogation gear either. He was quite certain he and *Goldenrod*'s doctor would find the right balance of medications and authorization codes to permit an anesthetized deep-sync link interrogation without more than two or three tries.

Waking her back up from the coma the implant would put her in would be relatively straightforward, too. Vigo *was* her commanding officer, after all.

She was silent again and he let her think.

"I think you owe me the truth, Lieutenant," he finally told her. "I selected you from RAMC's shuttle wings. I trained you. I *trusted* you. Talk to me."

Even his implants couldn't force a conscious and unwilling person to answer his questions—he would be able to tell if she was lying if she *did* speak, but he couldn't make her speak. And that was putting aside that forcing the connection on an involuntary subject was... well, gross.

"I don't know anything about the coup," she said after at least twenty seconds of silence. "I was 'recruited,' if you can call it that, by Major Hayes at Guard Central. She told me she had info on my family... From there, I don't know if she was lying or encouraging me."

Major Fenella Hayes was the head of personnel for the Adamant

Guard. It would have fallen to her team to attempt to track down Laurenz's birth parents. She had also been a previous section commander in Pentarch Benjamin's Brave Detail—a red flag to him now.

"I need to sync, Laurenz, or we can't trust what you say," he warned her. "Will you cooperate?"

"Can't stop you. Bit tied up at the moment. But... fine. Do it."

TWENTY-TWO

"I passed everything Laurenz told me on to Commander Cortez," Vigo concluded, nodding toward the Greenrock-native Chief Engineer. "All three of her... *patsies* feels like the best word? Whatever I want to call them, they were in Engineering."

"I prefer *idiots*," Cortez growled. "A Chief and two Petty Officers. Men and women I knew and trusted." She shook her head. "Zdravkov has them under quarters arrest until we can go over their stories and excuses."

The Marine CO was also in the room, along with Stephson, Savege, and *Goldenrod*'s gawky, dark-haired Tactical Officer, Lieutenant Commander Mattias Paris. Plus, of course, Pentarch Lorraine and Guard Corporal Alvarez.

Alvarez, at least, was standing guard by the door. The officers and Pentarch were clustered around the table at the center of the meeting room, useless as the chairs were in microgravity.

"How did we miss them being involved?" Stephson asked. "I presume Laurenz was covering for them when you did your sweep?"

"From what I can tell, we missed them because none of them actually *knew* they'd been involved at that point," Vigo said. It took quite a bit for him to say that calmly, but he'd got beating his head against the bulkhead out of the way already.

"Laurenz's control, the actual key agent for Pentarch Benjamin's plan aboard *Goldenrod*, was one of the administrative personnel who was on *Sultan* when everything went down—Lieutenant Wrona."

"Arnaq?" Stephson demanded, then cut herself off with a throwaway gesture. "She was... ambitious. I wouldn't have expected treason out of her, but I can see how the right bribe would have got her involved. But not involved enough to risk her life."

"From what Laurenz said, Wrona acted as control, but Laurenz was doing most of the grunt work," Vigo said. "We'll want to go through everything we can find about what Wrona was up to the last couple of weeks she was aboard, but Laurenz believed she knew all of the people involved in the scheme.

"Between them, they got three engineers to provide assorted levels of access to systems and to even, in one case, load software Wrona provided into key hardware," he concluded. "Laurenz set up the devices on Lorraine's ship and then the warheads in the magazine after we locked down the ship.

"From what she said, she was expecting to grab her shuttle and bail before the warheads could activate—at which point, of course, we went translight."

"What happens to Laurenz now?" the Pentarch asked. Lorraine sounded exhausted and Vigo had to sympathize. The security constraints had to be hard on his charge, but he *had* to keep her safe.

"She cooperated with the interrogation in exchange for a promise of her life," he told Lorraine. "I figure we'll be stopping somewhere after Ominira and can drop her off on a dock where she can't get back to your uncle's people quickly enough to cause us trouble.

"We don't have the ability to keep her in a cell forever, but I don't want to release her in the Kingdom, either."

"Fair."

Vigo knew Lorraine well enough to know that the chill in her tone was more exhaustion than anger or ruthlessness. So far. He worried about what this mess would do to her—but none of them had chosen this.

"And your NCOs, Cheng?" Stephson asked Cortez.

"They're *idiots*," the Chief Engineer repeated. "And once they'd been idiots, Laurenz had everything she needed to blackmail them. I'm going to let them sweat in their quarters for a few days, then sit them down with one of the Guard and tell them they're doing deep-sync loyalty tests or spending the rest of the trip in their quarters because we've nothing else to do with them."

She shrugged.

"I *think* all three will go for the test and prove out," she noted. "Worst case, we turf them wherever the Guard turfs Laurenz."

"Not Ominira, which means... where?" Savege asked.

Every eye turned to Lorraine. Vigo saw her straighten under the attention, like it woke something in her to realize everyone was looking to her for answers.

"We need to know what my uncle managed to do," she told them, reiterating the same position. The *only* possible position. "Ominira will have more recent news, and we *need* it. We're still three weeks away from that star system and any answer, and I'm wondering if we should have gone somewhere closer to Adamantine... but we're not running to the Concordat or the Directorate, so Tolkien or Greenrock would have only added to our final voyage time."

Beulaiteuhom would have been worse in *every* way since it was farther from Adamantine than Ominira *and* in the opposite direction from the wormhole. Maka'melemele, the sixth system of the Kingdom, was only a bit farther than Tolkien or Greenrock from Adamantine, but there was *nothing* of importance out past the binary system.

Tolkien, Greenrock, or Ominira were the only three directions from Adamantine leading toward nations who weren't utterly outclassed by the Kingdom.

"I guess the question is *what are we going to do in Ominira*," Paris asked. The holoprojector suite built into the table flickered to life at a silent command from the tactical officer, opening into a three-dimensional map of the star system in question.

Six planets and two asteroid belts hovered around the yellow F8 star of Ominira itself. Named for the Yoruban word for *freedom*, Vigo had always wondered if the North African engineers whose tech and skills had underlaid the Kingdom of Adamant's initial colonization wave had named the star ironically... or if they really had believed Alexander Adamant's hype and vision.

It took a lot of confidence in the man you'd crowned King to name the system you'd settled *Freedom*, after all.

"Ife Tuntun is the home base for the Ominira Station," Stephson observed. "*Dreaming* is a *Hope*-class battleship, older but refitted to the seventy-two-cee standard and effective enough. Lieutenant Admiral Tunison commands from her."

New icons flickered above the third planet, marking the location of the Ominira Station fleet base and squadron. Inward from Ife Tuntun hung the massive gas giant that fueled the system's reactors and a hot inner asteroid belt that fed the refineries.

Vigo doubted anyone except scientists visited the innermost planet of the system, a searing hot ball of stone less than a light-minute from Ominira itself.

"What does the Lieutenant Admiral have *other* than *Dreaming*?" he asked. "Obviously, the Station would be the best place for us to resupply and pick up information—but doing so under the Admiral's eye is risky."

"My uncle always spoke highly of Tunison," Lorraine added. "I don't think that counts as a recommendation now."

"Probably not," Paris agreed. "Ominira Station isn't part of the watch on the Directorate, but given that most of the nations we worry about are toward the wormhole, they still have a solid contingent. Plus, the Station serves as the home base for our trade protection and presence missions toward the heart of the cluster.

"*Dreaming* is the flagship, but *Corsair* is the real heavy hitter of the Station's squadron," the tactical officer continued, a second icon above Ife Tuntun flashing. "Newest of the *Pirate*-class battlecruisers, she's fast, heavily armed, and can shrug off fire from anything that *isn't* a battleship."

Vigo started to pull up the stats on the *Pirates*, but the Navy officers were ahead of him. The battlecruiser's icon expanded and moved to sit beside the star system above the desk.

"Other than the two capital ships, Tunison has four destroyers and twelve frigates," Paris concluded. "The Station is responsible for enough security and trade protection, above and beyond the long-range missions starting from Adamantine, that there's usually only four to six frigates in system."

"*Corsair* can catch us," Lorraine murmured.

Vigo remembered the conversation on the bridge, talking about how the *Pirate*-class ships had a full tachyon quanta, eight times light-speed, advantage over *Goldenrod* in translight.

"And if she catches us, we're dead," Stephson agreed. "So, we want to *avoid* that."

Vigo coughed.

"Could... someone unpack that for the non-naval officers in the room?" He gestured hopefully at Lieutenant Commander Zdravkov, trying to make it sound like he wasn't the only one wondering at the certainty in Stephson's voice.

"*Pirate*-class ships are newer than *Perennials*," Stephson explained. "When they designed the *Pirates*, the *Perennial* was the measuring stick. *Corsair*'s energy screens and missile defenses are *specifically designed* to guarantee a one hundred percent immunity to our weapons outside of ranges that are basically suicide."

"And *her* beams are designed to punch through *our* screens at fifty thousand klicks," Paris added. "If we put all of our shuttles up in interceptor mode, we can handle her missile fire at long range, but... not forever. And that's assuming *she* doesn't just go full alpha on us."

That, at least, Vigo followed. *Corsair*—like *Goldenrod*—split her missile arsenal between tube launchers linked directly to the magazines and launch cells that needed to be loaded from outside.

Launch cells were cheaper, easier to maintain, and could be packed into a lot less space—but also couldn't be reloaded in combat. In most circumstances, a Captain would stagger their cell-launched missiles through their first few salvos to give them a sustained heavier punch. *Full alpha* was launching *all* of them. In *Goldenrod*'s case, that would give them a single salvo of twenty-eight missiles.

In *Corsair*'s case, that single salvo was over *three hundred*. The battlecruiser had sixty missile tubes to the frigate's four, plus two hundred and forty missile cells to the frigate's twenty-four.

Of course, *Corsair* was five times as long, three times as thick, and almost twenty times the mass of *Goldenrod*. He'd known a fight against the battlecruiser was a losing proposition, but he hadn't realized that it was *quite* as guaranteed an imbalance as Stephson and Paris were saying.

"Can't outrun her, either," Lorraine said quietly. "It's *us* that limit the ship's ability to accelerate, not the tech. *Goldenrod* can pivot direction a bit faster, but she's got the same thrust-to-weight ratio and much the same delta-*v* in her tanks, too."

"We have some advantages," Stephson noted. "Mostly that three hundred forty souls can sort their gear out faster than twenty-five hundred people can. We can go to full emergency thrust faster even if the crews are equally trained."

She shrugged and grinned.

"I think *this* crew is better than *Corsair*'s, which helps too. But all we can do if *Corsair* comes for us is run and hope we can evade her somehow."

"Except she can follow us," Savege warned, the XO studying the battlecruiser's expanded image. "If *Corsair* or one of the *Martinez*-class frigates is around when we go translight, they can follow our tachyon trail. And because they've got a speed advantage, they can drop out regularly to make sure they're still behind us in a way the other frigates can't."

"I'm hoping *Martinez* and *Peralez* are out on patrol," Paris noted, though he added an expanded view of the new frigates—slightly bigger than *Goldenrod* but comparably armed—to the holodisplay.

"It's actually likely, too. They're the Station's fastest escorts and the Kingdom's newest and shiniest toys. Command *wants* them out showing the flag."

"But *Corsair* will be at Ife Tuntun," Vigo noted. "Which means we want to make sure we *aren't* at Ife Tuntun. What are our other options?"

Everyone's gaze returned to the system and considered it.

"Irin Tutu doesn't have a military supply depot," Savege pointed out, the mental attention moving out from the main world to the next planet. There were people on Irin Tutu, the fourth planet, but not many. The air was technically breathable, but an average temperature of sixty below zero meant that it wasn't *wise*.

The planet's unusually high density of fissionables and transuranics made it too valuable to ignore, though, so heavy surface mining operations took advantage of tectonic activity and the high oxygen content of the air to create artificial habitats to support the work.

"Ireti Ina has the supplies we want, but they're close enough to Ife Tuntun that I don't think the Navy maintains facilities at the gas giant, do they?" Vigo asked.

"No," Lorraine confirmed, his Pentarch working through the same thought process. "Contracts are in place to *buy* hydrogen and other gasses, but everything is for delivery to the fleet base at Ife Tuntun.

"But Ireti Ina isn't the only gas giant in system," she reminded them all. "And if you're not delivering to Ife Tuntun, making the translight run past the asteroid belt adds time and complexity that's not worth it."

The Pentarch highlighted the outer gas giant. Agbaye Lewa was a larger gas giant than its hotter cousin in the inner system. Its moons and single ring provided gravity anchors for a much smaller extraction and cloudscoop industry than orbited Ireti Ina, but many merchant ships—and warships and diplomatic couriers—preferred not to go deeper into a system than they needed to if they weren't stopping.

The facilities around Agbaye Lewa were the interstellar equivalent of a fuel alley in a small town next to a major transitway. Everything in those stations was set up to service ships stopping in for a minimum rest and resupply.

"There's a military logistics facility at Agbaye Lewa," Savege confirmed. "It's not big, but it's where we tend to stop when making a run toward the Republic from Adamantine."

"With the Pentarch aboard, even a trade-protection mission would have seen us stop at Ife Tuntun," Stephson said. "But if we can rig up the right papers, us stopping there won't seem unusual."

"Especially since we *need* to conceal that the Pentarch is aboard."

"News should be up to date there, too," Vigo observed, looking over at Lorraine. "Might even be a touch *more* up to date, as couriers heading toward Bright Dream or Kang Tao will stop there to fuel."

Which meant they might even get some *outside* perspective. There were non-Kingdom journalists in Adamantine, after all, and the death of the King was big-enough news to get some of them to break schedules and send couriers home early.

"Then we need to see what we can put together for orders," Lorraine said, her decision clear. "Something that looks right and can avoid trouble."

If they could get through Ominira *without* drawing more trouble, Vigo would thank every deity he could think of.

His expectations were *not* that optimistic.

TWENTY-THREE

"Translight exit in sixty seconds."

Captain Stephson's voice would be relayed throughout *Gold-enrod*, Lorraine knew, but she heard it directly this time. The Pentarch was strapped into one of the hotel stations behind the Captain, with her console set up in a simplified squadron-command role.

Perennial-class frigates were primarily designed for independent deployment, with squadron-command responsibilities usually falling on a larger destroyer or cruiser if they operated in formation.

Reality had, of course, ensued and RKAN had tested everything from cramming a flotilla commander with a staff of two into the hotel stations to giving the senior Captain three extra officers in the same place.

The latter worked better—but part of what the newer *Martinez*-class frigates' greater volume had gone to was a dedicated command space on every second ship. The RKAN learned from their mistakes where they could.

But the software for someone to run a small formation from *Gold-enrod*'s bridge existed, and Lorraine now had access to it. Her "formation" was just the single frigate, but she'd read the orders Captain Stephson had unsealed.

Regardless of her comfort level with the authority, Pentarch Lorraine was in command of this mission.

"Translight exit in thirty seconds. Thrust will commence ten seconds later at five meters per second, scaling up to one full gravity at one MPS squared per ten seconds."

That was the Navigator, Major Kagan Yildiz. The hawkish man was from Greenrock, a slow-speaking officer she had never known to make a careless mistake. He wasn't *perfect*, she figured, but any mistakes he *did* make hadn't hit the rumor mill shared through the ship's junior officers.

And that mill, in Lorraine's experience, was far too eager to share stories of mistakes.

The world flickered. It was barely noticeable, little more than a blink—except that it was followed by a *lot* more data appearing on the consoles across the bridge. In translight, *Goldenrod* was blind. Her entire mass was held in a faux-tachyonic state that even Lorraine had difficulty describing without math.

"Range to Agbaye Lewa is one million eight thousand kilometers," Yildiz reported. "We overshot the safety zone by more than I'd like."

The *safety zone* around any given planet was twenty times its radius—more a precaution against navigation error when traveling multiple light-years blind than anything else. For Agbaye Lewa, that was over one-point-one million kilometers. *Goldenrod* had emerged almost exactly a hundred and twenty thousand kilometers closer to the planet than they would have preferred.

"Given that we did two days of rapid random course changes with less than an hour to take your bearings when we were done, I can live with a hundred-thousand-kilometer error on a, what, seventy-six-*trillion*-kilometer journey?"

"If we'd been headed to Ife Tuntun, that error could have put us *in* orbital traffic," Yildiz pointed out, his tone level but clear on his error.

"And if we'd been headed to Ife Tuntun, we would have targeted emerging farther out for just that reason," Stephson said reasonably. "Good enough, Major. Any contact from Agbaye Lewa Orbital Traffic Control, Vinci?"

Major Solomon Vinci was the broad-shouldered and absolutely *gorgeous* Black man who headed up *Goldenrod*'s communications team.

"OTC is anchored on Okan, moon three," Vinci said in a velvety baritone that did *not* help Lorraine keep her thoughts appropriate. "We're still a few light-seconds distant, so we should be receiving about—yep, now."

"Hook them up," Stephson ordered.

A new voice echoed over the bridge speakers, its cadence and tone exaggerated to cover up its artificial origins. Lorraine had both heard *this* voice before and knew the type.

"This is the Speaker in Silicon, the Song of the Circuits and the Voice of Agbaye Lewa, this Beautiful World," the voice told them in a rapid-fire lilt. "You all can call me Speaker. I am the mind, the matter, and the words of Orbital Traffic Control here around Agbaye Lewa, and I am plotting your course.

"I have confirmed standard Kingdom English to be an acceptable language and idiom and have identified you as the RKAN frigate *Goldenrod*, out of Adamantine. I presume you are en route to the logistics base on Owo.

"Let's chat on your destination and purpose here while you forward me your course and I confirm it's clear. Idents and bona fides, please, though I'm quite clear on who you are."

From some of the body language around the bridge, not all of Stephson's bridge crew had known that Agbaye Lewa's OTC was run by a synthetic intelligence. The Kingdom had several thousand SI citizens—and since Adamant was a full signatory of the Asimov

Convention, they were unquestionably citizens!—but they still weren't common encounters.

"Forward Speaker our standard documents and our course to the logistics base above Owo," Stephson confirmed. "What's our time there, Yildiz?"

"Owo is moon six, much further out than Okan," the navigator replied. "Emergence was on a direct line; we are two hundred thirty thousand kilometers and change out. ETA to the depot in orbit, two hours forty minutes."

"Understood. How long until the main Ominira Station knows we're here?"

"Four hours, thirty minutes," Paris reported from the Tactical station. "Unless someone goes translight to tell them... Hard to predict, then."

The problem was clear, even to Lorraine. *Light* would take four and a half hours to reach Ife Tuntun, where Lieutenant Admiral Tunison's squadron waited. But a *ship* could make that journey in minutes.

That meant there was a hard time limit to how long they could be in Ominira—but if they increased acceleration past standard thrust, that would draw attention to where they were.

"Do we have any friends at Owo?" Stephson asked.

"Looks like two frigates are in orbit to keep an eye on things: *Bluebell* and *Peregrine*," Paris reported. "*Bluebell* is a sister *Perennial*. *Peregrine* is a *Kestrel*-class; we've got legs and guns on her."

The *Kestrel*-class were the oldest frigates still in RKAN service, limited to the same seventy-two-cee as the main battle line now. She still had energy beams and missiles, though, and Lorraine doubted her weapons were that much weaker than *Goldenrod*'s or *Bluebell*'s.

"Well, Captain," Speaker's voice lilted over the coms, "everything looks fine and dandy from my side. You are cleared all the way in to Owo, and I've loaded your course into the tracking system to make sure no one else slips. There's *more* than enough empty space to keep everyone safe here, for sure!

"Now, I remind you, I can talk to *everyone* in Agbaye Lewa at once if I need to, so don't hesitate to reach out with questions or concerns. Welcome to Ominira, all!"

Lorraine had to chuckle at the SI's effervescent cheer, earning her a questioning look from Stephson.

"You don't seem surprised by our host, Your Highness," Stephson observed.

"I accompanied my mother on a visit to the Republic of Bright Dream when I was fifteen," Lorraine told her. "Stopped here to refuel in the outer system and had a chance to talk to Speaker then. They found the chance to meet a Princess fascinating."

She shrugged. Her impression was that Speaker made a *point* of making time for kids on the ships who came through Agbaye Lewa. As the synthetic intelligence had noted, they could carry on a lot of simultaneous conversations—and Speaker liked children.

An SI in the Kingdom had the same guarantee of the basic necessities of life as any citizen—food, shelter, healthcare for a human; electricity and a network connection for an SI—but they were rare enough still to be looked at askance by many of their organic neighbors.

Speaker and several others of the more visible SIs took it on themselves to act as ambassadors for their kind. In Speaker's case, Lorraine believed it came quite naturally. Like some humans, some SIs just *loved* to talk.

"I assume you're not planning on resuming that contact," the Captain said.

"No," Lorraine confirmed. "The best thing for everyone is if no one in Ominira ever knows I'm here. Fuel and supplies are all good, but have we picked up the news updates yet?"

"Standard broadcasts are running," Vinci told her. "Now that we've a course set with traffic control, I've pinged Owo Station for the Navy packets. I'll have them in a minute or two."

"You can use the XO's office to review the news, Your Highness,"

Stephson told her. "The rest of us need to keep our eyes on the docket, but I think that might be the priority for you."

Unspoken was the fact that the news was probably going to hit Lorraine harder than anyone else and she *probably* wanted to look at it in private.

Or as private as she got at that point. Palmer was standing one step behind her seat, the Guard's posture relaxing slightly as acceleration took over keeping her on the deck from magnetic soles.

After over a month, Lorraine was *almost* used to the increased security her people were insisting on.

Almost.

THE FIRST THING Lorraine noticed as she took a seat at Savege's desk—it was amazing how good the ability to just *sit* felt after six weeks in translight and microgravity!—was that there were some odd gaps in the coverage she could see from Adamantine.

The largest news network in the Kingdom of Adamant was Moria News. While House Adamant had owned a good chunk of Moria since it had been founded as "just" a courier company, neither the government nor the Crown Trust that covered the King's expenses had any control. Moria News was *notorious* for being a thorn in the government's side, despite having a general pro-monarchy bias.

MN maintained a network of ninety-six-cee couriers throughout the Kingdom, and a much less dense network out in the rest of the cluster. They *should* have had direct news of their own from Adamantine, but she wasn't seeing it.

The usual structure was simple: the big news companies brought the news in on their courier ships. Either you paid for a subscription to them and got the news and analysis as soon as it was downloaded, or you were dependent on other companies who *did* pay for that subscription and syndicated their version of it for less. Several hours later, at least.

The one advantage she saw to the secondary news sources was that they generally subscribed to *all* of the big news companies *plus* getting the government updates *plus* buying news from any nonstandard courier that passed through the system, so often their later news would have a greater breadth of perspectives.

But Moria News's latest updates from Adamantine were from the day before the attack. It was like no courier from the network had arrived in Ominira since they'd left Adamantine. The couriers from the big news companies should have exploded out from the system within twenty-four hours of the death of the King.

That news should have reached Ominira nine days before *Goldenrod*—but her first pass showed *no* original news updates from the main four news networks.

The only news appeared to have come through the *government* courier service, with an update eight days earlier and another six days after that.

She glared at the blatant gap in the schedule, then checked a file in her neural link she rarely used. While her naval career had taken her out of the Adamantine System, she hadn't needed to know what secondary news services House Adamant and the Adamant Guard regarded as reliable in each system.

She had a list from both her House and her Guards, but she swiftly realized that they had different opinions on the value of the services there. She grabbed one news service that was ranked highly by both and selected what looked like their most recent overview article on the coup.

"Thank you for joining Black Raven News for our analysis broadcast," a woman's voice said in her ear. There was a visual layer to the piece, too, and Lorraine opened it in front of her, creating the illusion of a ten-centimeter-tall woman seated behind a desk... on top of Savege's desk.

"This afternoon's focus, as promised, is to catch people up on what we know about the attack on House Adamant. It's not as much as anyone would like, given that we are talking about the death of our beloved King Valeriya, and there are a *lot* of questions still in the air."

Lorraine was glad she was sitting. She'd thought she'd known. She hadn't doubted Roma's message, even without the extra evidence of the assassination attempts on her. She'd *known* her mother was dead.

It was still painful to hear it said by a news reporter, to have it confirmed beyond doubt.

Her breath ragged, she paused the recording—she'd lost several seconds staring at the wall and she needed to focus. She needed answers. She needed to *know* what had happened, as best as she could.

She focused on her breathing, calming her breath if not her emotions. Then, finally, she restarted the recording.

TWENTY-FOUR

"Thank you for joining Black Raven News for our analysis broadcast," the woman repeated, her tiny form still managing to show how impeccably coiffed she was. "This afternoon's focus, as promised, is to catch people up on what we know about the attack on House Adamant. It's not as much as anyone would like, given that we are talking about the death of our beloved King Valeriya and there are a *lot* of questions still in the air."

An image of Valeriya hovered behind the woman's head, in case someone had forgotten what their King looked like.

"Adding to those questions is that Crown Regent Benjamin Adamant is maintaining a news blackout around the Adamantine System for security reasons—only Royal courier ships have been authorized to leave while the capital system struggles with the scale of the catastrophe.

"All of the news we have received is therefore from official sources, which *normally* I wouldn't be much bothered by." The anchor smiled wryly. "But when even those official sources admit that the Adamant Guard turned on our King's family, everything only seems to open up more questions!

"First, the basics: we have confirmed that King Valeriya, her husband Frederick, and their two eldest children, Daniel and Taura, are dead. State funerals had been scheduled for all four, along with Daniel and Taura's partners—Lavender and Nelson—as of our last update from Adamantine.

"More openly in question are the fates of Pentarch Nikola and Pentarch Lorraine," the anchor continued—and Lorraine's attention was suddenly locked on the tiny figure.

Nikola's fate was in question? But Roma had thought he was dead, too!

"Officially, the updates we've received from the government say that Pentarch Nikola is dead and Pentarch Lorraine is missing. However, as I have said before, not all of the pieces add up."

The blue-and-green globe of Bastion rose up behind the woman's head.

"Before we get into that, let's finish laying out all of those pieces," she continued. "Pentarch Benjamin Adamant, our late King's older brother, has been appointed Crown Regent by Prime Minister Dakila Bayer.

"No date has yet been announced for the Royal Election, with the chaos on Adamantine a clear barrier to the proper process. There have been issues with rioting, and curfews have been imposed across the planet, with military law in place on Mithral— the southern continent, to those unfamiliar with Bastion's geography.

"While the *official* reports have given no details on why Mithral is under martial law, we here at Black Raven News have managed to acquire background information that wasn't released to the public in full detail."

The woman looked pleased with herself as she said that, and Lorraine chuckled grimly. She suspected that might be a more dangerous game than the reporter realized now. The Kingdom had a long history of freedom of the press on government matters, even when it had become a problem.

But if her uncle had already gone this far, punishing media for acquiring secret reports wasn't out of the question.

"According to our sources—and as always, viewers and listeners, I want to flag the question marks on this! We don't have multiple angles on this and I can't guarantee it's true—Mithral is under martial law because the Army troops in the military reservations are refusing to acknowledge the Regent's authority.

"As of our last update, the army units on Mithral weren't in open rebellion, but for units of the RKAA to defy the government is *unheard* of. Combined with reports of missing ships from the RKAN Home Fleet, there are some definite cracks around the edges of the official story."

The woman spread her hands wide.

"Now, listen to me, viewers and listeners. Our Kingdom has a long-standing tradition of transparency of government and freedom of the press. Where the truth gets put aside or concealed, it's often for a good reason—and this is a crisis situation, one where major questions are still being asked and the security of our monarchy is at risk!

"But poking at the cracks on the edges is what I do, so I'm going to tell you how *I* put these pieces together:

"First, I remind you all that Nikola Adamant is a Colonel in the Royal Kingdom of Adamant Army's First Armored Corps. Our Fourth Pentarch is the commanding officer of a strike brigade of power armor and tanks, some of the best the Kingdom has."

Icons started to light up on the globe, highlighting the position of the First Armored Corps—smack-dab center in the middle of Bastion's southern continent. The same one the reporter had told Lorraine was on the edge of open rebellion.

"First Armored, including the Pentarch's brigade, is based at Planetary Defense Center Mithral, the main surface installation of Bastion's anti-invasion defenses. The troops that are defying the Crown Regent are in the military reserve *around* PDC Mithral.

"Do you see what I see, viewers? *I* think Pentarch Nikola is alive and marshaling forces against his uncle.

"That raises ugly questions, of course, about what happened to Nikola's mother and siblings," the reporter added. "Especially as we have *no* information on what has happened to Pentarch Lorraine. Which ship she was assigned to in Home Fleet was kept secret, but some of the information we've been provided suggests that Home Fleet was attacked during the attempt on the Pentarchs' lives—most likely as an attempt on both Pentarch Benjamin *and* Pentarch Lorraine.

"Since we know ships were lost and Pentarch Lorraine hasn't been seen since, we can only conclude that either the youngest Pentarch is dead or that she has fled into hiding.

"In the latter case, given her brother's apparent rebellion and the attack on every *other* member of her family, we have to ask: Who is behind the attacks? Some outside threat like the Directorate, as is the current official high-probability scenario? I trust Prime Minister Bayer, people, but it will always be easier to point outside than in!

"Are we under attack from the outside? Or did our rebellious prince, now dug in to a mountain behind an army of loyal soldiers, turn on his siblings and parents to accelerate a chance at a throne? We don't know enough yet, my dear viewers, but I can assure you that Black Raven News is keeping our eyes and ears open for anything coming in from the capital!

"You may not hear it here *first*, but we always promise that Black Raven will give you the deepest take and the widest view of interstellar news!"

The recording ended, and Lorraine stared at the desk where her link had placed its illusion.

Nikola wasn't dead. *Nikola wasn't dead.* Nikola had possibly drawn the same conclusions as she had and might be in open rebellion against their uncle, but *he wasn't dead.*

"I need you to live, Nik," she whispered, as if he could hear her. "I don't know what to do." She chuckled. "I doubt you do, either, but at least you're at home."

The problem, Lorraine knew, was the analysis the reporter had made at the end. If a news analyst in Ominira was pointing a finger at Nikola without all of the information but *also* without the government right there to enforce their story, making him the scapegoat was going to look all too easy to her uncle.

She grimaced.

"Or I might be an even better scapegoat," she whispered aloud. "You're at least there to argue. I'm... *gone*. Possibly dead. Possibly on the run. Either way... I'm not arguing any stories you're telling about *me*."

They needed to go through all of the reports. She knew Paris's tactical team was already doing that, and she needed their analysis on top of her own. One reporter's take wasn't enough to set her plans in stone.

Even if it was enough for her to be sure of both the good and the bad.

TWENTY-FIVE

Vigo didn't need anyone to tell him everything was confirmed. He could see it in Lorraine's face as the key players gathered in Stephson's office. Savege was listening in, the XO focused on holding down the bridge against something unexpected happening.

That left him, Lorraine, and Stephson seated around the small breakout table, watching Lieutenant Commander Paris put together his thoughts.

"Lay it out, Guns," Stephson told him, using the ancient nickname for the ship's Tactical Officer.

"None of the news from home is good," Paris said. "Some of it is not *quite* as bad as we expected, but overall, it's a mess. My people have the Navy background briefing, which includes a few pieces not available to the public... but we've gone through it all and there's some definite censorship going on."

"Even of the Navy packet?" the Captain asked, surprised.

"Even of the Navy reports," Paris confirmed. "*Goldenrod* isn't mentioned anywhere, though..." He sighed. "There's a piece we didn't know about that's involved there, though."

"The beginning, Lieutenant Commander," Lorraine interrupted.

"If we go around in circles chasing the pieces that sound interesting, we may just run out of time. We have an hour to the fueling station. From there, we can safely assume we've only got two hours until Tunison comes looking for us."

Paris nodded gratefully to the Pentarch's interruption. Vigo himself waited silently, impressed. His charge was still feeling her way into her new situation and dealing with emotional blows he could barely see the edges of, but she had her mother's gift for cutting to the key points.

"The first wave of attacks—which we knew of thanks to Colonel Roma's message—hit the King's detail, Guard Command, and the details for the First, Second, and Third Pentarchs," Paris laid out.

"Four of those five attacks were complete successes," he continued. "King Valeriya and Pentarchs Daniel and Taura were definitively killed. Guard Command was taken out by a kiloton-range chemical explosive detonated *inside* the base."

Vigo winced. He'd figured it had to be something like that. The old fortress had been built to withstand orbital bombardment, with large chunks of it underground to withstand conventional surface attack. It wasn't a planetary defense center or anything of the sort, but it had been intended to serve as a fallback point for the Pentarchs under a wide range of threat situations.

It would have taken a nuke—a *big* nuke—to destroy Guard Command from outside, which would have had catastrophic impacts on the city around it. The fortress had been built on a hill overlooking Adamant City originally, but the capital had long since spread out around it.

An internal weapon was the only way—but a nuke would have been impossible to smuggle in. Even a conventional explosive of that size would have filled a *truck* at least—but CDX-225, for example, was something that *would* normally be present in the building.

"What about Daniel's kids?" Lorraine asked.

"Unclear," Paris told her, his tone grim. "What information we have says that the move on Pentarch Daniel was a direct attack with boots on the ground. While the reports confirm that Daniel and Lavender were killed, along with their entire Guard Detail, there is *no* information on the fate of the twins."

"Roma said some of Daniel's Guards betrayed him..." Vigo considered aloud, then looked at his Pentarch as he reached for a hope that might fuel them *both*. "Even Guards loyal to your Uncle might—no, *would*, I think—draw the line at allowing toddlers under their protection to be killed.

"Protecting the Princesses might have been part of the deal. They don't have a place in the Pentarchy, so they're no threat to Benjamin taking the throne. They're young enough that they could easily be adopted out as nobodies—or even raised as Adamants!—without being a likely threat to Pentarch Benjamin."

"The dearth of information suggests something similar to me," Paris agreed, surprising Vigo. "My team's projection is that the Regent either had the Princesses in hand or expected to in short order at the time of the last update.

"Revealing their survival might prove a valuable PR coup for him, if he gets the timing right. Either way, our news is from ten days after the attack. They *should* have been confirmed dead if that was the case. We have to assume they are now an asset in the Regent's hands—but they are alive."

Vigo knew the First Pentarch's children about as well as anyone *could* know a pair of toddlers. They were smart and active kids, still curious about the world around them and doted on by their parents and everyone around them.

He hadn't *quite* been twisting facts to fit what he wanted to be true, but it was still reassuring to have Paris support him—and while he hoped no one else could, *he* could see the slight relaxation in Lorraine's eyes and shoulders.

"What about Nikola?" she asked after a few moments of silence.

"It's not explicit in even the Navy reports, but it's pretty clear that someone in his Army unit decided they weren't quite sure about his Guard Detail. So, when one of *our* people overrode a security protocol to let an unmarked aircraft land at the field barracks for the maneuvers he was leading, they met some of the First Armored Corps's best armored assault troopers," Paris concluded. "It got... ugly from there, but it sounds like the brigade loaded up and rolled for heavier fortifications, Pentarch in tow."

"And Pentarch Benjamin's past gives him one giant headache," Vigo concluded. "Too many of the current senior officers of the Army were *on* Greenrock when he pulled out. Turnover or no turnover, enough of the troops in the First Armored, especially, were there.

"RKAA in general doesn't trust him, but the First Armored Corps? They *hate* Benjamin," he reminded them.

"According to the naval packets, the entire military reservation on Mithral is in a state of *questionable cooperativeness*," Paris said. "Given that includes the planetary defense command at PDC Mithral, I'd say Nikola is alive and digging in. I don't know what that's going to *look* like, especially when Benjamin commands the Fleet."

"Masada Protocols," Vigo said, almost unconsciously. Then he winced as he realized that he'd just hit *another* suppressed memory block. Most of the concealed information in his head was on his link, but certain situations and phrases would bring the mental keys to that information out of his memory.

"What?" Lorraine asked. "A counterpoint to Exodus, I'm guessing?"

"The other side of the coin," he told her. "One that might give Exodus a better chance of working. I don't have a lot of details," he admitted, skimming what limited information his link gave him on it, "because *you* would never be executing on Masada. It calls for... well, digging in to a planetary defense center, preferably PDC Mithral, and making an enemy dig the Pentarch out.

"The *assumption* is that the rest of the Kingdom will send relief," Vigo warned. "Which is much more in question than we ever thought it would be. But Nikola can still be a very present and *visible* living Pentarch to challenge Benjamin."

"I don't know how far that will go," Paris warned. "Prime Minister Bayer has already confirmed Benjamin as Crown Regent. The government seems to be in line behind the Regent so far, too."

"Dakila Bayer and my uncle go back a long way," Lorraine said. She chuckled grimly. "I've always heard people say that Alexander made being Prime Minister such a crap job that nobody wanted to do it."

The Prime Minister of the Kingdom of Adamant held one of two vetoes over legislation—an equal-but-separate counterpoint to the King's own veto. They had to be elected as a member of the House of the People, which required them to be part of a political party, but they had to surrender both their seat's vote *and* their party membership to serve as Prime Minister.

And only half of their cabinet could be drawn from their former party, which left the PM with an unreliable power base at best in the two Houses. Despite that, it remained a powerful position and the peak of ambition for most politicians.

Friendship with a Pentarch would certainly *help* someone rise to that spot—and to build the personal, nonpartisan alliances necessary to govern from it. But it also meant that Bayer wasn't going to push back against the new Regent's schemes.

"Where does that leave us?" Stephson asked.

"Outside my uncle's immediate worries or plans," Lorraine replied. "He'll be keeping an ear out for news of us—he always tries to plan for every contingency and *he* will know I fled on *Goldenrod*. I'm surprised he hasn't been more open about that, telling people to look for us."

"Two pieces to that, I think," Paris told them. "First, there was *also* an attack on Home Fleet. That's why the cruisers didn't come looking for us until after the lightspeed warning arrived. A freighter arriving in orbit dumped a couple dozen unmanned shuttles stuffed full of bombs aimed at the flagship, *Sultan*.

"At least two frigates were destroyed, and several larger ships damaged. Casualties are unknown but estimated at around a thousand. The official packet seems to imply that *Goldenrod* was in the losses from that—though we aren't mentioned by name.

"That said..." Paris sighed. "Vinci and I may have pushed harder than we should, but we confirmed that there have been *stacks* of encrypted and classified messages and updates sent directly to Lieutenant Admiral Tunison."

"Which means the Admiral almost certainly has more information and orders," Stephson concluded. "But Owo Station is a much smaller affair, and my conversation with Colonel Fitzwilliam hasn't raised any unusual questions. He's the commanding officer of the Owo orbital platforms, in charge of the defense and the supply base.

"The orders we put together cover our presence here and give us a departure date *before* the attack," she continued. "According to them, we did a deep-space-maneuver training exercise before heading here, adding about five days to our journey.

"Those orders call for Fitzwilliam to provide us with a full load of fuel and munitions—with the exercise covering that we weren't actually prepped for a long-range mission. From here, Colonel Fitzwilliam believes we're heading to the Rory System in the Glorious Reach for a trade-protection patrol through the Reach's territory."

Vigo pulled a reference on both the system and the Glorious Reach from his link. Rory was the closest system of the Glorious Reach, a four-star nation that served as a key trading partner of the Kingdom. The Reach was also, unfortunately, a demonstration of how systems created to keep colony financiers in power could go wrong.

While many star nations had clear and powerful first families, the Reach had an explicit aristocracy anchored on the Eight Dukes. Their elected legislature was more than a rubber stamp for the Ducal Council... but not by very much, as Vigo understood.

Between one thing and another, that seemed to result in the Reach never being *quite* able to provide security to key translight exit points. Ships would emerge *close* to planets on the scale of star systems, but that was still hundreds of thousands of kilometers away.

Not every nation was capable of patrolling even the standard bubble around a habitable world of six hundred thousand kilometers. That was what allowed piracy to *exist*—that, and unbelievably reckless pilots and crews who'd spend less than ten minutes in normal space before jumping back to translight!

While RKAN ran patrols through most of their neighboring systems, fishing for pirates, it was the patrols through the Reach that tended to turn up prey.

"A Reach patrol explains us stockpiling extra munitions, too," Paris observed, clearly running through much the same thought process as Vigo.

Though the Guard Major hoped that Paris hadn't needed to look up a glorified encyclopedia entry to get there!

"Exactly. Owo Station's logistics teams are putting together pallets of missiles, warheads, food, raw materials... everything a healthy warship needs to operate independently for a while," Stephson promised.

"What is the story about my presence?" Lorraine asked. "I know we don't exactly broadcast who the Lieutenant Commanders on a given ship are, but the Pentarch being aboard had to hit the rumor mill, and the question is going to get asked."

"It is and it was," Stephson confirmed. "Thanks to Major Vigo's people and our own systems specialists, we have some very clean-looking records saying you were transferred to *Sultan* to join Admiral Benjamin's staff. I hope you'll forgive me some very gentle grousing with him about nepotism and the House overprotecting the Pentarchs."

"If it keeps people in the dark, I'll forgive a lot," Lorraine promised.

"I worry that it's out of character enough to raise more questions," Vigo admitted. "The House is generally quite determined *not* to interfere in the Pentarchs' careers beyond sending people like me along as dead weight."

"There is the truth of the House... and there is about five thousand years of myth around kings and their families," Stephson pointed out. "It's sadly easy to lean on the latter to slander the former, I'm afraid.

"Plus, it's common knowledge in RKAN that Admiral Benjamin dotes on the niece who followed him into the service." There was a sharp, sad edge to the Captain's smile. "The House may have its traditions, but Pentarch Benjamin has always played around the edges, hasn't he?

"If anyone *would* go a bit beyond the norm to protect and promote a favored niece, it would be him."

If only that was the worst of the tradition-breaking Pentarch Benjamin had done.

TWENTY-SIX

Lorraine couldn't keep herself from the bridge now. Her instincts and training were screaming at her to be *doing* something—the shuttle flights were about to launch to pick up their supplies from Owo Station—but her weird new place on the ship meant all she could do was watch.

And she watched from the place with all of the information, seated behind Lieutenant Colonel Stephson and watching both the main tactical projection and the command displays set up for her.

Owo Station wasn't much to look at. A standard wheel-form orbital rotated at the center of a cluster of glorified shipping containers, providing pseudogravity for the base's permanent crew.

Peregrine, a hundred-and-eighty-meter-long older sibling to *Goldenrod*, was locked to the station's perimeter, rotating with it to provide her crew ongoing gravity while she played guard dog.

The other ship, *Bluebell*, was a near-exact copy of *Goldenrod*. She was in an active powered orbit well above the logistics station, maintaining one gravity of thrust to keep her crew's feet on the decks while they watched over the supply base.

Neither seemed to regard Lorraine's ship as worthy of question. It was the station commander's job to clear ships coming in, after all. They should still, in her opinion, have run a sensor sweep or *something* of *Goldenrod*—for crew training, if nothing else.

"We are on final approach now, Commander Chevrolet," Stephson said, speaking to Lorraine's old boss. "Shuttles are clear to begin cargo transfer."

"Understood," Chevrolet replied. "Charlie Flight will remain aboard—we've rigged them up as interceptors. Just in case."

Even on shipboard communications, they weren't mentioning that the third Flight were Guard shuttles. One of them currently had an RKAN *crew*, with the casualties Laurenz's betrayal had inflicted, but the shuttles remained Guard ships tasked with protecting Lorraine.

If something went wrong now, the best way to protect Lorraine would be to protect the entire ship she was sitting on.

"All hands, be advised, we are cutting to one-half gravity for ease of maintaining orbit," Yildiz said into his microphone. "Ten seconds. Five. Two. One. *Now*."

Numbers shifted on Lorraine's display as her own weight in the chair lessened. She focused her attention on the outside, watching first as the shuttles began to drift out of *Goldenrod*'s launch bay.

The first two Midas shuttles were in the massive *heavy transport* mode, fifty meters long and over *three* times the size of the shuttles in bomber mode. Only one heavy-transport Midas could leave the shuttle bay at a time, and the frigate only carried the components to rig two shuttles in that mode.

Once both of them were in space, the rest of the flights drifted out of the bay two at a time, in the more normal *standard* twenty-meter-long setup. The twelve spacecraft would need four journeys back and forth to fully load the frigate.

"Captain, Owo Station is offering to provide shuttle flights to accelerate the transfer process," Vinci reported.

Lorraine shivered. She couldn't see any easy way to say no without raising suspicions—but bringing in strange shuttles would make it very clear that *Goldenrod*'s shuttle bay had been heavily modified. Which would, of course, raise questions of its own—though Stephson's claim of her transfer to her uncle's ship would help cover them.

Maybe?

"Thank them kindly, Major Vinci," Stephson said. "Warn them we've got a very particular set of Deck Chiefs, and then send them the landing-instructions file labeled *Seventeen-K*."

"Yes, sir." Vinci sounded confused—but Lorraine could tell that the frigate's Captain was grinning at him from *behind* Stephson.

"Give them about thirty seconds and they'll start making excuses," Stephson told the coms officer. "Spin them out until they come up with something that sounds passingly reasonable, then let them off."

Out of curiosity, Lorraine looked up Landing Instructions 17K. It took her less than ten seconds of skimming the document to see Stephson's point. It read like the kind of excessively precise, overly procedural landing plan she'd occasionally seen in training.

No single piece of it was *completely* out of line, but between additional call-and-response sequences, an excessively precise approach vector and a general sense of treating the reader like an *idiot*, no pilot was going to want to deal with the Deck Chiefs who wrote that document for a real flight!

"Send my apologies to the Deck Chiefs, too," Stephson said drily. "I had them write that a long time ago to keep in my back pocket, but it *does* make them look like anal-retentive assholes."

Lorraine chuckled and turned her attention back to the broader display. Now that they were inside Owo's defensive perimeter, she had icons and details for the defenses themselves. Part of the same service or not, it was all too likely that those stations would turn their guns on *Goldenrod* before the day was out.

Most of the defenses, she quickly realized, were explicitly one-shot systems. About five hundred satellites, each equipped with two missiles, orbited Owo. Less than half of those could get a line of sight at any given point above the moon, but that was still enough to see off any particularly brave or foolish pirate.

A similar number of shorter-ranged mines—basically the terminal chassis of a missile without the main drive—were set up around the logistics station themselves. Currently, those mines were safed—sleeping, waiting on a command from the base controller.

Four manned forts hung at the outer end of "arms" of cargo containers reaching out from the main station. Neither the forts nor the cargo pods were hooked up to the orbital, and the stations had to be zero-gravity—less of a problem, she supposed, when the off-shift crew probably slept on the main station.

The station itself was surprisingly lightly armed, with its systems clearly focused on self-defense. Its energy screen was impressive, but its beams were clearly intended more as an antimissile system. The exterior forts had similar energy-beam systems to *Peregrine*—outdated but still effective.

It was enough to give her frigate a bad day. She had some faith in Stephson that they'd be able to break away, but if those forts turned their beams on *Goldenrod*, it might be over before they even knew new orders had arrived.

Lorraine glanced back up at the Lieutenant Colonel commanding the frigate. Stephson seemed relaxed, as cheerful as possible under the circumstances. Everyone knew there *was* a threat, but the Captain didn't seem to think it was going to come from the people already out there with them.

The real threat was the timer slowly ticking down on Lorraine's screen. The one marking when the light of their arrival would reach Ife Tuntun and Admiral Tunison.

A few keystrokes added a second timer. This one was much more of an estimate: how long it would take the shuttles to get everything aboard.

Each journey was about twenty minutes of flight alone. If the logistics base had set everything up correctly and were as efficient as they were *supposed* to be, they should finish transferring the last load at about the same time as Admiral Tunison realized *Goldenrod* was in his system.

Then it would come down to what orders the Lieutenant Admiral had—and whether he had someone he trusted enough to send immediately.

Lorraine didn't like her conclusions there. She didn't know Are Tunison, but she knew her uncle. And if the new Regent trusted Tunison, then Tunison would be ready.

Benjamin Adamant would tolerate nothing less.

AS THE SHUTTLES set to work, Lorraine forced herself to leave them to it and set to the task in front of her. They didn't have a great deal of time, and she knew that everyone was waiting on her.

The Exodus Protocols left her a lot of options. Roma had laid them out pretty bluntly, and Lorraine silently thanked the dead woman. She couldn't go around in circles right now.

The first option she made herself consider was the one with the most heartache: give up. Her anger had cooled somewhat, and the news that her nieces were likely *alive* undercut the most unforgivable of her uncle's crimes.

But only the *most* unforgivable. The funds she had immediate access to were enough for her to disappear. Included in the Exodus files were contacts who could source false identifications for her—she probably couldn't risk the one in Ominira, but there was an... *entity* called Bluelight in the San Ignacio System, two-thirds of the way to Bright Dream from Ominira.

She could buy a fast courier in San Ignacio. A ninety-six-cee yacht would be expensive but available to those who could afford it. Faster than that would be difficult; she'd have problems sourcing a one-oh-four ship in the Cluster outside of Bright Dream itself.

If Bluelight could be trusted—it wasn't clear from the files if it was an organization, a code name for an individual or even the real name of an SI—they could source new identities for her and her people, and she could take volunteers from her Guard and *Goldenrod* onto the yacht. Head off for parts unknown, where money would buy both comfort and discretion.

Lieutenant Colonel Stephson could go home, plead force majeure—Jarret's people had literally put a gun to her head, after all —and be fine. Everyone would be fine.

Except, of course, Nikola. Lorraine didn't have a lot of information about what her brother was doing, but she *did* have near-complete information on PDC Mithral. Digging him out of the fortress would be difficult without wrecking the entire continent, but it *could* be done.

Without relief or reinforcement, her brother could still hold out for a long time. Months. Maybe even a year or more—the PDC had powerful-enough weapons to force even Home Fleet's battleships to respect its arc of fire, which would reduce Benjamin's allies to a ground assault against the heaviest fortifications and best troops the Kingdom had.

But so long as their uncle had the support of the Short and Long Houses and the Prime Minister, the government would fall into line behind the Regency. Control of the military was fuzzy under Election rules, but it would fall to the Cabinet if there was any real doubt.

Even when there *was* a King, the day-to-day civilian control of the military was exercised by the Cabinet—and Lorraine had the sinking feeling that Daley had his Cabinet in line behind the new Regent.

Individual units—like the troops holding PDC Mithral around her brother and even *Goldenrod*'s crew—might defy the government, but the rule of law and civilian control of the armed forces were too rock-solid in the Kingdom for much more.

Nikola wouldn't be able to source reinforcements from a hole in the ground. If his sister went into exile, never to return, he would die.

Lorraine chuckled to herself. She'd put together the pieces of what running away looked like, but she had known that she wasn't going to do it. Following through the logic of what would happen to her last surviving sibling, well...

She *couldn't* do it.

Which meant there were only two real choices in front of her. Assemble a coalition of her mother's allies—and probably enemies!—to sail back into Adamantine and challenge her uncle with a fleet; or go to Earth and hope the United Worlds would give her a fleet to do the same.

In either case, she needed overwhelming force. An actual battle with Home Fleet above Bastion was her worst possible scenario. She needed to return with enough force to make it *unquestionable* she could win—combined with the legitimacy of her claim and her evidence against her uncle, that could convince Home Fleet and even whatever remained of the Adamant Guard to stand down.

The numbers took shape on the screen in front of her. She fed information from her link into the console and put the components up.

First, the Concordat of Amal Jadid. Her father's Griffin Family would back her, but it would be a lot to ask of the Concordat's government to risk the alliance that had been so carefully built over the last several decades.

Even if they *did* sign on, they couldn't put enough ships up. They only had three battleships, generally kept for defense of the Amal Jadid System itself. Their six battlecruisers made a useful fast wing when combined with the heavy battleships of RKAN, but they weren't meant to fight battleships head-to-head.

The Republic of Bright Dream was... probably a nonstarter, Lorraine knew. Their eighty-eight-cee battleships would count above their weight, especially for the *impression* she needed, but the Republic wouldn't jump without permission from their United Worlds corporate masters.

She could *probably* swing enough favors and promises to get some support, but that was in the range of *maybe* a single division of battleships and escorts. Two capital ships. Maybe.

Anything past the Republic was dicey in other ways. Adamant was known there, but the connections were more... generic, really. No one there would *care* much about a coup in Adamant, so long as trade was unaffected.

Some of the players—like Bright Dream's corporate puppeteers—might well see her uncle's coup as an opportunity. Lorraine knew her mother's economic stances had been politely described as *protectionist*—and impolitely described somewhere between *aggressive* and *colonial*.

Valeriya had kept outside corporations out of the Kingdom on one hand, while encouraging Adamant corporations to spread out with the other. That was the story, anyway, though Lorraine had read enough of the actual policies and decisions to know the reality was more complicated.

Corporations that were willing to play by the Kingdom's strict rules on lobbying, local involvement and general industrial regulation were perfectly welcome. Adamantine corporations that expanded into other star nations did so with the understanding that *they* were expected to play by local rules too.

Corps that tried to push local rules and came crying back to their home government found a chilly audience in both the Palace and the Houses. The galaxy had too much history of where letting business run roughshod over government led.

It didn't seem to be a lesson that had sunk in as widely as it should, in Lorraine's opinion, which was why places like Bright Dream were so badly in thrall to the corporate pocketbook.

There were other nations on this side of the Cluster—like San Ignacio—but few of them were wealthy enough to command powerful fleets. Fewer still had *enough* ships to spare anything from existing duties.

Best case, she could scrounge up another two to three battleships or battlecruisers there with months of work.

A desperate tour of every ally of the Kingdom that could take her a year or more would produce a fleet of maybe six allied ships. One equal, at best, to the Kingdom's Home Fleet.

Unless... a stylized cross flickered on her display as she brought up the information on the Richelieu Directorate. On *paper*, the Directorate was a democratic theocracy. The reality was, of course, much more complex. Only the current Director themself needed to be Catholic clergy at that point, but a lot of the form and pomp of the original plan remained.

Five star systems to the Kingdom's six, the Directorate had been her nation's rival for at least a century—aggravated by both of them trying to draw the smaller nations around them into their circle of influence.

Intelligence suggested that the Directorate had rebuilt from their fleet losses in the last war and now had twelve battleships of their own—though no battlecruisers. Official assessments put all of those battleships on par with RKAN's older *Hope*-class ships, but Lorraine had her suspicions about how rosy *that* assessment was.

Her mother's enemy might well give her the help to overthrow her uncle... but she doubted she'd enjoy the price. The *best* case she could see was a free hand on the part of the Director that could easily tip the long-term balance between the two states.

The numbers just didn't add up. Her answers didn't lie in the Bright Dream Cluster—they *couldn't*. Even allies of her Kingdom might not stand against her uncle, and Lorraine didn't think she could afford the price her Kingdom's enemies would ask for.

That only really left one option.

Earth.

TWENTY-SEVEN

"Well, Your Highness?"

Lorraine had barely stepped into Stephson's field of view before the tall blonde officer spoke.

"Were you waiting for me?" she asked wryly.

"If you were one iota less disciplined, Pentarch, you'd have been *muttering* to yourself as you stared at that console for the last hour," Stephson told her. "I can't mirror your console the way I can mirror my staff's at this point, but I can guess.

"Do we have a destination?"

"We do," Lorraine confirmed. "Do you want to pull Yildiz into this?"

"He's currently calculating his... seventh escape course out of Owo in the last hour," the Captain said. "Distracting him is probably a good plan. Major Yildiz! Join us, please."

The navigator started, then rose and crossed to them. The half-gravity of their current powered orbit was enough to keep his feet on the deck, but it was also light enough to give him a carefully managed bounce that probably made him look more eager than he was.

"Captain, Pentarch," he greeted them. "What do you need?"

Stephson tapped a command on her seat's arm, causing her main screen to rotate to horizontal and act as base for a holographic projection of the Bright Dream Cluster. Anchored on the Tavastar–Bright Dream Wormhole, the Cluster was a lopsided sphere, bulging toward Kang Tao and the wormhole there.

"Her Highness has a destination for us. Figure the three of us can rig up a course on our own if needed."

"Of course, sir. Where are we going?"

"Earth," Lorraine told him with a small smile. "But right now, the Bright Dream Wormhole."

The star system in question highlighted on the projection without her even asking Stephson. Her Captain had guessed that much, she supposed.

"Once we're through the wormhole, we're in the United Worlds and I have contacts to draw on that should get us access to the Charon Complex wormhole in Greenhall. All the way to Sol in the blink of an eye from there."

The actual wormhole transit would be a few hours, as she understood it, but compared to the *year*-long journey from Tavastar to Sol, it was nothing.

"Doesn't matter what's chasing us, either," Stephson observed. "The United Worlds is clear that their border is the wormhole—and anyone who comes through looking for trouble is going to *find* it."

Yildiz snorted.

"Always seemed odd to me, that," he admitted. "There are entire first-order clusters that are less travel time from Sol than Tavastar, but Tavastar is part of the United Worlds and they aren't."

Lorraine raised an eyebrow at him.

"You don't know?" she asked. It seemed an odd thing for a navigator to have missed, though she supposed it was covered more in history and politics—subjects *her* education had drilled into her—than even in the tachyon and wormhole physics a navigator *should* know.

"Presented as a bit of an established fact in the Academy," he said. "Never dug in to it, I guess. Just seems strange."

"You do know wormholes aren't *permanent*, right?" she asked carefully.

"Nothing's permanent," he agreed. "Even stars go poof eventually."

Someone, Lorraine realized, had misinterpreted part of what *was* taught at the Academy.

"Stars last millions of years," she told Yildiz gently. "*Wormholes* last thousands. Maybe tens of thousands, but the math isn't as exact as we'd like. So, we know our wormholes can just... go away.

"And it *happened. Twice.* The Tau Ceti Wormhole to New Hope was the big one, though. First major colony outside a wormhole, and it wasn't set up as self-sufficiently as we'd do it now."

She shrugged and could *see* the realization sinking in.

"Forty-two million people in two star systems were cut off. It took almost *sixty years* to get a confirmation back that they'd even *survived*. So, the UW made the rule: if they hadn't got there with a translight drive, it had to be self-sufficient in case the wormhole closed."

"Then a hundred years later, it happened again," Stephson added with a grim chuckle. "That was... Nuevo Santiago, I believe. A second-order cluster, though, so it didn't make quite as many waves beyond confirming that the UW was on the right path."

A green line had appeared on the hologram, and the Captain waved a hand toward it.

"A direct course from here to Bright Dream is a *long* haul. Hundred and twenty-eight days. We can do it, but it won't be fun for anyone." She shook her head. "We're not a cruiser or a capital ship, Your Highness. We don't have a hab pod."

Lorraine grimaced.

"I know... and please, can we skip the *Your Highnesses*? I can accept that I'm not Lieutenant Commander Adamant anymore, but... that one hurts."

The dividing line between a destroyer or frigate and a cruiser or capital ship was the habitation pods: detached sections of the ship that rotated to provide pseudogravity in translight or when otherwise immobile. They were designed to fold in line with the ship while under thrust, allowing the layout to be consistent for both modes.

They also took up quite a lot of space and mass, which meant that frigates and destroyers didn't have them. It was an ongoing argument for frigates, but the usual conclusion was that a frigate's role was best served by system-hopping *anyway*.

"We have a pseudogravity gym in Medical," Stephson noted. "One that our doctor says you haven't been spending enough time in... Lorraine. And the poor man isn't sure who to get to bug you about it."

Lorraine chuckled. The ship's Medical Officer was *right,* and she'd expected to hear from him by now. The question of who, exactly, to run even a minor rebuke through was confusing.

"While I will promise to be good, that doesn't make a four-plus-month journey in translight any easier on us," she agreed. "And I'd rather get updated news along the way somewhere, too."

"San Ignacio," Stephson told her, highlighting a star. "It adds a light-year and six days to the trip, but means we have an eighty-three-day stint and a forty-eight-day stint instead of one hundred-and-twenty-eight-day jump."

"And San Ignacio is studiously neutral," Yildiz pointed out. He still looked thoughtful from Lorraine's lecture on the wormholes. "No one is going to cause trouble there, which would mean we could give people some actual on-planet shore leave."

"That we haven't asked permission to send anyone over to the station or down to Owo is going to raise suspicions if it hasn't already," Stephson conceded. "Being under thrust is better than microgravity, but real gravity would be better for the crew.

"Right now, all of our shuttles are busy, but normally, I'd be planning to spend a day here and get everyone's feet on real dirt for a few hours."

"We can schedule it with the station," Lorraine suggested. "And then just bolt when we're done loading."

"That will draw attention more than just not booking the shore leave," Stephson countered. "If we're *lucky*, Tunison *doesn't* have any orders or information about us, and we can quietly finish loading up and vanish into the night. If we don't draw eyes here, we have a chance to get out of the Kingdom without trouble."

Lorraine nodded her understanding, turning her eyes back to the chart.

"Would we want to get shore leave short of San Ignacio, then?" she asked. "There aren't any good stops I can see."

There were two systems sort of on the way—one was part of the Directorate, which meant it was probably a bad idea, but the other was a single-system state like San Ignacio—but either of them would add at least four light-years to the journey.

"We'd lose too much time," Stephson said. "I think... coming here, there was a balance to walk between wanting to let news get ahead of us while not letting Regent Benjamin's people get ready for us. Once we're past here, time is tight but it's not *as* critical. We'll want to drop out of translight every ten days or so and spend a few hours under thrust to reset people's systems and brains."

"We could have done that coming here," Yildiz complained. Then he shook his head. "Except we were running on peacetime Home Fleet fuel levels, right?"

"Right," the Captain agreed, glancing over at Lorraine. "We had enough fuel to stop and refuel here in Ominira... and to make a second stop somewhere if we got chased out of here. But we needed to spend as little reaction mass sublight as possible."

Both the fusion engines and fusion reactors drew from the same pool of fuel, and the hydrogen for a single day of thrust could power the reactors for ten days. Lorraine had been watching the fuel levels herself, so she'd known the exact calculation Stephson laid out.

"That gives us our plan," she said quietly. "How long on the loading? I'll need to fill Vigo in on everything and get his opinion on some of our options along the way."

"They're not as fast as I'd like," Stephson admitted. "Yildiz, get started on that course."

The navigator saluted and turned away, leaving Lorraine alone with the Captain.

"It's been an hour, and they're only halfway through loading the second trip for our shuttles," she told Lorraine. "Forty minutes for the first turnaround. Another twenty for this one, and we have two cargoes left after that.

"We had two hours, give or take. But the loading is going to take two hours *and* forty minutes."

It should have been ten minutes to load the shuttles. That extra ten minutes per load was a problem.

"What do we do?" Lorraine asked.

"Get this load aboard and the next. And as we're coming up on the time window for Tunison knowing we're here, we get to make a choice.

"Do we blow any chance at cover we have *and* leave the system short a quarter of our fuel and rations by blasting out immediately? Or do we take the chance that Tunison either doesn't have orders for us or doesn't have a ship he can deploy in less than an hour and continue loading?"

"We could lose the cargo *and* have to abandon the shuttles if we do that," Lorraine said grimly. "But... even for one of the frigates, it's ten minutes to boot from cold. They need to maneuver to get clear of obstacles before they go translight... It *could* take forty minutes."

"Except that a competent commander—and Lieutenant Admiral Tunison *is* competent, believe me!—will have ships at full readiness in more-distant orbits to avoid just that problem," Stephson pointed out.

"So, the question then becomes *political*. Do we think Tunison will have Captains he can *trust* in those ready orbits with ships at ready one?"

Lorraine grimaced.

"No, Captain, that's not the question," she warned. "If he *wasn't* that ready, he wouldn't be my uncle's protégé. We have to assume that there are ships ready to deploy that he trusts without question."

Stephson exhaled sharply, then nodded once.

"That answers that, doesn't it?" she said. "I was hoping to get out of here quietly, but it seems that we are going to make Colonel Fitzwilliam live in interesting times after all."

"Better to have thirty-five thousand tons of fuel and sixteen shuttles than... well, thirty-five thousand tons of fuel and *no* shuttles," Lorraine agreed. "The risk is too high."

"I was leaning that way already," the Captain admitted. "And... well, at this point, this is your mission. If you *also* think we need to abort after three trips, that's the plan."

TWENTY-EIGHT

The Adamant Guard had almost all of its personnel and the vast majority of its resources in the Adamantine System, circling forever around the King and Pentarchs to secure the monarchy and the succession.

But their charges were the King and Pentarchy of the *Kingdom*. Traveling resources and personal details could only do so much, so the Adamant Guard had facilities and people in every star system of the Kingdom of Adamant.

And, most importantly, secure digital dropboxes no one else could even find. Vigo hadn't been sure there was one in Agbaye Lewa's datanet, but he'd had all of the codes to find it.

Of course, since that datanet was spread across two dozen stations and moons arrayed over several light-seconds, accessing the dropbox hadn't been a swift or easy process. He couldn't, after all, allow even the *Guard* to know he was in Ominira.

As the shuttles left for their third load of cargo, however, he had finally managed to backdoor the system and download the entire dropbox contents. He couldn't access all of it—not immediately, anyway, though he believed Klement's people could decrypt it all, given time—but once it was isolated, he could feed it his personal codes.

He was unsurprised to see two messages pop up for him. Both had arrived on the most recent courier from Adamantine—and he would have bet a rather large sum of money one of the senders hadn't known the other had access to the courier.

Vigo opened the first message, a mix of contradictory feelings swirling through him. Major Fenella Hayes' name had come up since they'd left Adamantine, and he wasn't surprised to see her. But for most of his career as Lorraine's bodyguard, the head of administration and human resources for the Guard had been a solid and reassuring presence, a source of sage advice and moral backup.

Now she wore the four gold pips of a Colonel, marking her as the new commanding officer of the Adamant Guard. A reward, he had to assume, for work well done enabling Pentarch Benjamin's coup.

"Major Jarret," she greeted him. "As you can imagine, this message is being sent to every Guard dropbox in the Kingdom in the hope we can catch you in time. I don't know what you believe is going on, Major, but from *here* it looks like your Pentarch has stolen a Navy warship and is on the run.

"I've attached a briefing on the situation in Adamantine. It is... *fluid*. I presume you've caught the news and know about the assassination of King Valeriya and two of the Pentarchs. Attempts were made on both Pentarch Nikola and Pentarch Benjamin. I am guessing that one was made on Pentarch Lorraine, but we have no evidence of that beyond her sudden disappearance.

"The blow to Pentarch Nikola's mental health has been... extreme. He appears to have lapsed into paranoia at best and delusions at worst. He has sealed himself inside Planetary Defense Command at PDC Mithral and has threatened violence against anyone who has attempted to reach him.

"Pentarch Benjamin has stepped up as Crown Regent with the support of the Prime Minister and Cabinet, but with one Pentarch locked inside a fortress with an army, there are questions over whether a proper Election is even *possible*."

Hayes sighed, lacing her fingers together and looking directly at the camera. Vigo was reasonably sure it was an act, but he could *see* the exhaustion and grief in her eyes.

"I hate to say it, Vigo, but there are questions being raised about Pentarch Lorraine's involvement and disappearance," she told him. "Some think she might be dead, a victim of the same attack, but the report from *Hermes* and *Agamemnon* suggests that she is still aboard *Goldenrod* and has evacuated the system.

"We are keeping that under wraps, but the idea has been floated that *she* is behind this. We need you to bring her home, Major. The only way we can quash that rumor is to give the public details of whatever attacks there were on her—and the Kingdom *needs* its remaining Pentarchs to show a united front.

"We have been grievously wounded, Major. But if Lorraine can talk her brother down, the Kingdom *will* survive. Please. Bring her home."

The message ended and he sighed, glaring at the screen.

"You know, *Colonel*," he told the screen, "that if you'd even *mentioned* Colonel Roma, I might have bought some of what you were pitching. But you're sitting there, wearing a dead woman's uniform, and you didn't even say so."

Vigo shook his head.

Part of it was that Hayes was making the exact pitch he'd expected. It was the cleanest and most likely approach from the coup's side. Bring Lorraine back home, get her to talk Nikola out of his hole. Accept the half-win they'd got, run the Election.

With Nikola having gone dark and Lorraine having *vanished* while Benjamin stepped up, the election wouldn't be open-and-shut, but the new Regent would have a decent chance of taking the crown.

The problem was that it was the *exact* same pitch they'd use to get him to bring Lorraine home so they could kill her. It was quite possible that they figured Lorraine *was* dead—most of the traps on the ship would have left zero trace of *Goldenrod*. But Hayes had sent her message out as a contingency.

"The question is whether I trust you more than Roma," he told the absent woman, then laughed. "Well, put that way, it's quite easy, isn't it?"

He started the second message. This one was audio only, but he knew the voice.

"This is Major Alexei Krupin," the voice said calmly. "This message is being sent to all Guard dropboxes under a covert code, one that I created myself with approval from the highest authorities at Command.

"If I've done this right and God is kind, you are listening to me, Vigo. This is a fucking mess, and the only *good* news I have is that no one knows what happened to Pentarch Lorraine.

"I failed at my fucking job, Vigo. One of my own shut down our scans, our security, everything. Let a kill team walk right into the damn camp for the training exercise. If the RKAA grunts around me had trusted me the way they *should* have, Nikola would be dead.

"As it is, I've IDed and handled two moles in my detail. Both were recruited by Hayes, our new *commanding officer*."

The disgust dripped from the two words.

"So far as I can tell, our new Crown Regent tried to kill everyone ahead of him in the succession. I've got Nikola safe for now, but God Himself couldn't convince an Adamantine Pentarch to keep his head down. We've got a couple of PDCs, a bunch of the Army, and one hell of a grudge.

"But I don't see a way out, Vigo. As I record this, no moves have been made, but Adamant City is surrounded by the entire damn RAMC. Even if Nikola decided to go for his uncle, that would be enough to tip a lot of neutrals against us.

"I'll keep my prince alive as long as I can, assuming I can do that better than I have, but I'm looking at a damned Regent in the City who I *know* killed his sister and her kids. I don't see a way out for us, Vigo. Not unless you can manage something from the outside.

"Tell Lorraine... Tell her that her brother will fight." Krupin snorted. "God knows I can't stop him. And we've got enough channels to make contact with the other systems of the Kingdom. We'll be a symbol. But we can't win this.

"I have to hope you and she are alive. We need friends, my old friend. God speed you on your mission."

The recording ended and Vigo sighed. There wasn't a lot of information in Krupin's message—the other Major had to assume that even secret Guard coms protocols were compromised at this point. But the confirmation that Nikola was alive from Guard sources was useful.

They weren't alone. Even if he was going to follow Lorraine to the far ends of the galaxy—or, rather, to its center as far as humanity was concerned—he knew he wasn't alone in this.

Maybe that would be enough.

TWENTY-NINE

Lorraine watched the fuel number stop increasing with a mix of satisfaction and frustration. The full load of fuel for the frigate was forty-five thousand tons, bringing the warship up to a hundred and forty thousand tons total mass.

As the fuel tank detached into Owo orbit, a beacon lighting up to bring Fitzwilliam's people to pick it up later, they were at thirty thousand tons. If they could complete their reload, the shuttles were supposed to bring three more five-thousand-ton tanks, but they'd already decided to abort the fourth flight and leave once the shuttles were back aboard.

"Captain Stephson, I apologize for the delay," Fitzwilliam said over the com. Lorraine had linked herself into the main command channel as an observer. *Stephson* knew she was listening, but Fitzwilliam wouldn't.

"We had the usual pile of problems that all manage to show up at the same time," the base commander continued. "Your shuttles are loaded and getting clear now."

"I'll admit, Colonel, I'm less than impressed with your cargo crews," Stephson told him. "We should have completed four trips by now. Instead, my third cargo load is only leaving your station!"

"I'm not... entirely sure what your rush is, Captain," Fitzwilliam said. There was something worrying in his tone. "Most ships that dock here want to stick around for at least half a day or so, let their crew get their feet on something solid. Nothing in your orders speaks to any real urgency."

"Well, Colonel, if I'd booked leave for any of my crew, I would now be in the position of telling them I had to postpone it for a few hours," Stephson replied drily. "I don't see a point in setting up shore leave until I know when I'm going to have my shuttles free."

"Right." Lorraine shivered at the Colonel's tone. "I should have taken a look at the exchange between my pilots and your deck crew earlier, I think. I can tell when my people are being blown off, Lieutenant Colonel."

That was a bad sign. It was not just against protocol but *rude* to call the Captain of a starship by their base rank while they were aboard their ship. For a *senior* officer to do it, they were making a very clear point.

"Your orders are bog-standard. Your mission is *so* usual that it's actually strange you came *here*, Stephson."

Lorraine quickly checked against her worst fear. The shuttles *were* clear, heading back toward *Goldenrod* at a regular pace.

The problem was that they were leaving the station when even the slow pace so far should have seen them reaching the frigate. And *that* meant they were already out of time. Lorraine's math said that Tunison's flagship and sensor arrays would have seen their arrival already.

It was a question of what orders the Lieutenant Admiral had given in terms of telling him about new arrivals and what her uncle's man would do. Every minute—every *second*—they spent now was a risk.

"Why take the risk of going deep in-system?" Stephson asked with a shrug, lying with a smoothness that impressed Lorraine. "We needed to refill from our exercises, nothing more. If I didn't know better, *sir*, I'd say you were causing problems out of some surfeit of caution."

"Maybe I just want some straight answers," Fitzwilliam told her. "I have too many questions, Stephson. By my authority as Owo Station Commander, I'm ordering you to bring *Goldenrod* in to dock with the station.

"Your crew will have spin gravity to stretch their legs—and you and I can have a long chat in person."

Lorraine saw him smile thinly.

"This isn't discretionary, Lieutenant Colonel," he said, repeating the focus on her junior rank. "I don't know what game you're playing, but the Kingdom is in crisis, and I have no patience for it. Report aboard the station, Stephson. ASAP."

The channel cut and Lorraine swallowed any response. This part was Stephson's job.

"We have received system lockdown codes from Owo Station," the junior officer at the Engineering station reported grimly. "Trans-light drive has been locked out, fusion drives restricted to half a gee."

"Not overly polite of the Colonel," Stephson noted. She sounded calm and collected—which was good, since Lorraine wasn't feeling *either* of those things.

"Sir, what do we do?" Yildiz asked. "They can't force me onto a course, but I've been *sent* one to lock us onto the station."

"Can we appear to follow that course in such a way that it will accelerate our shuttle pickup?" the Captain asked.

"It changes our vector enough that the best I can do is not *increase* our rendezvous time," Yildiz warned.

"Understood. Do that for now," Stephson ordered.

A new link popped up in Lorraine's vision as Stephson kept mirroring her coms to the Pentarch. The acoustics around the Captain's seat were *impressive*, both muting soft speech and projecting louder, clearer, orders.

Lorraine could hear most of the Captain's conversations from where she was seated, but the bridge was laid out to allow the Captain some privacy. Privacy Stephson was intentionally giving up to keep Lorraine in the loop.

"Cortez," Stephson greeted the Cheng. "We've been hit with override codes from the station. If I blow them away, can you make our systems send the right pings back to Fitzwilliam's people so they think we're locked down?"

"Yes. I need five minutes," Cortez replied instantly.

"You have *two*. And I need the translight drive stabilized for gravimetric interference."

"Did that an hour ago," the Cheng told Stephson. "On the code."

Gravimetric interference sent Lorraine back into memories of her old lecture notes. The safety zone around planets was mostly out of concern for *hitting* the planet during emergence. A ship didn't emerge from translight with a great deal of velocity—not enough to create a threat to a *planet*, at least... but a ship wouldn't survive emerging inside atmosphere, let alone the planet itself.

The *other* reason for the safety zone, and the reason why ships *entered* translight almost as far out as they *left* it, was gravimetric interference. Tachyons would pass through a planet and its gravity well without issues, losing only a tiny fraction of their number. *Faux-tachyonic matter*, however...

A ship had to be close to have real problems, but interference started at some distance. Going translight at their current distance from the moon and gas giant would be dangerous.

But Lorraine had to have faith. What else could she do?

"Can you override his lockdown codes?" she asked Stephson.

The Captain snorted amusement.

"If *I* couldn't, Major Jarret could," she replied. "But... well, I'd be a terrible Captain if I hadn't worked out ways around the lockdown codes. Their value isn't that I can't disable them. It's that Fitzwilliam will *know* if I disable them, in less time than it will take us to reboot the translight drive.

"So, we need to cloak that change, and that's *hard*." Stephson shrugged. "We look like we're obeying, we vector to pick up our shuttles and we keep our eyes open while the Cheng builds my cloak of shadow.

"We'll be fine so long as—"

"Contact!" Paris barked.

Lorraine absently realized that people had been drifting into the bridge for the last fifteen minutes and the room was now at full strength, with every console crewed to battle-stations levels.

That realization was buried as she pulled up the command interface and locked onto the source of Paris's shout.

"Translight emergence signature at five hundred thousand kilometers," the Tactical Officer continued. "They cut Agbaye Lewa's safety radius in *half, damn.*"

"I need more data, Guns," Stephson told him.

"Working on it. Contact's engines are coming online; we're reading five gravities of thrust. Mass is..." He paused, swallowing. "Mass is three million tons. Acceleration is stable; they are holding back from full emergency acceleration— Wait! New contacts!"

Lorraine saw them on the display even as more information filled in on her screen about the initial contact. Two ships, clearly *much* smaller than the big contact. Frigates, maybe destroyers. A quarter of a million kilometers back from the capital ship, they clearly hadn't pushed as far as the battlecruiser.

"Confirm identification," Stephson ordered.

"Confirmed, sir. She's *Corsair*, Commodore Nikostratos Wray in command. Her course is settling in—she's clearly picked us out on her long-range scans and is vectoring to intercept."

"Well, there goes playing nice with Fitzwilliam," the Captain said. "Cortez, Yildiz, Chevrolet! I'm wiping the lockdown codes—I need an emergency acceleration course for both *Goldenrod* and the shuttles.

"Keep us moving away from *Corsair*—but get the shuttles on board!"

"What do we do if Fitzwilliam orders the station to fire on us?" Lorraine asked softly.

"We keep running and we pray to whatever deities are listening that Paris and our screens can handle the blow," Stephson told her grimly. "Because I'm neither leaving our shuttles behind nor sticking around to tangle with a battlecruiser!"

THIRTY

"Frigate *Goldenrod*, this is Commodore Wray aboard *Corsair*."

Nikostratos Wray was a big man, large enough to loom over the bridge of his warship in the video feed he was sending. The space and arrangement around him were a near-perfect mirror of *Goldenrod*'s bridge, though expanded to handle three times as many people in each section.

"I know you are carrying Pentarch Lorraine Adamant, having fled the Adamantine System when cruisers from Home Fleet arrived to check in on her situation after the attack," he laid out calmly, in a smooth tone that lent itself better to soothing calm than implicit threats. "That, along with the evidence of Pentarch Lorraine *not* having been attacked when the rest of the Pentarchs were, has led to an unfortunate situation where Lorraine is now a person of *extreme* interest in the deaths of her family."

"We have grounds to suspect that Pentarch Lorraine has coordinated with both domestic terrorists and external threats, not least the Richelieu Directorate. My orders are that she is to be detained immediately for secure transport to Adamantine."

There was little stress in the Commodore's voice, marking neither the fact that he was tasked to arrest a Pentarch for regicide and fratricide or the fact that he was currently under no less than *five* standard gravities of acceleration.

Lorraine could see that stress on the crew around Wray, though they were putting on a good face as their Captain made his pitch.

"I understand that the situation as you see it may be different, Captain Stephson, but my orders are very clear. You will stand down and prepare to be boarded. Pentarch Lorraine will be transferred aboard *Corsair* for immediate transport to the home system.

"If you do not comply..." Wray sighed, a clear theatricality to the sound. "I will have no choice but to assume the worst-case scenario is correct. Flight will be regarded as complicity in Lorraine Adamant's treason.

"I will do whatever is necessary to bring the Pentarch to justice. Stand down, Captain, or I will *make* you."

The recording ended and Lorraine shivered. Wray had been no more energized or harsh when threatening than he had been when laying out the situation.

And *Corsair* was definitely capable of making *Goldenrod* stand down—if only by reducing her to very small pieces.

Stephson was silent for several long seconds after the message ended, then turned to Yildiz.

"Helm, report. What's our remaining time for intercept with the shuttles?"

It didn't help that *Goldenrod* was already pushing the same five gravities as *Corsair* in the opposite direction. They could accelerate faster, but they were also holding on to let the shuttles catch up.

The shuttles could burn harder but not *that* much harder.

"*Goldenrod* Flights are currently running at ten gravities, gaining velocity on us at fifty meters per second squared," Yildiz laid out. "Intercept is in seven minutes. We will be roughly seventy thousand kilometers clear of Owo at that time."

"Guns? *Corsair*'s status at estimated pickup?" Stephson asked Paris.

"She will be four hundred fifty thousand kilometers from Owo, roughly four-eighty thousand from us," *Goldenrod*'s Tactical Officer replied. "She'll have a slight velocity advantage over us, but she's not going to close the range without putting on more thrust. We can match her gee for gee—but Wray knows that."

The wild card in the deck was Owo Station's defenses. They were well inside the range of the missile launchers and energy weapons of the forts. If Fitzwilliam opened fire, their odds got a lot worse, *fast*.

"Get me vector possibilities on the two destroyers," Stephson ordered. "*Translight* possibilities. They might be seventy-twos, but that's enough to cut us off if they swing around."

The normal safety envelope for going translight was narrower than for exiting translight, but not by *that* much. The two Ominira Station destroyers—about twenty percent bigger than *Goldenrod* and with significantly heavier energy weapons—could get ahead of her and cause another layer of difficulty.

Wray had set up his gambit well. *Corsair* was the queen in his play: powerful and mobile, used to control the board and set the limits of where *Goldenrod* could maneuver. Owo Station was the pawns: dangerous but limited in range. If Fitzwilliam blinked, they'd get clear.

The destroyers were probably bishops or rooks in the chess analogy, Lorraine figured. They were more maneuverable in a very specific way, one that once again limited their maneuvering options.

"Any signal from Fitzwilliam?" she asked Stephson.

"Neither coms nor arms," her Captain replied. "We have legit-seeming orders but so does Wray. *Wray's* orders are more questionable, thankfully, so I *think* he's erring on the side of the orders that don't require him to fire on fellow RKAN spacers."

That was optimistic, Lorraine knew—but every moment they were unchallenged, they gained both velocity and distance from Placide Fitzwilliam's command area and weaponry.

"Do... Do either of you want to reply to the Commodore?" Vinci asked, the Coms Officer sounding nervous.

It took Lorraine a moment to realize he was including *her* in the people who might want to reply to Wray. She shook her head at the thought.

"Our best chance here is to keep the question of whether I'm aboard open," she told Vinci—and Stephson. "The last thing we want is for him to be *certain* I'm aboard."

"He might not be sure, but others are."

Lorraine turned—*carefully*—to see Jarret cross from the access hatch and take the empty hotel console. The third hotel seat was occupied by Corporal Palmer, with another Guard next to the hatch in full power armor.

The armor was the only thing allowing the man to stand under the ship's thrust, which made Jarret's strained-but-functional stride through *five gravities* impressive.

"Who?" Stephson asked.

"I have a *lovely* note from the new Guard Commander telling me to bring Lorraine home to convince Nikola to stand down," Lorraine's bodyguard replied. "The Regent's fully-in-the-loop people probably are still figuring we all died, but they *know* Lorraine was still on *Goldenrod.*

"We haven't had a real opportunity to transfer her off, so as long as *Goldenrod* exists, she has to be aboard her. Wray may not be privy to that level of information, but..."

"Tunison definitely is," Lorraine finished for him. Her gaze was locked on to her display with its icons for the ships—all marked green for friendlies.

The silence of deep thought that followed Jarret's update allowed her to adjust that. *Corsair* and the two destroyers were now orange—she couldn't *quite* bring herself to mark them as hostile yet—and Owo Station was a neutral yellow.

"No further coms from either Fitzwilliam or Wray," Vinci

reported. "I am picking up some scatter that suggests they're talking to each other."

They were close enough for a functionally live conversation, Lorraine supposed. Stephson could talk to Wray with barely a two-second delay. Their pursuer had sent his message as a recording so that they couldn't interrupt, not because a conversation wasn't possible.

"Three minutes until the shuttles are aboard," Yildiz reported. "They are adjusting thrust to match vee at the correct distance. *We* are moving to seven gees in one minute."

"Send the warning," Stephson ordered.

Even from five gees to seven was a difference that needed to be flagged. Five gees was *bad*, past their designed combat acceleration but not their true maximum acceleration.

The engines were rated for up to seven and a half, with *dire* warnings for going over seven. Seven gravities was generally regarded as the maximum even a military crew—with special training, careful preparation and ubiquitous light augmentations—could take, and the engines were designed to match that limit.

Shuttles, where the cockpits were literally flooded with antiacceleration gel in combat, were rated for up to twelve gravities. Without an explicit combat mission, the pilots were limited to the same training and augmentation as ship crews—plus a default level of specialty suits and other gear that was easier to justify for a small craft with a handful of crew than a starship with a crew of hundreds.

Hence, the Midases could pull ten gravities even without the gel. The problem was...

"Additional contacts," Paris reported as Lorraine spotted them on her screen. "Shuttles launching from *Corsair*. I don't have a number yet, but she carries twenty-four."

The battlecruiser had two shuttle bays to *Goldenrod*'s one, but Lorraine understood the bays to be basically identical with only a bit more working space. She could put four bombers into space at once, but it would only take her a minute to get all four of her shuttle flights into space if her deck crew pushed.

"Shuttles at twelve gees, heading our way. Mass suggests bomber configuration, no interceptors."

"Well, isn't that making assumptions," Stephson said wryly. "Lorraine, you'd know this: time to rearm from standard shuttle to interceptor mode?"

"Depends on how many we do at once," she replied instantly. "Can turn over one in fifteen minutes. Two in twenty. Four in thirty. Can't work on more than four at once, though—and swapping over from heavy cargo is a minimum of sixty."

Though none of that could be done while there was any cargo *in* the modules. The shuttles would need to be emptied, then refitted. Still.

"After unloading, we could put a short flight up in thirty minutes," she concluded. "But we already *have* a short flight loaded as interceptors."

Bombers were *useful* against capital ships, even if there was a perpetual trade-off between risk to the bombers themselves and accuracy of the attack. The farther back they dropped their charges, the larger the area they had to cover with the same munitions—*and* the lower the velocity they added to the weapons.

"They won't reach us before we can refit one of Chevrolet's flights, and eight interceptors could keep us clear of a bomber strike at any real range," Stephson observed.

"I think Wray put more weight on Fitzwilliam engaging us than he thought he was doing," the Captain continued. "Keep an eye on those destroyers, Guns."

Paris's response was lost in a grunt of exhalation as the acceleration countdown ended and even *more* pressure added itself to everyone on the ship.

Lorraine was now carrying a small cheerleading squad—something she'd *done* in her teen years, both before and at the Naval

Academy—and she wasn't going to be able to put them *down* in ten seconds like she would in a cheer routine.

At five gravities of acceleration, training and practice had been enough to keep her functioning. At seven, icons popped up in her vision as her link informed her that a number of her augments were kicking in.

The edges of her vision grayed for a moment and then flickered before returning to normal. She knew, from her training, that part of that return to normal was medication being injected to her bloodstream and part was her neural link adding the edges back in before the signal reached her brain.

Two minutes to the shuttles coming aboard. Fifty-two minutes after that to get far enough away from Owo—seven hundred and fifty thousand kilometers, roughly—to make a standard jump to translight.

And depending on the games the shuttles decided to play, they could get a bomb launch in before that. Putting *Goldenrod*'s flight into space to protect them would delay their escape, since they'd have to retrieve the shuttles.

"Any movement on the part of the destroyers?" Stephson asked, sounding only slightly perturbed by the faux gravity of their acceleration.

"Nothing material," Paris told her. "They're up to one gee for local maneuvering, but their maneuvers are clearly intended to keep them able to enter translight. Agbaye Lewa's planetary system is crowded enough to make a microjump risky, so my *guess* is that they're scanning for everything that might be in their path."

Gravimetric distortion and drive cycle speeds would make a jump of a handful of light-seconds difficult at the best of times. Lorraine wouldn't have trusted *Goldenrod*'s systems to handle a jump of less than a half a second—and she *knew* the frigate had more-refined drive controllers than the destroyers.

"They'll wait until we're closer to the safety zone to jump," Stephson concluded. "They want us to commit to a velocity vector we'll have a hard time shedding quickly. Plus, they know we know what they're doing."

She chuckled.

"Plus, the *threat* of them jumping ahead of us is more intimidating than if one of them jumps for four seconds instead of *point-four seconds*," the big blonde officer added. "And, frankly, I think that's *more* likely."

If the destroyers jumped nine million kilometers instead of nine hundred thousand, they'd remove themselves from the equation until their drives cooled down again—several minutes, at least. Jumping early might give them a chance to recover from that... but Lorraine doubted the destroyer Captains would expect to do any better on the second attempt than the first.

"First shuttles docking now," Vinci reported, the Coms Officer apparently linked in to the shuttle deck. "Heavy cargo units in first, then the rest. Estimate two minutes for full load."

Lorraine scanned their surroundings. They were out of the standard range of the energy weapons on Owo Station's fortresses. Nothing was stopping Fitzwilliam from launching missiles at them—some of his one-shot satellites were closer to them than the logistics base, even.

But despite his attempt to lock them down, the Colonel appeared to have decided this wasn't his problem and pulled his horns in.

"The Colonel is enough of a historian to recognize that he's looking at a dynastic conflict," Jarret said in her head. "And he's got enough legitimate orders to cover his ass if he does nothing. Best way to protect himself and his people if this turns into an all-out civil war."

"Which it will," Lorraine admitted, shivering against all that she *knew* that meant. The best chance she had was to come home with overwhelming force, a fleet that her uncle would *have* to surrender to without a fight.

"Jump!" Paris snapped. "And I just IDed the gal, too. *Longsword,*

Lieutenant Colonel Kawa commanding. We'll see if she... Clean jump, sirs. She's dead ahead."

"Kawa always was a show-off," Stephson said without heat. "Makes sense—*Longsword*, *Crossbow* and *Mangonel* are the destroyers here, and if *I* needed someone for a finicky bit of piloting, I'd send Sweeney Kawa."

Lorraine didn't know Kawa but it seemed Stephson did.

"Captain?" she asked.

"Sweeney Kawa and I were in class together in the Academy," Stephson told her absently. "He can be an ass but a fine officer. Push comes to shove, though, he's ambitious and his flag is hitched to his CO by default."

"Meaning Are Tunison."

"Meaning Are Tunison," the Captain confirmed. "Shuttles, Coms?"

"Last coming aboard... now."

"Helm? Do we have a course?"

"Cheng is promising stabilization to survive this, so yes," Yildiz confirmed. "We will adjust three degrees port and five up to make sure we miss *Longsword*, then punch it. Need to drop out in twelve hours for a small adjustment to get us lined up with San Ignacio. Won't change our flight time."

"It's a long-enough blasted trip no matter what we do, Helm," Stephson replied. "And I, for one, am sick of weighing several hundred extra kilos.

"Execute."

Every ship in the fleet could manage the same emergency acceleration, but frigates remained the most *maneuverable* ships in RKAN, able to turn multiple degrees in a second.

Lorraine barely had enough time to register *Goldenrod* rotating around her centerpoint before a flash of indescribable colors flickered over her vision and the weight on her vanished.

"Sublight engines down," Yildiz confirmed softly. "Translight drive online. Twelve hours to navigation dropout."

Lorraine couldn't keep herself from exhaling a long, drained breath.

"Order the ship to stand down from battle stations," Stephson said. "We got lucky; Fitzwilliam blinked."

She shook her head.

"The next time *Corsair* catches up to us, Wray won't be relying on anyone else. And *he* won't blink."

THIRTY-ONE

"How is my favorite niece?"

The holographic figure grinning at Lorraine from the desk was almost as familiar to her as her mother. Like Valeriya, he was tall, with a faded leathery look to his skin and the gold-centered eyes every Adamant shared.

Benjamin Adamant wasn't as slimly fit as his sister, though age hadn't yet robbed him of the muscle underlying his larger frame. Lorraine had watched that slow decay over the last decade as he had crept up on seventy, but the Admiral remained a physically powerful man whose dark gray uniform highlighted an impressive physique.

"You know I won't do you the disservice of answering your question about rumors," the message continued. The hologram was weeks old now, but the most recent one Lorraine had from him. She'd asked about the rumors around *Goldenrod* being deployed, knowing he wouldn't answer.

"I will note that *if* your ship was being deployed on a long-range patrol or similar endurance mission, your Guard Detail would have to be informed in advance to allow them to make special arrangements."

Benjamin grinned. "And we both know Vigo can't keep a secret from you to save his life."

Lorraine floated in the center of her new space. With the security upgrades mostly invisible from the inside, it was the most luxurious space she'd ever slept in aboard a starship. She presumed it was comparable to—or a step or two below—Stephson's quarters, but she'd only ever seen the Captain's dining room.

There was even a completely separate office, her current location. It was small enough that it would only take a minor movement to get a hand or foot on a wall, but it existed and had full communication and computer equipment.

Which allowed her to play her uncle's last message for the first time since she'd realized he was behind the attack, as if there was some kind of warning she'd missed. Some kind of clue that would explain everything.

In the hologram, Benjamin rose from his seat, the view following him as he crossed his own office aboard the battleship *Sultan*.

"I can't give any Lieutenant Commander in Home Fleet preferential treatment; you know that," he continued. "So, I won't say more. But rumors are rumors, and you will learn to judge which are worth listening to."

He shrugged and grinned again.

"You might have already. You were always bright. I'm still smarting over the game before last, you know. It's good to see you learning, but it stings to see my own trick turned around on me!

"I've attached my first move of a new game," he added, a holographic chessboard appearing above his head with one pawn moved. "I wouldn't count on winning *this* time, Lieutenant Commander!"

Lorraine eyed the board for a moment before it vanished. She'd gone over it a few times before sending her response, and she was certain she knew which array he was going for. But, of course, he was always trying to fool her.

And their second-last game, she'd managed to fool *him*. It had been a risky play, a bit more obvious in hindsight than her uncle's deceptive ploys, but she'd opened up his king to checkmate by her bishop.

"As for the rest of your last message..." Benjamin looked thoughtful. "I know how you feel," he told her. "I've been doing this for fifty years—fifty-two, I suppose, if we count from starting the Academy. The balance between officer and Pentarch isn't an easy one.

"The traditions of our House call us to serve, as officers or politicians or civil servants... To serve however we feel best, but to *serve*. Your mother chose the Diplomatic Corps, which worked out well for her and, it seems, for the Kingdom. You and I chose RKAN.

"I have never been prouder than the day Valeriya told me you were entering the Naval Academy, Lorraine. But I knew from the beginning this was going to be a hard path for you. Even the Army lets a Pentarch be on Bastion, available for the duties of being a Pentarch and a member of House Adamant.

"And despite what we like to pretend, those duties are real and demanding. It was in *that* role, after all, that I lost a leg and six months of my life."

And the Crown, Lorraine reflected. It wasn't something anyone had ever *said*, not around the younger generation, but she'd been aware of it. Benjamin Adamant had spent critical weeks of the Crown Election in a hospital bed, crippled in the same accident that had killed Lorraine's grandfather. He hadn't been physically *able* to make the Kingdom-wide personal tour practically assumed of a candidate for the Crown.

Which meant Valeriya had become King and he'd remained an officer in the fleet.

"I did my job," he said with a shrug. "But I will always wonder if I walked the right balance between the House, the Kingdom and the Navy. I'm not the right one to ask for advice on it, Lorraine. I'm not sure who would be, but I can only say that it's been a long, hard road for me."

Benjamin was silent for a moment, then grinned.

"I *will* say that I *do* read all of your evaluations, and I am almost as proud of you today as I was when you put the uniform on for the first time. I know you *will* find the right balance, just as I did."

She paused the hologram. There wasn't much left of the message, really, just the usual chatter of family. It was in this message where she'd learned her cousin Oliver had proposed to his girlfriend, but Lorraine didn't think there were secret messages in that.

There weren't any secret messages at all. This had been recorded four days before people he'd recruited had tried to kill her and every person on her ship. No sign of it. No hint of anything except the same warm relationship they'd had her entire life.

"Why, Uncle?" she asked the frozen hologram. Tears didn't fall right in microgravity, and she brushed them away angrily—nearly sending herself into a spin that took a moment to right herself.

There were new tears and she blinked them away furiously.

She felt so numb that even *anger* was welcome. She felt like there was something *wrong* with her, that she couldn't grieve her family properly—that none of this horror felt real.

Somehow, rewatching Benjamin's cheerful message drove the reality home. She would never have another happy conversation with him. She would never have conversations at *all* with her mother or father, but she knew that the next time she spoke to her uncle, it would be across a battlefield.

That felt more real than the absence of her parents and siblings. There was nothing she could plan or prepare for about the ones she lost. She *had* to plan and prepare for what to do about Benjamin, now Crown Regent with a pliant Prime Minister and Cabinet.

All of that was believable, hard facts supported by the news they'd downloaded. She suspected that locking down the news was going to turn out to be a mistake on her uncle's part, the source for a cloud of suspicion over his regency that would never quite fade.

The void in her chest where her heart should be was also real. It was just... *empty*. Denial, she thought, but she wasn't sure. Her grief was *there*, she could feel it, but it wasn't in her face.

It hadn't crashed in on her yet and she feared the moment it did.

It was only in Ominira that she'd *known*, for certain and without question, that everyone was dead. And their handful of hours in Ominira had been hectic, with no time to think.

Playing her uncle's message for the first time since the attack probably wasn't the *best* plan, but part of her had wanted to look his image in the eyes. It hadn't helped and she could feel other thoughts circling around the back of her mind.

The chirp of a message on her link was almost a relief.

"Adamant," she answered crisply.

"We're coming out of translight for course adjustment in fifteen minutes," Stephson told her. "I'm bringing the ship to battle stations."

There was a pause.

"I'm not sure where your battle station should be, but I think that observer console is as good as anything for now."

"We're in deep space," Lorraine murmured. "You think Wray will be there before we jump?"

"Fifty-fifty," the Captain replied. "The longer we're sublight, the higher the odds get. He's got the speed and the sensors to make this truly hard on us.

"So, yeah. Until I *know* he's not on our tail, we're operating as if *Corsair* is going to be right behind us every time we go sublight!"

THIRTY-TWO

The universe changed colors. Everything around Lorraine looked suddenly, inexplicably, more *right*. The feeling faded swiftly, but even without the announcement throughout the ship, the Pentarch would have known they'd dropped out of translight.

"Tactical, full defensive sweep," Stephson snapped. "CIC, scans?"

Lorraine's squadron-command display had a lot less detail on it than Stephson's ship-command systems. She didn't, for example, have the exact statistics on each missile launcher and fusion reactor, where Stephson *did*.

That meant that while Lorraine only had a computer-calculated summary of *Goldenrod*'s readiness—ninety-four percent, the primary issue being the missing supplies—she had a clear and immediate view of the situation around the frigate as the ship's Combat Information Center ran through the sensor data.

Twelve hours at full translight put them over a light-month from Ominira. The star was just a slightly brighter pinprick than most, marked out on the display because it was closest—and because it was their starting point.

The marker for the direction to Ominira was the only icon on the display. It was possible, even in the deepest reaches of the void between the stars, to find *something*. Asteroids, comets, even small planetoids were known to wander lost through the void.

The *math* said that there were bigger things out there, even up to major gas giants that were basically stars that had failed to ignite. Lorraine had seen the statistics—but unlike some of the people who told horror stories, *she* knew that anything large enough to actually threaten a ship in translight had a gravity signature on the surrounding stars.

And while humanity might not have sent ships to investigate every strange mass without light of its own, they'd *mapped* most of them, and any jump took into account the most recent data on the stars along the route.

That analysis, in fact, was part of what they'd dropped out of translight to complete. Their vector out of Ominira was also about eleven degrees off from a direct course to San Ignacio—closer to a direct line to Bright Dream, truthfully—and they had to drop out to make that major a change, but the more time Yildiz had to analyze the most recent stellar data, the cleaner their course would be.

"Area is clear," Commander Savege reported from the CIC. Even with the data on her own screen, Lorraine shared in the general sense of relief.

"Permission to launch a shuttle screen?" Paris asked. "Every extra set of sensors and energy weapons might help if we get surprised."

"Drives are cool in forty-four seconds, Guns," Stephson pointed out. "As soon as we've completed our turn and the drives are cool, our best defense is to not *be* here."

"Permission denied. Hold the shuttles aboard. Helm, the turn?"

It was a sign of how concerned Stephson was, Lorraine suspected, that they hadn't brought the main engine online at all. Even in deep space, the chance to provide acceleration pseudogravity was rarely passed up.

"It's not much of an angle," Yildiz replied. "Completed... now. Still running the mapping for the route."

"*Perfect* is the enemy of *done*, Helm," Stephson said quietly. Lorraine suspected she wasn't supposed to hear that, but Stephson had flipped her a neural-link connection the moment she'd entered the bridge.

Lorraine wasn't going to override the Captain without an amazingly good reason, but she appreciated both the trust and respect the gesture implied. It kept her fully in the loop while allowing her to, well, loom silently at the back of the bridge unless needed.

Yildiz clearly *hadn't* heard the Captain's comment, as he focused on his console.

Lorraine couldn't see what the Navigator was working on. She'd done the same kind of course work-up herself in the past, though, and she knew it wasn't a fast process. It wasn't *complicated*—not with learning-agent software to back you up, at least—but it was time-consuming.

And time was something none of them were sure they had.

"Sixty seconds since dropout," Paris announced. "No contacts."

There wouldn't be much warning if they *were* being pursued. Standard protocol would have *Corsair* drop out of FTL every few hours—or even every *hour*—to make sure they were still on *Goldenrod*'s tail, using her higher translight speed to make up lost time.

Unlike the frigate, though, *Corsair* didn't need to accelerate to provide pseudogravity for her crew. She'd probably be keeping her engines dark even sublight, leaving the habitation pods rotating in place to provide at least *some* space with faux gravity for the crew.

The side effects of starting and stopping the translight drive were noticeable, but they weren't dangerous, even in hourly doses. So long as Commodore Wray kept his crew's working situations consistent, they'd get used to the cycle.

The question wasn't even *would* he overshoot *Goldenrod*. It was just about certain that he'd drop out of translight somewhere past their current position for a check, then have to turn around and search the area to pick up their tachyon trail again.

Lorraine was grimly certain he *would* pick up the trail—in a star system, the trail could dissipate in as little as an hour or two, and the background impact of the star's general presence cut detection range significantly. In deep space, though, their tachyon trail could be followed for as much as a day and picked up at much greater distances.

"Maintain full readiness," Stephson ordered calmly and probably redundantly. "Set antimissile defenses to status ninety-nine."

There was a long pause.

"Sir, I'm... not familiar with that one," Paris admitted.

"That's because this is about the only circumstance under which ninety-nine is remotely useful, Lieutenant Commander," the Captain said drily. "It clears the defenses to fire on any and all movement within their range bracket.

"Right now, the only possible movement is *Corsair*. So, set the guns to ninety-nine."

A new icon popped up on Lorraine's display as Paris obeyed, a red warning sign next to *Goldenrod*—accompanied by a translucent red sphere marking the danger zone around the frigate.

The Asimov Convention was *mostly* about the rights and status of synthetic intelligences, but it had also set up agreed standards on what lower-level software—algorithms and agents and even simple match-recognition programs like status ninety-nine—were allowed to do.

Hand in the loop was the summary. No computer program was supposed to make the determination to fire a weapon system. An agent or algorithm could track the target, lay in the solution, even make the final decision of what exact millisecond to fire; but the *decision* to fire was supposed to be human.

It was a... *principle* rather than a law, as Lorraine understood it, and a vague-enough one to leave a lot of wiggle room. Her understanding was that, by and large, the basic principle was honored.

The fact that the United Worlds Navy stood behind the Asimov Convention probably helped. The UWN's enforcement of the various Conventions and Agreements and Treaties and suchlike was politely described as *spotty*, but few nations wanted to get on the wrong side of them either way.

And she supposed the advantage of uneven enforcement was that no one was ever quite sure *what* would be the step too far for whichever UWN officer had to make the call.

In this case, she figured status ninety-nine was *mostly* compliant because it wasn't a default state. They had to activate it, which counted as a human making the decision to fire. It was just such a *broad* decision to fire; it would be dangerous if they expected to see anyone else at all.

The bridge was quiet—not silent, no working space was ever *truly* silent—as the seconds ticked by.

"Five minutes since emergence," Paris reported. "No contacts."

Lorraine started running a comparison chart on her console. Even if Wray decided to be riskier with his translight jump than The Book called for, he'd still been vectoring almost directly toward Agbaye Lewa and Owo when they'd fled.

It would have taken him at least twenty minutes, she judged, to get onto a safe vector to jump after them. She took that minimum as her baseline. There was no reason for him to deviate from the standard doctrine: an eighty-eight-cee ship pursuing an eighty-cee ship would run in translight for fifty-four and a half minutes, drop out to check their trace, then jump back to translight on the hour.

Their average velocity would match up to *Goldenrod*'s, but they would be certain they didn't lose the frigate's trail. If her math was right and Wray was following The Book precisely, he'd drop out for his next check in around five minutes.

Corsair might still be behind them when he did so. That would be the best of all worlds for them, the battlecruiser carrying on thinking they were on track for another hour and *then* backtracking.

That would give them a clean break, enough time to play some games, maybe even lose the—

"Contact! Contact at seven light-minutes," Paris snapped. "We're resolving the signature, but I can't see it being anyone *else*."

The red icon flashed up on Lorraine's display, and she swallowed a spike of fear. If it was *Corsair*, the battlecruiser would have seen them the same time as they saw her.

"She arrived forty seconds before we did," Paris laid out crisply. "We have twenty seconds before she sees us."

And seven light-minutes was long enough to reduce the risk of overjumping inherent to a small hop. *Corsair* was going to be on them *fast*.

"Helm, I need that jump," Stephson snapped.

"Closing the calculations," the navigator confirmed.

He didn't say more. He didn't give a timeline—it wouldn't matter. If it was long enough to need a second emergency jump, Lorraine assumed Yildiz would have *said* so.

"They will have seen us *now*," Paris barked. "All defenses are at full power. Energy screen online. Beams on status ninety-nine. Religious gunners are praying."

There were a series of muffled chokes across the bridge, and while Lorraine hoped her own moment of humor was better concealed, she understood. Paris's crack cut the tension, clearing heads and focusing minds on the situation around them.

Just in time.

"Contact close!" Paris reported. "*Corsair* out of translight at thirty-two thousand kilometers. Firing main beams, firing all tubes and flushing cells one through twelve!"

The Tactical Officer hadn't even waited for permission to fire half of the frigate's single-use missiles. At this range, they wouldn't need their seven-minute flight times—but unless Yildiz had badly misjudged his calculations, they weren't going to be here to see them hit.

THE EXODUS GAMBIT   233

"*Corsair* firing," Savege reported from CIC. "They rushed it; screens held."

At thirty-odd thousand kilometers, *Corsair*'s beams should have punched right through *Goldenrod*'s screens. Only the ECM and other deceptions really gave them any chance against the battlecruiser's energy weapons within fifty thousand klicks—but that chance was enough. This time.

"Direct hit!" Paris half-cheered, but his tone was cooler a second later. "Screens took it. We need to get a *lot* closer to hurt her."

A timer was now ticking down in the corner of Lorraine's screen —the seconds until *Corsair*'s heavy beams would fire again. The number was not nearly high enough for her comfort. Wray's people weren't going to make the same mistake twice.

"And *there*," Yildiz snapped. "All hands, translight *now*."

There wasn't even enough time to *blink* before the world flashed and *Corsair* vanished from their screens—along with everything else.

Lorraine released a breath she hadn't realized she'd been holding. She doubted she was the only one, and she quietly unstrapped herself, walking to stand next to Captain Stephson, the *click* of her magnetic boot soles on the deck incredibly loud in her ears.

"Any damage?" she asked, pitching her voice to stay inside the Captain's bubble.

"More than Savege implied," Stephson replied. "Nothing serious. A few of the projectors for the energy screen overloaded. We have flash damage along one side of the ship, and there's a combat radiator Engineering is going to examine as well as they can from inside.

"For getting that close to a battlecruiser? We're brilliant. We should be debris."

"We needed this dropout." Lorraine wasn't asking or judging. They could have skipped some of the calculation-refining, *maybe*— but they had needed to drop out to adjust their vector anyway.

"We can't afford another one," she continued after a moment of waiting to see if Stephson would make the argument herself. "Wray was closer than he should have been. Seven light-minutes is a deep-space emergence error, not a fluke."

"He ran the numbers on our course and estimated our emergence zone, just as we did for his," Stephson replied. "We're all on the same playbook, and he read us better than we read him."

"Agreed. But that doesn't change my point, does it?" Lorraine asked.

"No. I don't *like* asking the crew to run eighty-three days without any time under acceleration, let alone spin or real gravity," the Captain admitted. "But you're right. He's got our number a bit too neatly, and he has enough of a speed edge to take risks.

"We make the run to San Ignacio in one jump."

"And what happens in SI?" Lorraine asked.

"The San Ignacio Defense Force has secured emergence zones, guarded by their warships," Stephson told her. "They are neutral and they are determined to *remain* so, no matter what the conflict. We might well end up docking and taking shore leave with *Corsair* in the blasted star system *with* us, but the Ignacians will *not* let either of us start a fight.

"It's the best chance for safety we'll have until we're at the wormhole."

That matched with Lorraine's knowledge of San Ignacio... but she had to wonder. Opening fire on another RKAN warship was a massive step to take, one Wray hadn't blinked at.

Was it that big a step from there to violating the neutrality of a nation without the power to threaten the Kingdom?

THIRTY-THREE

The shuttle bay was as silent as it could get. Even in translight, the compartment was usually busier than this, but Vigo had made quiet requests and been given what he needed.

Even designed to hold diplomatic functions, *Goldenrod*'s size meant there weren't many spaces that could fit a hundred people aboard. Vigo *could* have taken over the set of meeting and conference rooms that served double purpose as a diplomatic ballroom, but that wouldn't have been the right feeling.

The shuttle bay definitely *was*. Even with the shuttles and their modules tucked away into their storage bays and everything retracted as far as it would go, the open space was probably smaller than the ballroom would have been—but Guard and Navy alike knew how to improvise.

Vigo's audience were wearing magnetic soles and had locked their feet on every clear space of the bay's official floor, ceiling and walls. Every living member of Archangel Detail, Lorraine's Adamant Guard, was present except Jelica Laurenz.

Filling out the space were the pilots and techs of *Goldenrod*'s own shuttle wing. A few Marines. Captain Stephson herself, in a show of respect Vigo really hadn't expected.

Lorraine was present, of course. She was standing in the center of the Guard contingent, her eyes dark as she watched Vigo step out in front of everyone.

The flag in the Major's hands hung free, the small airflows in the shuttle bay ruffling it a bit but mostly leaving it straight and flat.

A white gauntlet and six blue stars on a field of dark gray. The exact same gray as every uniform in the shuttle bay. Alexander Adamant hadn't been one for *subtle* in a lot of ways.

The flag the first Adamant had designed, of course, had only needed three stars: Adamantine, Ominira, and Tolkien. Greenrock, Beulaiteuhom and Maka'melemele had come later: a requested annexation and two daughter colonies, respectively.

"Guards and guests," Vigo greeted his audience. "We are here to remember the fallen. One of our own, but... so many more, too."

The bay wasn't designed for this, and the lighting helped turn his audience into a bit of a blur. His link helpfully cleared some of the light from his vision, as well as dropping icons on Lorraine and other key people around him.

"Archie Patriksson was our Guard shuttle commander," he said. "That feels so... insufficient to describe a man, let alone what he *did*." He waved around the space. "This shuttle bay was built for twelve shuttles. When we came aboard, we needed it to hold sixteen. Even *I* am not always certain what was sacrificed to squeeze in four more shuttles, but Archie made it happen."

He *did* know that *Goldenrod* had given up a large chunk of her reserve ammunition. The frigate should have carried enough missiles to reload her outer racks twice. Instead, she'd given up a full quarter of her overall missile load—twenty-four weapons—to fit in the extra shuttles.

He also doubted that was everything.

"A man like Archie earned his job the hard way," he continued. "Twelve years in the Royal Kingdom of Adamant Navy, right through the war with the Directorate. He made ace in one of the last battles of the war, though he always talked that down as an ancient and silly tradition from another era.

"He was never in any of the big fights. Served on a frigate's shuttle wing, like this one," Vigo noted, gesturing around him. "You all know that the Guard isn't something you *apply* for. It's something you are *asked* to join."

The reality was more complicated, of course, but Patriksson wasn't one of the ones who found strings to pull. He *had* been selected based on his record—and then survived the grueling assessment of his loyalty to Crown and Kingdom.

"Archie was one of the ones who tried to argue," he continued after a moment, the memory bringing a smile to his face. "He gave me the names of three other pilots on his ship alone that he thought were better than him, better suited to the job.

"I told him I'd evaluated all three of them and they didn't fit my criteria. *He* did."

Part of those criteria, though not one Vigo had ever told Archie, was that the other three were all bed-hoppers who had recently had partners roughly the same age as Lorraine had been then. That hadn't been a concern with Archie.

He'd also edged out all three on reflexes, had ace wings where none of them did, and the Navy had been fighting to keep him in a way they didn't always.

"He actually ended up turning me down the first time. When I showed up the next day to make sure he was *certain*, he realized I was truly serious," Vigo concluded. "Like everyone joining the Guard, he got a paper demotion and a pay increase. I think he might have been one of the fastest jumps back to Lieutenant Major I know of, though!"

Most of the Guard, at least, knew that part. The shuttle pilots of his detail, especially, were nodding and smiling.

"We lost a good man, people," Vigo concluded softly. "The best kind of Guard—the one who understood that his job was to protect not only the Pentarch's life but also her ability to *do* her job... and her sanity."

Discretion was key. Vigo could count on the fingers of one hand the number of people who knew that Lorraine had brought a one-night stand into a shuttle—and that was *including* the young man who definitely hadn't realized what he was getting into! Archie had played more games with the official records than he should have to cover that up—but he'd told Vigo he was doing so.

He knew Lorraine well enough to pick out the embarrassed flush on her cheeks. She was likely thinking about the same incident.

"Lieutenant Major Patriksson's body is not here," he told the crowd quietly. "Just the flag. His remains are in stasis to deliver them home safely. Like all Guards who fall in the line of duty, he will be buried in the Field of Honor, in the shadow of the Adamantine Manse."

Technically, the Adamant Guard served the monarch, not the House of Adamant. But the difference was a vague line at best—and not one the House would ever let get in the way of acknowledging debts owed. The warriors who fell in defense of the Pentarchy were honored by Kingdom and House alike.

Many of the gravesites in the Field of Honor, tucked into a beautiful valley in the rolling hills west of Adamant City, were empty. The Guard went with their Pentarchs and Kings onto warships and to far-off places. Their bodies weren't always retrievable—but there was a plinth and a site for every Guard who fell.

"Present arms!" he ordered.

There should have been seven Guard *officers* to render the salute, the pilots and copilots that formed the core of Archangel Detail's Third Section. But with Jelica Laurenz in a cell, there were only six pilots left. The senior Chief of the Detail's shuttle techs had joined the firing line, bringing it to the traditional odd number of saluters.

"Fire!"

Crack!

The salvo was a touch ragged. Every Guard was capable of firing a carbine—the ceremonial carbines were modified training weapons, unable to load *any* type of ammunition but with the full weight of the real thing—but the shuttle crews didn't practice firing drills.

This audience, Vigo figured, would pick up the deep respect inherent in the pilots taking up the guns for the salute.

"Fire!"

Crack!

"Fire!"

Crack!

"Shoulder arms!"

All seven Guards slung their carbines. Six silently stepped backward into the crowd, but Lieutenant Dima Shwetz stepped forward. She *had* been the third-most senior pilot of Archangel Detail's Third Section—AKA *Goldenrod* Charlie Flight. Now, she was the senior officer of that Guard Section.

She took the other end of the flag silently, and they stepped through the ancient ritual of folding the flag with care. Finally, Vigo released it and she stepped back, the fabric package tiny to his eyes compared to the weight it held.

"Thank you," he whispered to her.

He could see the tears in Shwetz's eyes, and he knew his own weren't dry. They'd lost a good man in the worst possible way.

But Vigo still had duties to carry out, and he nodded to the junior officer as she stepped back into the crowd, and he faced his gathered people once more.

"Archie Patriksson died to treachery, shot down by one of our own," he reminded them. "Unfortunately, he wasn't alone. He wasn't even the first—but six weeks ago, no member of the Adamant Guard had ever been killed by another Guard."

From the mutter through the regular Navy crew in his audience, that wasn't as common knowledge as he'd assumed. The *Guard* knew. It had been a quiet point of pride that in three hundred years of the Kingdom of Adamant's history, not one Guard had killed another.

No personal feud had escalated to that level. No family squabble amongst House Adamant. *Nothing.*

Until forty-two days earlier, when everything had gone to hell.

"Among the data I extracted from our dropboxes in Ominira was a casualty list," Vigo told his people. "The Regent's people are placing the blame on *unknown terrorist elements*, believed to be in association with the Richelieu Directorate and possible traitorous Pentarchs, but the list of the dead appears to be mostly complete."

He could almost *feel* the mix of rage and grief tearing through them now. Much of it over their lost comrades. A not-insignificant part of it was directed at the implication that Lorraine had been involved in the attacks.

"At the beginning of March, there were six hundred and forty-three Guards buried in the Field of Honor," he told them. "The total strength of the Guard has been roughly eight hundred for most of the Kingdom's history... so you understand my meaning when I say that the Field of Honor is about to double in size."

Only Guards who died in the line of duty were always buried in the Field of Honor. Those who died after retirement had all of the usual options, decided by their families, though the House would often help pay for funerals and other costs.

There were a few retired Guards who'd ended up in the Field but not many. Mostly those who'd died in retirement without blood family to claim them—in that situation, their *other* family claimed them and took care of them.

"Five hundred and seventy Guards died in the attacks on the King, the Pentarchs and Guard Command," Vigo told them. "I will make the full list available to you all, but... with few exceptions, the survivors of the Guard are from the Regent's Brave Detail, an unknown number of Pentarch Nikola's Attila Detail... and us."

There was an angry growl in the room now, and Vigo didn't challenge it. He couldn't have stopped it if he wanted to—it took all of his effort not to join it.

"The honor of the Adamant Guard is *broken*," he told his people.

"Guard has betrayed Guard. If the hands that killed our King didn't belong to one of our own, one of our own cleared the way regardless. While many of our comrades-in-arms held true to our honor till the end, enough broke their oaths to bring us to the edge of failure."

Vigo let that sink in and then *finally* let his growl out.

"*But only to the edge,*" he told them all fiercely. "Archangel Detail has not failed! So far as I know, Attila Detail has not failed, either—but I can only speak wholly to what I see.

"And I see Pentarch Lorraine Adamant among us, alive and well because of *this* Guard. Because of *us*. The Adamant Guard has fallen —but *we* remain. True to our oaths. True to our honor.

"True to our Pentarch."

A moment of silence and he knew he had his people.

"*And so we shall remain!*"

The room exploded in loud agreement, and he met Lorraine's gaze through it all, his eyes carrying a silent promise he knew she could read.

Her Guard would not betray their honor. Would not betray *her*.

THIRTY-FOUR

Weeks in the dark without even false gravity *hurt*. Lorraine found the centrifugal gym attached to the frigate's medical bay excruciating in multiple senses, but every person aboard the ship was supposed to spend at least an hour a day exercising.

The *problem* was that the gym was sized to handle twenty people at once. It would be cramped with all of the machines taken, but with over three hundred people on the frigate, every time slot was normally at least half-full.

But even now, with a mole in a cell and everyone feeling certain of everyone's loyalties, her Guard wouldn't let her use the gym with the usual crowd. She was in the center of a row of machines, working through the series of exercises preprogrammed into the thing, and she felt even more isolated than normal.

The centrifuge was only ten meters across, too, which made its pseudogravity uncomfortably uneven. It was good for her muscles to do the exercises, but her inner ear *hated* the process.

She'd been slack enough that even the regular exercises were a stretch. With the only other occupants of the space her Guards, the half who were also doing exercises were pushing well past *regular* exercises.

Lorraine wasn't sure what foolish pride made her try to keep up, but she did. Which was why she *hurt*. The weights, shifts and motions of the Guard's exercise program were *doable* for her, but only barely.

"You know that pushing yourself isn't wise, right?"

She looked up from the machine to see Vigo floating at the center of the centrifuge, his hand on the central bar provided for ease of navigation. *He* wasn't getting any of the centrifugal force there, though she knew the rotation could be dizzying.

"It isn't exactly easy to be the one pushing ten kilograms when everyone else is moving thirty," she pointed out. "We can't let the place go *completely* unused when I'm in here, but your people are impressive."

"We need to be." He shook his head. "When you're done, swing by my office?"

They both knew there were fifteen minutes left on her exercise regime. Lorraine suspected that he *also* knew that she had run herself to the ragged edge and might not be able to push harder.

"I was just finishing up," she blatantly lied with a bright smile as she hit the shutdown button. "Give me a hand?" she asked as she unstrapped herself and rose carefully in the spin chamber.

She could walk to the end and climb the ladder into the middle, but she knew Vigo could manage this. To *talk* to her, he'd been half-consciously rotating himself around the center bar.

He couldn't reach all the way down to her, but she delicately hopped away from the deck—not the safest plan in a spin chamber, for obvious reasons—and he caught her arm easily, lifting her up to let her grab the bar.

"I need to clean up, but then your office?" she asked.

VIGO'S OFFICE hadn't changed in the last two months. It was the same utilitarian space built for a Royal Adamant Marine Corps platoon commander. The RAMC platoon barracks the Guard had taken over had been expanded in every way *except* its offices.

Lorraine's detail had crammed sixty-two Adamant Guards into a space meant for forty Marines. That had required fewer sacrifices than adding their four shuttles to the shuttle bay, she knew—and the sacrificed storage rooms had actually created a link from the barracks to the guest quarters.

That was more useful with her being *in* said quarters than when she'd been in the pilots' quarters a deck up, of course.

"What do you need, Vigo?" she asked him. After being strapped into an exercise machine, she didn't quite feel up to the mental and physical maneuver of "sitting" in space. For himself, her bodyguard folded himself into a vaguely cross-legged position above where his chair was mag-locked to the floor.

"To check in," he told her. "It's been three weeks since we left Ominira. Two months since all of this started. I know…" He sighed, waving a hand in the air and automatically adjusting his spin afterward.

"Grief is a weird and fucky process," he warned. "Very technical terms, those. And I know you've spoken to the doctors… but I know *you*. I'm not getting anything from the docs, which I assume means they aren't seeing anything worrying, but."

He shrugged.

"Your mind and soul are as much my charge as anything else," he concluded. "I am tasked not only to keep you safe but to protect who you are. I can't—I *won't*—hide you from the world or pretend things haven't happened.

"But I am here to support you, Lorraine. Whatever that means."

Lorraine wasn't sure *what* she'd been expecting—other than an excuse to skip the rest of her workout!—but she wasn't ready for an impromptu psych session.

"If there were concerns, Vigo, you'd be the first person I'd tell," she admitted with a sigh. "It's..."

The words didn't come. She didn't know how to explain to him how weird and empty everything felt. Dr. Major Stew Mackenzie, the ship's chief physician, had ended up taking over her care after his junior hadn't been able to get *anything* useful out of her in the first couple of sessions.

The Major, at least, seemed to be able to find the right questions to drag admissions out of her.

"I don't know if the sessions with the doc are helping," she finally said. "Mackenzie asks the right questions, I guess, because they *suck*. I'm not good at *letting the feeling go through me.*"

"No one is, Lorraine," her bodyguard told her. "You got the training before you made Major, let alone Lieutenant Commander. Handling subordinates with family losses. Handling losing your own people."

She nodded. She'd been remembering those lessons a lot of late.

"I went and pulled my notes from cold storage," she admitted. "I was hoping to find something useful in them."

"Did you?" he asked.

"Yes and no? For some reason, we don't cover *your uncle killed your parents and two of your siblings and now is taking over the Kingdom* in the abbreviated grief-counseling training we give officers."

Even now, it felt strange to say those words out loud.

"They teach you not to hate when you join the Guard, you know," Vigo said after a long stretch of silence. She gave him a questioning look. "They burn it out of us pretty hard, actually. It's part of why Laurenz's issues took me by surprise.

"We try to find the biases, the prejudices, and teach you to let them go. More than that, though, the Guard does everything they can to teach us that hate... revenge... grudges... That all of these things are contrary to the mission."

"I don't get it," Lorraine admitted.

"I didn't serve in the last war with the Directorate," he told her. "But I *did* serve in the one before that, lost friends. A lover, even."

That was a sore memory. He hadn't quite *forgotten* about Brian, but it had been a long time since the Navy officer had crossed his mind. It had been almost thirty years ago that Lieutenant Major Brian Kerensky's logistics ship had been caught out by a Directorate frigate and lost with all hands.

"And eleven years ago, I was the head of your bodyguard when you went on that state visit," he continued. "If I had held on to the hate I felt for the Richelieuans then, it could have been a real issue. The talks were doomed, as it turns out—but it would have been all too easy for your bodyguard's hate to sabotage them by *accident*, let alone on purpose.

"So, I was trained to put aside my hate, to see it as a risk. I don't hate the Richelieuans—haven't in a long time. I wouldn't *mind* some alone time in a dark alley with Director Emeritus François-Marie Dubois—but I suspect a large number of his *own* soldiers would like that too!"

Then-Director Dubois was the man who, so far as post-war analysis could tell, had single-handedly set up the last *two* Richelieu-Adamant wars. Partially as an effort at expansion by annexing Tolkien. But the second time, at least, though the Kingdom wasn't certain enough of this to make it public, also to create a distraction from a corruption scandal.

Lorraine could see how even letting go of personal feelings wouldn't take away the urge to... *educate* the man on the costs of his games.

"I don't know if I will be able to not hate Benjamin," Lorraine whispered. "After all of this. I can barely believe my parents are gone, but I know he did it. And I hate him."

"I know." Vigo let that hang. "Fuck, Your Highness, *I* hate him. Basically everyone I've worked with for the last two decades except my own team either betrayed us or is *dead*. That's going to take some handling.

"But we cannot let *hate* overcome *duty*," he told her flatly. "It may yet be necessary for you to cut a deal with him to find the best answer for the Kingdom. *Anger* is natural, necessary. So is hatred.

"We owe it to our people to bring this to an end with as little bloodshed as possible." He snorted. "While still stopping him from running roughshod over the Kingdom and our Constitution. I'm not asking you to abandon your plan, Lorraine. I'm just..."

"Looking out for me, as always," Lorraine finished after he trailed off. "I don't know my own emotions, Vigo. This is..."

"Hell." He let the word hang in the air. "The only hell your family would ever believe in—the inside of your own head."

She chuckled weakly, trying to find humor in the truth of that. House Adamant held to a sort of genteel agnosticism, demanding religious tolerance of both themselves and their Kingdom while espousing few real beliefs of their own.

Her father had followed his own faith with deep heartfelt belief, and no one had ever *objected*. But she wondered sometimes how hard it had been for him to let that go when raising his children. House Adamant had been willing to respect *his* choice, but she suspected there had been very real barriers to him sharing his faith with his children.

But Vigo was right. The only hell her family would ever believe in was being trapped inside their own heads—and if her grief was anything, it was that. Rattling around inside her skull, bouncing between empty and normal and broken at intervals she had no control over.

"I feel like I should... *feel* more," she admitted. "I wish I could find more to keep myself busy with, but even putting that aside, I just feel flat. Empty."

"Would it help if I told you that was normal enough?" he asked gently. "I felt lost for a long time after I lost my father. Felt guilty that it didn't feel like I hurt more—until..."

He sighed and she gave him a questioning look.

"Vigo?"

"It was *your* dad, actually," he told her. "I don't know how he talked to my doctor or why he got involved, but I was doing double duty about nine years ago when he and your mom were visiting the Academy for your graduation. Running your detail but also backstopping theirs.

"Work helped bury it, and believe me, guarding you at nineteen was a *lot* of work."

She felt a flush of embarrassment. In hindsight, she'd been a very good student and larval officer, but the moment she'd stepped off campus on leave, she'd been thinking with her hormones as often as not.

Vigo and the rest of her detail had dealt with that with enough calm discretion that she'd actually been *honest* with them about a lot of things she had never told her parents. She'd always been *discreet*, but she knew exactly what her bodyguard was talking about.

"But you talked to my dad about grief?" she asked.

"I don't even know how we ended up on the topic," Vigo admitted. "I was only half on duty—about as off-duty as any of the Guard get when there are Adamants around at all—and found myself sharing an observation deck with him.

"I'm not sure, even now, if it was happenstance or if he was there because he knew what was going on," her bodyguard told her. "I wouldn't have put the latter past the Colonel and him. He... He cared, a lot, about the people around him. He was always the heart to your mother's sword."

Lorraine could only nod, sniffling as tears refused to fall in microgravity.

"He told me that the empty feeling *was* pain. That the blank I felt, where I accused myself of not caring, was because I cared *so much*, I couldn't process how badly I hurt. Beating myself for not feeling was bad for me either way, he said, but I was also misunderstanding my own emotions."

Vigo shook his head, reaching out to hook himself over to a cupboard on the back wall. Lorraine was still digesting his story, her own emotions a roiling storm she still couldn't process, and missed what he was doing until he passed her a translucent bulb of red wine.

"Aren't you on duty?" she asked wryly.

"First job is to take care of the Pentarch," he replied. "A toast. To Frederick Adamant-Griffin, the heart of the realm that Valeriya brought home from another star. Your father."

"To my father." The wine-bulbs had a ring of faux glass so that they *could* be tapped together for a toast, creating a sound that was *almost* right.

The wine was surprisingly good, too. Lorraine wasn't much of a drinker of *anything*, but she had basic training as a sommelier—along with a *long* list of other esoteric skills—and she could pick out the quality and enjoy the flavors.

"The heart of the realm," she echoed softly. "Rumor in the palace is that he basically *wrote* the twenty-five-twenty-three treaty."

That document had ended the last war, recognizing the complete failure of the Directorate offensive and returning all borders and outposts to prewar status. It had called for reparations, but they'd been very specifically calculated to cover damage to civilian infrastructure and losses in Tolkien.

The indemnity hadn't been *small*, but it had been set up to be inarguable. The fact that the Directorate's capital-ship losses were almost twice the Kingdom's had left the Richelieuans in a hard place, but a counter-invasion would have been a nightmare. A balanced deal had been what was needed, but Lorraine knew a lot of people had held to *dictate terms in the burning ruins of Nouveau Versailles* as the only way to end the war.

"Not *just* him," her guard said with a chuckle. "But he was the one who talked your mother down from *burn them all* as a negotiating position and laid the framework of a fair deal. He was... good for the Kingdom *and* good for your mother."

"She was good for the Kingdom," Lorraine said, clinging to the memory of her mother. "Daniel was her choice to be King, I think. She wasn't done yet, though, not by a long shot."

She chuckled, brushing away stubborn tears to let them be sucked up by the air-handling system. "I think the most common over-under the bookies were running was whether she'd abdicate before the twins became Pentarchs. Seventeen years away, and the odds were that she'd still be King by then."

"Your father was dedicated to his family—Valeriya and all of you kids," Vigo agreed. "He served the Kingdom, but first and foremost, he supported his family. Your mother was a scion of House Adamant, the Kingdom first above all else.

"Our people and our realm were served well by your parents. I am grateful that this job let me get to know them as *people*, though," he told her. "I know neither of them would want to be forgotten. They would want you to face the task ahead, to find your strength where you must.

"But your grief is honest, my Pentarch, and no less real for it not *fitting* what you *expected*," he continued gently. "Do not blame yourself for not feeling what you think you should. Accept what you feel and know that you grieve them honestly and deeply.

"And that they loved you. Everyone who knew them knew they loved their children, all of you. I am here for you, whatever you need." He smiled. "Even if that's sometimes just to poke a bit until you cry in private."

Microgravity made the tears messy, even when they were flowing freely. But he was right and she let her grief flow through her.

There, in this room, she was safe. And in front of Vigo Jarret, there was no question that she could feel as much as she could—and if she felt too fiercely for it to even register as grief, as he said, well.

That was only human, and for all of the tinkering in Lorraine Adamant's genes, she was very much human.

THIRTY-FIVE

A swipe of Lorraine's hand, matched with a mental command and a habitually swallowed curse, scattered the hologram of Planetary Defense Center Mithral into pieces.

She glared at where the model of the fortress had hung, half-consciously shifting from one magnetic sole to the other to stretch her legs and let off *some* of the nervous tension she was fighting.

The tension levels aboard *Goldenrod* were high everywhere. No news in eighty days. No real human contact with anyone off ship in *four months*. Four months since her world had collapsed, but Lorraine had spent every single day of that time locked inside a steel box.

Seven days after the assassination attempt, Nikola Adamant had been alive and the fate of their nieces unknown. But she'd learned *that* thirty-six days after the attack. Eighty days ago now.

The math ran down her vision through her neural link for a moment before she sighed and reactivated the holographic projector in her no-longer-new office.

At coup-plus-seven, she knew that Nikola had fallen back into Planetary Defense Headquarters at PDC Mithral. Several other

PDCs and the military reserve had been implied to also be supporting him, but she was confident that PDC Mithral was in her brother's hands.

It was possible, of course, that her uncle—*the Black Regent* was the term *Goldenrod*'s crew had started to use—had cut a deal. Lorraine could see a few arguments that would convince her brother to lay down arms for the good of the Kingdom.

Mostly because they were the arguments that she'd had with herself. Benjamin had killed a *lot* of people to try to take the crown—and she craved justice and revenge alike—but a civil war would kill more.

Without knowing her uncle's *agenda*, she wasn't even certain that he'd be a bad King. Taking the throne by force wasn't a precedent she thought the Kingdom of Adamant could afford, but the price of stopping him could end up far too high.

"Except that Nikola lives up to the family name even more than the rest of us," she muttered. "*Our Realm. Our House. Our Will. Adamant.* He was the stubborn one even in *my* family."

She was three years younger than him, but she had memories of him as a teenager. Clashing with their parents, his bodyguard, his teachers... *everyone*. Nikola could be *convinced*, but he'd refused to be *bullied* from a young age.

Lorraine knew that RKAA's idea of "boot camp" was quite different from what popular media *still* perceived the training programs to look like—but she suspected it had still been a *fascinating* experience for both her brother and his instructors.

She doubted their uncle had talked him down. She *also* doubted that Benjamin had let *four months* pass without moving against him. The news might not have reached San Ignacio—a ninety-six-cee courier could make the trip directly from Adamantine in ninety-eight days versus the hundred and twenty-four they were taking, but that still left the news *months* out of date—but by now, Mithral was a battleground.

By now, her brother could be dead. *Goldenrod*'s files on Adamantine's primary Planetary Defense Center were frustratingly vague. There was enough for her to guess that even *Sultan* and the other *Monarch*-class battleships wanted to stay out of the fortress's field of fire, but the RKAN files didn't include *any* information on the surface defenses.

Given that PDC Mithral was built into a hollowed-out mountain, with underground aquifers and a mix of geothermal and nuclear power, she doubted it was a glass cannon that would fall easily to a ground assault.

But she had neither the data nor, if she was honest, the *skills* to judge if it was likely Nikola was holding out. She had to hope—had to *believe* that her brother could hold.

It would be two more months before they reached Sol. The time she would gain from the speed of her hoped-for United Worlds relief fleet she'd almost certainly lose negotiating to *get* that relief.

It had been four months since she left Adamantine, and Lorraine figured it would be eight more before she returned home. A full standard year—almost three months more than an Adamantine two-hundred-and-eighty-day year!

The dates flowed past her, and she swallowed her fear.

"If anyone can do it, it's Nikola," she whispered to the air. "I know you can, brother. I need you to.

"Nothing *less* than this is going to save our people."

She closed everything, putting both feet on the floor and crossing to the drink machine on the office wall. That was a *definite* step up from both her quarters and the office she'd shared with the two Majors in the shuttle wing: her quarters had only had a tiny coffee maker, and the shared office hadn't been much better.

The machine put in for a civilian guest was plumbed to the ship's water supply—through a secure filtration controlled by the Guard now—and had its own heating elements and refrigerated storage. At its simplest, it could pull a bulb of soda or wine from its storage unit—flagging to a supply computer if something ran low. At its most standard, it could brew basic coffee or tea.

At its most complex, it could handle everything from whiskey on the rocks to a properly proportioned Martian coffee (a latte with Asimov City's famous cream liqueur layered in) or a shaken martini.

The last suffered more than most for being served in a zero-gravity bulb, in her opinion. She'd had time to experiment, but most of the time, she settled on the same black coffee she grabbed now.

She could have slept away the entire day if she'd wanted, but her training as an officer had always been very clear: translight was safe but translight was boring. And bored spacers—*including officers*—could very quickly make a lot of things unsafe.

Lorraine needed work to do. And, thankfully, Captain Stephson had the same training.

"SAN IGNACIO, PEOPLE," Yildiz told the gathered officers and Pentarch, gesturing at a hologram of the system hanging in the middle of the room.

It spoke to the stir-craziness of effectively one hundred and twenty days in translight, with the break to supply at Ominira the longest time they'd spent in any facsimile of gravity, that Lieutenant Commander Paris was seated, cross-legged with one magnetic sole on the metal, *above* Major Yildiz.

The Tactical Officer wasn't the only one standing or seated oddly. Major Vinci and Commander Chevrolet were both standing on the bulkheads. Major Jarret was standing almost at attention near the door. Captain Stephson was across the hologram from the Navigator, and Lorraine stood with her.

Commander Savege was actually floating, her magnetic soles deactivated as she hovered near what would be the ceiling if they were under thrust, and while Commander Cortez had a hand on the ground, she was also free-floating with her mag-soles off.

A meeting of senior officers was probably the only place most of these people *could* goof off, Lorraine reflected, but that Stephson let the lack of military dignity stand said everything.

Four months incommunicado without gravity was *hard*. Frigates were meant to stop at each system they passed, both to provide security for freighters and to be seen by both allies and potential threats. They were tripwires and trade protectors, neither of which roles was well served when they were in translight.

Their flight to Ominira had been roughly the longest an RKAN frigate was expected to spend in translight. The Book limited them to ten light-years, a forty-five-day journey, but Lorraine knew that most frigate captains would try to avoid even a direct flight to Ominira or Beulaiteuhom.

Going via Tolkien to Ominira, for example, would turn the journey into legs of five and six light-years, adding two and a half light-years and eleven days to the *total* journey—but reducing the *maximum* translight flight by the same amount.

"San Ignacio is our local Swiss System," Stephson said into the silence.

Like Lorraine, the others probably hadn't even really *looked* at the model. The weight of their journey hung on everyone's minds.

"For those who aren't familiar with them, it means San Ignacio is two things: a major financial center *and* studiously neutral in all conflicts," the Captain continued. "The San Ignacio real is one of the major currencies of exchange in our cluster, coming in second behind the Bright Dream pound for local funds."

The Adamantine crown was third, at least in the half of the cluster on their side of Bright Dream. No one in the area where crowns were used would probably blink at being paid in Richelieuan francs, but they weren't a default unit of exchange.

The true default unit remained the United Worlds interstellar credit, but not every business could get their hands on enough of those to handle their transactions.

"We are going to be relying on San Ignacio's neutrality," Stephson warned. "We have no reason to believe that *Corsair* will be far behind us. Commodore Wray's people have every advantage over us for a long-range translight jump like this.

"His orders may not have stretched to this level of pursuit—but even if they didn't, he's likely already gone far enough that it would make more sense to finish the chase than leave it."

"If the Regent sent orders to pursue, he wouldn't have put any limitations on it," Lorraine warned. "That's not how my uncle works. He understands what he can communicate—that's why he made sure he had officers in place he could trust."

She had to wonder if he'd done that in *every* system of the Kingdom or just on the route toward Bright Dream and the wormhole. She suspected the former, though. He was nothing if not complete.

Lorraine just didn't want to believe he'd had that many senior officers who would sign on for a coup like this.

"Agreed. Which leaves us with two key choices to make as we approach San Ignacio," Stephson said. The Captain's words were for everyone, but her focus was on Lorraine.

"The first is where do we arrive? Like in Ominira, there is a stopover infrastructure around the outer gas giant—Vista Roja. There is also San Francisco itself, the habitable and inhabited world."

San Ignacio was a brilliant F3 star, its habitable zone falling farther out than Adamantine's. San Francisco was the fourth world, orbiting almost fifteen light-minutes from the burning furnace at the center of the system.

Vista Roja was a blood-crimson super-Jupiter at fifty-five light-minutes from the sun. A broad asteroid belt and a smaller gas giant divided the two key planets. Vista Roja was bigger and had a more useful gas mix than Vista Poco, the fifth planet.

"Regardless of which of the two we arrive at; we are left with the second choice: whether we play one hundred percent by the local rules or... *stretch* things."

Lorraine nodded slowly as she considered the star system. The only *real* reason to go to Vista Roja over San Francisco was to avoid the higher costs of visiting the planet. Fuel would be cheaper at the refinery stations themselves, and an inhabited planet always had a long list of fees to be paid to safely make orbit.

It wasn't a big-enough difference to worry her, given the resources she had. She couldn't conceive of a situation where a hundred thousand credits or so of fees would leave her unable to complete her mission.

"Which rules are we worried about?" Paris asked, the Tactical Officer looking at the second half of the question before Lorraine got there.

"The locals have established fixed arrival zones around both San Francisco and Vista Roja," Yildiz answered. A smaller green sphere flashed next to each planet. "They're roughly ten percent farther out than the usual safety zone but are kept under guard by the SIDF."

Lorraine had heard good things about the San Ignacio Defense Force, both about the quality of their ships and their sense of duty and honor.

"By arriving in a designated zone, we place ourselves directly under the guns of the local fleet," Stephson concluded. "That could be good *or* bad—but we *also* make our arrival location more predictable to any pursuit."

"And if we come in *outside* the designated zone, the SIDF probably won't shoot us?" Lorraine asked.

"Depends on *where* we come out," the navigator told her. A new translucent orange sphere appeared around both Vista Roja and San Francisco, drawn slightly inside the marked green sphere of the emergence zone.

"Inside these Security Zones, they will *probably* give us one warning before they open fire," Yildiz explained. "Standard military-reservation rules, effectively, but applied to their full local space. Once we're authorized and cleared, we're fine, but if we drop out of translight in those zones, we will be boarded and subject to *excruciating* inspection at the very least.

"We'll lose time and be fined—plus making the locals *very* grumpy—but our emergence can be as fully random as possible."

Lorraine nodded, considering the three-dimensional map. Someone—probably Yildiz—made an adjustment and it separated into two maps, focusing in on the planets of interest.

"Not much point coming out anywhere *except* at those two planets," Stephson said. "Nowhere else in the system will have infrastructure for fuel or shore leave."

"Better shore leave on San Francisco itself, I presume?" Lorraine asked.

"We can *breathe* on SF," the Captain pointed out. "Plus, real gravity. Last time I was at Vista Roja, we were only able to book time on one of the ring stations. Centripetal pseudogravity is better than nothing, but even a third of a gee of real gravity settles the brain in a completely different way.

"I'm told the domes on Vista Roja's moons are pleasant, but they're pricey and RKAN doesn't traditionally spring for it."

"So, if we want to put people on actual dirt, San Francisco might be cheaper anyway," Lorraine guessed.

"Potentially. It depends how long we're willing to stay here and what the goal is," Stephson said. She wasn't *saying* that it was Lorraine's call, but the implication was clear.

If Lorraine couldn't or wouldn't make the decision, Stephson *would*, but the mission was Lorraine's. The Exodus Protocols put her in charge and the whole mess was hers to run.

"We came through outer-system infrastructure in Ominira," she noted. "Wray may expect us to do the same." She snorted as she followed her thought through. "He might *also* expect us to do the opposite for just that reason."

She stepped carefully forward to examine the maps.

"There are files from the Exodus Protocols that I need to be on San Francisco to make full use of," she told the others. While there was a lot of money in the secured credit sequences—enough to complete the journey to Earth and underwrite her pitch there, she hoped—there were also account numbers and access codes.

She didn't know what was in those accounts or if they had other uses. It was possible that she had access to the standard diplomatic accounts for the systems she was passing through and draining them would leave the local Adamantine Embassies in trouble.

Without using those codes and checking the accounts, she couldn't tell—and the realities of modern banking meant that she could only do that in the systems those accounts dwelled in.

"While we *are* under a time constraint, we have also just put the crew through four months of microgravity," she continued. "I think the choice is clear: we go to San Francisco and we spend at least a couple of days on the planet, relying on the SIDF to protect us.

"*We* can't fight *Corsair*, but the SIDF has *battleships*. While we can't be certain that Commodore Wray will be intimidated, we need their support." She shrugged. "To me, that means we have to play by their rules and be at least *somewhat* transparent about what's going on."

"San Francisco, then," Yildiz said. "And the official arrival zone."

"Exactly," she confirmed. "And while I assume they'll order us to stand down our weapons, I *suggest* we arrive at battle stations. If Wray guesses right and I've judged him wrong—or he just jumps the gun without thinking!—we will need to... well, run for the SIDF's skirts."

That got a mix of wry and bitter chuckles from the officers. As they'd seen when *Corsair* had jumped them in deep space, they were badly outgunned. If the battlecruiser came after them, *Goldenrod* was going to need help.

Fortunately, the San Ignacio Defense Force followed what Lorraine understood to be one of the golden rules of neutrality: it was a *lot* easier to be neutral if you were both able and willing to make violating that neutrality *painful*.

THIRTY-SIX

"Ten minutes."

Yildiz's voice echoed through the ship and updated the timer in Vigo's vision.

The Guard commander had once more taken the right-hand observer console at the back of the bridge. Every seat on *Goldenrod*'s bridge was full, with the Pentarch in the central observer console and Corporal Alvarez in the far one.

Yildiz hadn't even needed to specify what the *ten minutes* was counting down to.

Goldenrod was still in her faux-tachyonic state, thirteen-plus light-hours away from the emergence zone above San Francisco and hurtling toward the planet at eighty times the speed of light.

The console in front of him was set up as a mirror of Lorraine's. He had no control codes in the command system she was using, but he had the same visibility to the ship's status.

Goldenrod was closed up at full battle stations. Her beams were online, though her offensive beams were set to lower power levels and active in a purely defensive mode. Every part of her energy screen that could be active in their current state was online—large pieces of the ECM component and the semi-physical energy shield that anchored the defense couldn't be activated in translight.

Combat radiators—more effective but both shorter-lived and more expensive than the non-combat systems—were extending all along the ship, their vane-like appearance turning her into something resembling an arrow as much as a wet-navy warship.

The biggest shortfall that Vigo could see was that there'd been no chance to reload the missile cells. All four missile tubes were green and ready to launch, but only twelve of the twenty-four single-shot cell launchers had weapons in them.

The missiles meant to reload those cells were in the same central magazine the tubes drew from, so they weren't useless. But if they somehow lived long enough to fire eleven salvos from the missile tubes, they were going to have had a *very* strange day.

"Five minutes," Yildiz announced. "Five minutes to translight exit."

Apparently, he'd felt he needed to remind people what he was counting down to this time. The Book, Vigo supposed.

The Major wasn't as familiar with the RKAN's standard rules and protocols as he'd once been. He'd been Lorraine's bodyguard for over twenty years, after all, and the Guard's Book was a very different document.

"You good?" he sent silently to Lorraine. "First time we're publicly presenting you as an envoy and ambassador."

That had been her decision. There would be no deception in San Ignacio—though they wouldn't tell the locals *everything*. Lorraine Adamant was there as an envoy of her mother, operating under emergency authority in the face of a coup. They were expecting pursuit by traitor warships.

It was the opposite of Ominira, where they'd needed to keep her presence secret. *There*, in San Ignacio, they needed to trumpet her presence to the high heavens. Politics, image and diplomacy.

Vigo Jarret had been trained in it so he could back Lorraine up, but he knew that *her* education on the topic put his to shame. Her formal qualifications might be in high-order physics, but the training she'd received as a known Pentarch was the equivalent of a double *master's* in economic and political theory—and practice.

He agreed with her plan, but it was her plan.

"I am ready," she replied by text, not even glancing at him. "Nervous. I think we have it in hand."

Vigo knew she was nervous—but he doubted anyone else on the bridge did. There was a calm readiness to her posture, a tilt and a tone to her motions and even her gaze that being strapped into the bridge chair didn't cover.

The only reason *he* could see through it was because he'd helped *teach* her that projection. He could tell the difference between her being calm and her *projecting* calm—but unless his own projections were less convincing than he thought, she was fooling everyone but him. Maybe not Stephson, he supposed.

The Captain would have had very similar training, after all.

"Check our codes, please, Major Vinci," Lorraine said aloud. She hit the perfect balance between *asking* while also letting her tone communicate that it was effectively an order.

The Pentarch's requests could be refused, but the officer doing it would have to have a *damn* good reason. With the authority Lorraine now wielded on paper, even a good reason might not be enough... except that it *was* Lorraine, and Vigo knew she'd listen to good explanations.

"We are transmitting the consular codes you provided, Your Highness," Vinci confirmed. "Your personal cross-confirmation codes as Fourth Pentarch are linked in to the consular identification sequence as instructed."

Second Pentarch. No one said it, but Vigo could practically hear the correction echo through the thoughts of everyone on the bridge. Lorraine was now the *Second* Pentarch of the Kingdom of Adamant.

Thankfully, that didn't change her personal codes. Everything they were transmitting was in the clear and should be recognized by any nation in the Bright Dream Cluster.

They shouldn't *need* to go quite that far, Vigo knew, but invoking diplomatic status was one more tool they had to secure the protection they needed.

"Three minutes to dropout."

Vigo went through a series of half-mental, half-physical exercises. He focused on and relaxed each limb in turn, letting the straps do the work of making sure he didn't float away from his console.

Things would have to go very wrong for his particular skills to be called for, but very little had gone *right* in the last few months.

THE FLASH of indescribable light was a normal strangeness, reassuring even in its defiance of his natural senses to understand what was going on.

"Contacts close." Paris's report was calm, expected. Icons flickered into existence across the bridge displays as the frigate's sensors drank in the light and other radiation around them. "Estimate sixty-plus contacts within a hundred thousand kilometers."

"Any RKAN ships?" Stephson snapped.

That was the risk. If Commodore Wray had judged everything correctly, *Corsair* might be waiting for them. Potentially with the kind of warrant that the SIDF would acknowledge, though Vigo couldn't see any way the man could have pulled that off.

"Negative," Paris replied. "Four civilian ships running Adamantine transponders, all freighters."

"Warships?" Lorraine's question was probably redundant, but it was the second point on everyone's mind.

"Looks like sixteen ships, none over a million tons," the tactical officer replied. "Processing IDs now—SIDF CruRon Four, DesRon Twelve."

Vigo knew enough about SIDF organization to know that meant two eight-ship squadrons. He'd been hoping for battleships, but eight cruisers *should* be enough to get Commodore Wray to back down.

Corsair outmatched any individual ship in the entry zone's guard force, though, and that was a problem. On the other hand, at least *Corsair* wasn't there yet.

"Incoming coms," Vinci reported. "I have a Coronel Superior Eiji Akabane, sir."

"Connect him to myself and the Pentarch," Stephson ordered. "Mirror to the screen, give him a double-feed on our side."

Vigo linked into Lorraine's coms as a silent observer. Coronel Superior Akabane—Senior Colonel, roughly equivalent to an RKAN Commodore—was a dark-skinned man with severe features and an even more severe expression.

"RKAN warship *Goldenrod,* we have received your diplomatic codes. We have also detected that your weapons systems and defenses are fully active. Per the San Ignacio AZA, you will be denied entry to our system unless you power down *all* combat systems immediately."

The *Arrival Zone Act* was the local law that laid out the structure of the area they'd entered. It gave the Coronel Superior the authority to protect the system's neutrality with a phenomenal amount of force if needed.

"Coronel Superior, we believe we are being pursued by rogue elements of the Royal Kingdom of Adamant Navy, commanded by officers participating in a coup against the Crown and Pentarchy," Lorraine told him swiftly. "They have already killed my mother the King, and I must see to my own security until I am certain they will not launch a surprise attack."

Akabane barely even blinked. He locked on to what Vigo suspected was Lorraine's gaze for him, assessing her with dark brown eyes that seemed to be doing a vast amount of silent math.

"I see. That is surprisingly aligned with the news we have received from the Adamantine System," he told her. "Though, of course, your *details* are quite different. Your navigator will receive a course. You will follow it. You will stand down your offensive arms *immediately* and your defenses in three hundred sixty seconds.

"Do you understand?"

Vigo sure as hell didn't, and his hand slipped toward his holstered sidearm. The gun wouldn't be useful in this situation, but it was the only tool he really had.

"We understand," Lorraine said in a steady tone. An image flickered across Vigo's console, mirroring what she was looking at, and he swallowed.

The provided course was going to take them *right* under the guns of two of Akabane's cruisers—a perfect cut between two ships separated by less than five thousand kilometers.

"We will comply," Lorraine confirmed. "Thank you."

The coms cut out.

"You heard the man and the Pentarch," Stephson said. "Yildiz, execute the course. Paris, shut down our offensive weapons. Shut down the missiles and their targeting systems... and dump power from the main beams, just in case."

The targeting sensors for the missiles and the capacitors for the main beams were probably the most obvious sign that *Goldenrod* was at battle stations. Without the active sensor beams, the missiles *could* launch, but they'd be half-blind.

The tubes and cells themselves were far harder to detect the status of, but Vigo saw the markers switch from green to amber as Paris followed his orders.

At the same time, the frigate's engines came up to a full one-gravity thrust and Vigo felt his body and mind *click* back into place in a way he couldn't quite explain. The downward pull still felt *right* after four months in zero gee.

He blinked as the acceleration kept increasing, up to what his link informed was a solid two gees of thrust.

"Three thousand kilometers before we cut the screen," Lorraine told him silently. "I suspect... Yep, there they go."

The two cruisers—each about eight hundred thousand tons fully loaded, almost six times *Goldenrod*'s size—were adjusting their own acceleration. New icons popped up as CIC identified the individual ships: *Numancia* and *Navarra*.

The SIDF's regulations and rules required that they shut down anything that might cause harm to another vessel—but their track record also said they fully understood the responsibility that laid on *them*.

No one had said anything officially yet, but the two ships' maneuvers made the intent clear. They were going to accompany *Goldenrod*, probably well into the emergence safety zone if not all the way to San Francisco orbit.

Vigo's job, of course, was to be the paranoid bastard.

"Are they targeting *us*?" he asked aloud. "We're assuming they're following their normal rules, but if we let them fall in around us and they turn hostile, we're in some serious trouble."

"It's a risk," Lorraine agreed. "I *am* relying on, oh, three hundred and twenty-seven years of San Ignacio history to judge them, though." Even so, her gaze flicked over to the Tactical console.

"Paris? *Are* they targeting us?"

"We got a once-over with what I *think* are defense targeting scanners," the Tactical Officer replied. "Nothing that stayed on us long enough for a lock. My guess would be that they were mapping us into their defensive perimeter."

"We're watching for them doing something... *odd*, yes?" Vigo asked.

"The XO and I are watching their every tiny move, Major," Paris promised. "So far, they're acting as I would expect for ships doing close-escort duty, whether they're officially taking that on or not."

"Are we *in* their defensive perimeter?" Lorraine asked.

Vigo figured she had a better idea of the answer than *he* did, but there was nothing on the overview display he was watching to mark where that line lay. For *Goldenrod*, the final inner defensive perimeter was roughly two thousand kilometers away from the frigate.

"About eighty seconds," Paris told her. "Assuming their beams are the same as our cruisers. They can't do much about something hitting us with beams of their own until we're a lot closer, though."

Vigo carefully did not give the Tactical Officer a questioning look, sending his question silently to Lorraine.

"What *can* they do about us being targeted by beams?" he asked.

His own understanding was *basically nothing*, but while he'd kept up his flight qualifications, the *rest* of his naval officer training was badly out of date.

"Assuming *their* cruisers have the same gear as our cruisers, if not better, they can project their energy screen away from their hull," she told him. "Ours can do about two hundred klicks. Enough to cover ships in very close company.

"I'm guessing theirs is better, but that's part of why they're vectoring to close up the range."

Vigo didn't dare to breathe a sigh of relief, his gaze locked to the displays showing the space around them. They hadn't even left the designated emergence zone yet—but they also hadn't seen *Corsair* yet.

He figured that meant Commodore Wray had guessed wrong. He could hope, anyway.

Given another couple of minutes, they'd be solidly under the protective umbrella of the San Ignacio Defense Force, too. That had to help. Even if only two ships were going to be flanking them, the *rest* of the two squadrons were nearby—and even Vigo could pick out the icons of the battleships in San Francisco orbit.

But it was Vigo's job to watch for where things could go wrong, and there were *so many* places this situation could still go up in flames.

"Yildiz, are we prepped for an emergency translight jump?" he silently sent the helm officer. He was probably pushing what he was supposed to without undercutting Stephson, but...

"Sixty-minute jump, but we have to rotate at least ninety degrees for a clear jump," Yildiz replied, equally silent. "Fifteen seconds, give or take."

Vigo nodded slowly.

"Thanks, Major."

Whatever Yildiz might have said in response was cut off by the interstellar equivalent of a belly flop, a translight emergence so close that *Goldenrod's* crew got the indescribable-light pulse of faux-tachyonic matter transitioning.

"Contact close!" Paris snapped. "Multimegaton contact at *five thousand kilometers! Fuck! It's Corsair!*"

THIRTY-SEVEN

Everything went very wrong, very fast. Their plan—Coronel Superior Akabane's plan, too—required *Corsair* to see the SIDF ships and be intimidated.

Except pure fluke had put the battlecruiser into death ground, the extremely limited-range zone where *Goldenrod*'s beams could actually hurt the much bigger ship. And there was no way for Commodore Wray to know that the frigate's beam weapons were offline.

Corsair fired first. Massive ultraviolet lasers blazed in the void, and for a single seemingly-eternal instant, Vigo *knew* he'd failed in his duty.

Goldenrod lurched underneath them all, and half the screens went dark around him. The "down" from the two gees of thrust vanished as the frigate's engines failed—and even the limited sensors left told Vigo that failure had saved the ship.

One beam had fired *just* enough milliseconds ahead of the rest to take down *Goldenrod*'s engines—and the rest of the beams blazed across the frigate's bow, missing her by little enough that new damage icons cascaded across the displays.

They'd survived by the same kind of perfect fluke that had let *Corsair* jump them—and then *more* heavy beams filled space around *Goldenrod*.

It didn't matter that the SIDF hadn't been in position to truly guard *Goldenrod*, or that they hadn't agreed to escort the frigate in to San Francisco orbit, or *anything*. Commodore Wray had opened fire inside the Arrival Zone, violating San Ignacio's neutrality without even *talking* to Coronel Superior Akabane.

"Engineering, get me engines," Stephson barked. "Helm?"

"I'm working on controls," Yildiz replied. "We've lost all primary connections for the engines *and* the maneuvering thrusters. All we can do is fucking *drift*."

"Translight?"

"Still online, but we're pointed *at* the damn planet."

"*Shit!*"

Vigo wasn't sure who had sworn. It might have been *him*, stunned at the brilliant flash of light as *Navarra* came apart under *Corsair*'s guns. The battlecruiser had stopped aiming at *Goldenrod* when the two cruisers opened fire on *her*.

At least she'd stopped aiming her *beam weapons* at the frigate.

"Multiple missiles in space," Paris announced. "At least a hundred, maybe more. Most of them are aimed at us!"

An SIDF cruiser was *gone*. *Numancia* was trying to get closer to cover them, but she was outclassed by her opponent and only really trying to buy time for the *rest* of the cruiser squadron to get into play.

As Vigo watched, *Corsair* flushed the *rest* of her cell launchers. With over two hundred missiles in space, there was no way to tell how many were aimed at *Goldenrod* versus the cruiser trying to honor San Ignacio's promises.

"Missile fire inbound from the other SIDF ships," Savege reported, the XO running all of the sensors in CIC.

"*Corsair* can take it," Stephson said flatly. "Helm? Cheng? I need news *now*."

Vigo wasn't quite as confident in *Corsair*'s ability to handle six cruisers flinging a thousand missiles at her—but he could do the math on *Goldenrod*'s ability to survive the fire coming her way.

The only reason they were still alive was that Wray could project their vector and angle. So long as their drives were down and they were pointed at San Francisco, they couldn't escape.

That meant he was dealing with the actual *threat* to his ship —*Numancia*—while preparing to take them down once he'd cleared the immediate board.

"Engines are at least five minutes," the Bridge Engineering Officer reported, the Lieutenant clearly at the limit of his ability as they hit the rare situation where the bridge engineer wasn't just summarizing the Chief Engineer's report. "The Cheng has a work detail on thruster control, but it's a mess. Getting them live could take—"

"Or we could all just owe Lieutenant Major Klement a giant beer," Yildiz told them. "I have maneuvering. *Hang the fuck on!*"

Vigo didn't even have time to ask what his Second Section Lead had done to give them the thrusters before everything tried to fly sideways. The rotation thrusters on the frigate weren't powerful—but he could *tell* that Yildiz had run them past any safe margin on the units.

Yildiz had said the turn would take fifteen seconds. It took them *six*—long enough for them to have a front-row seat to *Corsair*'s main beams drilling through *Numancia* the long way, coring the ship from bow to stern in a terrifying demonstration of why a cruiser shouldn't fight a capital ship.

Then the world shattered into a kaleidoscope and the San Ignacio System vanished.

THIRTY-EIGHT

"What the *hell* do we do now?" Paris demanded, the Tactical Officer's voice clearly stressed to Lorraine.

The Pentarch unstrapped herself, rising to her feet on her magnetic boots and stepping forward swiftly to stand next to Stephson.

"We complete the mission, Major," she told Paris before Stephson said anything. She hadn't coordinated anything with *Goldenrod*'s commander, but she'd somehow *known* this was going to be on her to handle.

"We made a mistake, assuming that Wray would play by the normal rules," she continued, looking around the bridge and the shaky expressions of the command crew. "We should have realized —I should have realized—that my uncle's core people *killed their King.*

"The rules are already broken, shattered into a thousand pieces. What's picking a fight with an entire star nation against betraying your most sacred oaths?"

Lorraine didn't know how many people a *Santa Maria*–class cruiser carried. She *did* know that *Navarra* and *Numancia* had died *fast*. They'd been on guard, yes, but they hadn't been at full battle stations. Even more so than normal, few of the cruisers' crews would have escaped their fate.

"There's only one choice from here," she continued. "We make the run to the wormhole—and we prepare to *fight* at Bright Dream. Wray isn't going to let us go—his orders from my monster of an uncle appear to be *very* clear."

"We can't fight a *battlecruiser*," Paris growled.

"Not head-on, no," Lorraine agreed. "So, we have forty-eight days, Major Paris, to work out a way to *sucker-punch* one. Like the SIDF, the Republic won't stand by while someone starts a fight near the wormhole, but we just saw how little that might matter."

That was unfair to both the SIDF and the Republic of Bright Dream Navy. Coronel Superior Akabane had assumed that putting his ships around *Goldenrod* would be enough to discourage any pursuer from starting a fight immediately—and he *should* have been right.

The intimidation power of a squadron of cruisers backed by a major star system's fleet was nonzero, after all—but *Corsair* had emerged too close to Lorraine's ship to even *realize* the protection was in place.

Their luck so far was awful enough that she was starting to wonder if Wray had some way to track their ship more precisely than the usual tachyon trail.

"*Corsair* is built to be immune to our entire arsenal at our best," Paris told her. "And we are *not* at our best anymore!"

"Then we will have to be very, *very* clever," Lorraine replied. "I have confidence in this ship and this crew, Major Paris. Don't you?"

The question was a trap and they both knew it. She almost felt mean for using it, but she *needed* Paris to calm down and focus.

"I do," he said. "But... we very nearly just got our own debris fed to us."

"We will find a way," Lorraine promised. She turned to Stephson. "Captain. Our status?"

"Paris isn't wrong that we're not at our best now," the blonde told her, pitching her voice so it didn't carry past the bubble.

"Lieutenant Major Kovac and I are still going through the reports we can get," Stephson continued, indicating the Bridge Engineering Officer with a nod.

That was worrying in itself. The BEO was a *backup* for when the Cheng was too busy. Unlike the Bridge Intelligence Officer—Lieutenant Major Ksenija Nazario, who was theoretically the relay from the Combat Information Center, but with the XO *in* CIC, they were almost always redundant—they were needed as often as not.

But if Commander Cortez was *still* too busy to check in with the Bridge after they'd jumped to translight, things were bad. *Real* bad.

"Fill me in by link," Lorraine instructed. She could *probably* manage to keep her voice pitched in the range that the captain's acoustic bubble would keep her words contained instead of projecting them, but she wasn't as practiced as Stephson.

Silence was better, and the flow of information into her neural link marked the Captain's agreement.

"The irony," Stephson told her silently as the status report filled a quarter of Lorraine's vision, "is that our offensive weaponry is almost untouched. We lost a good chunk of the cell launchers but only one that still had a missile. Primary beams are still passing remote self-check.

"Our *defenses* are in rougher shape," she continued. "We've lost about ten percent of the main screen projectors, plus a quarter of the close-in defensive beams. The *controllers* for the EW network are completely burnt out, so we won't even know the status of the jammers and countermeasures until that's fixed. And Cortez has bigger problems."

Lorraine could see them. Large sections of the frigate were flashing red in the schematic she was viewing, and the details were concerning.

"Translight is still online," she noted.

"And that's the only thing I'm sure of with our engines,"

Stephson confirmed. "I still need to confirm just *how* Yildiz got the thrusters online, because our main maneuvering control system is, well... *gone*. Shrapnel damage, from the DamCon party's report.

"Physical inspections are starting to suggest that whatever Yildiz did burned out at least half of our thrusters on top of that. Worth it— but our thrusters are designed to be replaced on a unit basis, *not* repaired."

"Which requires exterior access," Lorraine presumed. And they couldn't go outside the ship in translight. It wasn't even a matter of humans not being able to survive it. *Anything* that exited the main hull would basically *vanish*.

"In hindsight, the assumption that we'd be able to hide in deep space and carry out repairs underlies a lot of our ship-design methodology," Stephson confirmed. "The primary sublight engines are a *bit* easier to access, which is what Cortez is surveying right now.

"If they're completely done, it isn't going to matter how much confidence we have, Your Highness. We're down to hoping for a miracle."

"Understood."

Lorraine nodded to the Captain and concealed a deep inhalation as best as she could.

The situation was... non-optimal. But so long as they *had* engines, she was pretty sure they could make something work. She wasn't sure *what*, but they had a month and a half to sort it out.

And as far as unexpected tricks went, there was still a question she needed answered.

———

YILDIZ HAD the blank stare of someone who had just pushed past his limits and hadn't had a chance to fall back within them yet. The Chief sitting next to the Major nudged him with an elbow as Lorraine stepped up the Navigation section, and the officer exhaled slowly before turning to her.

"Your Highness," he said. "I... I probably need to run a translight course to Bright Dream, don't I?"

"Your emergency jump was sixty minutes, wasn't it?" she reminded him. "You can breathe for a couple, Major. You did just save us all."

"Never was too clear on what happens if we try to jump through a planet," the Navigator muttered.

"Didn't RKAN try to get you to study high-order physics?" Lorraine asked. Her own career had been about forty percent navigation and sixty percent shuttles, after all, and that was why *she'd* ended up taking her master's program in physics.

"Still bouncing options for the staff college," Yildiz told her. "Need *something* to make LC, but hadn't decided yet. Quanta physics locks me into navigation and staff officer, so... had choices to make. Not soon now, I suppose."

She let him babble. More than anyone else on the bridge, the Navigator knew how narrow the margin he'd cut to jump out had been. If Yildiz hadn't started his two-year correspondence program yet, he was probably actively slowing his promotion to Lieutenant Commander.

"Do you *really* want to know what happens if we hit a planet in translight?" she asked.

"Sure," he replied with a very false-looking grin.

"About forty percent of the time, we'd be fine," Lorraine told him. "Twenty percent of the time, we'd be yanked back to regular matter, *maybe* high enough to pull an emergency landing... but also quite possibly *inside* the planet."

He exhaled a sharp sigh.

"And the other forty percent?" he asked.

"No one's quite sure. That's the sixty percent we have data on. The *other* forty percent of tests and known incidents are never seen again," she concluded. "So, yeah. You saved everyone. Well done."

"Not me. I just plugged the orders in," Yildiz said quietly. "They wouldn't have gone anywhere without Klement."

"What did she do?" Lorraine asked. "I knew my detail's support section did damage control, but..."

"Apparently, while things were all being weird, Klement and her people installed localized overrides on all of the maneuvering thrusters," the bridge officer told Lorraine. "I think even *they* had forgotten they'd done it, until we lost the central controller.

"Then Klement realized that her overrides could still control the thrust units." He sighed heavily. "I figure they were there to turn the engines off, but apparently, the little toys *could* take full control. Getting everything linked took... well, almost too long."

"So... you took the ship through an emergency maneuver, above safety specifications for the thruster units, via a jury-rigged control node run through my Guard Detail's network and a set of emergency overrides meant to shut the ship down?" Lorraine asked, running through the sequence in her head.

There was a long silence, and Lorraine could see both Yildiz and the Chief at his side process that.

"I think so, yeah?" the Major finally said—as his Chief was looking at him with a new respect.

"I think that needs to go on your permanent record, Major," Lorraine told him. "Because I am *impressed*. That shouldn't have been possible, even if the overrides had the theoretical capability to control the thrusters."

If nothing else, it would have required aiming *each* of about sixty thrusters individually.

"I'm going to have to look up the regulations for field-expedient decorations, Major," Stephson agreed, the Captain stepping up beside Lorraine. "Because while I am not as intimately familiar with our navigation systems as you and the Pentarch, it sounds like you and Klement just pulled out all of the stops for us.

"Thank you."

THIRTY-NINE

Everyone on *Goldenrod*'s bridge—and, Lorraine suspected, the *rest* of the ship—breathed an audible sigh of relief when they jumped back into translight. Their dropout after Yildiz's emergency jump had been the absolute minimum interval, less than two minutes, but given that *Corsair* had arrived every *other* time they'd dropped out of FTL since leaving Ominira...

"Helm, are we good on the course to Bright Dream?" Stephson asked.

"Eighty-twenty rule," Yildiz said bluntly. "We're close *enough* that I can probably adjust it over the next six weeks. We'll be better if I can drop out and make a ten-minute calculation and adjustment at some point."

"What can you do two minutes at a time?" Savege asked from CIC.

"Not... much?" the Navigator said slowly, his tone confused.

Confusion was fair, in Lorraine's mind. No one on the bridge had stood down since before they'd entered San Ignacio.

"Because that looks like about what we're going to have," the XO said grimly. "We didn't see lightspeed data, but we got a ping on the tachyon receivers just before we jumped. CIC team is working on resolving, but it looks like *Corsair* dropped out about three light-seconds away just before we jumped."

A chill ran down Lorraine's spine. *Corsair* had a ten percent speed advantage, so she could have left several minutes later than *Goldenrod* and caught up to them, but the battlecruiser shouldn't have been able to track them *that* closely.

"How are they *doing* that?" Lorraine asked.

"I don't know," Stephson said grimly. "And once we can breathe, that will be a question we will need to investigate. For now, though..."

Goldenrod's commanding officer tapped a command and spoke to the entire crew.

"All hands, this is the Captain speaking," she said calmly. "We have reentered translight on our course to Bright Dream.

"I know we were all counting on being able to put real dirt under our feet and breathe on San Francisco, but it seems that our old friend Commodore Wray is *quite* determined that we don't get to rest anytime soon."

Stephson paused for a few moments.

"We will do what we must," she continued. "Today, that means a direct course to Bright Dream. Thankfully, that *also* means we no longer need to remain at battle stations. Bravo shift, remain on station. Alpha and Charlie shifts, unless you are assigned to class-one damage-control parties, stand down.

"I *suggest* you all rack out," she told them. "We may have time; we also have a lot of work to do. Some of it can't wait long, but most of it can at least wait for us to rest."

Another pause, then the Captain chuckled.

"And folks, while it may feel like we got kicked in a sensitive spot, let me remind you: we just got jumped by a *battlecruiser* at less than five thousand klicks and *lived*.

"I'm damn proud of you all."

The all-hands channel closed and Stephson surveyed her bridge crew.

"Same goes for you all," she told them. "Alpha and Charlie shifts, get off my bridge. Department officers, start checking in with your people and stations.

"You've twenty-four hours to pull together a full report on what works, what doesn't and what you need to turn the latter into the former. Get started."

LORRAINE DIDN'T HAVE a department or even a shuttle flight to run anymore. She still cleared off the bridge to let Stephson and her people work through what they needed to.

She took a copy of Yildiz's course and the sensor data with her, though. She wasn't going to undercut the Navigator, but quietly double-checking his work would make herself feel better and wasn't likely to hurt anyone.

But when she stepped into her quarters, leaving Alvarez behind with a nod, she found she couldn't bring herself to focus on the task she'd set herself.

She just... *stopped*. Magnetic soles kept her feet on the deck as she stared blankly at the walls—plaster over the steel bulkheads there, to provide the guest quarters with a touch more class than most of the ship.

Lorraine had promised the crew a break, a real chance to relax. She hadn't been sure they could afford the time, but she'd known they'd *needed* it. She'd run through the risks and the possibilities—but she'd never *truly* believed that Wray would go so far as to open fire on them once they were under the SIDF's protection.

Let alone fire on the SIDF itself. Alone without anyone watching, she pulled the full specifications on the *Santa Maria*–class cruisers.

CruRon Four wasn't the SIDF's best, but the *Santa Marias* were about as old as, say, *Goldenrod*. The San Ignacians had a newer class of cruisers, but the *Santa Maria*s appeared to be the current backbone of their fleet.

The SIDF didn't do the level of commerce protection and showing the flag as RKAN, which meant they were almost *entirely* a cruiser-and-battleship fleet, with a small number of destroyers and no frigates at all.

There were—or *had been*, at least—sixteen *Santa Maria*–class cruisers in the SIDF, making up roughly three-fifths of their cruiser strength. They were numerous enough and old enough that Lorraine's intelligence files had reasonably complete details on them.

Eighty-cee ships with a heavy missile armament focused on one-shot cell launchers. Despite their legs, they were clearly built to fight within hopping distance of their logistics base.

The number Lorraine *wanted* took some digging, but it was there: twelve hundred and eighty-six.

Each of the two ships that had died protecting *Goldenrod* had been crewed by twelve hundred and eighty-six human beings. Lorraine had seen the analyses for loss ratios in ships in assorted conditions, and *Navarra* and *Numancia* had been just about worst-case scenarios.

If even five hundred people had made it to safety out of those twenty-five hundred hands, she'd be stunned.

Lorraine knew there had to be deaths aboard *Goldenrod*. Those names hadn't been reported yet, but she knew they hadn't made it through the hits they'd taken without losses. She'd know those spacers individually, would attend their funerals.

She would never know who the officers and spacers who had died in San Ignacio were. Unless...

Her Royal Highness, Lorraine Alexis Elouise Nala Adamant, Second Pentarch of the Kingdom of Adamant, straightened on her magnetic boots and faced the consequences of her choices.

"They died for me," she said aloud. It wasn't *entirely* true—they'd died to protect their own people, recognizing that defending their neutrality was the only way to keep it—but that didn't change that at the moment, those two ships had been protecting her.

"I *will* know who they were," she promised herself and the air. "That's something I can find out, either on the way back home or afterward. I *will* know. They will be remembered."

It would take time before she could do anything about it—but even if everything failed and all she had left was the money from the Exodus Protocols, that would be enough for her to visit San Ignacio more anonymously and make certain the families were taken care of and the crews' names were remembered.

They hadn't fought *Corsair* to be remembered by a foreign Princess. Lorraine *knew* that. But what *she* owed them wasn't based on *why* they'd fought. Her debts were from their actions, not their reasons.

FORTY

Vigo had spent the day since they'd fled San Ignacio poking at a thought, a *concept*, that wouldn't go away. Following someone in translight was a complex, almost nightmarish task that effectively *required* a speed advantage—and would never have enabled the kind of precision arrival *Corsair* had now managed *three times*.

But that was because tachyon trails could only be picked up in regular space. He wasn't aware of any way they could be followed while the pursuing ship was also in translight space, but the worm in his brain sent him digging in to some of the deep archives that he generally regarded as pointless.

Why, exactly, did the Adamant Guard Detail attached to Lorraine need to be carrying a full backup of the Guard's classified intelligence files? Just the *presence* of those files, encrypted and on hard storage media as they were, was a security risk. There were pieces of information in the archives that he wasn't sure most of the Kingdom's *intelligence agencies* knew about.

As it turned out, the Exodus Protocol was at least part of the reason. They were on their own, heading farther and farther away from the Kingdom, with no ability to get updates or intelligence from home. Having the most complete—if not the most up-to-date—intelligence available might be critical.

And it meant that when he followed Lorraine into the staff meeting thirty-six hours after leaving San Ignacio, Vigo had some idea of *one* problem they faced. He just wasn't sure how it could exist in the first place... or how they were going to fix it.

"I know I'm pulling everyone away from a pile of work we still need to get through," Stephson said by way of introduction, "but we all need to be on the same page as to the status of our ship—and to make sure that the Pentarch knows everything about *Goldenrod* we do."

Lorraine's mask of calm was firmer than ever. Vigo had watched his charge refine the skills she'd already possessed over this hellish journey, rising to the challenge of being in charge of and responsible for the mission.

Stephson still commanded *Goldenrod*, no one doubted that, but more and more, Vigo suspected that the officers in that conference room, the frigate's key department heads, would follow Lorraine into hell.

Just as he would.

"Engines are probably the most important," Lorraine noted, glancing over at Cortez.

The Cheng didn't look like she'd slept. Her hair was visibly tangled, and while she'd clearly *tried*, there were visible smears of grease and ash on her face that her Spanish-descended coloring didn't conceal.

"We will *have* engines," Cortez said. "That's... a lot more than I could have promised twelve hours ago. We don't *currently* have them," she admitted, "but we *will* well before we reach Bright Dream."

She shrugged.

"Our emergency work to make sure nothing explodes or poisons us is done," she noted. "Right now, *all* of my engineering and damage-control people—except a critical systems watch—are unconscious or should be. We'll cycle back up to usual shifts over the next twenty-four hours and handle things in a steadier fashion, *without* fatigue-induced errors."

"How long?" Stephson and Lorraine asked in the same moment. Cortez chuckled at them.

"Replacing burnt-out fusion thruster linings isn't an exact science," she warned. "I'm eyeballing getting one primary engine back online a day for the next three days, then we'll move on to secondaries. Probably at about the same rate, so we'll have as much as we're getting in a week or so."

Vigo wasn't as intimately familiar with *Goldenrod* as the officers around him, but that still didn't sound quite right.

"Three primaries and four secondaries," Yildiz concluded, the Navigator the first to say it aloud. "That's... half the primary rockets and only a third of the secondaries."

"Might get one or two more secondaries," Cortez said. "But primaries two, five and six are done. The only value they're going to have for us at this point is gutting their internal assemblies for spare parts to fix the other three.

"Even a shipyard will have to tear them out and start again," the engineer concluded. "I can't even promise that the primaries we have left will stand up to full-power use. I won't have a hard recommendation on thrust limits until the work is done, but..."

"Three gravities at most," Stephson estimated, the Captain looking suddenly even more tired.

"Probably," Cortez agreed. "Might be higher. Probably won't be lower. Three is a good place to keep in mind."

That seemed to shake everyone in the room, but Lorraine leaned forward intently.

"We couldn't outrun *Corsair* even if we had our full engines," she pointed out. "We *need* to be smarter than them."

"Smarter won't help us much when she's faster, bigger and more heavily armed than we are," Savege pointed out. "*Corsair* was *designed* to run down frigates."

"If we give up, we have already lost," Lorraine replied. "We need to consider the options we *have*. Chevrolet, Paris. The shuttles and weapons?"

Of those two, only Paris seemed surprised to be called on, while the COSH smiled, like he'd been *waiting* for Lorraine to start asking sharp questions.

"The shuttle bay took some chain-reaction damage from internal overloads, but nothing major and nothing that damaged the shuttles," he told everyone. "Counting Charlie Flight, we have sixteen shuttles ready to deploy. We have the modules to rig every one of them as either a bomber or an interceptor."

Vigo blinked. That was news to *him*—he had no issue with integrating his Guard shuttles into the RKAN flights at this point, but his Third Section had come aboard with interceptor and personnel-transport modules.

He wasn't going to look a gift horse in the mouth, but *he* hadn't arranged for those extra four sets of bomb racks!

"*Goldenrod* herself is..." Paris hesitated, then shrugged. "Depending on the range, we've lost between a quarter and *half* of our offensive firepower. We're down two of six main beams and a quarter of the secondary defensive weapons.

"We've still got all four missile tubes, but we've only got eleven missiles in the cells and two-thirds of the empty cells are just gone. We got lucky in what cell launchers we lost—we only lost one loaded launcher—but even if we *could* load the four empties we have left, that would only give us fifteen birds.

"We've got fifty-one missiles left aboard and nine hundred–odd nukes to load them and the shuttles' bombs with, but we can't get enough shots in space to make *Corsair* blink."

"The shuttles can only carry a hundred and sixty bombs, total," Chevrolet admitted. "That's enough to give even *Corsair*'s targeting and defenses a real bad day. They may have designed her to take whatever a *Perennial* can throw at her, but *we* have more shuttles than they expect."

"They'll see that coming," Savege pointed out. "They'll see just about *anything* we can do coming. We could, I don't know, rig up the rest of the nukes as *mines* and it wouldn't matter—especially not if they keep dropping out right on top of us!"

The conference room was silent as they all chewed on that. The deep-space emergences hadn't been *quite* as close as San Ignacio had been—but they'd still been closer than they should have been.

"We need to think," Lorraine told everyone. "And I..." She swallowed. "I need to know who we lost."

Not, Vigo noted, *how many* we lost. *Who* we lost.

"Seven from Engineering, four Weapons, two from the admin team who were on DamCon," Stephson said instantly. "Another sixteen under Dr. Mackenzie's care."

There was a long silence before even *Stephson* caught up with the Pentarch's exact wording.

"I will forward you their names and files," the Captain promised. "Wounded and KIA alike."

"Thank you, Captain. I will stop by sickbay after this," Lorraine promised in turn.

There was a different tone to the silence now. It wasn't just the reminder of the losses, but Vigo also knew just how much Lorraine's gesture meant to even *these* officers.

Glancing over at where Senior Chief Roman was seated—at the Captain's left hand, silent throughout most of the meetings—he could see it in the Chief of the Boat's eyes. Even if someone *ordered* Roman to keep that part quiet, he wouldn't.

It would *matter* to the crew that Lorraine cared. And Vigo, at least, knew that Lorraine wasn't doing it to weld *Goldenrod*'s spacers to her.

"We've covered arms and engines," Lorraine said after a few more seconds of silence. "The rest?"

VIGO LISTENED to the list with everyone else. No one was really expecting an update from him—while Klement's Second Section had definitely been involved in damage control, they'd passed all of those reports up through Cortez.

Corsair would have needed to somehow board the frigate for him or Lieutenant Commander Zdravkov to have an important section of this meeting. They were both *present* along with the ship department heads, but the Marines had been in a similar position to the Guard.

Goldenrod had come away from her encounter with her pursuer intact, which was more than anyone would have expected. She was far from *undamaged* and too many key systems were irreparable in translight—or, like half of the primary fusion engines, just irreparable.

"For how close *Corsair* emerged, we got lucky," Stephson concluded once the run through was complete. "If Wray hadn't decided to focus on the SIDF cruisers, the fluke hit on our engines wouldn't have saved us."

"I *dislike* that our engines having a one-in-ten-thousand-chance cascade failure clearly saved our ship," Cortez said. "We have *multiple* controllers for the thrusters. Redundant plasma and control lines for *each* engine. That kind of cascade failure shouldn't happen."

"*Goldenrod* is too small," Savege told the Cheng, the XO sounding like this was an explanation she'd given before. "The *standard array* her engines are based on was built to simplify cruiser production—ten arrays per cruiser, so they had *twenty* primaries to our six.

"But a cruiser has the... well, the *rear end* to space them out," Savege continued with a weak chuckle at the near-unavoidable innuendo. "The *Perennial*s don't. The intervals inside the array are standard, but the arrays themselves are crammed together. If we could do a forensic analysis, I suspect what we'd see is that the cascade failure went from one array to the next and then *back* to the other engines in the original array."

Vigo didn't know enough about how the engines on the ship

worked to know if the XO was on to something. From the thoughtful look on Cortez and Stephson's faces, though, he figured Savege couldn't be too far off.

"That would make sense," the Cheng allowed. "How do *you* know that, XO?"

"Spent time pushing pencils for R and D," Savege told her. "Just after we lost *Viking*, there was a push to go over any and all possible flaws in our ships. The *Perennials'* drives came up. On the other hand, we'd already been pushing thirty ships to their limits and beyond for half a decade and it hadn't actually *happened.*"

"*Viking.*" Lorraine's echo of the single word drew everyone's attention and the Pentarch smiled thinly. "Not exactly RKAN's proudest moment, though I think it points out a sliver of hope for us.

"Fifth *Pirate*-class ship," she continued, clearly realizing that not everyone in the room knew enough details to follow her. "There were supposed to be six new battlecruisers, all eighty-eight-cee ships and the implicit deterrent to anyone deciding to hassle the Kingdom."

"Except that *Viking* had a critical translight failure coming back from her first training voyage," Stephson said grimly. "Exited translight in three pieces, two of which *exploded.*"

"Thankfully just a work-up crew, but even so... twelve hundred dead makes a lot of things move," Lorraine confirmed. "The last ship got canceled on the spot and our entire R and D and ship-design teams ordered to sort out just what had happened.

"They did and the four remaining ships got refitted." She shrugged. "Key interactions between translight and sublight systems had been miscalculated because our information on the eighty-eight drives we'd bought wasn't as complete as we thought. The vendor wanted to make sure we couldn't *duplicate* them, as opposed to cause failures, but the data was *just* enough off."

And because the error had been in how the ship interfaced with the translight drive, the Republic of Bright Dream corporation that had sold the Kingdom the drives had paid basically pennies and walked away.

If Wavetech BD had *just* been a Bright Dream corp, the Kingdom might have pushed it—but Vigo had seen the Guard's classified briefing on the affair when it happened. Wavetech BD was thirty percent owned by Dynastar Technologies, out of the United Worlds... and despite what the percentage looked like, *completely* controlled by the UW megacorp.

And the Kingdom couldn't afford to get on the wrong side of an Alpha Centauri–headquartered interstellar megacorp.

"My *point*, though, is that we can't think of *Corsair* as an invulnerable, unstoppable behemoth," Lorraine continued. "Wray doesn't have any magic weapons. *Corsair*'s missiles and beams are all things we understand. Yes, she's firing missiles with *four* independent warheads instead of our one, but they're still RKAN missiles.

"We know *Corsair* and her class are no more perfect than a *Perennial* like *Goldenrod*. We know more about her than she does about *Goldenrod*, frankly, because *Goldenrod* isn't a standard frigate of her class anymore."

"It doesn't help that they seem to keep doing the *impossible*," Paris muttered. "Following us is one thing, but to *keep* hitting the emergence zones like that..."

That was the cue Vigo had been waiting for, he supposed.

"I think I know how," he said quietly, the first thing *he'd* said in the entire meeting. "I'm going to need a *lot* of Commander Cortez's time to test the theory, though, and I don't think I'm going to like what we find."

He had everyone's attention now and he shrugged.

"The Adamant Guard has access to everyone's intelligence," he reminded them. "RKANI, RKAAMI, the Diplomatic Corps—and no, they don't even tell *us* who are diplomats and who are spies.

"Assuming there's actually a difference."

RKANI was Royal Kingdom of Adamant Navy Intelligence. RKAAMI was Royal Kingdom of Adamant Army Military Intelligence. Between those two organizations and the Diplomatic Corps, the Kingdom had a surprisingly in-depth level of intelligence on the rest of the Bright Dream Cluster... and beyond.

"But it's the Diplo Corps that gets us information out of the United Worlds," Vigo continued quietly. "And I went digging in that information to look up something I remembered. Took me most of the last day to find it, but I did."

"Find *what*?" Stephson asked sharply.

"The United Worlds Navy is decades ahead of everyone else in terms of tachyonic technologies," Vigo said. It wasn't even a reminder. It was just... the reality, but one key to the point.

"We acquired, though I have no idea how, some detailed information and abstracts on their experiments with a translight tachyon sensor system."

Lorraine's mask of calm was more solid than ever, but she slipped at that, inhaling a sharp hiss of breath that told Vigo *she* understood just how much of a qualitative leap that represented.

"Long story short: it sucks," he told the naval officers, watching them relax slightly. "We have the full conclusion of the experiments and testing, which was that it was a *valuable adjunct* to existing technologies but that its best value was reducing the dropouts necessary to maintain pursuit by fifty percent."

There wasn't much point in telling the others that the experiment, representing a technology light-years beyond anything the Kingdom had, had been almost twenty-five years earlier.

"But." He held up one finger. "They established one special-use case that required a *lot* of prep to make work. If the timing was basically *perfect* and effective real-space distance between hunter and prey was kept under a light-hour, the TTS would give the pursuing ship an exact moment of translight departure."

"So, you think *Corsair* has a TTS?" Lorraine asked carefully.

Vigo knew that tone. She could tell he hadn't explained everything yet and was prodding the key point.

"I don't know *how*," he admitted. "Frankly, I can't begin to think of a situation where the Kingdom would have a translight scanner and we'd put it in the Ominira Station squadron. Plus, I would expect that the possession of such a system would be *somewhere* in my files."

"So, Commodore Wray has a scanner that RKAN doesn't know about," Stephson said slowly. "That explains why *he* is the one pursuing us. Not just the scanner but the level of trust on the part of the Black Regent required to *give* it to him."

"We have already seen that Commodore Wray will go far beyond what we thought was reasonable or sane," Lorraine added. "The question of how my uncle might have even *acquired* such a thing is concerning, but you said *prep* was required, Vigo?"

"The major reason the UWN figured that wasn't an ability they could make use of was the timing," Vigo told them. "*One light-hour,* people. On ships traveling at eighty times the speed of light in our case.

"That would require *Corsair* to project our course with enough precision to get within that distance of us with enough warning to enter translight inside a forty-five-second window."

Vigo suspected the *actual* window would be much, *much* shorter.

"More than anything else," he continued, "in that scenario, *Corsair* would have matched our arrival far more closely every time instead of consistently being some minutes behind us."

"You have an idea of what is actually happening, don't you?" Cortez asked. "And it has something to do with *this* ship, doesn't it?"

"The TTS in itself wouldn't let him catch our emergences quite that closely," he confirmed. "Not without them being a *lot* closer than it seems like they're getting.

"But." He held up a second finger. "The UWN *also* discovered that the tachyon trail visible from translight is *different* from the tachyon trail visible in sublight. More unique, in some ways, to an individual ship.

"And in their experiments, they discovered that a ship's translight drive could be tuned to augment that signature. Dramatically." He sighed. "To about six light-hours, when combined with the TTS system.

"Enough of a range to make using that level of detailed pursuit *practical*—and give them even more detailed information on the target ship. Enough, given a number of nearby planetary and stellar masses to use as reference points, to nail the translight emergence location down within a few thousand kilometers."

The room was silent, a frozen chill seeping through mind and bones alike.

"We went in for a standard overhaul refit alongside the work for the Pentarch's quarters and the Guard shuttles," Cortez said quietly. "Engineering crew is usually aboard for most of that, but there was a point where I was told everyone was getting two weeks' furlough to allow for some classified systems to be installed for the Guard.

"We found a few things we probably weren't supposed to," she said with a chuckle and a glance at Vigo, "but not enough to really justify two whole weeks. I figured it was just the Guard being... well, the Guard."

"There were definitely systems and pieces installed that we didn't want the Engineering crew to see put in," Vigo confirmed. "I don't think anyone was ever so foolish as to think the Engineering Chiefs weren't going to find them all within a week, but the *installation* of some of that gear is messy enough to keep some secrets on its own.

"I don't recall that being two weeks, but I only signed off on what was being installed and sent a security detail to watch things," he admitted.

"Could they have done the tuning you're talking about in that kind of time?" Stephson asked.

"I... have honestly told you all as much as I really know," he admitted. "Cortez and I will need to go through the experiment data we have from the UWN together and see if we can find a way to find the tuning while in translight."

He wasn't sure they'd be able to *fix* it, but if they knew it was there... well, Vigo wasn't sure what that would give them, but it was better than not knowing.

"We all need to take some time to go through things," Lorraine said. "We get the ship fixed and we go through our options. Find new options. Like... can we fab more missiles and mines?"

Cortez shrugged.

"Easy. We only have the warheads we have, but we've got a stock of raw materials and key molycirc blocks I can turn into anything we need."

"We don't *have* any mines," Paris said. "They're not really a weapon our doctrine calls for. They're... quite visible when we drop them if someone has eyes on us."

"Difference between a mine and a shuttle bomb is, what, ten seconds of drive time and a sensor package?" Chevrolet asked. "Bomber tactics might help, if we look at them that way. Not a bad thing to throw around a simulator."

"We're going to be throwing a lot of ideas around simulators," Lorraine told them. "Because no one is wrong when they say we're on the wrong side of a power imbalance here.

"But we're not going to be able to *outrun* our good friend Wray. Not with our drives damaged. So, either we find a way to actually *fight* her... or we find a way to slow her down."

The Pentarch smiled, a chill to it that made Vigo shiver. It wasn't aimed at him or anyone else aboard *Goldenrod*, thankfully, but every so often Lorraine reminded him of her mother.

"We have forty-seven days," she reminded them. "And some of the smartest damn brains in the Kingdom.

"Let's find ourselves an answer, shall we?"

FORTY-ONE

Eight days to fix the engines and another week to go through the translight drives very, *very* carefully. All of it ended up with Vigo and Cortez standing in her office, studying the carefully assembled model of the exotic-matter arrays and the practically uncountable molycirc relays that managed them.

The engineer growled in the back of her throat.

"I have read over that damn experiment you gave me nineteen times," she admitted. "*Nineteen. Fucking. Times.* I'm still not one hundred percent sure I understand how this 'tuning' of yours works."

"If it helps, Cheng, I am one hundred percent certain you understand it better than I do," Vigo told her. "The only thing I think I understand is what it would allow *Corsair* to do. As far as this goes"— he gestured at the holographic model of their engine— "I am only really sure of one thing."

"And that is?" she asked. It wasn't a challenge, though Vigo was certain she'd seen everything he'd seen and a few hundred things beside.

"That this doesn't match the model that lives in *Goldenrod's* computers," he told her. "Nothing *huge*, but enough that there has to be a hidden mapping sequence somewhere for the control software that's hiding the changes."

"Yeah," she grunted. "I'd say we *should* have seen it, but..." She stepped *into* the hologram, tapping several of the sections that Vigo had been eyeing.

"These are the sections with the largest changes, and they're in places we rarely access with humans," she told him. "I'd have to check, but I'd take a solid bet that we haven't sent bodies into those sectors since the refit."

"I thought we'd surveyed every part of the ship," Vigo said. If they'd missed *this*...

"We have," she confirmed. "These sections would have been surveyed with drones under direct control—but we would be navigating those based on the map and model in the system. If the changes were masked enough for us to have missed them this far, the drones would have *automatically* adapted our orders to the real map.

"And because we were looking for threats, not vanes with a three-point-six-degree variance in recorded alignment, we wouldn't have noticed." Cortez sighed.

"Every time I think I can trust my own ship, I realize I didn't look deep enough. Now that I *know* this mask exists, I'm confident we can kill it with a couple of shifts' work, but it hid this from us."

Standing in the middle of the holographic model, light reflected off the tiny bits of sweat left on Cortez's skin in a way that caught Vigo's eyes for a few heartbeats. The engineer was taller than him, he noted absently, though lacking his own breadth and bulk.

He mentally shook himself as she looked back at him. He was *damn* tired if he was getting distracted by the Chief Engineer's skin.

"Beyond it being *different* than what it should be, which is enough to guess at the problem, what are you seeing?" he asked.

"Well, first, that I'm going to give my systems specialists a headache for the next week, because we are going to be going through our engineering software module by module, if not line by *fucking* line," she told him. "If there's one masking module in there to hide parts of our own system from us, I'm betting there's more.

"As for this, though..." She stepped out of the hologram and turned to examine the entire structure. "I need to run some numbers but, ironically, I think this configuration is actually more energy-efficient. We've been running under expected consumption in translight since the refit but not by enough to be out of normal variance. That we were *consistently* under meant I was starting to keep an eye on it, but I hadn't seen anything to *cause* it.

"Because, as it turns out, I was only looking at about half my actual drive most of the time." She growled.

"And the tracking possibility?" Vigo prodded.

"I can't be certain," Cortez admitted. "I can tell you that this configuration still works. Like I said, I can tell you that it appears to be more energy-efficient—and once I run the numbers, I may even be able to pull out enough of *why* to duplicate that in another ship! I can tell you that the adjusted structure and angles appear to be doing something *specific*.

"But confirming that it's somehow sending out a trail of marker tachyons that allow *Corsair* to track us? I..."

Vigo knew that pause. He hadn't heard it from Rose Cortez before, but he'd known too many engineers and scientists and generally *very smart people* not to recognize a moment of epiphany.

He waited.

"How are you at complex tachyon modeling?" the Chief Engineer asked him.

"I can hand you coffee and be a rubber duck," he admitted. "If you need someone to meet you out past lightspeed and talk numbers? You need the Pentarch."

The look she gave him somehow made him *very* aware of how warm and charming her brown eyes were, but he focused on the moment and her grin.

"That's right. She did the full nine yards heading up the Helm track, didn't she? So, not just a master's in tachyonic physics, but a *recent* one.

"I know Engineering has to be questionable from a security perspective right now, but you're right. I need her."

"We'll make it work," Vigo promised.

IT TOOK Lorraine less than ten minutes to shut down whatever she was doing and reach Engineering. Given that reaching Engineering from the guest quarters was easily a five-minute brisk walk, Vigo suspected she had leapt at any distraction.

Four Guards, led by Corporal Palmer, fanned out behind her. At a silent command from Vigo, they did a quick sweep of Cortez's office and then took up position outside.

"Major Jarret said you needed physics backup?" Lorraine asked, having waited patiently for her security to finish their job.

"We've built a new model of our translight drive based on direct scans," Cortez explained, restoring and expanding the hologram with a gesture. "Long story short, work was *definitely* done in our last refit that the computers were set up to hide from us.

"I'm starting to feed the information into the physics software I have, but while I can dedicate enough of *Goldenrod*'s computing power to this to make it *happen*, I want to make sure I'm looking at the right things."

Vigo made sure he was out of the way, doing the zero-gravity equivalent of leaning against the wall as he listened to two very smart women lay out the situation.

"We know that the UWN talked about tuning a ship's drive, but we don't know what that means," Lorraine murmured. "You want to pin down the key mechanism?"

"Exactly. If I know what we're *doing* that makes us traceable, I can disable it."

"Or manipulate it," the Pentarch suggested. "What are you thinking?"

"We know, in theory, that there's a whole set of properties that tachyons only possess while faster than light," the engineer told her. "When gravity pulls them out of that existence, we only get a relatively short blip of data and many of those properties are lost.

"Identifying a ship or estimating emergence points from what we see of the tachyon trail sublight is impossible. But if the UWN—and *Corsair*, it seems—are able to analyze tachyons *while they're still true tachyons...*"

"They can see all of those properties and details we don't normally," Lorraine finished. "Which would be part of why they need a *translight* tachyon scanner for the kind of pursuit and accuracy we're seeing."

"I *think*, if I can get the model set up correctly, I can calculate what kind of signature the modified drive is creating," Cortez said.

"And once we know what the drive could be creating, we have a better idea of what they're tracking. And how to block or fool it," Lorraine said. "Okay. What suite are you running for physics modeling?"

"RKAN standard: Theophysicist Twenty-Seven-Point-Four."

Vigo swallowed a chuckle. Betrayal, direct attacks, facing pursuit by a far superior ship, even *being directly under attack...* None of these had broken the shield of calm his Pentarch had mastered.

The name of the program Cortez was trying to use to model a tailored tachyon signature? *That* got a clear expression of disgust and concern.

"Okay," Lorraine said slowly. "So, *first* step is to send a runner back to my quarters and bring us my copy of AstroSynthesis Twenty-Five-Thirty.

"Because I don't think Theophysicist is going to handle something none of its coders predicted. AstroSynthesis has a much solider underlying model for projecting new things from old data.

"I promise!"

FORTY-TWO

Physics didn't lie. It didn't betray. It didn't spend your entire life being your favorite uncle, then murder your entire family and send people to kill you, specifically.

Most of Lorraine's practical work through her master's degree had been focused on tachyonic phenomena—things that a ship under translight could encounter—and how to avoid them. There were echoes of those oddities in the work they were doing.

"I think..." She trailed off, staring at the most recent round of data from their modeling suite.

"Your Highness?" Cortez asked carefully.

"Please, call me Lorraine," she replied absently, tracing a pattern in the data with a finger.

"If... you say so, Lorraine," the engineer said. "But you didn't finish the thought."

"Sorry, I'm staring at an old memory in a new context," Lorraine replied. "I worked on translight weather avoidance, basically, for my thesis. There were a couple of items that stood out in my testing, that I actually signed over to my thesis supervisor for *her* to investigate more deeply.

"Looking at this? I suspect *those* oddities might be the key to how the translight scanner works."

Because to avoid tachyonic phenomena, the "weather" of faster-than-light travel, they'd needed to *see* it. Lorraine had been one of six students—four of them naval officers, two civilians—with three civilian supervisors. All of them had been working on different aspects of the problem, prodding the edges of Adamant's understanding of tachyons as they found tools to predict and mitigate the risks.

Lorraine knew their work had turned into a sensor system that could measure, for lack of a better metaphor, the *atmospheric pressure* of a region of tachyons while inside it. It had just started testing when the coup started.

"You think we might have built one of our *own*?" Cortez asked.

"No," Lorraine said slowly. Wouldn't that have been a bitter irony? Her own research work the year before she'd arrived on *Goldenrod* used to track the ship and hunt her. "All of that was my final college work before I made Lieutenant Commander. I reported aboard *Goldenrod* within a few weeks of getting the final papers.

"All of this"—she waved at the modified translight drive and her model of its tachyon output—"was done *while I was doing that research*."

Cortez winced at Lorraine's tone, and the Pentarch inhaled, forcing herself back to her calm.

"Eighteen months ago now," she said, her tone more level. "*Fifteen* before the coup. *Fifteen months* before all of this, my uncle laid a trap to be sure I wouldn't escape."

It was hard enough to handle that her favorite uncle—technically her *only* uncle, though there had been half a dozen men of House Adamant she'd called that as she grew up—had betrayed her and her family.

But that he'd set all of it in motion *that* long before?

"You've got some idea what you're looking at, then?" Cortez

asked after a long pause, unable or unwilling to engage with the younger woman's grief and anger.

"Yeah." Lorraine closed her eyes for a moment, seeking her center more solidly before she tapped on the display.

"I ran this a second time to be sure," she noted. "Because I'd seen the pattern in our experiments. We weren't generating it, but we were studying all kinds of phenomena in models and lab environments.

"The drive itself leaks tachyons, always has," she continued. "We *know* that. It's a necessary balance feature of maintaining the ship as faux-tachyonic matter. Other than keeping an eye on it as a power-bleed issue, we don't pay too much attention to it because we can't *do* much about it.

"But this arrangement isn't just leaking ordinary waste tachyons. We figured, of course, but..."

"Aligned tachyons. Practically *braided*," Cortez said, looking at the simulation.

"I think it's the sequencing—the *braid*, as you said—that will stand out the most," Lorraine observed. "A stream of aligned tachyons might be a fluke. A long-enough one will draw attention, but I think producing a constant stream of aligned tachyons would have required a full rebuild of the drive.

"But having a sequence of specific alignments—a *repeating* sequence, based on the model we're running... If they have any way to read the tachyons while translight, it will stick out like a sore thumb."

The Chief Engineer looked over Lorraine's data and nodded slowly.

"So, now we can see what trail we're leaving," she noted. "Any idea how to *fix* it?"

Lorraine chuckled grimly and gestured at the hologram still hanging in the middle of Cortez's office, the one showing the layout of their translight drive with all its many and esoteric pieces.

"I know tachyonic physics and the way the universe *works* once everything is varieties of tachyons," she said. "And I know how to *fly* a ship in translight. But fixing and modifying a translight drive? I think, Cheng Cortez, that one is your specialty."

Commander Cortez nodded grimly and glanced from one display to the other.

"I was afraid you would say that," she conceded. "Well, we now know *what* the hardware is doing. Shouldn't be too hard for the engineer to work out *how*, right?"

FORTY-THREE

Throwing herself across the room into her bed was a *far* more difficult act in microgravity. It was also a rather pointless one, Lorraine knew, since she couldn't *sleep* in the regular bed—its mattress was still present, but the hammock hung above it was easier to use in zero gee —and there was no one to see her melodrama.

She'd thought. But about twenty seconds after she hit the mattress, there was a knock on her bedroom door—which meant that Vigo had probably been about to come in when she'd done her belly flop.

If he'd been watching link sync closely enough to know to enter the suite and knock on the bedroom door, he'd probably seen her frustrated self-launch.

"You may as well come in," she said, one hand on the bed allowing her to position herself to meet her bodyguard's gaze as he stepped in.

"In terms of acrobatics and skill in micrograv maneuvering, at least four out of five," he told her. "Melodrama points... *teenager* out of five."

Moments like that were when Lorraine wished she'd been

slightly less cultured to never swear. It was *undiplomatic*, her mother had told her. Code switching to match the vernacular of a group was often necessary, but there were habits it was wise to not get into.

"Are you just here to grade my frustration or is something up?" she finally asked.

"Mostly, I wanted to check in and see what you and Cortez worked up," her bodyguard said. "I'm guessing..."

"Nothing good." She stopped after that, taking a moment to breathe and calm down. "We now know what was done to *Goldenrod* to let us be tracked in translight. Your guess was bang-on; well done.

"But *knowing* doesn't help us that much."

"If Cortez knows what was done, can't she undo it?"

Lorraine knew Vigo knew better. But she also figured he *had* to ask.

"Ninety-six hours with the drive offline, give or take," she told him. "We *can* do it. But not in a time period that's going to help us. And it's pretty clear that the tuning you were worried about *was* done, so we can assume that *Corsair* has a TTS. Wray will pull the same damn move on us he pulled in San Ignacio, and the wormhole doesn't have secured emergence zones the same way."

A wormhole had a *massive* stability impact on the surrounding space, rendering translight travel impossible within about five light-seconds in any direction. As some people would come from Bright Dream and others would come from any star system nearby, there would be dozens of potential arrival vectors, all of them a long way from the actual wormhole itself.

Where San Ignacio set specific zones and guarded them, those zones were only a few hundred thousand kilometers from the planet. Heading to the arrival zones didn't really cost anyone much.

A similar zone at a wormhole would be badly off course for a lot of people. Even more than that, though, there was a question of *sovereignty*. There were no arguments about who owned local space around an inhabited planet and who had authority over it.

There were ongoing legal arguments and claims in various interstellar international venues that because a wormhole was easily *associated* with a star system, the owner of that system didn't *own* it in the same way as they'd own a planet.

No one was going to go quite far enough to attempt to transit a wormhole without paying the fees to do so—the Republic might not have the fleet to secure a ten-light-second sphere, but their forces at the wormhole could stop someone getting through! But enforcing arrival zones... That was harder.

Especially when the Republic of Bright Dream *needed* the revenue from those transit fees—and there was always at least one United Worlds warship in place to remind everyone of the UWN's commitment to *freedom of navigation.*

"Leaving us with nobody else to rely on and a battlecruiser on our tail," Vigo concluded. "Fuck."

"Yeah." Lorraine stared blankly at the wall. They still had three weeks left of this journey, but for all her insistence to the ship's officers, she wasn't seeing a way out.

"I..." She paused, then sighed. "I don't think I can even *surrender* fast enough to save the ship, Vigo," she told him. "The situation is sufficiently tilted against us that I have to consider it, but I don't think Wray is going to be listening when he drops out."

"No," Vigo agreed. "Like in San Ignacio, he's going to drop out and start shooting."

"We got lucky once. It's not going to happen again," Lorraine said. "I can't ask everyone on this ship to die *pointlessly*, but I don't even see a way for us to *give in.*"

There was a long silence.

"Your family doesn't give in."

It wasn't a judgment. That was the part that actually surprised her. She'd expected the words, but she'd expected them to be a push, a judgment—a call for her to do something *more.*

Instead, it was just a calm statement of fact. That Vigo Jarret, at least, didn't believe Lorraine was giving in. That *he* knew she wasn't actually giving up.

"If I saw one damn way out of this mess, Vigo, I'd be planning toward it," she told him. "But the one part of space travel where we *can't* be seen and tracked, my uncle's people have found a way around. The laws and rules that I might count on to keep other people safe, Wray has already demonstrated a reckless willingness to breach.

"Thousands of people died in San Ignacio to get us out, as damaged as we are. We can't even *keep the range open*. We don't know what our final acceleration will be, but Cortez is still figuring around three gees. Won't *know* until we fire the engines up for real."

"Giving *Corsair* four gravities on us."

"Exactly. They've got more and bigger... *everything*. More missiles. More beams. More shuttles. A better energy screen." She shook her head, glaring at the stupid plastered-over bulkhead. The false veneer of her quarters bothered her for reasons she couldn't quite put her finger on.

"I think it's an easily conceded point that we can't fight the *hardware* Commodore Wray has," her bodyguard said slowly. "Maybe you need to stop thinking about his advantages and start looking at his disadvantages?"

Lorraine snorted.

"You sound like my uncle, actually," she told him. "*Be where the enemy isn't.* Always harping on about how deception isn't about the tech or even the illusion you're portraying; it's about what's going on in your enemy's head."

"Benjamin Adamant might be our enemy now, but don't forget that he is probably the best fleet commander the Kingdom of Adamant has produced in three generations," Vigo pointed out. "You could do worse for a guiding light than thinking about what he has told you.

"If nothing else, we know that Wray was one of his protégés."

"Protégé of a protégé, I think, but fair. And he's probably at least *trying* to think like my uncle," Lorraine conceded. She locked a magnetic sole onto the deck and lifted herself away from the bed with a grunt.

"You're right," she told Vigo. "I'm not giving up, not yet. I don't see the way forward yet, either, but that doesn't mean it isn't there.

"I think I might even know where to start," she concluded as a thought struck her.

"Can I help?" he asked. "My job might be to keep you alive, Lorraine, but the only way any of us are getting out of this is if *someone* has a brilliant idea."

Lorraine gave her bodyguard a long look, not-quite-glaring at the man who had lived in her back pocket for twenty-three years and knew her every flaw, every vice, every weakness... and *still* believed she could do this.

Everything else could go burn in a star. She wasn't going to die. She wasn't going to fail her family... and she wasn't going to fail Vigo Jarret.

"I don't remember, actually," she admitted. "How are you at chess?"

FORTY-FOUR

"I used to win city competitions," Vigo complained several hours later, watching as the black bishop moved into the gap he hadn't realized he was opening. He studied the board. He'd seen *one* checkmate coming, and the move he'd just made had been about to turn the gambit back on his opponent.

Instead, he'd opened up his king to...

"That's checkmate. I don't know about this matching your *uncle*, but it's reminding me of the time I played with your *mother*."

He wasn't even playing Lorraine. In some ways, that might have been *better*. Lorraine walking all over him at a game of strategy was a good thing, something he could attach value to in several ways.

But he was playing against a chess-bot, a learning algorithm that Lorraine was feeding every game she'd ever played with Benjamin Adamant. His error, he saw, was a pretty classic one for humans playing against computers, too.

A computer knew the status and possible moves of every piece on the board. It would never make a mistake like the one he'd just made. The best chess players did the same, he knew... but while he'd won competitions as a *teenager*, he knew he'd never quite made that level. And his teenage years were long past, too.

"When did you play chess with Mom?" Lorraine asked, looking up from the console. This was the tenth game Vigo had played with the bot she was working on—and he'd won *one*.

"Don't you remember?" Vigo teased gently. "You were there. Of course, you were five."

He chuckled at her dirty look—and treasured it, too. Despite everything, she was still mostly unguarded with him. Her masks and self-control were hugely valuable to the man tasked to keep her alive, but it was still precious to him that she would be herself with him.

If nothing else, he knew all too well how dangerous it could be for someone to wear masks all the time and forget who *they* were.

"It was part of my interview to become head of your detail," he told her. "The Guard put me through two *weeks* of grueling physical and mental examinations and tests. Then they passed me on to your parents.

"I went golfing with your father. Played chess with your mother. Attended a state banquet as part of your mother's Guard, for *her* detail commander to assess me."

He chuckled.

"Beat your dad at golf, by luck basically. Lost to your mom at chess—*painfully*. Mate in nine moves. I'd never been beaten so quickly in my *life*. I knew I was rusty, but that was a shocker."

Vigo thought back to the moment and Valeriya's handling of the situation.

"Looking back, I think that's what she was going for," he realized aloud. "It wasn't about how I played chess. It was about how I handled getting *trounced* at something I thought I was decent at. I suspect if I'd been focused on something else as a teen, she would have found a way to create a similar scenario—but since I'd been city chess champion as a kid, Valeriya took it on herself to school me."

Lorraine looked thoughtful.

"Figure my dad let you win, too," she said after a moment. "Testing how you handled a slim victory and an unexpected crushing defeat—two points where humans can get pretty weird."

Vigo hadn't even followed the thought to that point, but he nodded slowly as he studied the holographic chessboard in front of him.

"Funny," he admitted. "That's literally something *I've* done when assessing people for Archangel Detail, but I missed it being done to me. Your parents ar... were *good*."

"Everyone tells me they single-handedly prevented war between the Kingdom and Concordat, turning one-time rivals into close allies —then followed that up by convincing the Directorate to back down from one near-war before leading the Kingdom through the war they *did* launch during Mom's reign," Lorraine said quietly. "While growing the national economy and keeping the interstellar megacorps out."

She chuckled, and Vigo could hear the irony in it.

"For some reason, very few people ever talked my parents down around me. From some of what Daniel said... the people who wanted to make things *change* after Mom's reign focused on him and Taura."

Vigo knew that there *were* people who thought Valeriya had been, if not a failure per se, a drag on the Kingdom. No one could argue that her carefully measured support of the military had delivered a fleet and army that had defeated the Richelieu Directorate *without* breaking the economy in peacetime.

But even the most measured approach left some people behind. He knew that Valeriya had judged her success by how much the state of the Kingdom's *poorest* had improved, but there were *always* people who lost ground. The poorest might be better off than they had been, but the people who through bad luck or poor choices *joined* those ranks wouldn't see that.

Yet... as leader of a Pentarch's Adamant Guard Detail, he'd had access to the most-classified intelligence briefings on internal threats to the Kingdom and the Pentarchy. It was, in his opinion and study of history, rarely the poor who started trouble. They were usually too busy *surviving*.

When the poor became trouble, either society had *truly* failed... or someone else was weaponizing them. Guns and propaganda didn't come from nowhere, after all.

Even more than it left people behind, a measured approach found itself with people who were *convinced* they should be further ahead. And the dangerous elements of *both* groups were the ones who were absolutely convinced that their current situation was entirely someone else's fault.

"A lot of people would rather follow their own desires than work for a shared good," Vigo said slowly. "To be grotesquely rich in a broken system rather than merely fabulously rich in a functional one. We have *lists*."

"I know. I'm not supposed to see them," Lorraine said drily. "It is the... *opinion* of the Crown that we must judge people for their actions, not their desires. So long as no one is actively selling out the Kingdom or actively trying to undermine our anti-colonial measures, we smile and play nice—and it's easier to do that if we don't know."

"There are people I would warn you about if I thought they were getting into your head," he noted. "Some of them spent a good while working on your brother."

"And I suspect I know who you mean," she agreed. "It's very easy to see the cash we'd get from letting the interstellars in. As we get closer to Bright Dream, though..."

She shrugged.

"There's a *reason* we have the anti-colonial laws we have," she concluded. "And it's Bright Dream."

Vigo knew what she meant. The Bright Dream Cluster had, until the Sol-Greenhall Wormhole opened, been of minimal interest to the United Worlds interstellar megacorporations. A year or more travel time from Sol to Tavastar had kept their stars of less interest than many first-order clusters and even some *second*-order clusters.

But the Republic of Bright Dream itself, just on the other side of the wormhole, had still been of interest. The interstellars hadn't dug their claws in deeply, but it had been clear for years that the Republic was beholden to powers on the other side of the wormhole.

The Greenhall Wormhole had accelerated that process. Now agents of the interstellars were cutting deals across the Cluster—and they'd collided with laws in the Kingdom that required minimum citizen ownership of operating entities.

There were other laws in place to limit external control of the Adamantine economy, but that was the most basic. For a corporation to own assets and conduct business in the Kingdom of Adamant, at least sixty percent of the corporate entity had to be owned by citizens of the Kingdom at no more than one degree of separation.

Both the interstellar megacorps and the kind of people who'd end up running their local subsidiaries found that restriction unreasonable—though Lorraine's understanding was that it was relatively common.

The interstellars had made their own bed, forging a reputation of banally extractive evil that went well ahead of them. But there were always those that felt they'd succeed in that system—or just felt that it was a moral wrong to prevent business from being done.

"Keep that in mind," Vigo warned her. "The Republic, for its failures and sins, has kept a measure of self-control by playing the interstellars off against each other—but *none* of their sponsors like your family."

"I know." Lorraine turned back to her console, making some more adjustments he couldn't see. "Worries me about the whole mission. We're hoping to lean on the United Worlds Stability Convention, but... I worry that the interstellars' setting up shop to get cheap goods for back home represents a more-honest face of the United Worlds."

Vigo wasn't sure how to answer that. He didn't think she was *wrong*, but at the same time...

"The realities of how a nation runs are rarely wholly in agreement with its ideals," he finally told her. "We know that. But that doesn't mean those ideals are forgotten or irrelevant.

"We can't ask the interstellars for help; we know that!" The worst part, to Vigo's mind, was that the big corps probably *would* help—but the price would be too high.

"But asking the Grand Assembly, the elected leaders of the United Worlds, to live up to their ideals? Challenging them to rise above the day-to-day and live up to what they swear by?"

He shrugged.

"It might not work," he admitted. "But you knew that going to the furthest extreme of the Exodus Protocol was a risk. High risk, high reward."

"Trying to put together penny packets of allies in the Cluster was a nonstarter," Lorraine told him. "And that was *before* we had a battlecruiser on our tail. The only option is to return home with over-whelming force, to avoid a fight by making it obvious Benjamin can't win.

"But first, we need to find a way around *Corsair*." She tapped a command and the holographic chessboard reset.

"One more time. I think I've got my uncle's strategy as mapped as I'm going to, so let's give it a final whirl."

"What's the point of all of this?" Vigo asked. "Playing chess against a simulacrum of your uncle? I can... sort of see using it as a basis for a simulation for tactical exercises, but..."

"It's one tool," Lorraine told him. "*Building* the tool has helped me understand some of what I need to know. Playing against it, once it's done, will help me think, help me go through those lessons of his you mentioned.

"A real-world tactical simulator isn't going to be much use. All that will tell me is how badly we're outclassed. If we're going to win, we need to come at Commodore Wray *sideways*.

"And that, Vigo, means I need to be thinking sideways before I even look at our actual weapons. So. Chess against a simulation of the best player I ever knew."

Vigo wasn't entirely sure he understood... but he *did* know that he was out of ideas for dealing with the battlecruiser. If Lorraine's sideways approach worked for her, it might help her find a chance.

So, he focused on the game and tried to plan how not to lose *this* time.

FORTY-FIVE

One of the keys with programming a simulation of a chess player was establishing how much to handicap the computer underneath it. Lorraine had access to copies of algorithms that would play a perfect game of chess every time, matching every move even a grandmaster made. Against code like that, few humans could even manage a *draw*, which made it... less than useful for simulating a human opponent.

The three games Lorraine played against the bot once she figured it was done felt *right*, in a way Vigo wouldn't have been able to judge. She'd watched her bodyguard take the sim on and used his play as a barometer, but she couldn't code the program and play against it at the same time.

The simulation was sneakier than a pure optimization program would be. That was how her uncle played, after all, but that *could* be a weakness. She'd *almost* caught its trick on the third game.

Well, truthfully, she *had* caught the trick. About one move too late.

Teaching a simple algorithmic program like this, which didn't even qualify as a full agent, let alone a synthetic intelligence, to *trick* people was always a challenge. It could only do so in chess, of course —it was simple enough that it could only do *anything* in chess.

She booted up a fourth game but, after a moment's thought, loaded her Profound Azure program as the second player instead of herself. A pocket-sized evolution of the computers that trained and beat chess grandmasters, Profound Azure was the type that made no mistakes and played a perfect game every time.

Her uncle had claimed that PA was a middling example of the type—and proved it by reliably checkmating the code when she'd asked him to. Even so, it should be more than a match for the simulation she'd set up.

It, after all, wasn't actually her uncle, and its need to play the trickery game the way he would limited it.

Three games unfolded in front of her in about ten minutes. The first one was what she was expecting. The technically competent Profund Azure bot played perfectly, negating the simulated Benjamin Adamant's trick by ignoring the attempt to divert its attention. Checkmate.

The second game was closer to what she'd have expected from her uncle playing the bot. The trickery that could be used against a computer was different from what worked on a human. It *relied* on your opponent having a full, always-correct catalog of pieces and possible movements. Against a human, you could play games with the focus of even the best players.

Against a computer, you couldn't do that. But you could still *bluff*, by creating a situation where the computer would project movements that could be a threat while you had no intention of taking those moves.

The Profund Azure bot still played a technically perfect game, though, so all that bluffing managed was a stalemate.

The third game, though... Lorraine didn't spot the chess-bot's error immediately. She realized it had moved its knight exactly how the simulation of her uncle needed when the program took an unusually reckless move to try to cover the gap it had created—two moves later and at least one move too late.

Even the perfection of a machine couldn't recover from the misstep the simulation had led it into.

Lorraine had expected the bot of her uncle's playstyle to stalemate Profund Azure at best, not *win*, and she looked at the checkmate very, *very* carefully.

Nothing had gone wrong in Profund Azure's code. Even the misstep had, from almost any perspective, been the correct move. It had been in answer to what had *looked* like an error.

She swallowed.

"The metaphor seems dangerously obvious, doesn't it?" she asked the air.

Profund Azure—powerful, capable, making few mistakes and capable of recovering from them—was the battlecruiser. If Lorraine and *Goldenrod* played by the usual rules and the logical best strategies, Wray and *Corsair* would run right over them.

If they tried to do something clever, it was more likely to fail them than anything else—that was the lesson of the first game between the two chess-bots.

What they needed to do was make *Corsair* do something clever and turn *that* into a misstep on their part. Only once *Corsair*'s crew was off-balance would they have the room to maneuver that might work.

She needed more information—all of which she'd asked for and should be ready.

She needed to know everything about *Goldenrod*'s weapons and even *possible* weapons.

And she needed to know everything about the translight tachyon scanner.

SPECIFICATIONS FLOWED through the air around Lorraine. On the one side of her, everything about *Goldenrod*. Her armaments. Her defenses. Her engines. Her damage. Most important of all, though, were her *fabricators*.

In a worst-case scenario, *Goldenrod* was intended to be able to drop into an uninhabited system and repair herself from scraps so long as she had an engine, a laser and a fabricator.

The other side of Lorraine laid out the details of the reason why that wasn't an option for them: *Corsair*, a *two-million-ton* battle-cruiser to their hundred-thousand-ton frigate. There was nothing reassuring in the comparison, but that wasn't *news* to her now.

She could hope that *Corsair* had damage of her own. She'd clashed with two cruisers at a range where even *Goldenrod* could have hurt her—and the rest of the squadrons in the Arrival Zone had sent a lot of missiles the battlecruiser's way, too.

It was even, Lorraine supposed, possible that the battlecruiser hadn't been able to pursue them this far or had at least lost the TTS.

She couldn't plan for that. Whatever scheme she came up with had to assume that Wray, his ship and his crew were in top form. Fully armed, fully fueled and wholly committed to their cause.

Their guesses on the abilities of the translight tachyon scanner moved over in front of her at a mental command. Ranges, cycle times, update resolution. All of it was purely theoretical, a mix of calculated projections from Cortez and herself and the data from the UWN experiments.

"What did you trade for vision, I wonder?" she muttered. "This is just *tech*, not magic. We know you're using our drive as a beacon, but how does that limit you?"

And in the middle of the notes from the UWN, the answer fell out.

We learned that translight tachyon sequencing still requires a starting point in regular space. Even using a modulated tracking signal, we were unable to track a ship out of and back into translight without going sublight ourselves.

A single paragraph lost in the report, a side comment in one officer's notes on a specific experiment. And in that paragraph, the first part of her answer.

Wray could see where they exited translight. But he couldn't tell if they *reentered* translight without following that exit. For almost any situation Lorraine could see, that wouldn't matter.

But *Goldenrod* needed space and time to make their run to the wormhole. It wasn't an entire plan, but it was a starting point.

One that would take the trick Wray was relying on and turn it against him. How better to put the Commodore off-balance and lay the groundwork for *her* next trick?

FORTY-SIX

"I hesitate to call this a *plan*," Savege said slowly. "But I'll be damned if it doesn't sound like more than any of us thought we had. Are we *certain* their TTS has that limitation?"

"No," Lorraine conceded, glancing around the frigate's senior officers with a grim look. "That's why I'm hoping to set up an exit-reentry-exit sequence that should give us a half-decent chance even if he sees the reentry. Unfortunately, I only see one way to do that."

"We can do it."

Every eye in the room snapped to Yildiz as the Navigator spoke, without even waiting to hear what Lorraine was suggesting.

"Helm?" Stephson asked.

"The Pentarch is about to point out that the cold equations say we've got two million tons' less mass than *Corsair*," Yildiz told them—to which Lorraine just nodded. She had been about to do just that.

"That means we're that much less vulnerable to the tachyon-flux effects of the wormhole. We *can* go closer than Wray can. The safety zone is just that, after all: a *safety* zone."

He shrugged.

"How unsafe do we want to be?"

Lorraine concealed her smile. The silence in the room spoke volumes. She'd done some hard calculations on it, but she also knew she needed these people, at a minimum, to buy in.

"Recommended minimum safe distance for a wormhole is two million kilometers," Savege noted, the XO sounding thoughtful. "The actual flux zone is only about... one five hundred, right?"

"Five light-seconds, give or take ten percent depending on the local stars and the wormhole itself," Cortez confirmed, the engineer clearly having been poking at the same numbers. "But the flux zone isn't stable, and if we get too close, we just... *cease to exist*."

"And *too close* is a variable of our mass," Lorraine said, reminding them of Yildiz's point. "My calculations say that wherever the true danger zone *is*, ours starts fifty thousand klicks closer than *Corsair*'s does."

"Helm says we can do it," Stephson reminded everyone, the Captain's tone level. "What number are you thinking *do it* gets us to, Yildiz?"

"Seventeen," he said instantly. "One-point-seven million klicks. Given the option that the Pentarch is suggesting to screw with *Corsair*, I'd suggest we drop out at two-point-five, wait out the drive reset, then hit a microjump for eight hundred thousand."

"I like it," Lorraine said. "If we weren't sure how they were following us, dropping out *way* outside the normal zone like that makes sense. If they were only guessing and got lucky at San Ignacio, there's very little chance they'd expect us to come out that far from the wormhole.

"So, it looks like we're playing clever games, but they know they have one up on us."

"And then when they drop out, we're already gone," Savege finished, nodding. "I see your point, Major, Pentarch—but all the way to *two hundred thousand klicks* from the estimated flux zone? The zone itself could easily be sitting at sixteen fifty."

"We're going to have *half* of *Corsair*'s acceleration," Stephson said. "We need every kilometer of space we can get. A stern chase is a long one, but no matter what we do, we have a long damn way to go."

Even at one-point-seven million klicks, which Lorraine had to concede was dangerously close, it would take over four hours for them to reach the wormhole at three gravities.

"Seventeen-fifty," the Captain decided, her tone making it clear the discussion was over. "It only costs us four minutes of total flight time, and it has that much less risk of instant death."

"I'll plot the course," Yildiz agreed. "Cheng, any idea what our minimum cycle time is going to be?"

"We've gone over everything with a fine-toothed comb now," Cortez told him. "I can tighten things up in interesting ways now—ways I would have *thought* I could do before, I'll note."

Lorraine shivered at the engineer's tone. The masking in Engineering's computers and drones had been more than good enough to handle day-to-day operations and even damage control and some level of pushing things.

But the translight drive had been sufficiently off from what the computer had been telling the engineers that taking it to the real limits could have been... bad.

"*Corsair* has been following us at about five minutes' flight time," Stephson said. "So, less than that would be good."

Cortez chuckled.

"Skipper, if I couldn't give you a five-minute drive cycle time, I would resign in protest at my own incompetence. This ship, this crew? Our *perfectly safe peacetime* cycle is three minutes. Two and a half, really. For this kind of craziness?"

She paused for thought—and drama, Lorraine figured.

"Seventy seconds," she concluded. "If we weren't jumping right at a wormhole's flux zone, I'd even say sixty—but for *that* stunt, I want to make sure everything is lined up."

"Wray might be closer on our ass than before, but I doubt he's *that* close on our ass," Stephson observed. "We'll be gone before he's out of translight. And drive cycle time on a *Pirate* is, what, five minutes?"

"Standard, yeah," Cortez replied. "I don't think any RKAN battlecruiser Captain or Cheng would accept that from the Engineering crew, though. Still, you can't yell at the laws of physics."

She shrugged.

"True emergency jump—say with a RBDN battle squadron bearing down on them? One hundred fifty seconds. For the pressure they'll be under to catch us? Three, three-and-a-half minutes."

"That will give us three minutes of full thrust, whatever we can coax out of the engines, plus however much margin risking the flux zone gets us," Savege said slowly. "If his people are running the same numbers we are, the latter should get us fifty thousand at least."

"Which will get us *out* of her beam range," Lorraine noted. "Her missiles will still be a problem. Thoughts there?"

She had plans for turning the whole mess around, but they needed to live long enough to manage that. From rest, the Galavant 2 heavy missiles in *Corsair*'s magazines and the Artemis 3 light missiles in *Goldenrod*'s had much the same range: one hundred and seventy-five thousand kilometers, mostly on a main drive pushing two hundred gravities.

"There are... possibilities," Paris said slowly. "We do have full specs on the Galavant Two, after all. The problem is that they have full specs on our missiles, and anything we do to their birds will just be telling them they can do it to ours.

"The stuff I can think of countermeasures for, so can they."

"And we have to assume they *have*," Lorraine agreed. "But *some* things can't be changed, can they?"

The Tactical Officer nodded and glanced around the staff room.

"We know the seekers and sensors on the Galavants," he told them. "I can tune our ECM to that knowledge. It's a risk—if they've picked up someone *else's* capital-ship missiles, we'll end up being more vulnerable.

"But by focusing our jamming and chaff at the zones and

frequencies I know *Corsair* will be using, I can degrade their missile effectiveness by at least twenty-five percent. That's a *hardware* limitation, too."

"They could have fabricated new sensor heads and seeker arrays," Savege warned, the XO looking thoughtful. "They've had time, same as we've had."

"It's a gamble each way," Paris explained. "Electronics like that are dependent on the molycirc modules we have available. It's a lot harder for us to fab molecular circuitry than it is for us to build more macro-scale gear.

"I can build you an entire Galavant Two more easily than I can build you a completely new sensor head for an Artemis," he concluded. "And that new sensor head will be notably *less* capable. If they've gone that route, they'll have given up five, ten percent of their missile effectiveness all on their own."

"So, they'll hold off on using them, even if they *have* them, until they see what games we're playing," Lorraine murmured. "That might help all on its own."

Everyone looked at her and she smiled thinly.

"This battle is not going to be won in the void between our ships with missiles and lasers, people," she told them. "If it comes down to the weapons and weight of metal in play, we lose.

"The only way we win this battle is to fight it inside Commodore Nikostratos Wray's head. The more he thinks he's been clever and is beating our tricks, the better off we are."

She got several concerned looks, but no one was arguing with her.

"We have a limited ability to handle *Corsair*'s full firepower," Savege warned. "To survive even a long-range extended duel, we'll need all sixteen shuttles up in interceptor mode."

"We can't fight *any* kind of extended duel," Chevrolet countered, the COSH speaking quickly and sharply. "All my people can do in interceptor mode is buy *Goldenrod* time. Maybe enough, but I doubt it. We're not exactly expecting anyone to come charging to the rescue, are we?"

"Even if the Bright Dream Navy decided to pick a side, there are unlikely to be any of their ships in position for us to hide behind," Stephson warned. "We can aim for any ships that are in the right area —it certainly won't hurt—but Bright Dream isn't as *forcefully* neutral as San Ignacio tries to be."

"Buying time won't cut it," Chevrolet concluded. "We need to slow *Corsair* down—preferably take her out.

"The best shot we have is the shuttles and an HVMD strike."

Lorraine didn't even bother concealing her wince.

"*High-velocity / minimum-distance* is a fancy phrasing for *suicide run*, Chevrolet," she told him. It called for the shuttles to accelerate the full distance between the two ships, getting up to the highest possible velocity and releasing their bombs at ranges measured in hundreds of kilometers.

Ranges where their bombs' limited engines would still suffice to cover the distance and hit the target while actively evading defenses.

The problem was that the shuttles would be in range of *Corsair*'s weapons for most of that run, and every shuttle shot down was ten fewer bombs in the final strike. Even with sixteen shuttles, Lorraine doubted they'd actually manage to get *anyone* close enough to deploy effectively.

"I know," the COSH said quietly. "My people have been poking at our gear since we left San Ignacio. We've worked out how to rig up a dead man's release on the bomb racks. It isn't pretty or even *safe*— but unless the bombs get vaporized when the shuttle gets hit, they'll release when the bird stops accelerating and deliver the strike regardless."

"The shuttles can't get close enough on autopilot," Vigo replied. "You have to put at least a pilot on board each of them. And you're more likely to pull it off with two."

"Every pilot and copilot, Guard and RKAN alike, has volunteered," Chevrolet said firmly. "It's... the only way we see to get everyone through."

"Thank you," Lorraine told him, making sure he turned to look at her. "And thank our people for me. I... don't have words for what the willingness to fly that mission means to me."

She held his gaze and smiled.

"And I'll admit I factored it into my planning. We may even have to do it. But I *do* have another option to try first."

Now she had everyone's attention. Still smiling, she turned her attention to Cortez and Paris as she sent a pre-saved message to everyone's neural links.

"Cheng, I've checked the Guard files, and it turns out we have a few fabricator schematics that *aren't* in the standard databanks," she told Cortez. "You should have a file for the Horatio Ninety-Nine in your messages now. Take a look. How quickly can we churn that out?"

She'd only told Cortez she had the message, but everyone else's eye movements told her they'd checked and seen it themselves.

"That's... What even *is this*?" Cortez asked. "I can fab it, yeah. Fit our warheads into it. But this isn't—"

"Ours," Lorraine finished for her. "It's not an RKAN design. Twelve months ago, it was the Bright Dream Navy's newest proto-type stealth mine. And no, I *don't* know how we got the fabricator schematics for that."

"It's as stealthy as anything in space can be, but that doesn't help as much as you'd think in our current situation," Paris pointed out. "They're practically invisible to radar, and their heat radiation is directional enough I think I can point it at us, but we don't have a way to launch mines quietly.

"We could drop a few out of airlocks, I suppose, but to get any kind of useful number out we have to use the shuttle bay. We open the bay, they're going to hit us with every active scanner they've got, and *nothing* is stealthy enough for that.

"We could sneak some out before they come out of translight, I suppose," he allowed.

"But we wouldn't know where they were coming from," Lorraine said. "You're right, Lieutenant Commander Paris. We *need* to deploy the mines once *Corsair* is in the zone and coming after us—and yes, just about every way we *can* deploy them in useful numbers is going to be blatantly obvious to Commodore Wray."

She smiled even more broadly.

"But while Wray aspires to be as good as my uncle, *I* have spent twenty years listening to Benjamin Adamant's stories and lessons. And my dear uncle always reminded me that you can't hide *anything* in space.

"Unless your enemy is looking at the wrong thing. We're going to give Commodore Wray a whole *lot* of things to look at. We're going to play tricks, sleight of hand, electronic-warfare games... and he's going to see through most of them, because RKAN didn't make him a battlecruiser Captain because he was an idiot.

"We want him to do just that. We want him to think he's seen through our tricks, that he's *better* than us. Because it's in the moment where Nikostratos Wray thinks he has won that we have a chance."

Lorraine's smile was cold now, colder than the void of space.

"Listen up. This is what we're going to do."

FORTY-SEVEN

"All hands, hear this, hear this. Translight emergence in fifteen minutes. All hands clear quarters and non-combat stations for maximum acceleration, then report to battle stations. Repeat: clear quarters and non-combat stations for maximum acceleration, then report to battle stations."

Vigo looked up at the call over the speaker and then down at the cards in his "hand."

Playing cards in microgravity was difficult at the best of times—but spacers had found a hundred thousand solutions to that over the decades. The virtual game he was playing with the three shuttle flight leaders was one of the simplest iterations of poker software he'd ever seen—and almost omnipresent in the neural link storage of shuttle pilots.

His complete garbage of a hand certainly wasn't a reason to delay his response to the call.

"I hear our mistress calling," he told the three pilots. "Time to get to work."

"And you're just saying that to save your money from the pot, aren't you?" Chevrolet asked with a grin.

"The *pot* is currently eleven shillings," Major Watanabe pointed out. "Barely a full crown. I think Major Jarret is more concerned about his pride than his *money.*"

They hadn't been playing for real money, after all. Shilling-ante poker was only to get the betting part of the game involved.

"Are you ready?" Vigo asked the three pilots. He unfolded himself from his floating position, locking a sole to the deck and surveying the shuttle bay around him.

He was glad he wasn't going to be trying to cram *his* bulk into the space around the Guard shuttles. He suspected that Charlie Flight's pilots were just as happy too. Every time Vigo had flown, one of the pilots had been left behind.

The Guard didn't distinguish between pilot and copilot, rotating the roles to keep everyone fresh. That meant that losing Patriksson and Laurenz had only left them short *copilots*—and the two older men with RKAN Chief Petty Officer insignia standing with his people were the answer to that.

Both were from Lorraine's old Bravo Flight, crew chiefs who had turned out to have the qualifications to run *everything* on the shuttles they managed. Vigo suspected the two old hands could take over for pilots if needed, let alone serving as copilots.

"I think my pickups are better than some of my pilots," Lieutenant Juturna Deering told him. Deering was one of his, an ex-RAMC shuttle jock who'd served twenty years in the Marines—as an NCO and then a mustang officer—before being picked up by the Guard.

Older than Patriksson, she'd still been the fourth-ranked pilot in the Guard's shuttle flight. Now she was second-in-command—and if anyone on the ship knew how to judge whether a noncom could handle the job she needed, it was the mustang Marine-turned-Adamant Guard.

"Since I *know* how good your pilots are, I'm going to say that means you're ready," Vigo told her. "Chevrolet? Watanabe?"

"We're fine," Chevrolet told him. "We might not *officially* carry spare pilots, but we know who on the frigate has their wings—and it's hardly a coincidence that all of our *pickups* are Crew Chiefs."

Vigo chuckled and shook his head at the pilots. The shuttle bay had already been secured for heavy acceleration, but the pilots and copilots were starting to drift toward their shuttlecraft. Even so, they were clearly looking away from the nuclear weapons already mounted on the ships.

Between the bomb racks and a dozen other clever ideas in the space, there were a *lot* of warning trefoils in the shuttle bay. Part of the reason Vigo was even down there, playing cards with the flight leaders, was to remind people that the bombs *were* safe to be around.

For people with Naval implants. Mostly. Assuming they kept up their regular doctor's appointments.

"If it will make you feel better, I *fold*," he told his poker players, canceling his hand with a mental command that showed his cards to the others. Jack high after the second draw was *not* something he was going to write home about.

"I'm not sure that does help, actually," Watanabe replied, folding her own hand to reveal a *nine*-high. "I think this deal just hated us all."

"Hated *you*," Deering said wryly, revealing a straight flush, jack of spades high.

"Are you *kidding* me?" Chevrolet's glare could be *felt* even before he tipped his own *four aces* into the digital middle. "Just hope I didn't burn luck I'll need later. This plan..."

"Is better than suicide-charging and hoping you get enough bombs through," Vigo said quietly. "Are you good?"

"The Pentarch scares me," he replied. "Worse, I *still* think her uncle might be better at this, so that scares me too. But yeah, I'm good."

"I'll judge the plan after it's over," Watanabe said as she pushed the eleven-shilling purse over to Deering—at ten to a crown, that might buy him a cheap coffee somewhere. "Because if the chips fall wrong, we're right back to *burn the whole squadron to get one bomb in*."

"No," Vigo corrected, grim and quiet, making sure only the three flight leaders heard him. "If the chips fall wrong, we'll never know."

Because between the wormhole tachyon flux and the battlecruiser's main guns, there were all too many ways for them to die without ever knowing what hit them.

"Get your depressing ass to the bridge," Chevrolet told him. "We'll do our part. You do yours. Keep the Pentarch ticking—if we live through this, it's because of *her* plan."

FORTY-EIGHT

The strange colors of translight emergence flickering across Lorraine's vision brought a equally strange sense of relief. They were committed now. They had *been* committed, really, for a long time.

But now they were in realspace in the Bright Dream System, less than ten light-seconds from the wormhole to the United Worlds. Still hours of actual *flight* away, with a battle against a far more powerful opponent to come first, but the first key barrier was in sight.

We're going to pull this off, Mom. For a moment, her emotions surged, and she let them. She had no role to play in this particular seventy-second sequence. Anything she added right then would only be complexity they didn't need.

Her father would have understood. He wouldn't have *liked* it, but Frederick Adamant-Griffin had been a generous and peaceful man. Not a *pacifist*—no scion of the key families of a twenty-sixth-century star nation could be a true pacifist—but violence was far down his personal solution list.

Even so, Lorraine doubted her father would have wanted her to walk away from this. Despite his personal distaste for it, he'd always

had a keen sense for when the sword and the missile were the only
answer left.

She *knew* her mother would have wanted her to fight. To honor
Valeriya Adamant's memory by shattering the scheme and
conspiracy that had killed her. It should not have happened, and it
wasn't fair.

Lorraine knew that wasn't even the inevitable opinion of an
orphan. It was just... true. Her uncle *shouldn't* have turned on her
entire family. It *wasn't* fair that her mother had died because
Benjamin Adamant had needed to be King.

She still wished she could talk about it with either of them. Both
of them. She had been closer with her parents than with her two
eldest siblings, but she also wanted to talk to *them*. She'd lost... *so
much.*

We can't always get what we want, sadly. She remembered
Daniel's words with a shock. What had they been talking about?
She'd been... sixteen. He'd been twenty-eight, the age she was now,
and had just been dumped by the man he'd planned to marry.

At the proposal, in fact. Daniel had asked Reinhardt to marry
him, and the other man had... Well, Lorraine hadn't been there, but
the phrase one of the Guard had used when she hadn't thought
anyone in the family could hear was *freaked out.*

Daniel hadn't got what he wanted. Reinhardt had walked out,
never speaking to anyone from House Adamant again. Lavender had
come along half a decade later, and Lorraine had *always* suspected
that the elders of House Larsen and House Adamant had pushed
their pair of unmarried thirtysomething heirs together.

But Daniel had understood what had happened with Reinhardt,
in a way Lorraine hadn't, and that had been his explanation. The
power and wealth of being the First Pentarch came with a long list of
expectations and responsibilities. Reinhardt could be the First
Pentarch's boyfriend, but he couldn't be the First Pentarch's *husband*,
the Prince-by-marriage, with the attendant requirement of child-
rearing (if not *-bearing*, in his case).

"Engines are live. We're at three gees and tentatively pushing up with Engineering watching the gauges," Yildiz reported from Navigation.

Lorraine was half-present in reality, half-considering her family and letting her grief run through her.

She'd liked Lavender well enough, but she'd grown up in the one clear noble family of the Kingdom of Adamant. House Larsen might not *explicitly* share that status, but with their family trust owning several key industrial enterprises and information networks, they might as well.

By the time Lavender had entered her life as her brother's partner, Lorraine could smell an arranged marriage from half a planet away. Despite her own... hormone-driven activities, she'd always half-expected to end up in one herself. Her *romantic* entanglements had been... minimal and unsatisfying.

"We are at three-point-five gravities and Cortez says to hold there," Yildiz reported. "It's all we're getting, sirs."

"That's half a gravity more than I was expecting," Lorraine told him, surprising herself with the balance of her thoughts. "We're doing fine."

"My compliments to Commander Cortez, Major Kovac," Stephson agreed, addressing the Bridge Engineering Officer.

"Time to translight?"

"Thirty-two seconds and counting," Yildiz confirmed.

Lorraine exhaled slowly, letting her grief, her memories, flow through her. She hated how empty and flat her emotions felt, how hollow even her *grief* felt—but that same flatness served a purpose.

When her grief hit her, she had to let it. She feared her emptiness too much for anything else. But there were times when the emptiness itself was a tool—and that time was upon her.

She'd had the moment to be just Lorraine... but now it was time to be Pentarch Lorraine Adamant.

"DO we have an update on contacts at the wormhole itself?" Lorraine asked. "And ships between us and the flux zone?"

The seconds left before they could return to translight were ticking away. The only reason they might change their planned emergence was if there were potential friendlies they could use as a shield against *Corsair*'s pursuit.

"Should be on your screen... now," Paris told her. "There's only one group that we could potentially use as a backstop, but they're eleven degrees around the safety zone, and, well, whether we want to provoke the *Directorate* is a political call."

Her command display updated as he spoke, and she followed his flag to the key group he'd flagged.

Three ships, sitting at seventeen hundred and eighty thousand kilometers from the wormhole. As Paris had noted, they were at a sufficiently different entry angle to make emerging from translight near them tricky—and to turn a seven-hundred-thousand-kilometer straight-line distance into well over a million kilometers via translight.

A battleship and two cruisers would make for a spectacular backdrop to her plan, though. Without an ID on the battlewagon, Lorraine couldn't be sure the ship was a match for *Corsair*. The battlecruiser wasn't built to fight the slower and more heavily armored ships of the line, but she was *very* modern—and the Richelieu Directorate fleet had some very *old* battleships.

The Flotte Étoilée's capital ships averaged younger than RKAN's ships, but that was because they'd lost two-thirds of their fleet in the last war. It was a problem Lorraine had known her mother was thinking about—but it was a toss-up whether the Directorate would send one of their new ships or old ships on what was presumably a diplomatic visit to the United Worlds. The new ships were needed to watch the Kingdom, and since the UW was probably going to dismiss *anything* they sent as obsolete...

Lorraine figured old. Even an *old* battleship could make *Goldenrod* go away if her crew panicked and opened fire when they came out too close—and *nobody* from the Directorate was going to take the arrival of an RKAN warship lightly!

"Let's stick with the plan and trust ourselves," she said clearly. "No changes, Helm."

"Yes, Your Highness," Yildiz confirmed.

Stephson could have made the call, but everyone was looking to Lorraine as head of mission. It was still a strange feeling—one made easier to handle by *knowing* that Stephson *would* have made a call before they had to jump.

Fifteen seconds left, and Lorraine turned her attention to the center of everything. The wormhole itself was only visible on the tachyon scanners, a strange continuous burst that almost but not quite resembled a ship perpetually jumping to translight.

There were a *lot* of ships and space stations around it, though. At least a hundred civilian ships, Lorraine judged, and two dozen military and civilian stations.

Her focus was on the RBDN. Despite the strictures the Republic worked under there, the Tavastar–Bright-Dream Wormhole was still the single largest key economic asset they had. Any travel from the home stars came to the cluster through Bright Dream—and anyone who was heading *to* the home stars had to leave through Bright Dream.

Eight battleships, positioned in divisions of two, orbited the sphere of stations marking the wormhole's position in space. Four cruisers accompanied each division of battleships, which meant that the RBDN had almost as many cruisers at the wormhole as RKAN had in *total*.

The real queen of the wormhole's defenses was the group of seven ships "above" the wormhole by Bright Dream's ecliptic plane. The "destroyers" were easily six hundred thousand tons, seventy percent of the size of the Bright Dream cruisers, but it was the six *million* tons of United Worlds Navy carrier that calmly dared anyone and *everyone* to oppose proper freedom of navigation.

None of those ships, unfortunately, *mattered* at that moment.

Between the UWN carrier group and the RBDN battle squadron, there was enough firepower around the wormhole to take on most Bright Dream Cluster nations' entire *navies*.

The duel between *Corsair* and *Goldenrod* would be over before any of that firepower could get into play. UWN combat shuttles were significantly more dangerous than anything the Bright Dream Cluster built, but they still had the same squishy organic bits in the middle, limiting acceleration.

"Still no sign of *Corsair*," Stephson told her silently. "We might be lucky."

"We *know* she arrived when we dropped out to recalculate our course," Lorraine replied, the messages flying between their links and hidden from everyone.

Well, except Vigo. As was becoming standard, Lorraine was in the central observer station with Vigo to her right and Palmer to her left. Her bodyguard was fully synced to her neural link, too, following everything she saw and heard.

She doubted he would interrupt—not unless she was *truly* screwing up or he saw something she needed to.

"Waiting puts us in more danger than jumping," she continued to Stephson. "We might be lucky, but I'm not counting on it."

Lucky hadn't summed up their flight from Adamantine so far.

"Major Paris, jump to translight when ready," the Captain ordered aloud.

"It's a very short jump," the navigator warned. "Stand by. Entering translight...

"*Now*."

FORTY-NINE

In and out of translight in less than a second was even stranger than usual. Lorraine's eyes and mind didn't even manage to lose the impossible perception of going translight when the equally impossible feeling of dropping sublight hit.

She blinked, her vision blurring entirely for half a moment.

The gap in *Goldenrod*'s acceleration was just as obvious as the strange lights—more so, really, even with the compounding double effect of the in-and-out. They were in microgravity for about three seconds before the fusion rockets came back online.

"Holding at three-point-five gravities," Yildiz reported as several enthusiastic cheerleaders climbed onto Lorraine's chest.

A timer popped up in the corner of her vision, counting down their estimated minimum time to *Corsair* catching up to them. Based on the previous pursuit, about four minutes to the warship's arrival, plus four more minutes for their drive to cycle.

Lorraine had a second counter running next to the one Paris was sending her. *That* one cut two whole minutes off the estimate. She didn't have enough of a basis for her estimate to push it back to Tactical, but she *knew*, in her gut, that *Corsair* wasn't going to take almost ten minutes to catch up.

"We have eyes on our emergence zone," Paris announced. "Time lag, approximately two-point-five seconds."

"Sirs, we are receiving a hail from Tavastar–Bright Dream Wormhole Control," Vinci reported. "Um. It's addressed to both Lieutenant Colonel Stephson *and* Pentarch Lorraine Adamant."

"Fascinating," Stephson said calmly. "Your thoughts, Pentarch?"

Lorraine turned her grimace into a calm smile.

"It's a twelve-second turnaround for messages," she noted. "Too long for a live conversation. Let's see what they have to say."

She'd *had* semi-live conversations with a twelve-second time lag, but it made for a useful excuse to give them time to think.

Her console and the main display both lit up with a woman who rivaled Stephson for sheer Valkyrie impressions. Taking in the control station and other people around her, Lorraine realized the golden-haired stranger was actually *bigger* than Stephson—both at least fifteen centimeters taller and easily thirty or forty kilos heavier.

The local's uniform was ever so slightly unkempt, too, like she'd *tried* to make it presentable but it was an ongoing losing battle.

"RKAN vessel *Goldenrod*, commanding officer Lieutenant Colonel Sigrid Stephson and known transport of the Pentarch Lorraine Adamant," she greeted them crisply. "I am Rear Admiral Hilde Ljungborg, commanding officer of Tavastar–Bright-Dream Wormhole Control.

"You have overjumped into the T-BD Wormhole Safety Zone, a violation of local regulations requiring the impounding of your ship until a review takes place and a fine can be assessed. You will be provided with a vector on which to surrender to T-BDWC officers. You will comply."

The message ended and Lorraine smirked, knowing everyone had half an eye on her.

"Does anyone need the translation from political chicanery to normal language?" she asked drily.

"Bribe me?" Paris suggested.

Lorraine shrugged and chuckled.

"Not *quite*... but close enough," she conceded. "Captain Stephson, do you want to take the lead? We want to be honest about our situation with *Corsair*, and we are prepared to pay the fines, but we need to transit to the UWN upon arrival."

"I think... this may be a *diplomatic* conversation, Your Highness," Stephson told her. "Do we follow the vector they've provided?"

Lorraine didn't sigh. Even the limited instruction she'd given was a sign that the Captain was right—if it *wasn't* political and diplomatic, she could have left it to Stephson to handle.

"We'll stick to ours. There can't be that much difference at this point; we're still a long way from the wormhole. Any adjustment would be in the last fifty thousand klicks."

"Looks like," Yildiz confirmed. "Stick to the plan?"

"Stick to the plan," Stephson agreed, glancing back at Lorraine. "I think the Rear Admiral is yours, Pentarch."

"Agreed. Major Vinci, give me a feed," Lorraine ordered.

A tiny light on the console turned orange, warning her the camera was live but not recording yet. Her neural feed handily gave her a screen-in-screen image of what the camera was seeing.

Three and a half gravities of thrust left her hair flattened to her scalp and sharpened her already-aquiline features. She took a moment to make sure she had her gaze focused on the pickup dot, then gave the Bright Dream officer her calmest expression.

"Admiral Ljungborg, I am Pentarch Lorraine Adamant," she greeted the other woman. "We are aware that we overjumped the safety zone in violation of Bright Dream regulation. As such, I see no problem with paying the necessary fines.

"However, if you review the diplomatic codes attached to this message, you will see that I am traveling under consular authority and diplomatic protection that extends to my entire ship. I am tasked by my mother, the late King Valeriya Adamant, to bear her final messages to the Grand Assembly of the United Worlds.

"As such, I must make an urgent consular transit, as authorized by the twenty-three-sixty-six treaty between our nations. Per that treaty, I cannot be detained or impounded." Or fined, technically, but paying the fine gave a face-saving way out for everyone.

"I also must advise you that my vessel is being pursued by a rogue RKAN warship believed to be under the control of the conspirators who killed my mother," Lorraine finished. "While I respect the authority and sovereignty of the Republic of Bright Dream and would *prefer* to refrain from lethal force in your territory, I do not expect my pursuers to give me a choice.

"My people will use all necessary measures to protect our ship. My scans suggest that there are no vessels close enough to be endangered by this conflict, but I ask that Wormhole Control vector any new arrivals away from this area.

"I cannot guarantee their safety and I do not expect our traitors to try."

She smiled, a relaxed expression far from her actual feelings.

"Please forward us the amount of the fines for our jump and provide a timing and vector for our priority passage through the wormhole. Thank you, Rear Admiral Ljungborg."

She thought-clicked a command, sending the recording on its way. Everything she'd said was true, but she wasn't sure if Ljungborg would go along. The situation she'd laid out covered the Republic and its Admiral on both *need* and *reputation*.

But that didn't mean things were going to go according to plan.

"Emergence!" Paris barked. "*Corsair* has emerged at our original entry point! I'm resolving... Damn, they'd have been just as on top of us as they were at San Ignacio!"

He wasn't wrong, Lorraine saw. *Corsair* would have been a bit farther away this time—but only by enough to keep her out of the danger zone of *Goldenrod*'s beams. With the damage they'd taken, Stephson's ship hadn't been able to turn to present her main energy weapons before they'd fled the system—but Wray had clearly recognized the risk and changed his approach.

That was what Lorraine had expected. Her opponent was smart and capable. He wasn't going to make the same mistake twice.

In many ways, that was what she was *counting* on.

THE TWIN QUESTIONS now were how fast *Corsair* could cycle her translight drive and how far Wray and his people would push the flux zone.

Lorraine figured they weren't planning on sticking around to pay the fines for coming out of FTL within two million kilometers of the wormhole. She wouldn't push the battlecruiser past one-point-eight herself, but she also knew she'd have taken the optimistic one-point-seven range for *Goldenrod* herself.

They were seventeen hundred and fifty thousand kilometers from the wormhole, burning toward its surrounding collection of stations at three and a half gravities and building velocity as fast as they could. A stern chase was a long chase, but *Corsair* was going to have twice their acceleration.

Every scrap of speed and distance they could create before their pursuer jumped closer was going to be critical.

"New message from Wormhole Control," Vinci reported. "Directing to your console, Pentarch."

"Thank you."

Lorraine had the message playing the moment the Amazonian local officer appeared on her screen. There was... something to Ljungborg's expression she couldn't quite read. Not confused or amused, but somewhere in the area of both.

"Pentarch Adamant, I will admit that your... description of your situation is fascinating to me," the Admiral said brightly. "Per the news out of the Kingdom of Adamant, the investigations around the death of King Valeriya and her other children currently have *you* as the primary suspect."

Lorraine was glad she was both pinned to her seat by their acceleration *and* watching a recording. She'd expected that accusation, but it still hurt to hear it.

Any news Ljungborg had from Adamantine was a hundred and thirty–plus days old—but that still put Bright Dream's information as being from a *month* after the attack. They needed to get the information the ninety-six-cee couriers had brought before they moved on.

That wasn't her immediate priority, though, and her attention was still mostly on her timers and the battlecruiser. Assuming four minutes to cycle the warship's drive, they still had three minutes left.

Lorraine's shortened timer said ninety seconds. *Corsair* had arrived sooner than even her worst case, which was pushing how much time she had to play with the local Admiral—before the battle, at least. If they lived, she'd have a couple of hours to sort things out.

"I don't need you to give me your story or defend yourself, Pentarch," Ljungborg told her. "I imagine it is a dark tale of treachery and kinslaying, much like the one your government is sharing.

"From my perspective, it is irrelevant. The Kingdom of Adamantine has not delivered an Interstellar Warrant to the Republic of Bright Dream. We have not been asked to arrest or extradite you.

"Equally relevant, your diplomatic and consular codes are entirely valid, and I am treaty-bound to honor them." The local smirked. "A fine of one million, two hundred and fifty thousand pounds will be levied against the standard account of the Kingdom of Adamantine for your overjump, per your verbal authorization.

"Traffic control has been advised of your approach and consular priority. Expect to receive an entry vector and time when you arrive. I imagine we will not have time to speak in person, Pentarch Lorraine..."

There was a long pause, one that Lorraine wasn't sure how to read.

"Allow me to extend my heartfelt deepest condolences for the loss of your parents, brother and sister," she finally said. "I knew Taura Adamant well when she served in the embassy here, and I met your father, long ago. They were bright souls, Your Highness, and they will be missed."

The message ended as Lorraine's heart fell at the surprisingly honest words. For a moment, her shield against her grief crumpled and she had to fight back tears.

"Emergence!" Paris snapped. "Contact at one-oh-one five hundred klicks! *Corsair* jumped."

FIFTY

"They knew exactly where we were," Paris noted. "Wray blinked."

"I'm not sure *blinked* is the right word," Kovac pointed out. "Our drive is in pretty rough shape. Nothing mission-critical, but the Cheng says we'll need a solid two hours of work before we can safely go translight again."

"Good news is that we'll have that time," Stephson told her crew, calming everyone with an ease of tone that Lorraine knew she needed to master.

"What's our friend up to back there?" the Captain continued.

"We've been pinged with targeting scanners, but I haven't detected any weapon launches," Paris reported. "I'm pinging *her* too, but holding per the plan."

Lorraine didn't want them to fire first. Any chance to talk Wray down was worth it—but more than that, the same treaty she was using to claim priority passage limited just what an Adamantine warship could *do* in Bright Dream space.

Goldenrod could defend herself, but starting a fight was a violation of the treaty, one that would have long-term consequences. From the Kingdom's perspective, it didn't *matter* who fired first—so long as there was a battle between the two RKAN ships, there was a treaty violation—but so long as Lorraine didn't violate the treaty herself, she had safe passage through to Tavastar.

If they lived.

"Incoming coms, sir," Vinci reported. "Live channel, no attention-to specified."

"I think this one is mine, Pentarch," Stephson told Lorraine. "Connect him, Coms."

A mirror of the feed popped up on Lorraine's console, but she wasn't recording or included in the conversation.

"Lieutenant Colonel Sigrid Stephson," Wray said flatly as his scowling face appeared on the screen. "I am forwarding you orders from RKAN Command. You are to stand down *immediately* and surrender Pentarch Lorraine Adamant.

"She stands accused of regicide, treason and murder in the first degree. If you do not surrender, I will have no choice but to take your ship in by force."

"Commodore Wray, you've already committed at least one act of treason yourself," Stephson told him sweetly. "Or so we *used* to classify unauthorized acts of war against neutral systems. I don't know what hellhole you've dragged our Kingdom into, but your attack on the San Ignacio System is a violation of *so many* laws and articles of military justice, my legal officer threw up their hands and summarized it as treason."

"Daring words from a woman harboring our King's murderer."

"I have my own damn suspicions about who killed our King, Commodore," Stephson replied. "*I* am operating under Class One Orders, countersigned by the Cabinet and the King. *You* are a murderer, arguably a pirate and, from where I sit, *definitely* a traitor.

"So, back the *fuck* off before your crimes taint your family name for all time."

Wray listened impassively to Stephson's words, then shrugged.

"The Courts will judge who is guilty, not us," he told her. "But you are set on your path and so am I. History will be our court, then, but I suspect you will see it rather sooner than I.

"May God have mercy on your souls."

The channel cut and *Goldenrod*'s bridge was very silent.

"There are times I truly, deeply understand why my family chose to ban any state religion in the Kingdom," Lorraine said softly. "I didn't expect today to bring one of them."

"Vampire!" Paris snapped, reality intruding on her moment of reflection. "Missiles launching from *Corsair*. *Holy fuck! Two hundred–plus incoming!*"

A moment earlier, there had been two icons on the command display—now narrowed to the immediate battlespace of the two RKAN warships. Now *Corsair* was surrounded by a swarm of red triangles, each of them marked with codes showing they were accelerating toward *Goldenrod* at two hundred gravities.

"Weapons free, Commander Paris," Stephson ordered. "Engage as specified."

THE FIRST STEP was mostly showing off. Matching the arrival time of their alpha strike—the salvo where Paris fired all eleven of their remaining cell launchers alongside the four missile tubes—to the arrival of *Corsair*'s first launch was hardly *necessary*.

But it was another weapon in Lorraine's arsenal, another tick to shape the mental model she knew Wray was building of his opponent.

"Total flight time three-twenty-seven seconds," Paris reported. "Remaining flight time three-ten. Our missile flight time matched, three-ten to impact. Two-ninety to terminal strike."

They were well inside the range of the missiles on both ships. The standard RKAN weapon, in both its light and heavy variants, accelerated at two hundred gravities for three hundred seconds, then launched a terminal munition that pulled a thousand gravities for *twenty* seconds.

The problem was that the two hundred and twenty missiles *Corsair* had launched were Galavant 2s, carrying *four* such warheads.

"Why two hundred and twenty?" Stephson asked. "I was expecting three hundred."

Even two hundred and twenty was far more than *Goldenrod* was expected to handle—but Lorraine saw the Captain's point. A *Pirate*-class battlecruiser had sixty missile tubes and two hundred and forty cell launchers.

If he was launching a full alpha strike, Wray's ship would have put three hundred missiles into space. But if he *wasn't*, eighty was a strange number to hold back of his cell launchers.

"We have a better look at her now than we did before," Lieutenant Major Nazario reported, the Bridge Intelligence Officer to Stephson's left mirroring the Engineering station to the Captain's right. "She definitely took some solid hits tangling with the San Ignacians. She might have lost that many of her launchers."

Or Wray, like them, was playing games.

"Watch for those extra missiles," Stephson ordered, "but we'll take the gift horse as it comes this time. Paris, do we have a handle on their seekers yet?"

"We're still too far out," he replied. "We've got a few probes scattered in our wake for extra data, so I'll know well before we can actually range on them."

New green icons appeared on Lorraine's display as *Goldenrod*'s second missile salvo blazed into space. They'd never had a chance to rearm their cell launchers, which meant they were now down to just the tubes and salvos of four missiles apiece.

Even the *fifteen*-missile salvo didn't have much of a chance against *Corsair*'s defenses, but they had to try everything. And the missiles they'd carried in their tubes had a few extra tricks up their sleeves, toys they couldn't rig up for the missiles in the external-access cells.

"*Corsair* has not fired a second salvo," Savege reported from the CIC, linking directly to Stephson and Lorraine rather than relaying through Nazario. "Since none of our scans support her having lost, oh, *all* of her missile tubes... Wray is doing something clever."

"Or he's assuming two hundred and twenty missiles are more than enough to handle us," Stephson replied on the same private channel. "Which, if Paris is, oh, only nine-tenths as good as he thinks he is..."

"It wasn't *just* his plan, skipper," the Executive Officer reminded her. "It was also mine and yours."

"Oh, good," Stephson said. "If we die before we even get to the *clever* part of the day, we're *all* at fault."

Lorraine bit down her chuckle. It was easier than it might have been, since the battlecruiser's opening salvo was just as overwhelming as Wray clearly thought it was.

RKAN didn't pick their capital-ship commanders out of a hat, and Wray was clearly a member of her uncle's faction, well briefed on the whole plan. The Black Regent might have picked people for personal loyalty, but she *knew* her uncle.

Anyone *he* put in command of a starship for a key role in his plan was going to be good. Competent. Smart. Capable of inspiring the undying loyalty of their crew and leading them all into treason.

That meant that Wray was *looking* for the tricks and traps in everything *Goldenrod* did. He knew as well as they did, how badly they were outmatched and how bad their options were.

There was no way in stars and worlds that Wray would bring his ship inside the range where *Goldenrod*'s beams could hurt *Corsair*. He'd work through his solution list calmly and carefully, recognizing that *he* controlled the range and held all of the cards.

Almost all of the cards, Lorraine realized as the datafeeds on her display updated. One of the few things where *Goldenrod* actually came close to matching *Corsair*'s equipment list was in sensor probes. Paris had dumped almost half of the frigate's allotment of the drones behind them, with their drives physically disabled to stop them from giving their positions away.

Their only active communication was a tightbeam link to the frigate, undetectable from *Corsair*'s position—but even their passive scanners could give Paris a lot of information as the missiles flew past them.

"All missiles are flying with the standard LK-Twenty-Nine sensor kit," the Tactical Officer reported. "We are ready for Dazzle."

Dazzle hadn't been meant to handle this many missiles. Lorraine had been expecting the standard doctrine of spreading cell-launched missiles out over multiple salvos from the tubes.

"Dazzle was always going to work best the first time we fired it off," Savege observed on a general channel. "In some ways, this works to our advantage."

"It does," Stephson agreed. Lorraine could tell that the Captain's attention was riveted in the same place as hers: the vague sphere in space where the missiles would enter the range of *Goldenrod*'s defenses.

Against smaller targets like shuttles and missiles, the lack of energy screens was offset by smaller targets and higher maneuverability. Their beams would be able to hit the missiles at around... *now*.

"Execute Dazzle on your discretion and engage," Stephson ordered.

At the same time, the incoming missile icons on the command display fuzzed out. The missiles carried their own jammers and ECM, reducing the frigate's ability to track them.

Except that Paris's people had spent weeks going over every detail of the missiles, and countering the Galavants' deceptions wasn't even part of Dazzle. The contacts firmed up again, and Lorraine smiled thinly as the frigate's beam weapons opened fire.

At this range, their hit rate should have *sucked*. Instead, they immediately began to slice through the incoming fire. Every missile they shot down now was *four* terminal weapons they didn't have to shoot later.

The next fifty seconds were the most critical for just that reason—and normally where their defensive fire was least effective.

"There's no modifications to these missiles at all," Paris observed. "Our hit rates are at least four times what I'd expect at this range. T-minus forty on Dazzle. Decoys in space now."

Five new green icons appeared on Lorraine's screen, spreading out from the frigate in a pentagonal pattern as they paralleled her course. The decoys were matching the warship's acceleration but otherwise staying quiet.

Corsair might have picked them up. They might not have. At this range, it could go either way—*they* couldn't see any that *Corsair* had deployed, though the battlecruiser crew might figure they didn't need them. A third of their first salvo of missiles was already gone, which was about the normal rate Lorraine would expect against their opponent.

The missiles incoming on *Goldenrod*, however, were being *slaughtered*. The complete failure of their ECM was worse than Lorraine had anticipated—and when Dazzle kicked in, ten seconds before the missiles hit separation, it only got worse.

The decoys maintained their acceleration, but their carefully designed engines were suddenly putting out heat signatures to rival *Goldenrod*'s own—and their electronic siren songs were coded specifically to the LK-29 sensors.

By separation, it was clear that only a fraction of *Corsair*'s missiles were still heading for the frigate—and with the warhead ECM no more effective than the missiles' systems had been, not one made it within a dozen kilometers of the frigate.

FIFTY-ONE

There was a stunned silence on *Goldenrod*'s bridge.

"Report," Stephson finally ordered.

"Everything from the ECM countermeasure to Dazzle worked even better than projected, sir," Paris told her. "We lost two of the decoys. Nothing else. Our missiles were all shot down before separation..."

"But?" Lorraine jumped in, catching his hesitation.

"They pulled some of the same tricks we did," the Tactical Officer replied. "They were trying to be sneakier about it, but knowing what we did, I can see it in their firing patterns. Our tube-launched missiles did better—but we *did* swap out their sensors."

"Cortez did better than I expected with the replacement seekers," Stephson agreed. "How much are we losing on those birds?"

"Probably five percent resolution on scanners, but we're hitting completely different wavelengths than they're expecting. If they prepped for standard Artemises the same way we prepped for Galavants... well..."

"Spit it out," Stephson told Paris.

"We made a mistake," Savege concluded before the tactical

officer spoke. "Mixing unmodified missiles with the modified ones gave them a decent look at our new seekers alongside a set that they could shoot down easily."

"It wouldn't matter," Lorraine argued. "Even if the other eleven missiles were more vulnerable, they still added a layer of distraction that the four with improvised seekers wouldn't have on their own. Yes, Wray will have his people adjust for nonstandard seekers for the next salvo."

They were already seeing that, she suspected, as their second set of missiles crossed the line.

"The stacked salvo with modified seekers hidden in it was our best chance to get missiles through. Wray knows that too."

"He's going to cut through our remaining salvos with ease," Paris predicted.

"Which is fine," Stephson agreed. "If we'd got a hit, that would be a win, but convincing him we're desperate has a value all its own."

"New vampires!" one of the Tactical Chiefs declared. "Looks like fifty-eight, plus/minus three."

"Sixty, almost certainly," Stephson said. "Took them two minutes to launch, so expect fully refitted seekers, Guns. The first salvo was probably every cell launcher he had left—and he never took the time to refit the sensors on them. They're using the data they collected to refine these salvos."

Unlike *Goldenrod*'s crew, Wray's would have been *able* to take the time to pull and rearm the missiles in the cell launchers. But it would have been a risk of time and resources, and he'd clearly settled for just reloading them for everything he'd fired in San Ignacio.

"Can you handle that, Guns?" Savege asked softly.

"Launching new decoys now," Paris replied. "We still have the probes in space between us, which will give me a solid look at them as they approach. It's not as good as having full schematics on their seekers and electronic-warfare systems, but we *know* they can't improvise anything as good as the gear the missiles were supposed to have."

"Assume they can," Lorraine told him. "We still don't know where they got a translight tachyon scanner, after all."

Several faces turned back toward her, looking slightly sick before they returned to their duties. The TTS, after all, was a *United Worlds Navy* system. If *Corsair* had weapons from the same source... *Goldenrod* was well and truly doomed.

"Well, if we want to convince the Commodore we're desperate, we're on our way," Stephson said on a private channel to Lorraine. "He knows we've got two options with the shuttles. Since we haven't launched interceptors, he has to be expecting Chevrolet's plan."

"If he *isn't*, well, that might make this even easier," Lorraine said drily. "Timing on the launch?"

"Well, do we want him to think we believe our trick is going to work again?" Stephson replied.

"He won't buy that for a second," the Pentarch said. "He knows he did the same thing, and he'll figure we'll work it out—just as we did. He's a good officer, so he'll assume *we're* competent, too."

"I think we let the missiles get far enough for us to confirm they're nonstandard seekers, then we drop Chevrolet and Pandora's box."

Lorraine snorted. There was no *official* name for that part of the plan, but the descriptor fit.

"They'll pass the probes in about thirty seconds, about ninety seconds from their launch," she told the Captain. "Wray almost certainly knows the probes are out there, but if we hit the timing too closely, he might just localize them, and we don't want that.

"Two hundred seconds before the missiles reach us," she decided. "That will give Chevrolet lots of time to get his formation in order before the missiles are a threat to him—and then both our shuttles and their missiles will buy Pandora the cover she needs."

THE PROBLEM with so many of the plans they'd considered and rejected was simple: they had two means of deploying real weapons other than their beams. The first was the four missile tubes, which were needed to launch their actual *missiles*, and using them for anything else risked costing them the only one of their main weapons that could reach *Corsair*.

The second was by opening the shuttle bay, but even with a hundred thousand–plus kilometers between the two ships—*Corsair* had gained enough velocity now to be slowly gaining on the frigate— opening the shuttle bay was *very* obvious.

There were ways to minimize that, of course, and *Goldenrod*'s crew was doing all of them. The bay had been evacuated of air before they opened the main doors. The internal lighting had been cut down to the absolute minimum for safe work. As many energy signatures as could be muffled *had* been.

But Lorraine knew all of that was theater to make themselves feel better. Wray's people knew exactly where *Goldenrod*'s shuttle bay was. The moment they opened the hatch, the other ship knew about it.

The Midas combat shuttles launched in pairs. Like everything else, their launches were kept muted, with them drifting out of the bay on minimum thrusters.

Despite the designers' best efforts, though, bomber mode wasn't all that stealthy, and Lorraine *knew* Wray's people had dialed in the bombers as they cleared the frigate. The only point of the attempt at sneakiness was to cover the bombers from missile fire as they got set up anyway—and that was the other reason for launching well before the missiles reached *Goldenrod*.

Plus, well, they had a *small* hope that Wray and *Corsair*'s crew hadn't been briefed on *Goldenrod*'s extra shuttles and the sixteen shuttles would help spook the Commodore.

They lit off their drives ten seconds after the last bomber was clear, all of them forming up as one and adjusting their courses swiftly. Sixteen parasite spacecraft carried a hundred and sixty fifty-kiloton warheads, making them the single biggest threat Lorraine's people could field against *Corsair*.

"Definitely got their attention," Paris announced. "Active scanners pinging the shuttles."

"Godspeed, Commander Chevrolet," Lorraine said. She was careful to speak just loud enough that everyone heard her.

"Pandora?" she silently asked Savege.

"*We've* lost track of her already," the XO admitted. "But the box is out there. Just have to hope he opens it at the right moment."

And that we live long enough to see it.

"One hundred eighty seconds to missile impact," Paris reported loudly. "Decoys are standing by to go active at impact minus forty. Multiple salvos in space behind them."

There was no good way to spin this part. In some ways, *Goldenrod*'s best chance for survival was for Wray to assume the shuttles were launching a high-velocity / minimum-distance run. In the absence of any clever plans, it might be the best chance they had... and by refusing to use up their shuttles, Lorraine might be making a mistake.

"*Corsair*'s shuttle bays are opening," Nazario reported, running key sensor analysis while Savege tried to manage Pandora. "We have Midas deployment, one group of six. Not enough data for modules yet, but the number implies interceptor mode."

There was a pause, then Nazario visibly nodded to herself.

"Second group launched, six again. That's three launching from each shuttle bay on a twenty-five-second interval. Scan data so far aligns with the projection that they're interceptors."

"Understood. Paris, kill them," Stephson ordered.

Goldenrod's missile tubes had been silent since the first exchange. Now they woke once more, hurling their remaining missiles into space to try to remove *Corsair*'s escorts. Even covered by the battlecruiser, the shuttles would be much easier targets than the warship herself.

And for the kind of HVMD strike they wanted Wray to worry about, stripping his defenses was absolutely essential.

"You're good at your job," Lorraine muttered, half to herself and half to her distant enemy, studying the icon of the enemy ship on her display. "You know the best chance we have to hurt you, and you see us putting it in play. What are you going to do?"

Wray had clearly expected the move, or he wouldn't have had all of his shuttles rigged up as interceptors. The question to Lorraine, now, was whether he'd divert his missiles to aim at the bombers.

"Missiles in beam range."

Paris was *trying* for a calm report, but the tension leaked through, to Lorraine's ear. They didn't have the ECM for this round perfectly dialed in, which meant he was operating on more-normal terms.

And against sixty missiles, *she* would have loved a few dozen more advantages.

"We have them dialed in from the probes," the Tactical Officer continued after a moment. "It's not as handy as knowing their exact spectrums, but it's helping."

Lorraine's display handily marked the beam weapons—almost invisible to the naked eye—with clear lines. Even the frigate's main beam weapons were involved at this point, their slower tracking more than made up for by the guarantee of a kill on even a glancing hit.

Not all of *Goldenrod*'s beams could fire behind her, but enough could to make a halo of coherent energy the missiles had to pass through. The incoming weapons were dying, if not nearly as fast as Lorraine would have liked.

Ask me for anything but time. The Napoleon quote—originally shared with her by her uncle, of course—echoed in her mind.

Time was distance. Every second was a few dozen kilometers closer to their destination. Every moment let their shuttles close the range with *Corsair* that much more.

But once the missiles started arriving again, it would be a steady metronome of sixty missiles every fifty seconds. *Time* for her plan to work meant time that Paris and his people needed to keep *Gold-*

enrod alive, and Lorraine's fingers twitched with the urge to do *something*.

Anything.

Instead, she remained silent and watched her plan unfold.

"Separation! Warheads incoming!"

There were too many missiles left on the screen, and they split into *far* too many warheads, the terminal munitions blazing toward them.

When the last missile detonated, wiping away a decoy they could ill afford to lose, Lorraine slowly relaxed.

"Report," she and Stephson said in the same instant.

"Lost three decoys," Paris said. "Closest detonation to the hull was seven hundred twenty meters. Some radiation burn on sensors, and I think we just cut a few hundred hours off the useful life of the stern combat radiators, but no major damage."

The combat radiators were lower-profile and vented heat a *lot* more effectively than the cruising heat-radiation systems, but a solid radiation pulse would damage them. Fixing that would involve releasing the damaged pieces into space—but since the radiators worked by melting themselves and releasing the molten metal into space, cutting off the damaged pieces cost them both immediate effectiveness and long-term life.

"Hold off on ablating the radiators till we want blood in the water," Stephson ordered. "You have eyes on the next salvo?"

"Entering the engagement perimeter now." Paris paused, then continued with a grim smile audible in his voice. "They weren't expecting us to shoot at the interceptors. Got one."

"Keep it up," Stephson ordered. "Each interceptor down is a better chance for Chevrolet."

"New decoys are up," Paris's Chief reported. "We've got one spare left."

"Let's try not to burn up three of them this time, then," Paris replied. "Probes and the last round have given us a bit more data. Let's play them a tune."

It took Lorraine a bit of poking at her console to get the squadron-command routines she was running to give her enough detail to follow what the frigate's tactical department was doing. Even then, it was a simplified summary that mostly just flagged which decoy was currently outputting the largest signature.

She wasn't getting the full effect of Paris's "tune," but she could get the gist. The decoys were swapping signatures with each other, creating an ever-changing array of heat and electronic signatures that didn't just expand *Goldenrod*'s target area but regularly changed its centerpoint.

Smart as the enemy weapons were, it couldn't fool all of them, but each time the decoys shifted, the missile swarm moved with them. And *that* made the incoming fire ever so slightly more predictable.

"Clear," Paris announced as the last missile vanished from the scopes. "We're down a decoy, but closest detonation was at three klicks. No further damage."

"Get the last decoy up and prep for blood in the water," Stephson ordered. "It's time."

Lorraine nodded her agreement, watching the next missile salvo blazing toward them. Wray's people would be spending the current moments sending new code to the weapons' silicon brains, updated algorithms based on human judgment and learning agents operating on the ship's systems to handle their new trick.

That meant there was a very real chance that they'd take a hit on the next round. *Corsair*'s crew was demonstrably capable and competent—but Lorraine knew her people had proven the same.

Wray's people doubled down on her impression a moment later, when missiles from the *next* salvo—the one well outside of range of *Goldenrod*'s weapons—suddenly separated. The entire salvo of sixty missiles converted to terminal warheads well away from Lorraine's ship.

And dove in on the half-dozen stealth probes Paris was using to prepare his defenses. Wray's people had failed to narrow down the sensor platforms closely enough to actually *hit* them… but forty fifty-kiloton nukes layered through a bubble about fifty kilometers across was enough.

"Three probes gone, the others disabled," Nazario reported from the Intel console. "We had a second set attached to the hull; I'm releasing them now. We'd lose them at blood in the water anyway."

They wouldn't get *any* real benefit from the new probes unless they fired up their engines, but if the duel lasted long enough, the drones would drift back into *Corsair*'s path like the first set had.

"We've got a handle on their missiles, but *they* have a handle on our games," Paris reported. "Once the tricks are all out, it's a numbers game."

He didn't need to tell them how *that* was going to work out. The numbers all shook down one way: *Corsair* had more of *everything*.

"Separation! Forty-eight warheads inbound!"

Despite his complaint, Lorraine noted, Paris had still taken down almost fifty missiles before they'd split into attack munitions.

They had twenty seconds, but those were in the optimal defense range—that was *why* the terminal mode had vastly higher acceleration, after all.

The problem was that for blood in the water, they needed to let a nuke get far enough to *look* like it hit them—and even against less-overwhelming firepower, that was a terrifying balance to get right.

Paris didn't manage it—and three nukes went off right on top of them in a blaze of light and fire that overwhelmed the bridge screens.

FIFTY-TWO

The screens were back in a few seconds, the darkness solely a glare-management safety feature. The engines were still burning underneath them, and Lorraine still had two and a half cheerleaders sitting on her chest.

Those were the good signs. That many nukes going off that close was still bad news, and Lorraine mentally bit her tongue to stop herself demanding reports and updates.

"Blood in the water fired as planned," Kovac reported from the Engineering console. "We had a *lovely* visible blast of oh-two and flames out the side of the ship.

"Unfortunately, we have some very real metallic debris instead of just ablating rods from the combat radiators," the engineer continued. "We've lost screen projectors, jammer dishes, armor plating, beams... We've lost local automatic control in sectors S-D-Eighteen through -Twenty."

That was the last thirty meters of the ship on the starboard underside.

"No drones and minimal sensors," Kovac warned. "We know what isn't reporting back to their main systems, but we don't know what's actually gone. We're leaking atmosphere from SD-Nineteen, but airtight bulkheads appear to be sealed."

"Hands?" Stephson asked.

"Seven local control stations for weapons and DamCon," the engineer said grimly. "Twenty-five crew. Local controller loss prevents automated check-in, and we don't have direct reports yet. Only one station is inside the sealed area at the breach."

Lorraine had pulled the schematic as the report came in. The scarlet wash on the rear of the cruiser was concerning—especially as it included part of the lower sensor tower.

The breach was at the upper part of the tower, which meant the station was part of the tower's control team—and a *seven*-crew station, not a two- or three-crew position.

"Chevrolet is following on from blood in the water," Vigo said, his voice cutting in to Lorraine's channel with Stephson. She gave her bodyguard a quick look, and he shrugged against the gravity.

Everyone else was distracted, that shrug told her. And her chief bodyguard was as qualified to backstop the shuttle ops as anyone else on the ship—and his words were accompanied by a flag on the sensor feed highlighting the shuttle maneuvers.

Because it *was* Vigo flagging it, Lorraine's screen lit up with swift notes as she zoomed in on their shuttles. At first glance, it looked like a chaotic mess, the result of the pilots looking back and seeing their only way out on fire. Even a few seconds of flame in space was a bad sign for the ship that had your stuff, after all.

Two shuttles made turnover, flipping end for end, then burning for *Goldenrod* at twelve gees. Even the *best* crews could break, Lorraine knew. Any officer, any spacer, any pilot could reach their limit.

Even if she *had* committed them to a suicide run, she would have expected a good chance of at least one shuttle breaking off before the point of no return. She *wouldn't* have expected what happened next, but she had seen it in combat footage and training videos.

A third shuttle followed a second after the first two. Then two more—followed a couple of moments later by the remaining seven Midases of *Goldenrod's* organic shuttle flotilla.

For ten solid seconds after that, the four Adamant Guard shuttles continued their charge before, appearing abandoned by their backup, they broke off as well.

It looked even worse than she'd feared when she'd asked for it. Even to *her*, it looked like the shuttle flight's will had broken and they were falling back in disarray.

But she also knew that Wray would look deeper. If nothing else, he'd be looking for the *bombs*—and they were there. Vigo's notes marked the sequencing, the careful timing that had kept all sixteen shuttles' munitions moving for a time-on-target hit.

It was a clever trick, one that might give her opponent a moment to believe he had everything in hand. But she expected Wray to look past it, to focus his active sensors on where the shuttles had launched.

If he really bought the display and didn't look for the bombs, well, there was a good chance *Corsair* might find herself eating a few dozen nukes, and that would be that. Lorraine wasn't counting on that, though.

She was counting on him seeing through this deception, too. Finding the bombs would require him to focus active and passive sensors on a narrow window of space that would approach his ship at over a hundred kilometers a second.

"Fourteen minutes," Vigo told her. "The bastard has to run out of missiles sometime, *right?*"

Lorraine wasn't taking any bets. *Corsair* would have had a full load of missiles leaving Ominira, which even at her most optimistic assessments of their use in San Ignacio would have seen the battle-cruiser arriving in Bright Dream with twenty-five salvos' worth of weapons for her missile tubes.

The one now hurtling toward her ship was only salvo number four.

EVASIVE MANEUVERS TWISTED *Goldenrod* through space, her faster turning angle undermined by her limited acceleration. A steady, grim rhythm filled the frigate's bridge, and Lorraine sat silently at the back of the bridge, watching death come for her and her people across the void.

The shuttles were still getting closer to the battlecruiser, though they were all accelerating for *Goldenrod* at their maximum thrust. *Corsair*'s shuttles were pulling slowly in front of their mothership, only burning at nine gees to their mothership's seven.

Like their mothership, the interceptors were sweeping space for the bombs they knew Chevrolet's people had launched. *Goldenrod*, unlike her opponent, was now out of missiles, so there wasn't even a *threat* to the shuttles as they casually swept for the incoming projectiles.

They knew roughly where Chevrolet's bombs would be, and they were focusing in on that zone. Every so often, an interceptor fired its lasers, but they were missing as often as they found something.

Over a dozen salvos had now crashed down on *Goldenrod*, and Lorraine had no idea how they were still alive. Over a *thousand* missiles had been thrown at the frigate, and they were still there.

They'd been hit. Nine times now, *Corsair*'s people had punched nukes through everything Paris and Yildiz could manage for deception and maneuver, but their engines were still online and most of their antimissile defenses were still operational.

The decoys were long gone. Lorraine had suspicions about whether their main beams were online, and half of their combat radiators and other obvious surface installations were waste metal. But *Goldenrod* lived.

Everyone knew the timing. The bridge officers and specialists all had the same countdown to the bomb strike on their consoles and neural links that Lorraine did. Wray and his people could calculate it, and she could see that knowledge in the tightening maneuvers and scan patterns of the interceptors.

"Scans are still focused on the bomb strike," Stephson noted quietly. "Pandora is still hidden."

"Any idea how many bombs we've lost?" Lorraine asked Vigo.

"*Corsair*'s gunners have done better than I hoped but far worse than I feared," he told her. "I can't be certain at this point, but I think they've only hit about twenty."

A hundred and forty bombs. Once they went live, they'd be *very* visible, and they had a lower starting velocity at that point than the missiles would. But it was the best shot they had, the only way to clear the way for Pandora.

"And now."

Lorraine wasn't sure who'd spoken. The shuttle bombs lit off their drives, visible again as green sparks on the display as seventy-three weapons hurled themselves forward.

Like the chaos of the shuttle turnover, the partial activation had a purpose. Unlike the chaos of the shuttle turnover, this purpose was probably easier to work out—and at this point, it didn't matter.

The interceptors had put enough distance between themselves and their mothership to let bombs aimed at *them* light off ten seconds earlier than the bombs aimed at *Corsair*.

The pilots were *good*, she noted absently. They realized what was happening, and they made the right call, the one no pilot ever knew if they'd truly make until they had to.

The interceptors focused their fire on the bombs aimed at their ship. Their own defense was an afterthought, and a cascade of nuclear explosions cleared the board as Lorraine mentally saluted them. It was a hard choice—but the right one. A bomb that killed a shuttle couldn't hurt *Corsair*, and the battlecruiser had over two thousand people aboard. Two interceptors made it through, but their chaotic maneuvers suggested major damage as they pushed to get themselves out of the line of fire.

Only sixteen bombs survived the interceptors' stand to hurl themselves at Wray's ship, and they had no chance. Lorraine was already starting to shift her attention to the last string in her bow when someone shouted in surprise.

"Holy shit! *They got her!*"

Lorraine snapped her attention to the bridge's main display as a mixed schematic and visual image of *Corsair* expanded to fill it. The same fire and debris that they'd *intentionally* vented to cover their turnover was now flying free of the bigger ship.

"Direct hit," Savege reported from CIC. "Still localizing where, but we got her, and we got her *hard*."

"Well done," Lorraine said loudly and clearly. "Let's... see what Commodore Wray does."

The damage wasn't fatal; she could see that at a glance. They'd hit the dorsal sensor tower, about halfway up... and as she watched, the upper half of the tower broke free. It was *bad*, but *Corsair* could still fight.

But just as she would have allowed for the risk of the shuttle pilots blinking at the point of no return on a suicide charge, it was *possible* that Wray would turn back.

Even on a two-million-ton battlecruiser, that strike was more than a bloody nose. There were key sensors and targeting systems in the dorsal tower, systems *Corsair* no longer had.

"Damage assessment?" Stephson finally asked.

"They've lost their primary sensors and coms systems with the main tower," Paris reported. "They're doing what they can, but it's clear many of their missiles are no longer under direct control. Our chances of handling them just went *way* up... but they've also stopped launching missiles at all."

"He doesn't need them anymore," Stephson warned. "Time to her beam range?"

"We'll hit fifty thousand klicks in thirty seconds," Nazario reported. "I... am guessing the point where we can hurt *her* isn't relevant."

"No."

One way or another, *Goldenrod* wasn't going to be shooting at *Corsair* when they hit five thousand kilometers.

FIFTY-THREE

No one aboard *Goldenrod* had ever seriously expected to carry the day *without* ending up in beam range of the big battlecruiser. Cortez's people had gone over every piece of the energy screen, every electronic-countermeasure projector—*everything* they had that could slow or weaken the incoming fire.

At maximum range, it wouldn't take much extra to disperse the beams. And like the seekers on the missiles, they knew a *lot* about *Corsair's* lasers. More than they should, thanks to the classified files Vigo's Guards had handed over.

He hoped it was enough. It was his job to keep Lorraine Adamant alive, but almost *none* of his skills were relevant there. He was acting as a relay for the shuttles because he *could* more than because it was necessary. The Deck Chief in the shuttle bay was perfectly capable of whispering in Captain Stephson's ear if needed.

The Chief seemed happier to have Vigo acting as an interface, but there also wasn't that much to say. The bombs had hit. The interceptors were gone, and *Corsair* was half-blinded. It might just be enough.

As warning lights flashed and screens darkened, he felt his heart try to stop. A beam weapon was invisible *from the side*. It was a lot more visible from the target's perspective, as all of the light from every particle it incinerated along the way arrived with it.

The bright flash said that *Corsair* had fired, but the fact that the computers had been operating to darken the screens at all said they were still alive.

"Clean miss," Paris reported. "Not even our ECM, I don't think. Shot was off by at least a full degree."

"She's lost half her scanners," Stephson noted. "But that would be... Were the *emitters* damaged?"

It didn't seem likely to Vigo. Their one hit had been in the sensor tower, after all, not just at the back of the ship but well away from the main hull where the beams lived.

The screens darkened again.

"Clean miss again. There's definitely something wrong with her emitters, but *we* didn't do that," Paris said grimly.

"We certainly *helped*," Savage said, the XO interjecting over a wider channel. "But we're close enough to get a solid look. She's taken *serious* beam damage along her bow—looks like the SIDF left her a parting present."

A third set of shots blazed across the display, and *this* time, Vigo felt the ship shiver around them.

"They *fixed* their damage, but losing the upper tower threw off their sighting," Savege guessed.

"They're narrowing in faster than I like," Paris replied. "I'm eighty percent sure our ECM forced that miss."

"I need *one more minute*," Lorraine warned. "Chaff 'em."

Vigo couldn't argue his charge's order. It *shouldn't* be necessary— the work everyone had done should get them through a couple of hits at long range. But she wasn't wrong. They were *so close* to opening Pandora's box, as Stephson had described it.

"Chaff deploying... *Fuck me!*"

The screens turned near-black for a second.

"Report," Stephson barked.

"Clean hit on the rear screens," Savege reported, leaving it to Paris to handle the defenses. "Chaff was deploying, but the screens themselves were breached. Leftover energy hit the chaff mid-deployment."

Chaff, in this case, was thousands of ribbons of mirror-bright metal that would absorb and disperse the energy of the beam. Fired like canister from special launchers, it was often held back for closer-range beam clashes... but Lorraine's push might have just saved the frigate.

"No damage," Nazario reported, the engineer's voice tight. "But we're down half our chaff launchers now."

"We tuned the damn screens," Stephson growled. "That should *not* have punched through at this range."

"He knew he would," Lorraine snapped. "Undo whatever screening you can. He's *using* it!"

Vigo swallowed a curse. It would have been a *lot* easier if Wray weren't so damn good at his job.

"Chaff is up; setting all remaining launchers to maximum fire rate," Paris reported. "It's going to look like we're panicking, but we'll have maximum coverage for thirty seconds from *now*."

Vigo's link automatically picked that up, and he started a countdown. The chaff wasn't a perfect shield by any means, but backed by the energy screens and the range, it *should* carry them through.

More warning lights flared across the displays, and he turned his attention to Lorraine.

He had access to her vitals, and he *knew* she wasn't as calm as she appeared. As he watched, she clearly checked the time and distance on Pandora. Even as *Corsair's* beams lashed out, frustrated by the chaff and screen but burning closer with every shot, she was watching it.

"And if Wray is half as good as I think he is," she murmured, "he's going to realize about... *now*."

It was three whole seconds later before the beam fire suddenly cut off—*Corsair* suddenly had *far* more critical things to do with her beam weapons!

"Pandora's box is open," Lorraine announced loudly. "Drives activating *now*."

Vigo saw her math. She'd figured *Corsair* would pick up the mines at five thousand kilometers. Forty-seven hundred klicks wasn't *that* much closer, but at a closing speed of a hundred klicks a second...

Pandora's box was the result of Cortez taking over every fabricator on the ship for a week and turning them to one purpose: manufacturing Horatio-99 knockoff casings for the nukes they didn't need for their missiles and their one bomb strike.

Two hundred and fifty-eight mines had been drifting back toward *Corsair* since they'd launched the shuttles. They weren't *quite* as stealthy as the real Horatio-99 would have been, but they were both better than and *different* from the mines *Goldenrod* could have built from her own databases.

Now, with only forty-three hundred kilometers between the minefield and the battlecruiser, their drives came online. Identical in most ways to the terminal attack mode used for their shuttle bombs, they blazed toward *Corsair* at a thousand gravities.

Vigo felt a twisted moment of pride and horror. Horror because he'd *been* aboard a ship—a battlecruiser, even!—taking a swarm of warheads they couldn't stop.

Pride because he'd seen Lorraine's plan play out, as they'd played trick after trick, each of them quite possibly effective in their own right, but their *main* purpose being for Wray to find them and catch them—and, in so doing, have his attention held, focused, *managed*.

As over a hundred fusion warheads crashed in on the pursuing battlecruiser, Vigo Jarret knew his charge had been right: they hadn't won the battle in deep space against *Corsair*'s weapons and armor.

Lorraine had won the battle in Nikostratos Wray's head, because she'd known how a competent officer would think and used it to control his attention.

Thirty seconds after *Corsair* saw the mines coming, it was over.

FIFTY-FOUR

"In hindsight, we very much appreciate the heads-up that you were being pursued, Pentarch Lorraine," Rear Admiral Ljungborg told her wryly. The Wormhole Control commander shook her head. "While I have to admit that we would strongly prefer that no one use fusion mines in our space, I don't see anything in your actions that isn't covered by the self-defense clause of the treaty between our nations."

"Thank you for stating so," Lorraine replied. The statement would be recorded, and they would bring it up if someone tried to make trouble later.

"I do have to ask, however. You deployed a *lot* of mines. Are you certain they are all handled?"

"All were set with timed safeguard detonators," she promised the local. "Any that were missed would have detonated by now."

Goldenrod was in the final hour of decelerating toward the wormhole. The battle with *Corsair* was hours past, and *everything* they'd deployed would have hit its safeguard detonation times by now.

"The same is most likely true of any weapons deployed by *Corsair*," she noted. "I cannot *guarantee* that Commodore Wray was following standard RKAN procedure, however. Treason isn't generally part of said procedures, after all."

Ljungborg managed not to choke on her coffee, but Lorraine thought it was closer than the Bright Dream flag officer would have preferred.

"No, it is generally not," she agreed. "We have search-and-rescue ships approaching the likely vectors for escape pods as we speak. They're running active scans, just in case, but they'll check with any survivors who would know."

"Before we detain them," the local finished chillily. "While I imagine you would denigrate the legitimacy of the current government on Bastion, they are the ones we will be negotiating with.

"Commodore Wray broke a long list of our laws alongside the treaties between the Republic and the Kingdom when he attacked you. If he has survived, he will answer for his actions. If he has not... the negotiations between the Kingdom and my government for his remaining crew will likely be straightforward. And expensive."

Lorraine just nodded. There was nothing for her to say. As Ljungborg guessed, she was unwilling to acknowledge the legitimacy of the Black Regent's government—but she also couldn't take responsibility for Wray's people.

Benjamin Adamant didn't have *quite* as much control over the news leaving Adamantine as he'd like, she suspected, and the cost of the control he *was* exerting was already visible in the news she was accessing.

Twenty-sixth-century media did *not* like heavy-handed censorship.

"Are we clear for our wormhole transit, Admiral Ljungborg?" she asked.

"You are, Pentarch Lorraine," Ljungborg confirmed. "Priority passage and all. Traffic Control should have sent you your course already. The situation in Adamant appears... complicated, Pentarch, and I feel that even wishing you luck would seem like taking a side.

"I wish you safe travels. No one in Bright Dream will bar your way from here."

"Thank you, Admiral. I hope the Republic is... untroubled by any result of my actions, at least. I mean your people no harm."

LORRAINE STAYED on the bridge as she went through the data they were receiving. Part of it was that she wanted to see the wormhole transit. Part of it was that she couldn't bring herself to be anywhere else after the last few hours. Twenty-six members of *Goldenrod*'s crew were dead... and they'd probably killed over *two thousand* people aboard *Corsair*.

The battlecruiser had a listed complement of twenty-five hundred, including four hundred Marines. Some would have survived. There were a lot of features built into a modern warship to save the crew, after all, and they would have been at battle stations in shipsuits that acted as emergency space gear.

But she had to face the truth: most of them hadn't. Too many nukes had gone off in close proximity. The crews of the damaged shuttles would live, but even people who made it to escape pods or safety vaults might still die from radiation poisoning before the Bright Dream ships could retrieve them.

The RBDN search-and-rescue crews had launched the moment the shooting had stopped, blazing out from the stations at a ten-gravity acceleration that suggested specialty designs for the small sublight ships, but it would still take them hours to match the vector of the debris.

Lorraine's clever plan had killed thousands of people who had sworn loyalty to her kingdom and her family. She'd saved herself and the people she was responsible for. That was... what she'd had to do.

Her own survival was key to continuing her mission. The Tavastar–Bright-Dream Wormhole ahead of them was the only thing that made her chosen gambit out of the Exodus Protocols possible. It would take her six hundred and twelve light-years toward Sol in the space of a few minutes.

"Pentarch."

She looked up as Nazario stepped up to her console.

"Lieutenant Major," she greeted the Intel Officer. "What do you need?"

"Since we... survived, I've been going through the news we have from Adamantine," he told her. "The Regency has been exerting a high level of control over the information coming out, but there are definitely some pieces I can put together."

"Not least, from the tone of the couple of reports I had time to review, because the news agencies are *pissed* about that," Lorraine noted. "That level of control is almost unheard-of in the Kingdom."

Goldenrod's crew had started calling Benjamin the Black Regent a while back. It had surprised her to see the phrase *Black Regency* in one of the written articles—a *very* hostile article that drew a line from the information control to the theory that Benjamin was behind the assassinations.

"This one won't stay quiet for long, no matter how hard he tries," Nazario said grimly. "Our news is from early May, but it looks like assault landings hit Mithral on the twenty-eighth of April.

"It took your uncle almost a month to put together enough loyal troops to move, but the landings appear to have been a success. As of four months ago, Mithral was a war zone—and *Hope* was destroyed when the Regent sent her in to support the landings."

Lorraine bit down her immediate reaction with the ease of long practice. Nameship of her class, the battleship *Hope* was the oldest capital ship in RKAN... but she was still a two-million-ton warship with almost three thousand crew aboard.

But if her brother controlled PDC Mithral as they'd guessed, *Hope* had been badly outclassed. If she was close enough to support the landings, she was close enough to be hit by the PDC's kilometer-long mass-driver cannon.

"Civil war, then," she murmured. "Thank you, Lieutenant Major. I needed to know that."

Nazario nodded, walking stiffly back to his station as Lorraine considered the future.

Mithral was a good-sized continent and, by the sounds of it, most of it was at least partially aligned with Nikola. The attack might have started four months earlier, but Lorraine doubted her uncle's troops had even managed to invest PDC Mithral itself.

In their place, she'd go after PDC Ironhand first. The *other* planetary defense center on Mithral was smaller but still lethal. So long as Nikola could reliably command both—or even command one and neutralize the other—he was going to be nearly impossible to dig out.

She had time. Not a lot... but time.

She was going to need it. Lorraine had no illusions about how easy the task she'd set herself was.

"We have the final course from the locals," Yildiz reported. "Transit in thirty-two minutes. Arrival in Tavastar seventy-eight minutes later."

The Tavastar System was an uninhabitable wasteland. But, like there in Bright Dream, there was a massive complex of space stations around the wormhole itself. The Tavastar Wormhole Complex was ten light-hours from the star and a *lot* bigger than the stations on the Bright Dream end.

This side, after all, had a planet nearby to live on.

The Complex on the Tavastar side was the permanent home to forty-three million people. Among the stations that held them were several major permanent facilities for the United Worlds Government.

Including the closest office belonging to the United Worlds Stability Convention Fund.

Lorraine didn't know whether she really *could* convince the UW to save her nation. But one way or another, *that* part of her mission started in Tavastar.

Lorraine's story will continue in the United Worlds in *The Old Guard*, book #2 in the House Adamant series, arriving in September, 2024.

Want the most reliable release notifications? Visit glynnstewart.com and join the mailing list.

JOIN THE MAILING LIST

Love Glynn Stewart's books? Join the mailing list at

GLYNNSTEWART.COM/MAILING-LIST/

to know as soon as new books are released and for special announcements.

ABOUT THE AUTHOR

Glynn Stewart is the author of *Starship's Mage*, a bestselling science fiction and fantasy series where faster-than-light travel is possible–but only because of magic. His other works include science fiction series *Duchy of Terra*, *Castle Federation* and *Vigilante*, as well as the urban fantasy series *ONSET* and *Changeling Blood*.

Writing managed to liberate Glynn from a bleak future as an accountant. With his personality and hope for a high-tech future intact, he lives in Calgary, Alberta with his partner, their cats, and an unstoppable writing habit.

Want the fastest way to get updates on new books? Sign up for the newsletter at glynnstewart.com.

- Chat with us on the Facebook Group
- Check out my Facebook Page

The following people were involved in making this book:
Copyeditor: Richard Shealy
Proofreader: M Parker Editing
Cover Artist: Elias Stern
Publishing: Jack Giesen
Typo Hunter Team

And a sincere thank you to my Patreon subscribers!

Made in the USA
Las Vegas, NV
14 January 2025

16315385R00236